W9-BSO-934
KOKOMO-HOWARD COUNTY
www.KHCPL.org
3 9223 039385342

KOKOMO-HOWARD COUNTY
PUBLIC LIBRARY

THE FEVER KING

THE FEVER KING

FEVERWAKE: BOOK ONE

VICTORIA LEE

This is a work of fiction. Names, characters, organizations, places, events, and incidents are either products of the author's imagination or are used fictitiously. Any resemblance to actual persons, living or dead, or actual events is purely coincidental.

Published by Skyscape, New York
www.apub.com

ISBN-13: 9781542040174 (hardcover)
ISBN-10: 1542040175 (hardcover)

ISBN-13: 9781542040402 (paperback)
ISBN-10: 154204040X (paperback)

Cover design by David Curtis

Printed in the United States of America

First edition

For Ben,
who fell in love with me as I was writing this book

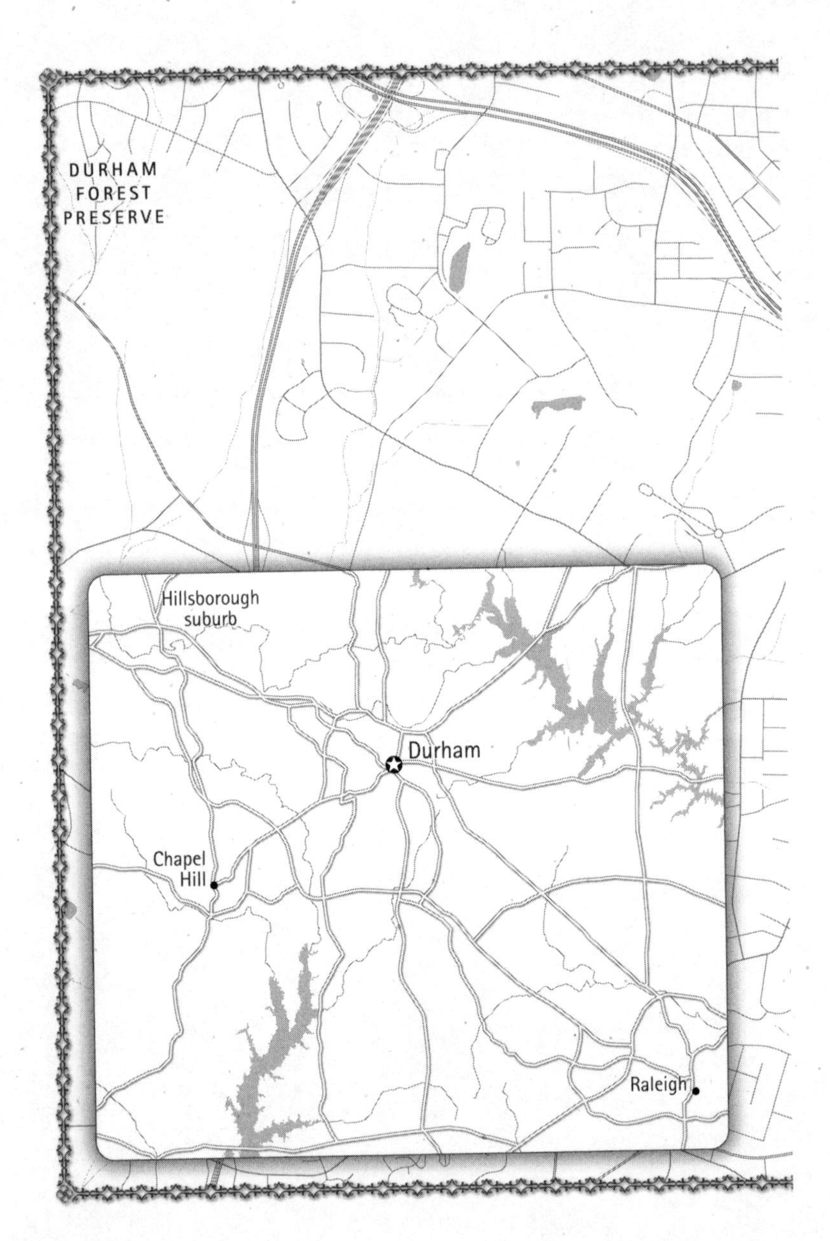
DURHAM
FOREST
PRESERVE
Hillsborough
suburb
Durham
Chapel
Hill
Raleigh

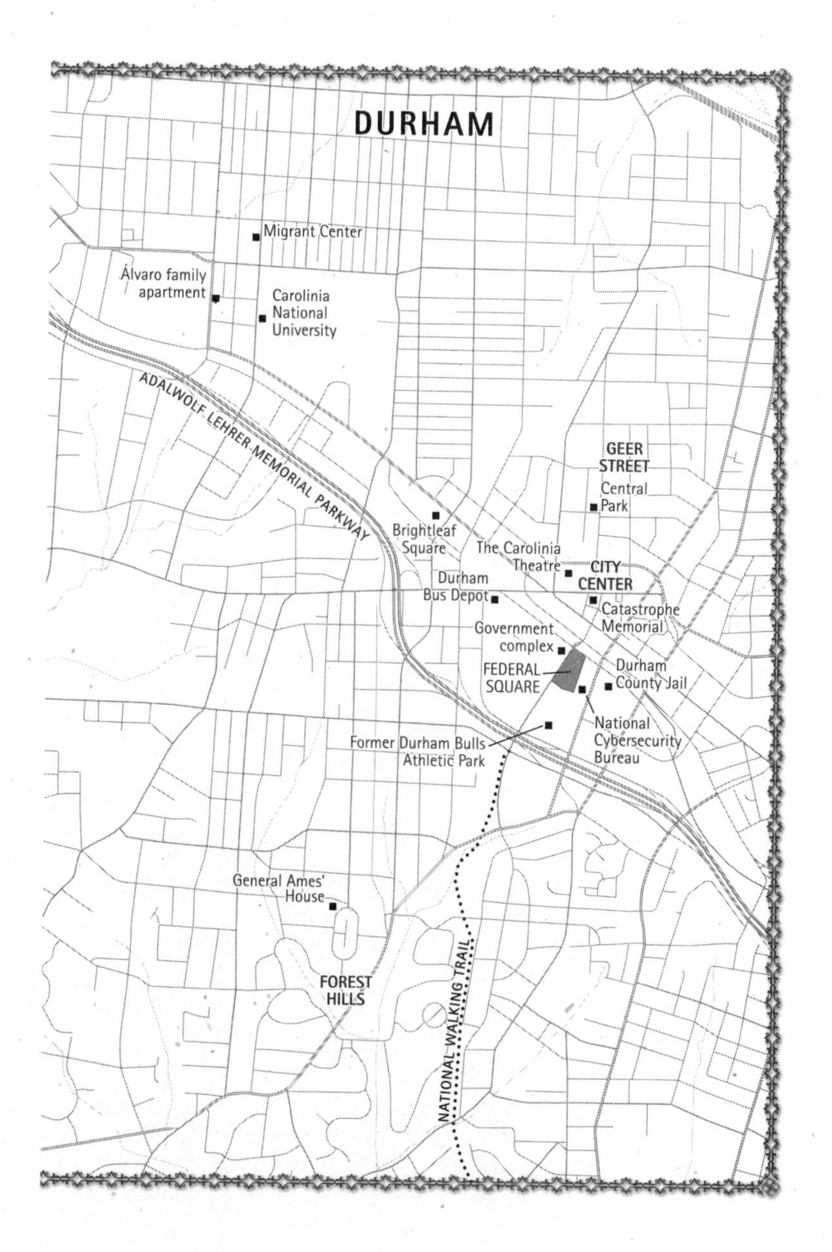
DURHAM
Migrant Center
Álvaro family apartment
Carolinia National University
ADALWOLF LEHRER MEMORIAL PARKWAY
GEER STREET
Central Park
Brightleaf Square
The Carolinia Theatre
CITY CENTER
Durham Bus Depot
Catastrophe Memorial
Government complex
FEDERAL SQUARE
Durham County Jail
National Cybersecurity Bureau
Former Durham Bulls Athletic Park
General Ames' House
FOREST HILLS
NATIONAL WALKING TRAIL

CANADA
Syracuse
YORK
Boulder
MIDLANDS
Refugee Camp
(site of virus
outbreak)
Durham
CAROLINIA
ATLANTIA
Montgomery
TEXAS
San Antonio
ATLANTIC
OCEAN
Gulf of
Mexico
AZTLÁN
PACIFIC
OCEAN
0
500
1,000 Miles
0
500
1,000 Kilometers

March 9, 2018

Calix,

As I write this, they're packing up the fighter jets. Your virus gets packed into the belly in these big crates. Frozen, of course, so the magic doesn't get loose while we're in the air.

Did you know viruses aren't actually alive? They're useless without a host. They're just chemicals. Even magic. The problem is they can infect just about anything, from people to animals to plants to bacteria.

Of course, you knew this already. You know everything, right?

I still don't know if I'm going to DC because you fucked up your order and I have to or because I want to. I've decided it doesn't make a difference. I'm going, and that'll be the end of me.

Don't get angry. I can tell you're unhappy, Calix, and I know it's my fault. I've always been like this. I hurt people just being around them. Usually it's by accident, but with you it was on purpose, at least at first.

I'm trying to make up for that now.

Power's a nasty thing, and none of us are immune. Get out, go to college, and get some kind of doctor degree and save the world—just don't try to save it the way I did. The war will be over soon, and I want you to move on. Promise me. Please. If it helps, you can consider it my dying wish.

You're the best person I know. Always have been. You just need to learn how to feel something again.

Maybe when I'm dead, you'll at least feel something for me.

I love you, little brother.

Wolf

Letter stolen from the personal archives of Calix Lehrer, on behalf of H. Sacha

Chapter One

Outbreaks of magic started all kinds of ways. Maybe a tank coming in from the quarantined zone didn't get hosed down properly. Maybe, like some people said, the refugees brought it up with them from Atlantia, the virus hiding out in someone's blood or in a juicy peach pie.

But when magic infected the slums of west Durham, in the proud sovereign nation of Carolinia, it didn't matter how it got there.

Everybody still died.

Noam was ringing up Mrs. Ellis's snuff tins when he nearly toppled into the cash register.

He all but had to fight her off as she tried to force him down into a folding chair—swore he'd just got a touch dizzy, but he'd be fine, really. *Go on home.* She left eventually, and he went to stand in front of the window fan for a while, holding his shirt off his sweat-sticky back and trying not to pass out.

He spent the rest of his shift reading Bulgakov under the counter. He felt just fine.

That evening he locked the doors, pulled chicken wire over the windows, and took a new route to the Migrant Center. In this neighborhood, you had to if you didn't want to get robbed. Once upon a time, or so Noam had heard, there'd been a textile mill here. The street would've been full of workers heading home, empty lunch pails in hand. Then the mill had gone down and apartments went up, and by the 1960s, Ninth Street had been repopulated by rich university students with their leather satchels and clove cigarettes. All that was before the city got bombed halfway to hell in the catastrophe, of course.

Noam's ex used to call it "the Ninth Circle." She meant it in Dante's sense.

The catastrophe was last century, though. Now the university campus blocked the area in from the east, elegant stone walls keeping out the riffraff while Ninth and Broad crumbled under the weight of five-person refugee families crammed into one-room apartments, black markets buried in basements, laundry lines strung between windows like market lights. Sure, maybe you shouldn't wander around the neighborhood at night draped in diamonds, but Noam liked it anyway.

"Someone's famous," Linda said when he reached the back offices of the Migrant Center, a sly smile curving her lips as she passed him the morning's *Herald*.

Noam grinned back and looked.

Massive Cyberattack Disables Central News Bureau

Authorities link hack to Atlantian cyberterrorist affiliates.

"Haven't the faintest idea what you're talking about. Say, have you got any scissors?"

"What for?"

"I'm gonna frame this."

Linda snorted and swatted him on the arm. "Get on, you. Brennan has some task he wants finished this week, and I don't think you, him, and your ego can all fit in that office."

Which, fair: the office *was* pretty small. Tucked into the back corner of the building, with Brennan's name and **Director** printed on the door in copperplate, it was pretty much an unofficial storage closet for all the files and paperwork Linda couldn't cram anywhere else. Brennan's desk was dwarfed by boxes stacked precariously around it, the man himself leaning close to his holoreader monitor with reading glasses perched on the end of a long nose and a pen behind one ear.

"Noam," he said, glancing up when the door opened. "You made it."

"Sorry I missed yesterday. I had to cover someone's shift at the computer store after I got off the clock at Larry's."

Brennan waved a dismissive hand. "Don't apologize. If you have to work, you have to work."

"Still."

It wasn't *guilt*, per se, that coiled up in Noam's stomach. Or maybe it was. That was his father's photograph on the wall, after all, face hidden by a bandanna tied over his nose and mouth. His father's hands holding up that sign—**REFUGEE RIGHTS ARE HUMAN RIGHTS**. That was in June 2118, during the revolt over the new, more stringent citizenship tests. It'd been the largest protest in Carolinian history.

"Linda said you had something for me to work on?" Noam said, tilting his head toward the holoreader.

"It's just database management, I'm afraid, nothing very interesting."

"I love databases." Noam smiled, and Brennan smiled back. The expression lifted the exhaustion from Brennan's face like a curtain rising from a window, sunlight streaming through.

Brennan oriented him to the task, then gave up his desk chair for Noam to get to work. He squeezed Noam's shoulder before he left to help Linda with dinner, and a warm beat of familiarity took root in the pit of Noam's stomach. Brennan might try to put up boundaries, clear delineations between professional life and how close Brennan had been to Noam's family, but the cracks were always visible.

That was pretty much the only reason Noam didn't tell him up front: database management was mind-numbingly tedious. After you figured out how to script your way past the problem, it was just a matter of waiting around. Once upon a time, he'd have emailed Carly or someone while the program executed. But they were all dead now, and between the Migrant Center and two jobs, Noam didn't have time to meet new people. So he sat and watched text stream down the command console, letters blurring into numbers until the screen was wavering light.

A dull ache bored into Noam's skull.

Maybe he was more tired than he thought, because he didn't remember what happened between hitting "Execute" and Brennan shaking him awake. Noam lurched upright.

"You all right?" Brennan asked.

"What? Oh—fine, sorry. I must have . . . dozed off." Noam seized the holoreader, tapping at the screen until it lit up again. The script was finished, anyway, and no run-time errors. Thankfully. "It's all done."

The thin line between Brennan's brows deepened. "Are you feeling okay? You look . . ."

"Fine. I'm fine. Just tired." Noam attempted a wan smile. He really hoped he wasn't coming down with whatever it was Elliott from the computer store had. Only, he and Elliott had kissed in the back room on their lunch break yesterday, so yeah, he probably had *exactly* what Elliott had.

"Maybe you should go on home," Brennan said, using that grip on Noam's shoulder to ease him back from the computer. "I can help Linda finish up dinner."

"I can—"

"It wasn't a request."

Noam made a face, and Brennan sighed.

"For me, Noam. Please. I'll drop by later on if I have time."

There was no arguing with Brennan when he got all protective. So Noam just exhaled and said, "Yeah, all right. Fine."

Brennan's hand lingered a beat longer than usual on Noam's shoulder, squeezing slightly, then let go. When Noam looked over, Brennan's expression gave nothing away as he said, "Tell your dad hi for me."

Noam had arrived at the Migrant Center in the early evening. Now it was night, the deep-blue world illuminated by pale streetlight pooling on the sidewalk. It was unusually silent. When Noam turned onto Broad, he found out why: a checkpoint was stationed up at the intersection by the railroad tracks—floodlights and vans, police, even a few government witchings in military uniform.

Right. No one without a Carolinian passport would be on the street tonight, not with Immigration on the prowl.

Noam's papers were tucked into his back pocket, but he didn't need to deal with Chancellor Sacha's anti-Atlantian bullshit right now. Not with this headache. He cut through the alley between the liquor store and the barbecue joint to skirt the police perimeter. It might be a longer walk home from there, but Noam didn't mind.

He liked the way tonight smelled, like smoked ribs and gasoline. Like oncoming snow.

When he got to his building, he managed to get the door open, even though the front latch was ancient enough it probably counted as precatastrophe. Fucking thing always got stuck, *always*, and Noam had written to the super fifty times, for what little difference that'd made. It was November, but the back of Noam's neck was sweat-damp by the time he finally shouldered his way into the building and trudged into his apartment.

Once, this building was a bookstore. It'd long since been converted to tenements, all plywood walls and hung-up sheets for doors. The books were still there, though, yellowing and mildewed. They made him sneeze, but he read a new one every day all the same, curled up in a corner and out of the way of the other tenants. It was old and worn out, but it was home.

Noam touched the mezuzah on the doorframe as he went in, a habit he hadn't picked up till after his mother died but felt right somehow. Not that being extra Jewish would bring her back to life.

Noam's father had been moved from the TV to the window.

"What's up, Dad?"

No answer. That was nothing new. Noam was pretty sure his father hadn't said three words in a row since 2120. Still, Noam draped his arms over his father's lax shoulders and kissed his cheek.

"I hope you want pasta for dinner," Noam said, "'cause that's what we've got."

He left his father staring out at the empty street and busied himself with the saucepans. He set up the induction plate and hunched over it, steam wafting toward his face as the water simmered. God, it was unbearably hot, but he didn't trust himself to let go of the counter edge, not with this dizziness rippling through his mind.

Should've had more than an apple for lunch. Should've gone to bed early last night, not stayed up reading *Paradise Lost* for the fiftieth time.

If his mother were here, she'd have dragged him off to bed and stuck him with a mug of aguapanela. It was some sugary tea remedy she'd learned from her Colombian mother-in-law that was supposed to cure everything. Noam had never learned how to make it.

Another regret to add to the list.

He dumped dried noodles into the pot. "There's a checkpoint at the corner of Broad and Main," he said, not expecting an answer.

None came. Jaime Álvaro didn't care about anything anymore, not even Atlantia.

Noam turned down the heat on the stove. "Couldn't tell if they made any arrests. Nobody's out, so they might start knocking on doors later."

He turned around. His father's expression was the same slack-jawed one he'd been wearing when Noam first came in.

"Brennan asked about you," Noam said. Surely that deserved a blink, at least.

Nothing.

"I killed him."

Nothing then either.

Noam spun toward the saucepan again, grabbing a fork and stabbing at the noodles, which slipped through the prongs like so many slimy worms. His gut surged up into his throat, and Noam closed his eyes, free hand gripping the edge of the nearest bookshelf.

"You could at least pretend to give a shit," he said to the blackness on the other side of his eyelids. The pounding in his head was back. "I'm sad about Mom, too, you know."

His next breath shuddered all the way down into his chest—painful, like inhaling frost.

His father used to sing show tunes while he did the dinner dishes. Used to check the classifieds every morning for job offers even though having no papers meant he'd never get the good ones—he still never gave up. Never ever.

And Noam . . . Noam had to remember who his father *really* was, even if that version of him belonged to another life, ephemeral as footprints in the snow. Even if it felt like he'd lost both parents the day his mother died.

Noam switched off the heat and spooned the noodles into two bowls. No sauce, so he drizzled canola oil on top and carried one of the bowls over to his father. Noam edged his way between the chair and the window, crouching down in that narrow space. He spun spaghetti around the fork. "Open up."

Usually, the prospect of food managed to garner a reaction. Not this time.

Nausea crawled up and down Noam's breastbone. Or maybe it was regret. "I'm sorry," he said after a beat and tried for a self-deprecating grin. "I was . . . it's been a long day. I was a dick. I'm sorry, Dad."

His father didn't speak and didn't move his mouth.

Noam set the pasta bowl on the floor and wrapped his other hand around his father's bony wrist. "Please," Noam said. "Just a few bites. I know it's not Mom's cooking, but . . . for me. Okay?"

Noam's mother had made the most amazing food. Noam tried to live up to her standard, but he never could. He'd given up on cooking anything edible, on keeping a kosher kitchen, on speaking Spanish. On making his father smile.

Noam rubbed his thumb against his father's forearm.

The skin there was paper thin and far, far too hot.

"Dad?"

His father's eyes stared past Noam, unseeing and glassy, reflecting the lamplight outside. That wasn't what made Noam lurch back and collide with the window, its latch jabbing his spine.

A drop of blood welled in the corner of his father's eye and—after a single quivering moment—cut down his cheek like a tear.

"Mrs. Brown!"

Noam shoved the chair back from the window, half stumbling across the narrow room to the curtain separating their space from their neighbor's. He banged a fist against the nearest bookshelf.

"Mrs. Brown, are you in there? I—I'm coming in."

He ripped the curtain to one side. Mrs. Brown was there but not in her usual spot. She was curled on the bed instead, shoulders jutting against the ratty blanket like bony wings.

Noam hesitated. Was she . . . no. Was she dead?

She moved then, a pale hand creeping out to wave vaguely in the air.

"Mrs. Brown, I need help," Noam said. "It's my dad—he's sick. He's . . . he's really sick, and I think . . ."

The hand dropped back onto the blanket and went still.

No. No, no—this wasn't right. This wasn't happening. He should go downstairs and get another neighbor. He should—no, he should check on his dad. He couldn't. He . . .

He had to focus.

The blanket covering Mrs. Brown began to ripple like the surface of the sea. Outside, the hazard sirens wailed.

Magic.

Dragging his eyes away from Mrs. Brown, Noam twisted round to face his own apartment and vomited all over the floor.

He stood there for a second, staring woozily at the mess while sirens shrieked in his ears. He was sick. Magic festered in his veins, ready to consume him whole.

An outbreak.

His father, when Noam managed to weave his way back to his side, had fallen unconscious. His head lolled forward, and there was a bloody patch on his lap, yellow electricity flickering over the stain. The world undulated around them both in watery waves.

"It's okay," Noam said, knowing his dad couldn't hear him. He sucked in a sharp breath and hitched his father's body out of the chair. He shouldn't—he couldn't just leave him there like that. Noam had carried him around for three years, but today his father weighed twice as much as before. Noam's arms quivered. His thoughts were white noise.

It's okay, it's okay, it's okay, a voice kept repeating in Noam's head.

He dumped his father's body on the bed, skinny limbs sprawling. Noam tried to nudge him into a more comfortable position, but even that took effort. But this . . . it was more than he'd done for his mother. He'd left her corpse swinging on that rope for hours before Brennan showed up to take her down.

His father still breathed, for now.

How long did it take to die? God, Noam couldn't remember.

On shaky legs, Noam made his way back to the chair by the window. He couldn't manage much more. The television kept turning itself on and off again, images blazing across a field of static snow and vanishing just as quickly. Noam saw it out of the corners of his eyes even when he tried not to look, the same way he saw his father's unconscious body. That would be Noam soon.

Magic crawled like ivy up the sides of the fire escape next door.

Noam imagined his mother waiting for him with a smile and open arms, the past three years just a blink against eternity.

His hands sparked with something silver-blue and bright. Bolts shot between his fingers and flickered up his arms. The effect would have been beautiful were it not so deadly. And yet . . .

A shiver ricocheted up his spine.

Noam held a storm in his hands, and he couldn't feel a thing.

Chapter Two

Noam drowned in a sea of white heat and electric current. A dizzy free fall into the ocean, salt water drenching his lungs.

Then the tide receded. The storm cleared. Noam opened his eyes to bright light.

Everything hurt.

God, everything . . . his body was a knot of pain and exhaustion. Noam shivered as he shoved the bedsheets down, pushing upright. His mind blurred, and he couldn't remember—

Noam tipped his head back, a fresh wave of heat searing down his spine.

Where was he?

The room smelled of spoiled meat. He looked to the left.

A girl lay on the bed next to his with her mouth open, her face a solid gray mask, frozen midbreath.

Noam lurched out of bed, ankle catching in the sheets and sending him crashing sideways into an abandoned metal cart. The girl stared back with white eyes.

Jesus—how long had she been there? Days? Perhaps even weeks, her flesh rotting into the mattress three feet away while Noam shook through his fever and never noticed.

Door. There was a door. Get to the door.

Noam stumbled across the room, bare feet sticking to whatever fluid had congealed on the tile. He swore—*swore*—he could feel the bones of the building, cameras overhead, little electrical signals sizzling down the wires.

Hallucinating, that was it. Identifying patterns in the world, seeing himself—but from the outside, all edges and too-long pants.

Madness.

The hall was a long white ribbon stretching toward a pair of steel doors.

And silence. The sort of silence that suffocated, pouring into Noam's nose and mouth and ears like black water.

A camera gazed dispassionately down from the ceiling. Noam gazed back.

"Hello?"

His voice didn't sound like his own.

A crash behind him. Noam spun around, half expecting to see the girl from his room with skeleton fingers reaching for his throat—but there was nothing. Just empty hallway, fluorescent lights flickering on tile.

He had to get out. Anywhere was better than being in this dead air.

Noam faltered toward the double doors. He had made it three feet before they crashed open, spilling a small army of aliens in strange white space suits, oxygen tanks strapped to their backs and gloved hands held aloft.

"Hey, there," one of them said. His voice came out sounding odd, synthetic. "Hey, now. Take it easy. Stay where you are."

"Who—" Noam's throat was raw. It hurt to speak. He staggered against the wall and leaned there, cheek pressed against cold plaster. "Who are you?"

"We're doctors," the space suit said. "We're here to help. You've been very sick." He gestured at one of the others, who stepped toward Noam, dragging a stretcher. "Just relax. It's all okay."

I am relaxed, Noam wanted to say, but he could barely keep his eyes open. He slumped farther down the wall. It was almost a relief when the other doctor reached him, grabbing Noam's arm to help hoist him onto the stretcher.

The doctor injected him with a clear fluid.

"Whassat?" Noam mumbled.

"Sedative. Just to keep you calm, honey. Can't have you accidentally blowing this place to high heaven, now, can we?" The doctor patted him on the sternum with one huge gloved hand.

Noam tipped his head back and closed his eyes. He felt like he was spinning in place. Something buzzed between his ears like static.

He was distantly aware of the other space suits moving toward him, a low hubbub of untranslatable conversation. Someone plastered sticky sensors onto his chest.

"What's happening?" he managed to get out.

"Shh, it's all right. We're gonna get you out of here."

He gave up arguing.

They rolled him out those double doors, through an air lock that sprayed some acrid disinfectant all over him. Then out again, into a white-walled maze of corridors and too many machines, beeping, buzzing, the sound loud enough it shuddered down into his bones.

It was only after he'd been settled in a new bed that he managed to get his thick tongue working again. "Is this . . . hospital?"

"Yes it is, sweetheart," someone said.

Noam opened his sluggish eyes. Not a space suit, this time—a regular woman wearing scrubs. *Nurse*, his mind provided helpfully, if a beat too late.

"How much do you remember?" the woman asked.

His thoughts slogged along like heavy boots trudging through mud. "Nothing."

Only, that wasn't true. He remembered the dead girl. He remembered how she smelled.

They'd left her there with him. They'd left her with him because they had no reason to think he would live.

He gagged, and the woman made a soft noise in the back of her throat, dabbing his sweaty brow with a cloth. "You had the virus, sugar. Magic. There was a bad outbreak in west Durham."

Magic. *That's right.* The electricity in his hands. The blood on his father's face.

Noam rubbed chilly fingers against his temple and squeezed his eyes shut. There—he got sick, they all got sick, there was—he'd *survived.* That meant—

"Where's my father?" The words were sandpaper scraping against his throat.

"You need to rest," the nurse said. "The doctor'll be in later. He'll answer any questions."

Tar oozed through Noam's stomach. *Dead. He's dead. My father's dead.* "Where is he?" It wasn't a question anymore. "He's alive." *He's not alive.* "He's okay."

The nurse couldn't look him in the eye. Noam pushed himself upright. This time, she didn't try to stop him. He was falling, falling toward a ground that kept getting farther away.

"Tell me!"

She pressed him back against the pillows with one hand. "I'm sorry, Noam. You're the only one who made it."

Noam didn't hear what she said after that. The words were a language he'd abruptly ceased to understand, ears filled with the beep of his heart monitor and the shallow heave of his own breaths. The noise from the oxygen machine was a distant roar.

If once he'd hoped his father might get better, might wake up from that catatonia one day, might read the books Noam gave him, kiss Noam's cheek on early mornings and say, "Te amo, mijo"—that future had crumbled to dust.

The nurse said something else as Noam pushed himself farther down in the bed and put his back to her, closing his eyes. That made her stop talking. She just cut off midsentence and left, though not before patting him twice on the shoulder.

Something clawed at his chest, leaving long gouges in its wake. The wounds were bloodless. Nothing rushed in to fill them, not even the relief he'd feel if he believed the dead went to a better world.

He only realized later what that really meant—later, after he'd let an endless stream of doctors run tests and draw blood, after they'd put little objects on the table and asked him to levitate them. After they'd shined lights in his eyes and interrogated him: *What can you feel? Anything unusual? Anything useful?*

Magic killed his father and left Noam alive.

His body had fought magic and conquered it.

That made him a witching.

Witching. The word was practically synonymous with power, but Noam had none of that. His body was fragile, spun-sugar bone and translucent skin. If magic swam through his blood, he couldn't feel it. He held a hand over his head and stared at the greenish veins snaking along his fingers and down toward his wrist. The virus was still in there, wild and alive. He imagined it as blue ink, bleeding into every cell.

He tried summoning that storm again.

Nothing.

Maybe he'd be the first. A medical mystery. A witching without the witch.

Fuck witchings, anyway. Noam'd rather have his dad back.

Two days later, after he was off fluids and able to walk around, someone knocked at the door. Noam tilted his book down, realizing only then that he'd lost his place, had been turning pages without really reading them. The thought of another doctor prodding and poking him was unbearable.

"Come in," Noam said anyway. Apparently the manners his mother'd instilled in him were stronger than resentment.

The door swung open, and a man stepped in. He was taller than anyone Noam had ever seen, swallowing up the length of the doorway, his angular face as artful as if sculpted from marble. The creases of his suit could have cut Noam to ribbons. "Noam Álvaro?"

"Yes?"

The man shut the door. "I hope I'm not disturbing you. Do you have a moment?"

There was something strange about his voice, though perhaps it was just the accent. Noam couldn't place it. European, maybe.

Noam folded down the corner of his page and set the book aside. "I have lots of moments."

The man didn't take off his coat or gloves, just advanced into the room, his movements as precise and measured as everything else about him. Noam couldn't stop looking at him—like he was the center of gravity around which all things must orbit.

Why did he seem so familiar?

The man took the chair opposite Noam. He was far too long for the seat but didn't seem to notice.

"I'm told," the man said, elbows perched on his thighs, "your dynamics are quite impressive. It's been a long time since I've seen antibody titers as low as yours. I wanted to meet you myself."

He didn't look like a doctor.

But maybe all that meant was that he was a fancier doctor, seeking another publication for his curriculum vitae.

"I won't make a very good case study," Noam said. His father was dead because of this virus. That made it hard to care about antibody levels, yet antibodies were all anyone talked about.

No one really knew what made some people witchings and others not. Witchings had the same viral load as those who died, so it wasn't any kind of natural resistance. Whatever the secret to survival was, it ran in families—though clearly it hadn't run in *Noam's* family.

He folded his arms across his chest. "I can't do magic. Everyone's already tried."

The doctor waved away Noam's argument. "Sometimes it can take a few weeks. That's not unusual. Would you like to see?"

It took Noam a second to realize he meant the blood results. Noam shrugged, which the man took as consent. He pulled a slim black phone from his pocket and tapped a few times on the screen. "There," he said, passing the phone to Noam. "Beautiful, isn't it?"

It was a photograph. A GIF, actually, a brief recording at magnification showing the antibodies glowing like alien green lights on his blood smear right alongside the tangled threads of the virus, keeping it in check. A banner of nausea unfurled through Noam's gut. He couldn't help imagining that virus festering inside him even now.

"They look like worms," he said. He passed the man back his phone.

"Worms can't do what this virus does to people," the man said, almost reproachfully. But then he put the phone away and offered his hand, palm up. "May I?"

Noam nodded and placed his arm in the man's grasp. The man pressed two fingers to Noam's wrist and closed his eyes, concentrating on Noam's pulse. Noam was amazed he could feel anything at all through those leather gloves. They were real leather, too, despite how expensive meat was these days. Did doctors make that kind of salary?

He swore his skin tingled where the man touched it.

"I'm sorry about your father," the man said when he opened his eyes. He squeezed Noam's arm before releasing him, though he didn't lean away. "I lost my parents, too, when I was a few years younger than you are now."

Noam swallowed around the tight feeling in his throat and glanced down at his lap. His skin itched beneath the gauze over his old IV site; he picked at the tape with his thumb. "The virus killed them?"

When he looked up, the doctor was giving him a strange look. "No." A pause, long enough that Noam started to wonder if he'd said something wrong, but the man went on. "Nevertheless, I understand what you're going through. I won't promise it gets easier. But you learn to live with the grief in other ways."

Noam turned his face toward the window so the man wouldn't see the wetness stinging at his eyes. Now that both his parents were gone, the world was much larger than it had been before—gaping around him, sharp toothed and hungry.

"I should let you rest." The doctor unfolded that long body to stand, buttoning his coat. Noam quickly rubbed the heel of his hand against his face while the man was distracted, though it occurred to him that maybe the man was just offering him a chance to pull himself together in relative privacy. The man gave him a small smile. Not pitying but . . . soft, somehow. Understanding. "Get some sleep, Mr. Álvaro. I'm sure I'll see you again soon."

The next day they discharged Noam from the hospital.

Not to go home, though. Not even to Charleston, where so many new witchings went for basic training.

They sent him to the government complex.

From Tides of History: Shifting Political Power in the Modern West, *an Atlantian eleventh-grade textbook from 2098. Illegally imported copy found in the personal library of C. Lehrer.*

The first new nation to rise from the ashes of the catastrophe, Carolinia, established itself in May 2019 under the leadership of committee-elected monarch Calix Lehrer. Texas followed in June. But by late August, the rest of the former United States remained a shambles of fire- and nuclear-bombed wasteland, surviving communities separated by hundreds of miles of land infected with lethal magic.

The difficulty of transporting resources across these distances—especially considering Carolinia and Texas both closed their borders to travel, trade, and immigration—was perhaps the primary reason why Texan president Marcus Harlow called an emergency summit of representatives from the largest remaining communities. Originally, this event was to be hosted in Dallas. However, Carolinian leadership refused to meet at this location, citing concerns about Texan antiwitching sentiment. The location was changed to Boulder, in the present-day Midlands.

The Boulder Summit marked the decision to form nations from the remaining major communities in the former United States. A single-state solution was vastly considered impractical, both due to infrastructure difficulties in navigating the quarantined zone as well as

Carolinian refusal to rejoin with any nation that would not commit to legislative protection of witching rights. Therefore, borders were drawn based on a combination of natural landmarks (e.g., rivers, mountain ranges), cultural similarity (e.g., the historical Deep South states of Mississippi, Alabama, and Georgia, which became modern Atlantia), and, of course, consideration for the boundaries of the quarantined zone, where endemic magic and residual nuclear fallout made the land uninhabitable.

The Boulder Summit was also meant to host the signing of both a peace treaty between all the new nations as well as a mutual support agreement in pursuit of developing a magic vaccine. These plans went unmet, with competing claims as to why the treaty was not signed: Carolinian propaganda stated that other nations—including Texas and Atlantia—demanded an 80 percent reduction in witching population from Carolinia as a gesture of goodwill. Atlantian officials claimed that no such demands were ever made and that the refusal to sign a treaty was a strategic move by Lehrer and others to establish Carolinian military dominance in the region.

The true series of events at the Boulder Summit remains unclear to historians, as the original classified records were destroyed in a freak fire in 2063. With other witnesses since deceased, Calix Lehrer (then king of Carolinia, prior to his abdication in 2024) is now the only one with accurate knowledge of the Boulder Summit. Given limited diplomacy between Carolinia and other nations, it is unlikely these secrets will ever be told.

Chapter Three

The car arrived on schedule: a sleek black vehicle with tinted windows and cushioned seats. Durham sped past, a blur of ancient brick buildings and glittering neon nightclubs paving the way to the government district. They passed the old stadium, lit up for some event or another. Here the streets were peppered with green-uniformed Ministry of Defense soldiers. Not too many, not enough to frighten, but enough for Noam to get the message: *don't try any shit.*

Noam tugged at the sleeves of his new sweater to pull them down over his wrists, little linty flecks detaching to float down onto his thighs, and avoided his chaperone's gaze. They weren't far from Noam's neighborhood—although that was probably a firebombed shell by now. Best way to stop a virus spreading, after all, was to burn everything infected to the ground.

In that neighborhood, people lived two families to a home and boiled swamp water for drinking. He knew every person who lived in the bookstore, from old Mrs. Brown to the family downstairs with six kids who never slept. There was mold damage on the ceilings and a rat nest that came back no matter how many poison traps Noam set out.

The government complex was nothing like that.

It used to be an old tobacco warehouse, then was repurposed, and repurposed again, renovated year after year before magic made the world fall into ruin. During the catastrophe it had been a barracks.

Then it became a courthouse. Now it belonged to Chancellor Sacha. The brick walls smelled like history, remortared so many times that they were more mortar than brick. The people here dressed so well they had a new set of clothes every day of the week—and the more important they were, the better they dressed, all the way up to the ministers, with their crisp suit jackets and papercut collars.

These were the people Noam's father had spent half his life trying to undermine.

Now Noam was one of them.

Level IV, they'd told him in the hospital, was the highest rank of the witching training program, practically a factory for generals and senators and future chancellors. They said it was modeled off the same training Adalwolf Lehrer gave his militia before they overthrew the US government in 2018. They said this was the seat of all real power in Carolinia, that Noam's blood test made him the perfect Level IV candidate.

Noam reckoned he'd stay the perfect candidate right up until they remembered he was Atlantian. Then it'd be all, *thanks for your time* and *conflict of interest.*

"Wait here," Noam's chaperone said and disappeared through a heavy wooden door. Noam was alone.

It was a cool night, autumn perched on the blade of winter, quiet even in the center of the city. *Someone's magic,* Noam thought—and shivered.

He sat on a bench and braced his hands against the seat, leaning his head back. In that strange silence, the seconds stretched out like dark molasses. Noam imagined he could feel radio waves arcing over the city—a cobweb trawled by government spiders and their all-seeing eyes. He thought about his father, about that same sky curving over his now-dead neighborhood, and shut his eyes.

He ought to feel more than this. He hadn't cried over losing his father since feverwake three days ago, and now it felt wrong to be upset, as if he had the chance to grieve and missed it.

"I hope you haven't been waiting long," a voice said from behind Noam's left shoulder. His eyes snapped open.

Him. It was him. The doctor from the hospital.

Only he wasn't a doctor at all.

"You," Noam forced out, and Minister Lehrer's mouth twitched into a small smile.

"Me. Enchanted to make your acquaintance properly, Mr. Álvaro."

How the hell hadn't Noam recognized him before? His grandmother'd had a photo of Calix Lehrer hanging *in her house.*

This time, Lehrer was unmistakable. In his military uniform, tawny hair combed back, he could've been freshly clipped from a newspaper photograph.

The air caught in Noam's throat, oxygen suddenly something he could choke on. Reading about Lehrer, discussing him in history class and over the dinner table, wasn't quite the same as seeing him in person. The uniform made him seem even taller.

Which, fuck, Noam was still sitting in the presence of the *defense minister.* He started to get up, but Lehrer touched his shoulder and gently pressed him down onto the bench again.

"That won't be necessary," he said. "Next time perhaps we can stand on ceremony, but today, I think, exceptions can be made."

Lehrer stepped forward and sat on the bench beside Noam, both feet flat on the ground, his shoes so shiny they reflected the lamps overhead. The wind caught his hair and blew strands of it loosely across his brow, making him seem less formal, though he still didn't seem human. He looked the same as he did in that photograph Noam remembered, like he hadn't aged a day.

Impossible to believe he was over 120 years old.

Noam was too aware of his own breath, exhaling as quietly as he could.

Lehrer was . . . well. *Legendary* came immediately to mind. At sixteen, he'd survived the catastrophe. At nineteen, he overthrew a nation. At twenty, he was crowned king.

Now, even though he occupied one of the most powerful positions in the world, Minister Lehrer could walk into the courtyard of the government complex utterly alone, without bodyguards, and not spare a thought for safety. He was untouchable, more myth than man. To look at Lehrer was to see a man who was everything Chancellor Sacha was not: Revolutionary. Principled.

Witching.

That was the one thing Noam had never quite been able to grasp. Why did Calix Lehrer, who'd sacrificed so much to build his utopia, allow a man like Sacha to rip his nation apart?

A question for later. Not now, with Lehrer so close that Noam felt his body heat.

His magic.

"What now, sir?"

"Let's not talk about that yet," Lehrer said, and this time when he looked at Noam, it was with a warm smile—one that reminded Noam, painfully, of his father. "Let's just sit a spell. I don't get to do that often, you know."

It was a strange silence, Lehrer gazing at something far off in the distance and Noam wondering what this scene must look like to anyone watching: Defense Minister Calix Lehrer, reclining in the government complex courtyard next to a teenage boy in a too-small sweater.

Noam didn't dare move. What if he accidentally knocked Lehrer's elbow or brushed up against his thigh? He stole a glance at Lehrer's wristwatch, visible below the cuff of his jacket, and his heart stammered to an abrupt stop. Before, Lehrer had worn leather gloves, but tonight his left hand was bare in his lap, long fingered and elegant.

The lines of the black *X* tattooed between his thumb and forefinger were blurry now. Just looking at it felt like an act of violence.

"It didn't hurt as badly as you'd expect," Lehrer said.

Noam jerked his gaze away from the mark as if burned, even though it meant meeting Lehrer's eyes instead. They were unusually pale, more colorless than gray.

"I'm sorry, sir. I wasn't—I didn't mean to stare."

Lehrer smiled. "Don't apologize. There's no harm in curiosity."

Maybe not. But Noam didn't fancy risking it either way.

He tried to imagine a Lehrer as a child sitting in some bureaucratic office in the old country while a state official dipped the tattooing pen in ink. Noam'd read how Lehrer used his power to erase the scars of torture. Why leave this one?

Maybe he didn't want anyone to be able to forget. Everyone who had lived through the catastrophe was dead . . . except Lehrer. And as long as Lehrer had this mark, the descendants of those men who'd tried to wipe witchings off the earth could never sanitize history.

"It was a long time ago," Lehrer said. He lifted his left hand, holding it to the light. He didn't seem upset, just thoughtful. "Sometimes I feel as if all that happened to someone else." A small, dry laugh. "Or perhaps I'm just going senile."

Noam seized the opportunity to change the subject, desperate to talk about anything, *anything*, besides genocide. "You don't look your age. Sir."

No shit, Álvaro. Still, Lehrer was the only witching who'd been able to achieve something close to immortality.

Lehrer laughed. "If you thought I looked any older than forty, my vanity would never recover." He turned toward Noam, hooking his elbow over the back of the bench. He searched Noam's face. "I will be blunt with you, Noam. You cannot understand what I'm asking of you."

Noam thought he had a pretty good idea.

Lehrer went on, his gaze unwavering. "I'm asking you to make great sacrifices. But then, you've sacrificed before, have you not? I read your file. What you gave up, when your father became ill, was more than should be asked of any child. And as for your work with Tom Brennan, I think I, more than most, understand that sometimes individual freedom is an easy price to pay in exchange for justice."

Wait—wait, was Lehrer saying . . . was he *actually saying* what Noam thought he was saying? He stared at Lehrer's unlined face, breath stilled in his throat.

In Noam's old neighborhood, everyone had worshiped Lehrer because they thought he might champion refugees the way he'd championed witchings during the catastrophe—as though Lehrer was the personal hero of the downtrodden and the oppressed. Noam liked Lehrer well enough as a historical figure, but he'd thought the rest a touch idealistic.

Maybe he should have paid closer attention.

Sympathy isn't action, Noam told himself. Chancellor Sacha was still the one in charge of Carolinia. Lehrer's power was hamstrung by the same laws he'd drafted after abdicating the crown in 2024.

Still. Noam's chest was alight with a dozen fluttering butterfly wings, all of them beating the same rhythm.

"I'm not very patriotic."

"Not for Carolinia as it is," Lehrer said. "But perhaps for what it could be."

The chilly wood dug in against Noam's palms where he gripped the edge of their seat. He kept seeing Lehrer's hand draped over the back of the bench, too aware of how near it was to his shoulder, of how he could tip slightly to the right and Lehrer would be touching him. "What are you saying?"

"I'm saying I wouldn't ask you to join Level IV if I didn't think you could make a real difference in this country. I'm trying to convince you to stay."

"Carolinia needs witchings. When the doctor said I was joining Level IV, he didn't make it sound like a choice."

Lehrer smiled, but it seemed incomplete. "There's always a choice." A moment's pause. "Of course, I would like you to make my preferred choice."

Always a choice? Not unless Lehrer meant enlisting in the military as disposable cannon fodder or being commissioned as an officer. Witchings weren't exactly in heavy supply these days, and everyone who was anyone in this country graduated from Level IV. The signing bonus they gave witchings who joined the military could make a huge difference if Noam donated it to the Migrant Center. And at least this way Noam could do something worthwhile.

The thing was . . .

The thing was, Noam was nobody. To date, his greatest accomplishment was hacking immigration records and getting thrown in juvie for it.

Needless to say, he hadn't exactly changed the world from inside a jail cell. Instead he'd watched four friends get deported to Atlantia. All of them had caught the virus within a week.

All of them died.

Ever since feverwake, he'd seen the world through a haze of shock and grief. Now, possibility glimmered just out of reach. Lehrer was here, Lehrer was sitting *right here*, the most magically powerful man alive, even though he worked under Sacha—and he wanted Noam to be part of his world.

He wanted to give Noam power.

If Noam gave this up, he'd be giving up a chance to do something *real*. To amount to more than his parents had.

Of course, just thinking that was enough to make him sick with himself. There was nothing wrong with being a refugee. But could he walk away from this? From Lehrer, with his incredible abilities and immortality and the faded mark on his hand that suggested he—if no one else—might understand what it was really like in Carolinia today?

"I understand," Noam said. The promises—to trust Lehrer, to be a good soldier—should have come pouring out of his mouth, but they congealed there instead. Whatever Lehrer might say about information and consent, people like Noam didn't have other options.

Perhaps Lehrer recognized that, too, because he said, "I'll push you harder than you think you can go. Some days you might wish you'd said no to me here. Or that you'd died in fever, like your father."

That cut deeper than Noam was willing to admit.

He wanted Lehrer to trust him, though, even if Lehrer shouldn't. So he smiled, making himself the frail, nervous little thing Lehrer must expect him to be. "There's nowhere else for me to go. But I'm stronger than I look."

"I'm relieved to hear it," Lehrer said. He reached out that same marked hand to clap Noam on the shoulder. "We need strong men and women to protect the ones who are weak. If you make it through training, you won't just be powerful, Noam, you'll be able to use that power to help people. That's far more important than a little pain."

Lehrer got to his feet and reached out to help Noam up. Noam felt dwarfed next to him, even though he'd always been the tallest in his class. Or maybe Noam was now small, shrunken by the virus into something fragile and easily subsumed.

Noam met Lehrer's gaze and smiled again.

After 123 years, that was one thing Lehrer might appreciate.

Everyone else might be dead, but Noam was *still fucking here.*

And as long as he was, he had a war to win.

Level IV was housed in the east wing of the government complex, a building attached to the administrative west wing by a series of now-empty halls. Lehrer seemed oblivious to the silence. The nails in the soles of his fine leather shoes clicked off the hardwood floor, echoing toward high ceilings, his presence leaving no room for intruders. Even so, the shadows seemed to move in the corner of Noam's eye, though every time he looked they stood still. This place was beautiful, Noam decided, but there was something about these walls that he didn't like—walls that closed in on him, that had teeth.

"You grew up near here, didn't you?"

Noam startled, and when he met Lehrer's gaze he almost flinched. How long had Lehrer been watching?

"Yes," Noam said. After a moment he dragged his gaze away, toward the windows and the few skyscrapers peppering the downtown skyline, the banks and office buildings visible through the evening fog. "Ninth Street."

"You know your way around, then. Have you been to this part of town before?"

"Some. Mostly on field trips."

"It's lovely, isn't it?"

Noam wasn't sure he'd use that word. When Noam thought about *lovely places*, he thought of faraway cities in books. New York, before it was destroyed. Berlin and Kyoto. Places people had visited before Carolinia closed its borders but were now elusive as daydreams. Still, he thought he understood what Lehrer meant. If he could look at Durham for the first time, he might find beauty in the brick warehouses, the oddly crenelated roofs, the ancient and crumbling smokestacks.

And all this was Lehrer's creation, of course. He and his brother built Carolinia from the ashes of the catastrophe, a nation cut from what used to be three states, now sewn together and made whole. It was lovely because it was loved—because it was *alive*.

"Yes," Noam said, a little surprised with himself for saying so. For being sincere.

They turned one last corner and stopped in front of an unlabeled door. Noam tried to memorize its featureless face, its location in the hallway, to recall how they got here so he could do it again on his own, but all the seconds leading up to this moment were just a blur. And at the center, like the focus point of an old film: Lehrer.

Lehrer delivered him to a steely-haired woman named Dr. Howard, who was in charge of supervising Level IV cadets. She gave him a cursory tour of the barracks, not that Noam remembered much by the time he was ushered to the boys' bedroom and left alone in the dark. He lay awake for hours, feeling like he'd swallowed a storm. The other boys' breathing rustled out from the shadows, too loud. It reminded him of the noises that hid around corners in the bookshop: his father's soft snores, the pad of his mother's feet on the floor when she got up for a glass of water, neighbors bickering downstairs.

All of them were dead now.

It was too large, too terrible, to comprehend: that a fever could wipe his world clean like a dishcloth scrubbing a dirty countertop. Heat burned his throat. Noam turned his face into the pillow, squeezing his eyes shut even tighter. *Don't cry.*

Don't think about those little details: The way Carly laughed when she had a secret, the cut of his father's grin that time Noam managed to get an illegal stream of the Colombia-Argentina game on his holoreader. Noam's mother, asleep with a book draped over her face.

His grief was a grim specter on the other side of a shut door. And if he opened that door, he'd be consumed. He'd go fevermad, like the raving cretins scurrying pestlike through the gutters, ranting about evolution and viral gods.

No. He was finally where he needed to be. Where he could use whatever powers the witchings taught him to undermine the foundations of their world and rebuild it into something new. Something *better*.

He couldn't break.

He wondered if Brennan was still alive. If he knew that Noam had survived. If he also lay awake on the other side of the city—had texted

Noam, not realizing Noam's phone burned with all the other contaminated artifacts of his old life.

Noam rolled onto his stomach and sucked in a mouthful of air. It tasted like detergent.

Brennan was like Noam. He didn't have anyone else either. His kids died in Atlantia, and he'd never married. It was just him and Noam's dad and Noam himself, the crooked edges of their broken families fitting together imperfectly but *right*.

Noam had to believe Brennan survived. Brennan didn't live in the same neighborhood as Noam, so he might not have been blocked in by the military perimeter set up to stop the infection. Anyway, magic was transmitted by contact with infected body fluids, right? Noam hadn't coughed on him or anything. (Or kissed him, like he kissed Elliott—Elliott who was most definitely dead.)

Only the virus wasn't just transmitted through fluids. Noam remembered reading something, insomniac at four in the morning with his holoreader propped on his knees: a research study suggesting magic might transfer through physical contact as well. Noam had always thought it was just paranoia and poor science education, people worrying about catching the virus when witchings used magic around them.

But what if it was true?

When Noam went to the Migrant Center, when he fell asleep over the keyboard Brennan would keep using, when Brennan touched his shoulder and Noam jerked awake—was he already contagious then? Did magic seep through Noam's skin, between the fibers of his sweater, and poison Brennan's fingertips?

Stop it, Noam ordered himself. *Stop thinking like this. Go to sleep.*

Eventually he must have, because he woke hours later to an empty room.

Shit. Was he supposed to be up early? No one said anything about classes or early training. Noam fumbled out of bed and hastily made up the sheets. He'd slept in his clothes, so being dressed was just a matter of pushing his feet into his shoes and dragging his fingers back through his hair—not that it helped.

But when he emerged from the bedroom, the apartment was eerily quiet. People could have been there moments before: dishes stacked on the rack next to the sink to dry, someone's book left open on the table with a clean fork tucked between the pages to mark the spot. It was impossible to guess anything about the people who lived here. From the state of the kitchen—all gleaming chrome and a bowl of fruit sitting on the counter—someone clearly tidied up the place every night. Everything had its purpose, down to the bland mass-produced artwork hanging on the walls. None of it felt like a home, though it was far nicer than anywhere Noam had lived before.

He wandered through the other rooms branching off from the hall: a gym, a classroom, an office for Howard, another bedroom that must belong to the girls. These rooms were equally as neat, all sharp edges and military precision.

There was no phone that Noam could see. No way to ring up the Migrant Center and ask if Brennan was around. Eventually Noam returned to the kitchen and sat at the table, staring across at the open book. The letters bled together as Noam's eyes unfocused. Maybe everyone had gone to school. But then why hadn't Howard left a note? Annoyed, Noam shifted in his seat to tuck one foot under his thighs and reached for the book, pulling it closer. The fork clattered onto the tabletop.

Invitation to a Beheading. Noam smiled despite himself; he'd read this book at least four times. The bookshop had multiple copies, so there was always an *Invitation to a Beheading* lying around somewhere to be picked up when bored. He pressed a thumb against the pages and let them flitter against his skin, a papery *fwip* until there was just the cover in his grasp. He peered at the book jacket, intending to read the summary, but someone had scrawled a note:

Dara Shirazi, return to owner.

The latch turned. He shut the book, pushing it across the table just in time as the front door swung open. A series of teenagers spilled into the room, all wearing identical olive cadet uniforms: one boy, two girls. Last night's anxiety rushed back in all at once, thickening like nausea in Noam's throat.

"—an ego thing. Swensson'll never admit you're right, so you might as well let it go. You only *just* got off his bad side, anyway . . ."

The girl who was speaking seemed to realize Noam was there only as she finished the sentence, words faltering, then trailing off in uncomfortable silence. Probably wondering how much Noam heard and how much she trusted him to hear it.

But then the silence cracked like an egg, and the girl brushed past the others to smile at Noam. The expression was bright and sincere seeming on her young face.

"Hey. You're the new guy, right? I'm Bethany."

Up close she looked to be around fourteen or fifteen, white with curly blonde hair pulled into a bouncy ponytail, like one of those perfect golden girls Noam used to know, the ones always knotted together and whispering in groups. Upon inspection, even the way she smiled reminded Noam of his ex-girlfriend. Carly'd had that same carelessness about her, as if she believed the world could orbit around an undocumented Atlantian girl living in the slums.

But Bethany wasn't Carly. And she wouldn't die like Carly had, deported to an infected homeland she didn't remember.

She extended her hand. After a moment, Noam took it.

"Noam," he said. Her grip was surprisingly firm. "Was I supposed to be up early this morning?"

"Free pass, since it's your first day and all. All you missed was basic—lucky, really."

She perched on the edge of the chair just across from him, and after a taut moment, the other two took her cue, joining Noam and Bethany at the table.

"This is Taye," she said, tilting her head toward the tall black boy with a toothpick sticking out of his mouth like a skinny cigarette, "and Ames," the other white girl, who had flipped out her phone as soon as she sat down and was now furiously tapping out a text. "Ames is a bitch," Bethany said after a beat; Ames gave them all the finger without lifting her gaze from her phone. Her finger, like most of the rest of her Noam could see, was tattooed.

"It's nice to meet you, Noam," Taye said, and he reached past Ames to shake Noam's hand. "Have you been to aptitude testing yet? I hear you came from outside."

He said *outside* like it meant something, like the world beyond the Level IV program was some foreign place he'd never been. Maybe he hadn't. Most people who survived the virus were a lot younger than Noam. If Taye came from one of the other programs, promoted into Level IV rather than being assigned to it directly, he might not remember anything else.

"Not yet," Noam said. "Dr. Howard didn't mention anything about tests." Should he be worried? Was this the kind of thing he ought to study for? Or was it just assumed he'd *know* all about aptitude testing, the kind of thing he would've learned if he'd ever taken a civics class?

"Don't worry about it," Bethany said. "It's not a big deal. You'll do fine. I mean, if you got sent straight to Level IV, you've got to be pretty talented, right?" She glanced at Taye and Ames, as if for confirmation; the latter had finally put down her phone.

"I don't know about that," Noam said. "I haven't even done any magic yet." Judging by the looks on their faces, that was the wrong thing to say. "Lehrer just showed up in my hospital room and told me I was coming here. Something about my antibody titers."

"Wait, *Minister Lehrer* sent you?" Taye shot a meaningful look at Ames. "Do you think Dara knows?"

"Don't think he cares," Ames said. Still, she fixed Noam with a narrowed gaze. Noam got the abrupt impression he was being observed and summarily analyzed, as if Ames were jury, judge, and executioner of the Level IV social scene. "Where you from, Noam?"

"Here," Noam said. He gestured vaguely toward the window. "On the west side. Ninth Street."

"Ooohh, right." Taye tugged the toothpick free. "That's super Atlantian territory now, right? I heard it's pretty overcrowded, with all the refugees."

"Yeah. I guess it's"—what the hell was he even saying?—"super Atlantian."

All of them watched with bated breath, like he was supposed to keep going. Under the table, Noam hooked both ankles round the legs of his chair.

Stay calm. Stay calm. He wouldn't be able to help Atlantians if he got thrown in jail his first day in Level IV.

"It's a little crowded," he added.

That seemed to be what they were waiting for, because Taye nodded knowingly and said, "It was only a matter of time before there was an outbreak."

Noam's whole body was on edge, waiting for someone to say it. Someone *was* going to say it, any second now. Carolinians just couldn't help themselves—

"Border control is shit," Ames agreed. She hadn't stopped watching Noam. "You flood a small neighborhood with a bunch of rednecks who're probably infected already, and it's gonna be a shitshow."

And there it was.

Noam felt a thin layer of frost crystallize under his skin before he even opened his mouth. "How long is the virus incubation period, d'you reckon?" he asked as lightly as he could manage—as if he didn't know. As if every Atlantian hadn't learned all too well from the constant fear that seethed in the slums and the refugee camps, the silent and savage knowledge they could be next.

"Twenty-four hours," Bethany said.

"Ish," added Taye, but Bethany's expression had gone oddly still, her hands in loose fists atop the table. She, at least, had cottoned on.

Noam smiled, sickly sweet.

"Wow," Noam said. "It took my dad way longer than that to get sick after he came here from Atlantia."

It was worth it just to see the looks on their faces, staring at him like he was the unholy incarnation of Typhoid Mary. Taye's toothpick hung forgotten in his hand.

Noam propped his elbows on the table, smile widening. Spite tasted like bile in his mouth. "No worries. I survived, so pretty sure I'm not contagious anymore."

"Of course you're not. And we couldn't get infected again, even if you were." Bethany actually scooted closer to him, not away, and gave him a tiny grin. "Though you're about to be in a world of trouble all the same. Have you been reading this?"

The change in subject was so abrupt that at first he didn't know what she was talking about, until he looked down and saw her pointing at *Invitation to a Beheading*.

"Oh," he said. "Not really?"

Bethany shook her head. "That's Dara's book. I'd be careful if I were you. He doesn't like people touching his things."

"Maybe he shouldn't have left it out, then," Noam said. Across the table, Ames lifted a brow.

"That's a risky stance to take," she said. "Good luck with it."

It was such an ominous thing to say that Noam almost laughed, biting the inside of his cheek to keep from making a face. He had no idea who Dara was, but if he was another student, then he couldn't be older than eighteen. Noam found it difficult to imagine any boy, even one who survived the virus, being worthy of that kind of warning.

Then again, he'd heard stories. They'd all learned about that kid back in the '50s who came out of feverwake with the ability to split atoms. He didn't have control. It was an accident.

He'd leveled his whole city with a nuclear blast twice the size of the one that destroyed New York.

"So," Taye said, "what's your presenting power?"

Noam didn't get a chance to answer; that was the moment Dr. Howard returned, tapping her watch and declaring the others were about to be late for class. Noam stayed where he was while the cadets' lives eddied around him: showers and quick snacks eaten over the sink, shouts down the hall in pursuit of lost socks, wet-haired teenagers wandering through the den in various states of undress. The barracks felt smaller with people in it. Noam preferred it that way.

Was this going to be his life now? Clean halls and real doors, the chance to go to *school* again?

He wanted that, but he hated himself for wanting it. All this . . . all of it was bought and paid for with the blood of dead fevervictims. Carly, Noam's old juvie friends, deportees. Noam's own father.

"Noam?" Dr. Howard zeroed in on him the second the other students had been ferried out the door. "It's time for your aptitude testing."

Noam didn't move. "What does this 'aptitude testing' entail, exactly?"

She glared disapprovingly, but the carefully blank look on Noam's face didn't falter.

"We need to know what you can do and how well you can do it," she elaborated at last. "We need to know more about your magic—any special affinities, boundary conditions. It's standard operating procedure, Mr. Álvaro. There's nothing to worry about. Now come with me."

Noam really, really didn't want to go with her. He couldn't imagine anything less appealing than being asked to make a fool of himself in front of a whole bunch of government officials.

Still. He was admittedly interested in figuring out what kind of magic he could do.

He got up, dusted off his trousers—though there wasn't much he could do to make the old hand-me-downs presentable—and followed Howard out into the hall.

Now that it was daylight, the corridors swarmed with government officials, tall and cold and blank eyed like ghosts from another world. Their gazes lingered on Noam as he went past—as if he had *contamination threat* painted all over him. Like Atlantia was written on his skin as much as in his blood and bone.

Just wait. He pushed the thought back at them and their smug faces. *I'll learn magic. I'll become a witching. And I'll use everything Carolinia teaches me to help Atlantia instead.*

They might've been in the west wing, the wing that usually housed high command, but Howard didn't bring him to someone's office. Instead they went down, following a narrow spiral staircase into the basement. There was a single door. Howard knocked.

"Enter."

"Go on, then," Howard said.

Noam looked at the door, at its unassuming steel knob.

He wouldn't be any use to Brennan or the cause if he was intimidated by a few men in suits.

He opened the door.

The room within was not the kind of room you'd expect to find so far underground, not unless they'd torn out the ceiling to merge it with a room on the floor above. It had a tile floor and soaring rafters, with streams of light cast down from tiny rectangular windows near the ceiling. The space was empty, if you didn't count the two tables at the far end—one bearing a whole mess of objects, the other surrounded by people in military uniforms.

A ripple of shock ricocheted through him: Minister Lehrer was among them.

Lehrer was also in uniform, although his had a commander's circle of silver stars on its sleeve instead of lesser insignia. Noam managed not to falter, but it was a near thing.

Lehrer met his gaze, a small smile crossing his lips.

"Noam Álvaro," one of the others said, reading off a folder in front of him. "Álvaro—is that a Carolinian name?"

Jesus, people just couldn't quit today, could they?

Noam raised a brow. "Are you trying to find out if I'm Atlantian or just if I'm white?"

That, at least, earned him a reaction. The man's throat convulsed and he frowned, then tipped his head closer to his holoreader to cover his expression. "The former."

"Yes. My parents were Atlantian."

The man looked up. "Documented?"

"No," Noam said. "But I was born here, if you'd like to see my papers."

"That won't be necessary."

Noam desperately wanted the man to say something else about Noam's father. Fuck going back to prison, and fuck self-control.

Calm down. He'd chosen this for a reason; he had to remember that. His heart pounded in his chest, and he forced himself to breathe, unsteady little gulps of air that didn't make him feel any better.

The young woman intervened, tapping the table. "Come closer, please." Noam approached until she said, "That's far enough. Ivar, if you will . . . ?"

The last man, black haired and wearing a colonel's phoenix insignia, said nothing. Did nothing. He sat there and looked at Noam, unblinking, until Noam's skin itched.

Maybe he was having some kind of seizure.

Noam was about to open his mouth and say something when the man finally twisted toward Lehrer and spoke. "His dynamics are well within range for Level IV. You were right about that much, sir."

"I usually am," Lehrer said benignly; he didn't seem to find the remark insubordinate. He gestured toward the other table. "Mr. Álvaro, why don't you go have a look at all these. Let us know if anything stands out."

Another test. If Noam really was Level IV, he'd probably send the whole table spinning up toward the ceiling. He'd turn it invisible. Light it on fire.

Instead he walked over to look down at the items spread like some bizarre buffet before him. There was a baseball bat, a bowl of water, some matches, what looked like metal ball bearings . . . even a couple lamps, their cords dangling off the edge of the table, one snaking along the floor to plug in to an extension cord and the other simply hanging loose.

What if his presenting power turned out to be something dumb, like changing his eye color? They'd probably kick him out.

He glanced back at the others. "What exactly am I supposed to be looking for?"

The woman shrugged. "You tell me."

All I see is a bunch of random shit.

Noam pretended to be interested anyway, poking around a stack of magazines, an ancient-looking and incredibly ugly necklace, a pile of misshapen rocks. He rolled one of these around between the palm of his hand and the table, bemused by the way two of the adults suddenly leaned forward in their seats, anticipatory, only to seem disappointed when he moved on to the next thing.

There was no magic. No moment when his fingers grazed metal, or wood, or stone and he felt a telltale spark.

Useless.

"This is a waste of time," one of them—the black-haired man—muttered.

Lehrer cleared his throat and picked up a pen to make a note on a pad of paper.

It was oddly gratifying to watch the way the others' faces went pale. All gazes swung back round to Noam, as if he were suddenly the most important person in the world.

They made him stay at the table for ten minutes. Ten excruciating minutes examining every last piece of yard sale nonsense before, at last, Lehrer said, "That's enough, Mr. Álvaro. Thank you."

"So," Noam said, returning to the center of the room and stuffing his hands into his pockets. "Did I pass?"

Judging from the disappointed looks on their faces, the resigned set to the woman's mouth, that was a no. Noam fought the strange emotion bubbling up within him, a hot mixture of anger and embarrassment. What did they expect? They brought him in here, told him nothing, propped up a table full of garbage, and expected him to perform miracles? He fucking *told* Lehrer he couldn't do any of this shit, but Lehrer had let him get his hopes up anyway, had let him believe for one second he wasn't damned to the same life as his parents. That he might ever amount to more than just another unemployed slum rat with a criminal record and a foreign last name.

Stupid. He should have known better.

The woman drew out a tablet and began typing, brow furrowed. The man who had first greeted Noam swiped at his holoreader with a frown on his face. The black-haired colonel was bland and utterly unreadable.

Lehrer just sat there, chin resting on the heel of his hand, watching Noam.

The silence was relentless, broken only by the obnoxious click of the woman's overlong nails on her screen. Probably typing about just how fucking useless Noam would be in Level IV, considering he couldn't do shit.

"Do that again."

The typing stopped. The older man froze as well, pen in hand. All looked to Lehrer, who had straightened in his seat, leaning slightly toward Noam. His voice was sharper than before. This was not the calm and collected man Noam had seen on television or even the mild one he'd met in person.

Noam faltered, hands curling into fists.

"I'm sorry, sir," he said after a long pause. "I don't know what you mean. I didn't do anything."

Lehrer made a dismissive gesture. "No. You did something. I felt it. I want you to do it again. What was that just a few seconds ago, right before I spoke?"

"Nothing," Noam said incredulously, shaking his head and forcing himself to flex his fingers. "I was just thinking."

"About what?"

"I was imagining what she was writing." He nodded toward the woman.

Lehrer's brows flicked up. "What did you imagine? Verbatim, please."

"Despite negative antibody staining present at very low dilution, one in two, prospect shows no signs of useful magical skill or ability. Do not recommend for officer candidacy."

From the moment Noam started speaking until the last bizarrely specific word dropped out of his mouth, as naturally as if he'd been reading off a sheet of paper, it felt as though his heart stopped beating. Lehrer watched him the entire time, perfectly unruffled. And when Noam was done, the woman slid her tablet across the desk for Lehrer to see. He peered at the screen, scrolled down a few lines, then glanced up.

"Exactly correct," he said. He sounded pleased but not surprised.

"Telepathy?" the woman said, aghast and staring at Lehrer with wide eyes. "What are the odds, after—"

Lehrer shook his head. "Technopathy, unless I miss my guess. Equally rare, as presenting powers go. I don't think I've ever met a presenting technopath before." He was still smiling, the expression small and oddly private, like it was meant for Noam alone.

"I seem to recall from your file that you have a lot of experience with computers," the older man said, finally showing some interest in Noam now that he was useful.

"One of my jobs is at a computer repair shop, and I do some programming on my own time." No doubt that file was full of all the felonious details.

Which, it seemed, they were all polite enough to ignore.

Well. *Polite.*

"And yet," the man continued, tapping at his holoreader without looking up to actually meet Noam's eye, "you never graduated from the eighth grade. Is there a reason for that?"

Noam's mouth twisted. "Sure, there's a reason."

"Your mother's suicide?" the woman said archly. Noam nodded. "Were you suffering from depression yourself?"

"No." At the disapproving looks his tone received, Noam revised, softening his voice as best he could: "No. My father was sick. I left school so I could work to support us. It's not uncommon. At least, not where I grew up."

"Perhaps not." The black-haired man was as cool and crisp as crushed ice. "But it is quite uncommon for Level IV. You may not be aware, given your limited education, but magic requires specific knowledge in order to be used. To move a ball across the room without touching it, one must have some understanding of physics. To deflect a tornado from hitting the city, one must know meteorology."

"I know that," Noam snapped. "I'm not a total idiot."

"Then you also know you can't attend the same classes as the other students without passing a placement exam. Without knowledge, magic is useless. We expect our Level IV students to develop abilities beyond their presenting powers, but you'll never amount to anything more than a technopath."

Abilities *beyond* his presenting power?

Noam knew that was possible; of course he did—no matter what these people seemed to think, he'd cracked open a book a time or two. But if being a witching was rare, and being a technopath rarer still, having more than one ability was . . .

Noam had never met someone like that.

Only that wasn't true, was it? He glanced at Lehrer, whose unreadable smile lingered.

"I can learn," Noam said, staring back at Lehrer. "I don't need to go to the shitty Ninth Street public school and sit in a tiny overheated classroom with three hundred other students to figure that two plus two equals four; I can read pretty well on my own. Let me take the test."

The adults exchanged glances. Most looked to Lehrer for their cues. For one reeling moment, Noam was certain he was about to get thrown out on his ass, but Lehrer's expression remained unchanged.

"I don't see why we shouldn't let him try," the woman said.

Could Noam sense a change when she shut off her holoreader—as the electrical cells stopped spitting data back and forth and went to sleep? Or was he only imagining it?

"He can take the exam this afternoon while the others are in class," she continued. "We'd be fools to pass on a low-antibody technopath just because he comes from a spotty background."

Noam wasn't sure he liked being discussed as a business acquisition much more than he liked being looked down upon for his parents' nationality, but this time he kept his mouth shut. There was probably some cosmic quota for the amount of sass you could get away with in one day, and Noam wouldn't be surprised if that cold black-haired man was keeping score.

"Why not?" the older man agreed after a moment. He looked to his left. "Ivar?"

The colonel sighed and arched a brow, which the others seemed to take as sufficient response.

"Excellent. Mr. Álvaro, you'll return to the barracks in the meantime. Colonel Swensson will be along later in the afternoon with your exam materials, and then we'll see about where to put you."

A dismissal, even if it wasn't phrased that way. Noam fought the urge to bow or salute and instead simply inclined his head in their direction. Mostly for Lehrer's benefit. Lehrer was the only one who had stood up for him, after all.

Upstairs, everyone was still out for classes, the barracks empty except for the paper shuffling Noam could hear from Dr. Howard's office. He found a few basic textbooks gathering dust in the corner of one of the bookshelves and tried to learn at least a thing or two about physics.

Turned out, learning physics required a little bit more than knowing how to read. Growing up in a bookstore, surrounded by the classics, by everything he'd ever want to learn about the British Empire, books upon books written in dozens of languages, didn't begin to lend him the kind of knowledge he'd need to answer a question about organic chemistry. Who cared that Noam read fluent Russian or that he could hack his way into the housing association's servers in less than six minutes? The only thing he remembered from science class was that the cell membrane was a lipid bilayer. Helpful.

Maybe, Noam thought when two o'clock rolled around, maybe he could use the time set aside for the exam to try to access test records and change his score to reflect a passing grade. He'd never tried cracking a government firewall before, but if he really was a technopath, he could probably figure it out. Right?

But when Colonel Swensson arrived, he carried a folder filled with printed paper and a black pen. Analog. The sardonic look he gave Noam as he slid the exam packet onto the kitchen table suggested he knew what Noam had been planning—knew and thought less of him for it.

"You have three hours," Swensson said and sat himself down just across from Noam. Presumably to make sure he didn't find some other way to cheat.

Don't panic, Noam ordered himself as he finally reached for the pen and wrote his name in block letters on the first page. *It's fine. It's just critical thinking. You can do this.*

But it wasn't, and he couldn't. The questions weren't logic based; they were factual, designed to appeal to someone skilled in rote memorization. Whether Noam was or wasn't that kind of person was irrelevant since he'd never memorized the right things. Despair had settled like a black rock in his gut by the time Swensson's stopwatch went off, and he passed the exam materials back.

"Dr. Howard will let you know your results either way," Swensson said, his cool gaze traversing Noam's face. "Therefore I'm sure we won't meet again."

I'm still a witching, Noam reminded himself once Swensson was gone, lying on the plush sofa with an arm flung over his eyes to block out the window light. He could do magic. He'd done it in that room, even. If he didn't pass this test—*although* he didn't pass this test—he'd still have a place in the military, even if just as an enlisted soldier.

Not that he'd ever go to Charleston. The whole point of signing up for Level IV was that it brought him close to Lehrer—and, by extension, to Sacha. If he wasn't here, in the government complex, then fuck it. Noam would take his power and go rogue, figure out some way to use technopathy to erase every piece of data on the government servers.

Great plan.

Noam swung his legs off the sofa and crossed back into the kitchen to grab *Invitation to a Beheading* off the table. He carried the book over to the chair by the window, setting it open facedown on the armrest, as if he'd abandoned the book midway through reading. He hoped this Dara, whoever he was, had a conniption.

As Swensson promised, Dr. Howard found him a few hours later, after Noam had raided the fridge for expensive-looking snack items but before he'd chosen a new book from the broad library collection. He spun around a bit guiltily when she said his name, even though he'd technically done nothing wrong.

"I failed, didn't I?" Noam said, deciding to preempt the soft breaking-of-the-news he could tell Howard was working herself up for. "It's all right. I figured."

"I'm sorry," Howard said. She genuinely did seem sorry.

Noam's heart felt strange, like it was being crushed in a giant fist. *It doesn't matter. I don't care.* "Cool. Guess I don't need to pack." It wasn't like he owned anything. "Mind if I keep the toothbrush?"

"You'll stay here," Howard told him, perfectly matter-of-fact. "You failed the exam, but Minister Lehrer has offered to personally oversee your remedial education until such a point as you can join your peers in regular course work."

What? "What?"

Howard repeated herself, the words the same as before. Lehrer had offered to tutor him. Defense Minister Lehrer, socialist revolutionary hero of the catastrophe, was going to teach Noam algebra? It was the most ridiculous thing Noam had ever heard. He pressed the heels of his hands to his eyes, clenching them tight, as if he could cast off the insanity of the situation and see things more clearly. But when he opened them again, nothing had changed.

"I don't understand," he said, and goddamn it, his voice was quivering. "Why? Why would he bother?"

"To be honest, I don't know. He's a very busy man. But then again, he finds time to give private lessons to Mr. Shirazi as well. Perhaps he sees you as an investment."

Noam frowned.

Interesting. So, Calix Lehrer had a good use for technopathy, did he?

What was he planning? And more importantly, was Noam smart enough to stay one step ahead of him?

"Okay," Noam said. "But tell him if I'm doing this, I want a new computer. And I want to be allowed to keep my job at the corner store and to keep volunteering at the Migrant Center."

Noam wouldn't be one of those assholes who turned his back on where he came from. Besides, if Lehrer wanted Noam here badly enough to give him private tutoring, he'd agree. And if he agreed, that in itself would be useful data.

Howard gave him an arch look. "Tell him yourself. You start lessons tomorrow after lunch."

In the archives of the Carolinian Ministry of the Interior: a documentary, never broadcast

FADE IN:

INT. CAROLINIAN NATIONAL HISTORY MUSEUM - DAY

Focus on an exhibit displaying instruments of torture used in US witching research programs during the catastrophe.

NARRATOR (V.O.)

By 2011, over two million witchings had already died at the hands of the US government. Dr. Granley is a history professor at Duke University and a world-renowned expert on the catastrophe.

INT. DR. GRANLEY'S OFFICE

DR. GRANLEY

Especially powerful witchings—usually those with multiple abilities or unusual presenting powers—were enrolled in massive federal experiments designed to understand how witchings attain new powers, with a secondary goal of developing a vaccine against magic. The . . . the sheer sadism of these experiments cannot be understated.

INSERT – PHOTOGRAPH OF ST. GEORGE'S HOSPITAL

NARRATOR (V.O.)

One such hospital is famous, not only for particularly extreme cruelty but because of the famous witching who survived it.

In 2015, four years after the US began rounding up witchings for extermination or experimentation, Adalwolf Lehrer's militia liberated the witching patients of St. George's Hospital near the historical town of Asheville, North Carolina.

INSERT – PHOTOGRAPH OF ADALWOLF LEHRER AND HIS MILITIA, VICTORIOUS AFTER THE BATTLE FOR S. CAROLINA

NARRATOR (V.O.)

Of the patients they saved, only one ultimately survived: Adalwolf's own brother, the future king of Carolinia, sixteen-year-old Calix Lehrer.

CHAPTER FOUR

"I'm glad you're staying," Bethany declared over dinner that evening, with the decisive tone of someone who'd considered her thoughts on the matter carefully. "We need new blood."

"Aw, sick of us already?" said Ames, smirking.

"I grew up with all y'all since I was eight. Of course I'm sick of you."

Taye snorted.

Ames popped a hush puppy into her mouth. "Nah, you love me, B. You know it, I know it, even the new kid knows it. I'm lovable."

"Since you were *eight*?" Noam interrupted before Ames could keep going—and she looked like she wanted to. "How young do people usually start?"

"I was nine," Taye said helpfully. He wasn't eating a proper dinner, just picking the red pieces from a bag of sour candies. He'd accumulated quite the pile next to his lukewarm potatoes.

"Seven," said Ames.

Seven. No wonder none of them thought Noam belonged here. They'd spent their formative years studying Rousseau and physics; Noam had spent his taking shifts at the corner store.

He abandoned his dinner, propping his elbows up on the table and clasping his hands in front of his mouth.

Why was Lehrer letting him stay?

It was all well and good to talk about antibody levels and "dynamics," but Swensson was right. Noam couldn't learn additional powers. Not quickly, at least. He was little use to Carolinia as a soldier either, considering his record for undermining legal authority. Was technopathy just that good?

Of course, working for Lehrer wasn't the same thing as working for Sacha. There'd been a big scandal in all the papers a couple years back, right after Sacha'd been elected. The two loathed each other, or so the gossip went. Lehrer thought Sacha too capitalistic, too eager to build Carolinia's economy at the expense of the working class, that the only thing Sacha cared about was making peace with the notoriously antiwitching Texas and Britain. And Sacha kept trying to push through all these reforms: health care, pensions, lower taxes . . .

So Lehrer had threatened to step down as minister of defense.

Whatever Sacha thought of Lehrer personally, he'd backed off right quick after that. No one wanted to be the chancellor who made Calix Lehrer resign.

"I suppose Lehrer must think I can catch up," he mused aloud. "Otherwise he wouldn't tutor me."

That got their attention.

"Lehrer's tutoring you?" Taye asked through a mouthful of candy; he'd moved on from picking through his sweets to devouring them.

"You are talking about *Minister* Lehrer, right?" Ames said dryly.

Noam shrugged. Taye and Ames exchanged looks. Taye lifted an eyebrow, and Ames shook her head ever so slightly.

Bethany set down her fork. "I guess that means you'll be sharing lessons with Dara. I can't imagine Lehrer has time to teach both of you separately."

Right. The mysterious Dara.

"I suppose. Howard said Dara's getting tutoring from Lehrer too."

At least Noam wasn't the only one so far behind.

Taye waved a dismissive hand. "Dara's a special case. He's top of our class. Lehrer raised him since he was four."

Oh.

"Yeah, I heard he's a *prodigy*," Ames said, and both she and Taye snickered at some indiscernible inside joke. Even Bethany smiled.

Noam sat in silence, at the same table as the rest yet not there at all.

He wished he had an excuse to get up and go back to the bedroom. Maybe sit on the floor of the shower and pretend for a while that he was back home in the bookstore. That any second now a neighbor would rap at the door, demanding he hurry up. That his father waited back in their apartment, gazing out the window across his city.

"How long's Lehrer keeping him, anyway?" Bethany said eventually. It took Noam a moment to realize she was still talking about Dara. She looked at Ames. "He's been gone three days."

"Why're you asking me?" Ames said. "I already said he didn't leave a note or anything." She dumped more salt on her plate. "He's liable to show up soon enough. Lehrer probably has him off doing fancy training for people with fancy powers. It's fine."

Something about the way Ames said it made Noam think maybe it wasn't fine.

"Listen, don't stress out, okay?" Taye nudged Noam with his elbow. "You'll catch up in no time. Just do a lot of reading."

"I grew up in a bookstore," Noam said, but Taye was still looking at him with that same expectancy, Ames stirring the salt mound into her potatoes, Bethany smiling. "Yeah," Noam said and sighed. "Lots of reading."

That night, as Noam sat in the common room with an algebra textbook—he figured he could get a bit of that *remedial education* done early and maybe not look so stupid in front of Lehrer and Lehrer's clever protégé—he looked at Bethany reading with a pencil in her mouth and wondered what his father would say if he could see him now.

None of these people, Dad would tell him, *give a shit about you or anybody you know.*

His father had said just that at the dinner table, brandishing his fork like a spear. His mother rolled her eyes, but Brennan—who'd come over for Shabbat dinner—had agreed. *Don't trust anyone in a suit*, Brennan had said. *Especially ones bearing government insignia.*

Government ran screeching through the halls wearing only wet towels. Government watched bad detective movies and ate only the red candies and sketched out new tattoo ideas by the window light.

Noam hated the government, or so he reminded himself as Taye gave him a dramatic tour of the barracks and when Ames let him borrow shampoo and Bethany made sure he had a set of drabs to wear tomorrow. He hated the government. He was here to tear their castle to the ground.

That night he barely slept, and come morning, his alarm went off at five. He choked down a few sickly bites of porridge, and then it was out to a field and the care of an eagle-eyed sadist named Sergeant Li, who put the cadets through the steps of basic training.

Noam used to run track, back when he'd still gone to school, but that was a long time ago and before the fever wasted his strength. Trying to run a seven-minute mile was grueling, the air bone cold in November and the frosty ground crunching underfoot. Noam barely managed to finish the mile under nine. Noam thought it was over, but no, then it was fartleks, and hurdles, and an obstacle course. Finally, after so many crunches and push-ups that Noam suspected he might throw up all over the icy lawn, Li blew her whistle and sent the cadets in to shower. The others headed off to their lessons afterward, leaving Noam alone in the Level IV common room to wait.

Howard showed up around nine, the sound of the front door startling Noam from where he'd fallen back asleep on the sofa. But he refused to leap up like a scolded child, even when Howard gave him a pointed look. He just stretched his arms up overhead, arching his back, and smiled. "Hey, again. Time for class?"

"Minister Lehrer won't like to be kept waiting."

"Let's go, then." Noam swung his legs off the sofa and stood, tugging the hem of his uniform shirt to make it appear a little less wrinkled.

Howard frowned. "Where's your satchel?"

"My . . . what?"

She sighed, tapping the countertop. "Your satchel, Mr. Álvaro. There was a satchel provided for you, containing notebooks and pens and other school supplies. It should be in your bedroom."

"Oh. Right. Hold on."

Noam remembered the bag from this morning. It hadn't been labeled with his name or placed anywhere near his dresser, so he'd just assumed the bag belonged to someone else. But there it was, leaning against the wall, a practical brown leather satchel with a strap and handle on top. Much nicer quality than anything Noam had owned before—and they were just giving it to him. To a *cadet*.

"Minister Lehrer's office is in the other wing of the building," Howard said as they set off, moving fast down the narrow halls, Noam's sore legs barely able to keep up. "You are not allowed in that part of the government complex unless accompanied by a ranking adult—do you understand? This is where the ministers and the chancellor have their offices. It's no place for an unsupervised cadet."

"Of course not," Noam said and smiled his best innocent smile. Howard didn't look convinced.

Nor should she be. Noam's blood felt sharp in his veins the moment they stepped into the central atrium of the building, where the walls were glass, sunlight streaming in from the courtyard on one side and the open street on the other, wooden floors gleaming underfoot. The glittering chandelier must have taken weeks to build—all those hands threading crystals on string. Men and women in gray military uniforms walked in every direction, people in suits jabbered into their phones or stared at screens in their hands, guards stood alert at the doors and watched with narrow eyes. The cobalt-blue flag of Carolinia hung over the entrance to the administrative wing, emblazoned with the sign of the white phoenix.

Noam was going to be here *every day*. He'd be surrounded by the most important people in the country: Lehrer, García, Holloway, the home secretary whose name Noam forgot. Chancellor Sacha himself.

If he could get in here sometime—alone, not with Howard, and not on his way to see Lehrer—he could do a whole lot of damage.

He had to get in touch with Brennan. If Brennan was still alive, Linda would know—Noam just had to find a way off campus.

Howard pressed her hand to a screen beside the towering wooden door to the west wing, leaning in to allow a tiny laser to scan her eye. Noam noticed with a burst of adrenaline that he could actually *feel* the computer working this time, as if his aptitude testing had been a switch just waiting to be flipped, and now he could sense the little electrical signals jumping between pins, the flicker of data packets being transferred, a whole buzzing ecosystem contained behind that panel and visible to Noam alone.

In that moment, he wanted to sink down onto the floor and just sit for a while, letting the tech wash over him. Binary was something he'd only known about on the theoretical level, something he'd considered while writing code or fixing someone's computer. It wasn't something to feel in one's bones, a new sensation as sharp as sight and sound.

Other countries—England, and Canada, and even York—had spent the past hundred years developing the kinds of tech no one in Durham could dream of. And yet when Lehrer closed the borders back in 2019, he'd frozen Carolinia in time. Noam only knew about foreign tech because he'd hacked a Canadian newspaper once. Carolinia relied so much on magic that it barely bothered developing new tech anymore.

But imagine . . . just *imagine* what it might have been like. How much Noam could've done if tech research hadn't ground to a halt in 2019.

Noam was a technopath in Carolinia—but that could have meant so much more.

Then again, being a witching anywhere else probably wouldn't bode well for him, considering all those other countries had a bad habit of locking witchings up in secure facilities for public "protection."

The latch clicked on the door: *1*, binary code. Entrance approved. An awed Noam trailed after Howard into the next hall, now blind to the people around them. He was too focused on the things they carried.

Cell phones and tablets. Medical implants. Tracking devices. Holoreaders tucked away in padded cases. Now that he was paying attention, they gleamed in Noam's awareness like beacons, information content washing over him in tiny humming waves. He tried to translate the data, but no luck.

Soon, he told himself in giddy anticipation. After Lehrer, after he knew magic.

Soon, he'd make sure this place had no secrets left.

They went up two flights of stairs and through a new maze of corridors. When they stopped in front of a plain, unmarked door, Noam realized he hadn't paid the slightest bit of attention to where they were going. And now they stood in front of what must be Lehrer's office, no sign or security panel in sight.

Howard didn't knock. She just turned the knob and let them in.

The room was relatively small, for one—no more than half the size of the common room back in the barracks. The best word for it was *cozy*. The walls were painted deep blue, the furniture upholstered in a soft burgundy fabric that appeared again in the patterning on the worn Persian carpets draping the floor. Everything here seemed at least a hundred years old and well loved, as if the decorator had stubbornly refused to acknowledge the passage of time and trend in favor of staying locked in a familiar microcosm.

And there was no technology whatsoever. Noam's power just hung there uselessly, somehow a strange sensation, although he'd only learned to notice tech the day before.

"I imagine Minister Lehrer will be along soon enough, so I'll leave you two be," Howard said.

Noam frowned, because there was no one else here, but then Howard stepped back out into the hall and pulled the door shut. There was another chair in the far-left corner that had been obscured by Howard's body and the open door, and someone sat in it.

He was older, seventeen or eighteen, brown skinned with unruly dark hair that fell in tousled curls around a perfectly symmetrical face. He had one leg drawn up onto the seat and an open book perched against his knee, the sleeves of his uniform rolled up to his elbows as if he'd decided to wear his drabs for fashion purposes rather than practical. He looked up over the pages of his book at Noam, a small frown tugging down the corners of his mouth, and Noam realized he was staring. It was hard not to. The boy looked like he belonged in a magazine.

As if he could tell what Noam was thinking, the boy raised an eyebrow.

"Hello," Noam said, trying to cover awkwardness with false bravado. "I'm Noam. I take it you're Dara, then?"

"I must be."

Noam waited for him to keep going, to say whatever else polite people usually said when meeting someone new, but that appeared to be all Dara had in him. He'd already turned his attention back down to his book, disinterested. Fighting a twinge in his stomach that felt suspiciously like embarrassment, Noam cast his gaze around the room. Was he supposed to sit down? How late was Lehrer going to be?

He looked back at Dara, lifting his satchel. "Is there somewhere I ought to put this?"

Dara glanced up. "Hmm? Oh." He tilted his head toward one of the other armchairs, the one nearest the window. "Right there's fine."

"Thanks." Noam carried the bag over and dumped it on the seat. He hovered there a moment, trying to figure out if it would be rude to go examine the bookshelves. Lehrer had a broad collection, it seemed, everything from glossy new titles to tomes so old the binding had worn away to expose hand-sewn pages.

Noam settled for sitting instead, choosing the chair nearest Dara. He stole a glance at the spine of Dara's book. *Ava.* Another Nabokov, just like the one he'd left on the table back at the dorm. Noam seriously doubted that was assigned material. He thought about saying something else, *That's a good book*, maybe, to try to draw Dara back into conversation, but that was probably pointless.

This close, barely a foot between their chairs, Noam thought he detected the shadow of a bruise on Dara's brow, only just obscured by the fall of his hair.

The door opened. Noam's gaze jerked away from Dara as he leaped to his feet, wondering if he ought to salute. He was glad he didn't, because Dara hadn't moved from his spot in the armchair, still looking at his book as if he hadn't noticed his commanding officer walk in.

Lehrer, for his part, didn't correct either of them. He smiled when he saw Noam, the door falling shut and cutting off the brief noise that had filtered in through the hall. "Good," he said. "I see you found the place all right, Mr. Álvaro."

Noam nodded, the back of his throat dry. Once again, that uniform made Lehrer look far too tall, like he wasn't built to exist in such small spaces. "Yes, sir."

Lehrer's gaze slid away from him to Dara, who was still reading. Then he looked away without saying anything, moving toward the armchair by the window. He made as if to sit, then paused, brows raised. He pointed to the satchel. "Whose things are these?"

"Mine," Noam said at the same time as Dara said, "His."

The nape of Noam's neck burned as he moved to retrieve the bag from the chair—from Lehrer's chair, Dara had him put his bag in *Lehrer's* chair—unable to look Lehrer in the eye as he retreated back over to his spot in the corner, his hands white knuckled around the satchel's strap.

Lehrer sat down in that chair, long legs crossed at the knees and his hands folded in his lap. His expression was impassive. "I gather the two of you made acquaintance," he said. His tone was as dry as dead leaves.

Noam nodded. Dara did nothing.

"Very well. Noam, you'll just be reading today. I put a book on the table there. Read through chapter four, do all the practice problems, and check them against the answer key. Let me know when you're done. Dara, you're with me."

Noam and Dara both got up, Dara finally abandoning his book in the chair and crossing the room to Lehrer. That left Noam to grab what was on the coffee table: *Algebra and Trigonometry, Book 2.* He sat on the sofa and tugged the book into his lap, opening up his satchel for a spare pencil.

This wasn't what he'd imagined when Lehrer said he'd tutor him. But then, Lehrer was still the reason Noam was even here at all. He turned to the first chapter.

Polynomials. Basic enough—even if the later sections looked like they were gonna be hell. What was a radical function? But for now, solving polynomials meant it was only too easy for Noam to get distracted by what was unfolding between Lehrer and Dara just five feet away.

Dara had taken up the seat nearest Lehrer's, frowning down at the small table between their chairs. There was nothing on the table; Dara was just looking at it. Opposite him, Lehrer sat with his elbow perched on the armrest and watched. He'd lit a cigarette. Every now and then he'd take a drag and then exhale the smoke away from Dara's face, toward the open window.

How the hell had Lehrer lived to be over a hundred years old if he was a smoker?

He imagined Lehrer's lungs staining black, crumpling in on themselves like burned paper, only to heal themselves and expand, pink and fleshy. Over and over again.

Noam wrote down the answer to the problem he was working on, then traced over the numbers again with his pencil.

"You can use gesture, if you must," Lehrer told Dara.

Dara lifted his hand, holding it palm down over the table, and almost instantly an apple appeared beneath it. Noam, startled, pressed too hard on his pencil, and the tip broke off. He hunched over, using the excuse of digging around in his bag for a fresh one to keep watching Dara and Lehrer.

The apple rocked once, twice, as if touched by a hand, then went still. It was green darkening to red, only barely ripe, and a little bruised toward the base.

"Good," Lehrer said, although he sounded dubious, as if illusion were nothing and not the most impressive piece of magic Noam had seen in his life. "But how complete is the illusion? Is it merely aesthetic?"

Dara didn't say anything, just picked up the apple and bit. The apple's juices leaked over its skin, trickling down onto Dara's wrist as he chewed, then swallowed. That appeared to answer Lehrer's question. He smiled and took the apple from Dara's hand, tossing it into the air once. The fruit vanished before it could fall back into his palm.

"Not bad. I'd like to see you do it without the gesture next time. You won't always have that crutch to rely on, especially if you're trying to fool someone who expects magic."

Noam turned the page in his textbook and started working through the next set of problems, but it was hard to concentrate with Dara practicing his illusions just a few feet away. He wanted, more than anything, to perform magic like that. Dara made illusion seem so easy, but Noam couldn't fathom how he was doing it. If your ability to do magic was based on how much you knew about whatever it was, like knowing physics to do telekinesis, then what kind of knowledge was required to make someone see and feel and taste something that wasn't there? You couldn't just change the way light was refracting off the air; you'd have to influence the signals sent by the nerves in Lehrer's hand when he touched the apple to get the weight and texture right. Then you'd have to titrate *those* when Lehrer threw the apple into the air, making quick and miniscule adjustments as fast as Lehrer could decide he wanted to throw the apple in the first place. And how did you manage taste? He supposed Dara could have faked that part, since he was the one who had bitten the apple, not Lehrer, but even so.

Dara was obviously every bit as powerful as the others said he was. He deserved to be here, getting private lessons from Minister Lehrer. Dara was the kind of person Level IV recruited . . . not middle school dropouts who didn't even understand radical functions.

If Noam hoped to ever catch up to Dara—if he hoped his power would be any use to the cause—he had a long road ahead of him.

Saturday, Noam had been in Level IV for a week, but all he'd accomplished in his lessons with Lehrer was to sit quietly and read remedial math. He hadn't even left the government complex. He'd thought about sneaking out to find Brennan, but he wouldn't get his new ID card until Thursday, and without ID he was pretty sure he wouldn't be let back in. Then on Friday they sprayed the city with some kind of chemical that allegedly sanitized everything and prevented viral outbreaks—not, of course, that anyone believed that actually worked. Even so, nobody was allowed outside for eight hours, and by then it was dark.

That left Saturday.

The others spent their free day in the common room, all four caught up in some poker game Dara had roped them into with a buy in Noam couldn't afford. Noam sat in the corner chair with his books and notes and watched as Ames threatened to fight Taye and Bethany for the spot on Dara's team. Ames sat in Dara's lap and refused to get up even when Bethany laughed and tugged at her hands; Dara smiled and locked his arms neatly round Ames's waist.

None of them seemed remotely aware—triumphantly trading chips, Taye accusing Dara and Ames of cheating with his typical melodramatic flair—that outside these walls there was a whole world where the money Ames scraped off the table into her lap could have fed an Atlantian family for three weeks.

Finally, Noam just left. No one seemed to notice.

Even the guards at the front door didn't stop him, although Noam had wondered if they might—and then Noam was free, stepping into chilly winter air and the seething warren of the city.

The first thing that hit him was the tech.

The whole world was a sea of data, so many electrical impulses sparking from pockets and tablets and streetlights and cameras and drones. It was like someone had plugged in a cord and turned on the galaxy.

The streetlight: yellow in three seconds. hey don't think i'll be home for dinnr but i'll see you later ok? $59.21. The weather today is forty-nine degrees and sunny. Breaking news. In twenty feet, turn left on West Pettigrew Street. The CIP is down 1.2 percent.

Noam struggled just to see properly, eyes refusing to focus when there was so much . . . so much *everything* spinning out all around him, from here to the horizon. It was too much, dizzying, a wild free fall that left Noam breathless and grasping at the rough brick wall to keep from losing balance. Inside hadn't been as bad. Why?

He blinked, hard, sucking in several deep breaths. Eventually the noise retreated to a quieter murmur in the back of his head, still there but not overwhelming.

People started giving him weird looks as he stood there staring at the street with his mouth open. Noam grabbed his new Level IV–issued phone and looked at it like he had somewhere important to be. He set off north.

The Sunday afternoon market that had built up around the sidewalks was nearly impassably crowded. Vendors shouted their wares, fresh chickens and cantaloupe and apples shipped in from the mountains. Noam bought a foam cup of hot cider for five aeres—insane, absolutely insane, that Level IV gave him an allowance that meant he could afford this—and drank while he walked, the sweet spices heating him from the inside. He paused for a while, too, in front of a cart that was piled high with fabrics of every hue: deep, bruised purples to silky scarlets. Cheaply made, but the shock of color was exotic after being in the government complex, where no one wore anything but drabs and dress grays.

They used to buy food here when his parents had been alive. He'd have the cash from his paycheck folded in his back pocket, would argue the shopkeepers down to a reasonable price for eggs and buckwheat. He'd go home, where his mother would have made lunch already. He'd eat arepas in his favorite chair in the history section and read a book in front of the window light.

He missed that life.

Which was stupid, of course. His parents were gone, and he was here. Better get used to it.

"Oh, *Noam*," Linda said when he showed up on the front step of the Migrant Center, just five blocks from where he'd been living. She had flour on her hands from prepping the lunch service, although she did her best to dust them off on her trousers before pulling him into a tight embrace. She gripped him so hard he worried he might bruise. "I heard what happened. Oh, honey, I'm so sorry about your father. Are you doing okay?"

She pulled back just enough to peer at him with her kind brown eyes, gaze skimming over his face and then down to his body, lingering briefly on the cadet star sewed onto the sleeve of his uniform. She rubbed her hands up and down his arms like she was trying to warm him up.

She was alive.

She was alive.

"I'm okay," Noam said and managed a smile.

"We thought you must be in Charleston—what are you doing here? Are you on leave?"

Right—he supposed they wouldn't have any way of knowing he'd gone to Level IV. Survivor names were printed in the paper, but it wasn't like they publicized Level IV admissions.

"I'm training in Durham," he said, deciding on impulse not to mention the specifics. *Level IV* sounded so cold. People on the street shied away from him when they saw his drabs, like they thought he was catching. He couldn't blame them. Parts of the city still smoldered after being firebombed during the last outbreak—he could smell the smoke from his old neighborhood from here.

Or maybe it wasn't fear of contagion. These were Atlantians, after all. The one thing they hated more than the virus in this neighborhood was government, and when they looked at Noam now, that was what they saw.

Linda's mouth twisted with concern. "You're so thin. Aren't they feeding you?"

"Sure," he said. "It's just . . . the virus, you know . . ."

"Of course, honey. I'm sorry. You're still recovering, aren't you?"

If she was afraid of him, of his uniform or the magic in his veins, it didn't show.

"I'm all right," he said firmly and squeezed her arm. "I came to . . . I mean, is Brennan . . ."

His breath was frozen. Impossible to exhale, impossible to imagine the possibility, now, that Linda might shake her head and say—that Brennan might be—

"He's alive," she said.

Relief crashed into Noam all at once. If Brennan had died . . . if Brennan had died, that would have been it. The last fragile root buried in the soil of Noam's old life, ripped up and thrown away.

Brennan was alive.

"Can I see him?"

"Oh," she said, flustered. "Oh . . . I bet they've got you spread thin already. You don't have to worry about us."

He could read between those lines easily enough. "I want to help. Just because the government owns my magic doesn't mean they own *me*. I haven't become one of Chancellor Sacha's acolytes overnight." A beat. "Actually, I've been working more with Minister Lehrer."

And *there* was that reaction, widening eyes and a sharp breath. "You have?"

"Yes. He's tutoring me personally."

Linda glanced over her shoulder into the building, like she expected to find Lehrer standing right behind her. "Well. Well, that's . . . I'm so proud of you, Noam."

Should she be?

The thought lanced into his mind, subtle as a spider bite. Even though Noam was here, bearing promises of technopathy and open doors, it wasn't like he was a prisoner in Level IV either. He'd volunteered.

This had been his choice, for better or worse.

"Can I see Brennan?"

"Maybe. He's so busy these days," Linda said, still fiddling with his collar. Had it been askew?

Too busy to talk to Noam? That was a new one. Noam bit the inside of his lip to keep from frowning. "Okay. That's fine. Just let him know that I'm here. Tell him . . . tell him it's important." He bit the inside of his cheek. "Um. Is there anything else I can do?"

Linda's next smile didn't reach her eyes. "Of course." At last she stepped back into the foyer, tugging him after her. "Come on now, sugar. Let's find something for you to do."

She set him up in one of the guest offices with an ancient two-terabyte computer and another database management task. He thought about using his newfound power to try to make it go even faster than what he could manage with a bit of LOG, but if he got caught by someone who didn't know better, he might not be allowed to come back. *Better stick to scripts.*

Even so, he wrapped his power through the wires and pins, caressing each packet of information as it flowed by. It was like realizing he could see a new color nobody else could, like a part of his brain hadn't been functioning properly, but now he could see the world as it really was.

The whole damn city was alive with light.

He'd been at it for a couple hours when someone knocked. Noam turned and immediately leaped to his feet.

Brennan looked—*good.* He looked good. The circles under his eyes were darker than before, perhaps, but he didn't have the flushed cheeks or glassy eyes of someone battling a fever. He wasn't too thin and weak, like Noam was now. No magic flickered over his skin like lethal electricity.

He really was okay.

Noam darted across the space between them and threw his arms around Brennan like he was twelve years old again. Noam couldn't stop shaking, a bone-deep tremor; when Brennan's hands rose to grasp his shoulders, Noam's fingers twisted in the fabric of his shirt.

But Brennan didn't smooth that touch down his arms, didn't stroke his spine or whisper comforts against his cheek. That grasp tightened instead, and Brennan pushed him away.

Noam couldn't name that look on Brennan's face, or define the oddly flat set to his mouth.

"Please," Brennan said. "Take a seat."

Noam obeyed. He felt colder without the press of Brennan's body heat against his chest.

"I'm very sorry to have heard about Jaime," Brennan said. He didn't step closer. He kept one hand on the knob, like he might leave at any second. "Your father was much loved by all of us. He did great things for the cause."

Before Noam's mother died, went the unspoken conclusion. Before he drowned himself in his depression and forgot he cared about anything, never mind politics.

Just hearing his father's name was like dropping below the surface of a frozen lake. Especially when Brennan's voice sounded like that, so formal, as if Brennan and Jaime Álvaro hadn't been best friends.

"Thank you," Noam said, a little awkwardly. His hands curled into fists against his thighs, and an unexpected nausea rippled through his stomach.

Brennan's gaze skimmed the length of Noam's body, lingering on his sleeve. "And I see you're doing well."

Why did Noam get the feeling that wasn't a compliment?

"I'm better," Noam said. He lifted his chin to look Brennan in the eyes, flattening his hands again. "I'm a witching now."

"Yes. I heard."

Brennan surveyed him in cool silence, long enough that Noam thought about trawling through the phone he could sense in Brennan's pocket and finding out if there was something going on. This was—weird. Brennan had always been reserved, but this wasn't his usual reticence.

So what the hell was going on?

He'd actually reached his power out into the circuit board and started parsing binary when Brennan said, "I don't think you should be here, Noam. You should go back to the government complex."

Noam paused, all that data still humming at his fingertips.

"What? Why?"

Brennan shook his head. "It's like you said. You're a witching now. You should be with your own kind."

It took a moment for that to sink in—and then it was like being shot in slow motion. Brennan's words tore through Noam too hot, too fast, stealing the blood from his veins and leaving him cold.

"*My own kind?* Are you serious? They don't even want me there. You should have seen the way they looked at me when they heard I'm Atlantian."

"Be that as it may," Brennan said, unruffled, "you're working with Minister Lehrer. I'm sure he wouldn't like you to get mixed up in refugee politics when your actions could reflect poorly on the administration."

Noam couldn't believe he was hearing this. His whole life he'd lived in tenement housing. He knew all the people who came to the Migrant Center by name. This was his home every bit as much as that burned-out hole that used to be his neighborhood. Brennan had been, if not a father, then like an uncle to him. He came to Shabbat dinner every Friday night. He gave Noam handmade birthday presents. Noam had organized the cyberattack on the Central News Bureau servers; he'd gone to *every* fucking protest. And now—now that he actually had a chance to make a real difference—Brennan wanted nothing to do with him?

He now recognized that look on Brennan's face. It was the same look he used to give the government witchings who accompanied Immigration on its raids, the same look they had given him in return: a twist of the lips and a narrowed gaze.

Contempt.

"You aren't getting it," Noam said, trying to be calm. "That's the point. I'm Level IV. Fuck DDOS attacks; I can do something *real.* We can stop the deportations. I'm a technopath now—I can get you anything you want off the government servers. We could prove what Sacha's up to. We can prove there's no *real* contamination threat from the refugees. If I can find a way onto Sacha's computer—"

"That's illegal," Brennan said.

"You didn't care about that when I was taking down CNB," Noam retorted. His hands were in fists again, tight enough his nails dug into his palms. "You didn't care when I went to fucking juvie. Back then it was all, 'Oh, I'll talk to your public defender, don't worry Noam, you're doing the right thing.'"

A threatening heat prickled at his eyes. God. If he started crying he would never forgive himself. He squeezed his eyes shut and willed the tears away, sucking in an uneven breath. He sensed Brennan still there, watching.

"And we are grateful," Brennan said at last, voice soft and nearly paternalistic, "but we never asked you to do any of that."

"Right. Because you couldn't ask me. You had to keep your distance from it. But you knew what I was planning, and you didn't try to stop me."

When Noam opened his eyes again, Brennan looked tired, dragging one hand back through his hair and avoiding Noam's gaze. "If you regret what you did . . ."

"That's not what I said. I don't regret it." Only that wasn't true, not entirely. Noam had done it for the cause, but he'd also done it to prove to his father—and to Brennan—that he could help, that he was good for something. And now being a witching erased all that.

Noam's legs ached with the need to get to his feet. To pace around this tiny office. He stayed where he was.

"I'm telling you I want to do more. I'm telling you I *can* do more, and all you can say is that you don't want my help anymore now that I'm not working two jobs and practically living on the street."

"You do have certain privileges now—"

"My father is *dead*!"

And Noam was on his feet after all, dizzy with the rush of blood away from his head and his veins burning. It was hard to breathe, like he'd plunged underwater and given up on air.

Brennan watched him in silence, eyes dark and unreadable even in the office fluorescence.

Whatever else Noam had planned to say was gone. All his thoughts were white noise. He grabbed his jacket from the back of the office chair and slung it over his arm, stalking past Brennan and slamming the door behind him.

Out on the street he only felt worse, anger exposed under the bright sunlight and impossible to avoid. This had been his life. This had been his life, his father's life, and now it meant nothing.

Noam had magic. He was one of *them* now.

Noam meant to go back to the government complex, but in his foggy rage, that wasn't where he ended up.

He found himself ducking under red quarantine tape instead, stepping off the sidewalk and onto a softer ground of black ash. Soot plumed underfoot, a cloud of it that tasted like charcoal and made him cough. Once upon a time, this street had teemed with people, street carts selling candied plums and pulled-pork sandwiches, kids playing, families on their way to church.

All those buildings, the street carts, the children and families—all just dust in Noam's mouth.

It didn't matter what Brennan said.

Noam thought about his father, draped over that useless chair and refusing to speak. There was medicine that might have made him better if they'd been able to consistently afford it.

Noam could still see the sign in the pharmacy. **No Papers, No Pills!!**

When they were rounding up people to take to refugee camps, his father had fit perfectly into the cabinet beneath the sink, thin and frail as a moth.

Noam looked out at his ruined neighborhood. He exhaled soot and bone.

He'd break into the government complex. He'd find out what Chancellor Sacha was planning next, and he'd bring it to Brennan. He'd prove what side he was really on. And then.

And then.

Diary of Adalwolf Lehrer, from the private collection of Calix Lehrer, stolen and delivered to Harold Sacha, October 2122

February 4, 2015

I still can't believe it's him.

He doesn't even look human now.

February 5, 2015

Calix is out of surgery. Raphael managed to get that damn metal gag off his face, but now he's a mess of open wounds. If he survives, he'll have scars.

I didn't read Raphael's report. I don't want to know the details of what they did to him in that place. All that matters is he's here.

Calix reacted badly coming out of anesthesia. To be expected. Will have to talk to the men about it next meeting, must try to *explain. He couldn't help it. He was scared. Magic doesn't behave the way you'd like when you're scared.*

G-d. He's just a kid.

February 8, 2015

C. was sick last several days, infected central line. Doing better now. Raphael expects him to recover.

Damn kid demanded I bring him books from the stacks. Wants to read Wittgenstein.

Who the fuck is Wittgenstein.

February 10, 2015

Seriously, I thought 16-year-olds were supposed to be into comics and girly magazines, not Husserl.

Guess it's reassuring to see C. hasn't changed a bit.

He's still having the nightmares. I've started sleeping in his room just so he isn't alone. The way he screams sometimes makes me want to tear my own ears out. I can't stand it.

February 11, 2015

Prep for CDC mission. Israfil and Nakir have everything in order. Will be ready by May deadline.

April 24, 2015

Calix joined us for the prep meeting. I think being around him makes the others nervous. Maybe because he's powerful, more likely because of his face. Even I don't like to look at it.

He sat silently in the back, though, which is good.

April 28, 2015

I take back what I said about silence.

May 2, 2015

Final preparations. Not getting much sleep, thanks to Calix.

Raphael says he needs therapy. Dunno where we're gonna find that in NC these days. Does he think shrinks set up shop in bombed-out supermarkets and give out pills at the Shell station?

Psychiatry's a pseudoscience anyway.

May 6, 2015

CDC tomorrow. Driving to Atlanta before dawn. I'm too recognizable, so I stay in the car. Nakir and Suriel take the new wing. Raphael first and second floor west. Gavriel first and second floor east. Michael and her team take the rest, while Azriel/Calix keeps security in line.

If anything goes wrong with the plan, I'll be losing all my best people. Nothing better go wrong.

May 8, 2015

CDC mission massive success, mostly thanks to C. Starting to think letting him help out isn't such a bad idea. He's always been clever, not surprising that applies to military strategy too. Raphael says having C. think about this shit is a bad idea, says he's too young or too traumatized or some BS. He doesn't know my brother.

Will have Calix look at specs for June mission, see what he thinks.

Chapter Five

Autumn dragged into winter with a slurry of ice and snow. Noam met with Lehrer every weekday, and every weekday he was assigned a corner and a book to read, long blocks of problem sets, and chapters from *A Physics Primer*. Noam slept in the barracks, cold and austere, no mezuzot to touch as he went through doors. No one to take care of but himself. Weekends he spent reading ahead in his textbooks, feverishly late into the nights with sheets pulled over his head and flashlight in hand.

He had to study. The best way to prove his utility to Brennan, at this point, was to use his power and bring Brennan everything he could find from the Ministry of Defense servers. No way was he good enough to break past their firewalls with code.

But if Noam could use magic—Carolinia's most treasured resource—for the Atlantian cause, then maybe being a witching wasn't such a bad thing.

Studying meant he had an excuse to avoid Dara, at least. After that first lesson, Dara had made a point of never speaking to Noam. Everything about him was baffling. Dara never met Noam before that day in Lehrer's study, presumably hadn't even known Noam was Atlantian. He just took one look at him and hated him. The best justification Noam had come up with was that Dara thought Noam was here to steal his special lessons with Lehrer.

A huge stretch, considering Dara was there every day to see what little regard Lehrer had for Noam's ability to do more than p-sets. But whatever. Dara could take his good looks and cool power and bewildering popularity and fuck right off.

The only glimmers of respite were Noam's daily meetings with Swensson, who disliked Noam every bit as much as he disliked everyone else but was a remarkably good instructor all the same. He helped Noam practice his technopathy, assigning him four new programming languages to learn and ordering him to write a basic integer-sorting program without using a single one of those languages (indeed, without touching the keyboard at all). Noam spent the whole hour of their lesson sitting in front of a computer, willing it to sort the damn integers, half-convinced this whole thing was a government conspiracy to make him look like an idiot.

"You're not thinking this through," Swensson accused him after two sessions, looming over Noam with his arms crossed. "You understand how magic works, surely. Why are you a technopath and not, say, a telekinetic?"

Noam sat very still, certain that if he moved an inch his frustration would boil over. "Because I understand computers but not physics."

"Exactly. So why are you sitting here, thinking how nice it would be if this machine just did what you wanted? Think about what you *need.* Think through each and every step, then tell the computer to execute them."

But what was the point of writing a program in his head when he could type it out just as quickly? What was the point of being a technopath if it just came down to doing what he could've done anyway with a perfectly good Ursascript?

He obeyed all the same, and to his simultaneous frustration and delight the computer spat out an elegantly efficient radix-sorting algorithm. When he asked Swensson why he didn't just write a code to do the same thing, Swensson said it would get easier the more he practiced, that eventually he'd accomplish impossible technological feats with just a thought.

It was a minor victory when, a month after he first began lessons in Level IV, Noam managed to get a computer to connect to the internet, open a browser window, bypass security measures, and send an email from his account to Swensson's, all without coming within ten feet of a holoreader.

"Twelve seconds. Not bad," Swensson said, "for a juvenile delinquent."

The next lesson, Noam did it in five.

His success with technology didn't mean much to the other cadets, though. Somehow word got out that Noam hadn't just failed the placement exam but that he hadn't gone to school at all for three years. It wasn't clear just how much else they knew, but Taye and Dara both started locking their dressers when they left for classes in the morning, like they thought Noam would steal their socks if they weren't careful.

"I'm sure it's not personal," Bethany reassured him one evening. They were both up late with curriculum work, Noam's intro math books sprawled next to Bethany's *Cardiovascular Physiology*. Her presenting power was healing, apparently. Bethany had her toes tucked under Noam's leg and holoreader propped up against her thighs, slouched so far down on the sofa her head was below the armrest. She was the only cadet willing to spend time with him—and that, he suspected, was just because she was nice.

"Not personal?"

When Bethany glanced up to meet his gaze, Noam made a face.

"Dara's a really private person," she said. "Taye's probably just taking his lead."

As usual, just hearing Dara's name sparked a new flame of irritation. Of course Bethany made excuses for him. Dara was perfectly charming when she and the others were around, all smiles, but as soon as it was just him and Noam—or him and Noam and Lehrer—all that switched off like a lamp going dark.

Noam took it as a compliment. If the only person Dara despised as much as Noam was Minister Lehrer, then Noam must be doing something right.

"Where do you reckon they are, anyway?" Noam asked, tipping his head toward the empty barracks.

"The others like to go to this club over in Raleigh on off weekends," Bethany said, tapping her holoreader screen. "I expect they're still out."

And Bethany hadn't gone with them. Was that because she didn't want to go, or because she felt sorry for Noam staying home alone?

Noam had never really enjoyed partying. After Carly died he went out some, mostly from a misguided sense that he needed to move on, to meet somebody. And yeah, he met people. But he'd never been able to muster the energy for the kind of relationship they wanted from him. Those romances fizzled out, quick and ephemeral as the rush from a tequila shot.

He chewed the inside of his cheek to keep from saying anything he might regret and tried to pay attention to precalculus—a difficult task, as he couldn't quite ignore the little blips of electrical current every time Bethany's word processor autosaved.

"Do you ever get to go home?" Noam asked, giving up. "Your mother's still alive, right?"

Bethany snorted. "Yeah, she's alive. I never see her, though."

Noam tried to imagine not visiting his mother, if he had the option. He still saw her body sometimes, when he was trying to fall asleep, her face swollen and red and her neck bruised where the rope bit into her skin. Her limp feet dangling inches above the floor.

He put his book aside and twisted to face Bethany properly. "Why not?"

She shrugged. "My mother doesn't understand magic. It's like she's in awe of me and scared of me at the same time. The way she acts, you'd think her real daughter died in the red ward and I'm some impostor come to replace her."

Noam hadn't considered that. His mother died a long time ago, but what if his father hadn't gotten sick? What if Jaime Álvaro had survived the outbreak, only to watch Noam transform into a witching and be snatched away to Level IV?

There was a strange guilt about witchings among the older generations. Seeing a witching was to remember your grandparents' sins, a stain that wouldn't wash out. Noam went to the memorial with his school once, the black basalt monument carved with more names than Noam could count.

His parents fled Atlantia because they were worried about the virus outbreaks there. They thought Carolinia was safer.

They'd been wrong.

Atlantians didn't share Carolinian guilt over the catastrophe, even though their ancestors were equally complicit in the genocide. To them, witchings represented Carolinia—Carolinia, with all its careful protections against the virus, with its militarized QZ border, weekly disinfectant sprays, and government-subsidized respirator masks—Carolinia, which refused to use those same protections to shelter Atlantian citizens. Carolinian armies, which marched south with promises of humanitarian aid and then refused to leave.

No. If Noam's dad survived, he'd hate Noam just as much as Brennan did.

"I'm sorry," Noam said.

"Why? It wasn't your fault."

"I know. It just felt like the right thing to say."

"Anyway, she's the reason I got the power I did, I think. So I'm grateful to her for that." Bethany gave him a slight smile. "She's a doctor, so I was exposed to a lot of medical stuff growing up. She used to take me in with her to work and let me watch the med students dissect cadavers."

"That didn't gross you out?"

"Me? *Nothing* grosses me out. Seriously. Try me."

Noam grimaced. "I'd rather not," he said. "I just ate."

She laughed and kicked his thigh.

They worked in silence for another hour or so until Bethany went off to bed, taking her books with her. Noam stayed. Sleep seemed a long way off, chased away by an anxious determination to read just one more chapter, two more, three. Everything was finally knitting together, concepts he learned in math reappearing in physics, the physical laws threaded into the fabric of chemistry, chemical reactions shaping biology . . .

He could catch up. He *could.*

Ames and Taye returned around one, draped in clubbing clothes and exhaustion.

"Hey, Noam," Taye said. He was so drunk that when he waved, even his hand looked slurred.

Noam's grip tightened on his textbook. "Hey." A beat, Noam turning the question over in his mouth a few times, before deciding he didn't give a fuck what they thought of him for asking. "Where's Dara?"

Ames tried tugging her jacket off and got her arm stuck in the sleeve. She laughed, stumbling as Taye tried to help her get free. "Dunno," she said at last. "Probably went home with someone. Probably suffocating himself on dick as we speak."

Right. Noam tapped the tip of his tongue against his teeth. It wasn't any of his business what Dara did. "Does that a lot, does he?"

Taye laughed. "Can't take him anywhere."

Ames's mouth twisted, her expression somewhat less amused. "He usually makes it about fifteen minutes before abandoning us for better prospects."

She must have seen the look on Noam's face because she shook her head. "Whatever. If he hasn't given himself alcohol poisoning again, I'm sure he'll stumble back here eventually."

Noam felt like they were talking about two totally different people. Dara being an asshole was unsurprising. Dara losing his grip on that perfect self-control for even a second, on the other hand, struck Noam as less characteristic.

Ames and Taye departed for their separate bedrooms, leaving Noam in the common room still clutching his math book. Any hope of sleeping tonight had evaporated; Noam got up and made himself coffee instead of following Taye to bed. No point in wishing he'd gone to Raleigh, too, when he could barely summon an electric charge. Better to focus on p-sets. Better not to be such an embarrassment to Level IV. And then maybe one day Lehrer would say, *I'm impressed, Noam—you learned this so quickly*, and Noam would perform feats of magic far more magnificent than eating a goddamn apple.

He wasn't worthless. He *wasn't.*

The door finally opened again around five in the morning. It was still dark out, the world blanketed in a midwinter silence broken only by the click of Noam's keyboard and the turn of the latch. Dara slipped inside. He didn't see Noam at first, too focused on pulling the door softly shut and glancing down at the glowing white screen of his phone. His hair was messy, like someone had been dragging their fingers through it over and over, party glitter caught in the curls and dusting the line of a cheekbone.

"Ames and Taye got back ages ago," Noam said, just to watch Dara startle. A dark twist of schadenfreude coiled up through his gut. He smiled. "Where've you been?"

Dara stuck his phone in the back pocket of his jeans, which were tight—really tight. "At the library," he said.

Noam arched a brow and sank back against the sofa, coffee cupped between both hands. He was exhausted, and he'd held his tongue for weeks now—so he said, in a light tone that was very nearly teasing, "Oh yeah? Those jeans're so tight I can see your religion. Does the librarian make you bend over to get the good books?"

His words didn't quite garner the reaction Noam anticipated. Dara, usually so cold and dispassionate, turned a delicate shade of red. It was fascinating, a sea change that sent little shock waves of anger radiating between them. Or it would've been, if Noam didn't suddenly taste magic crackling in the air.

I've gone too far.

Dara looked like he wanted to reach for that magic and fashion it into a weapon. Like he might be far more dangerous than Noam anticipated.

"I don't need to pull all-nighters to do well," Dara said at last, voice laced with frost but steady—too steady. He started off past the common room toward the bedrooms, but he paused right by Noam's sofa. Noam could smell the alcohol on him.

Dara's gaze dragged over the books Noam had scattered across the coffee table and seat cushions, the discarded eraser nubs and scribbled notes. It lingered on the cover of *A Physics Primer*, then lifted to Noam's face. Dara's eyes were black wells, pupils bleeding into iris.

"You can study all you want," he said softly. "It isn't going to make a difference."

And then he vanished down the hall, leaving Noam to clutch his coffee and stare at those same notes, wishing Dara hadn't carved out the guts of what Noam already feared was true.

Noam couldn't get Dara out of his head. He'd set up shop there right alongside Brennan, the imaginary pair of them watching Noam and judging him every time he fumbled when trying to learn electrical magic or went to bed at the end of another day without making himself useful to the cause. It was all well and good swearing to Brennan that his magic would save them all, but so far Noam had only managed to glare at Chancellor Sacha's photograph in the papers and think nasty thoughts.

Brennan didn't answer when Noam called his cell, and when Noam did manage to get hold of Linda, Brennan had always conveniently "just stepped out."

Fine. Noam hacked the Central News Bureau all on his own. He could find a way into the government complex servers without help too.

The next several times he went to the west wing for lessons with Lehrer, Noam paid attention. He noticed tech whenever he could, everything from traffic control to people's texts. It didn't count as snooping when he spied on people he didn't know, or so he'd decided—although that meant he now knew way more about strangers' hemorrhoids and marital problems than he'd have liked.

He tried to notice, too, the inner workings of the biometric security system between the training wing and the government complex. But when he dipped his magic into the circuits, it slid right off like oil on water. He tried a second time, and a third, fumbling with the wires and pins and failing to comprehend the engineering at all.

The problem wasn't his magic; he knew that much. He could easily fiddle with people's holoreaders or the electrical system. But trying to influence the biometric reader was like chasing a vanishing horizon. Some kind of antitechnopathy ward, maybe?

He should've known. Why had he assumed the government would be stupid enough to leave its system open to powers like Noam's? That would've been an egregious oversight, considering Noam's ability was on record with Level IV.

He pushed his power into the next biometric reader he passed, trying to sense the shape and structure of the magic blocking his access, but it was impossible. He wasn't that good.

When he reached Lehrer's study, Dara was there—outside, in the hall, leaning against the wall with a book perched in hand. He didn't look up when Noam approached. With his head tilted over the pages, chewing on the inside of one lip, Dara seemed too absorbed to notice his presence at all. But then when Noam reached for the doorknob, Dara spoke.

"Don't go in there."

"Why not?"

Dara didn't answer.

It was so goddamn tempting to ignore him. But if Dara was just trying to make Noam late, well, he was making himself late too. So Noam found a spot on the opposite wall and sat on the floor, pulling out his phone and pretending to read something on-screen. He prodded his technopathy against the wards on the government servers once more, that hard kernel of frustration in his chest winding tighter as his power slid right off the shields. *Again.*

No wonder Brennan didn't trust Noam. Noam had no real power—just magic-contaminated blood and a cadet uniform. A uniform that was, apparently, made by some famous fashion designer and tailored to the cadets' personal measurements, because of fucking course that was a thing. Noam couldn't call himself an anarchist when every single thing he owned was bought and paid for with federal blood money.

Being here, in the government complex, trusting Lehrer, was probably one of the stupider things Noam had done of late. Working with Lehrer would buy him nothing. If Noam was going to save the world, he'd have to do it alone.

The study door opened, jolting Noam back to the present. But it wasn't Lehrer's imposing figure that stepped out into the hall.

It was Chancellor Sacha.

Chapter Six

He was smaller than he looked on TV.

That was the first inevitable realization that fluttered across the surface of Noam's mind, chased by an immediate surge of something terrible and acidic burning through his chest like bile.

Harold Sacha was shorter even than Dara, who was five ten at most. He had bland gray hair and a bland face and wore a bland suit, but the gaze that shot out from beneath heavy brows was keenly intelligent. A fresh tremor ricocheted up Noam's spine, and he was on his feet before he knew he was moving. His right hand twitched, a reflex; Noam had nearly reached for the gun he had trained with in basic that morning, a gun that wasn't there.

No fewer than six bodyguards spilled out of the room on Sacha's heels, all wearing iridescent antiwitching armor that took on a strange gleam under the hall lights. Noam's attention slid from Sacha's face to theirs—or where their faces would have been had they not been obscured by heavy masks.

When Noam looked back at Sacha, the chancellor was watching him.

"You must be Álvaro. Minister Lehrer's new student, yes?"

Noam hardly dared open his mouth. He didn't trust what might come out if he did. And of course Dara just stood there, reading his book, completely unfazed by the presence of a war criminal not two feet away.

Noam nodded.

"Excellent," Sacha said, looking grotesquely pleased with himself. "I'd hoped to run into you at some point. Calix has such an eye for talent. He found our friend Mr. Shirazi, of course."

Noam glanced at Dara, who turned a new page in his book.

Sacha stepped closer, and Noam took a half step back, only to meet the wall.

"Why *do* you think Calix has such interest in you?" Sacha asked him. His eyes searched Noam's face, then briefly dipped down Noam's body.

"I don't know." Noam managed to get out those three words, at least.

"I read your file," Sacha said.

He meant Noam's criminal record.

Noam felt as if his chest was caving in on itself, a clenching pain that shot from his heart all the way down to the tips of his fingers. He imagined closing those fingers round Sacha's throat.

"Leave the boy alone."

Lehrer stood in the doorway, one hand on the frame. His expression was very cool.

"The polite thing would have been to introduce me," Sacha commented mildly.

"And now you've been introduced. Dara, Noam, come into the study. We've wasted enough time."

Noam sidled around Sacha, who looked as if he would've loved to tell Lehrer off for insubordination but was too afraid to, which . . . *good.*

He trailed Dara into Lehrer's study, glancing back just long enough to watch the door shut on Sacha and the antiwitching soldiers. He expected Lehrer to say something. To at least comment on the chancellor's presence in his office, or apologize, but Lehrer just directed him to the corner with a physics book. Again.

So Noam was left alone to keep prodding his technopathy against the government complex servers and watch Dara move little lights across the ceiling. He could use the time he was meant to spend reading to try and break the ward, he supposed. Lehrer certainly wasn't paying attention.

Noam tilted his book up, leaning in like he was trying to work out a difficult problem, and expanded his mind. Lehrer didn't have so much as a holoreader in this entire damn room. There was just his phone on his desk—ward protected, of course—and Dara's, tucked into his back pocket.

He hesitated there, mental fingers poised over Dara's data. God, it was tempting to drag his power through those circuits and find out some kind of nasty secret. Or better yet, chase Dara's network connection up to the cloud and erase the whole thing.

Only, unlike the phones of all the low-level government workers out in the atrium, Dara's was protected by the same antitechnopathy ward as Lehrer's.

Noam glanced up.

Dara was looking at him.

A jolt of static shot up Noam's spine, and he snatched his power away from Dara's phone on reflex. Ridiculous how guilty he felt, especially since Dara had no way of knowing what Noam was thinking. But he felt oddly observed as he flipped to the next page in his textbook without reading it, like Dara had tangled himself up in the wires of Noam's mind and Noam couldn't cut him out.

What if, though—he scribbled a meaningless line of notes—*what if* he convinced Lehrer to take down the ward? Lehrer was powerful enough.

It was an insane idea, but Noam was willing to entertain just about any solution at this point. Lehrer was one of the few who had spoken out against Sacha's treatment of refugees, one of the few who could afford to. He had the cachet of being the only living survivor of the catastrophe, of his revolutionary past, of having been Carolinia's king before he gave up the crown. Lehrer and Sacha famously loathed each other. But even Lehrer hadn't accomplished much to stop Sacha from doing precisely as Sacha pleased.

Was that because he couldn't? Or because he didn't want to?

Noam had to believe Lehrer cared. He glanced up at him again over the edge of his book. Lehrer had caught one of the little yellow lights in his hand; a faint glow emanated from the cage of his long fingers as Lehrer smiled at it and praised Dara, who looked annoyed.

Lehrer even cared about Dara, for all Dara was indifferent to everything Lehrer gave him. Lehrer cared about Noam, enough to intercede for him. And when witchings were being oppressed, Lehrer had risked his life to save them.

But on the other hand, Lehrer's department enforced Sacha's laws. And after the outbreaks in Atlantia got bad, it was Lehrer's army that had marched south to help.

The Atlantian government called that an act of war, and Noam was inclined to agree.

"That's enough for today," Lehrer said to Dara, releasing the little light, which vanished. Noam looked back down at his book. He hadn't even finished reading the first of the three chapters he'd been assigned.

"Dara, I want you to keep practicing with this tonight. Noam, chapters fourteen through sixteen in this book, and then finish the last chapter in *A Physics Primer* along with its problem set. Also, I need to speak with you. Stay behind."

That was new.

Noam took his time with his things, lingering over the organization of his notes and pretending to fumble with his satchel straps. Dara didn't even bother putting his book in his bag before leaving, door slamming shut in his wake and rattling one of the paintings on the wall.

It was just Noam and Lehrer. Lehrer drifted over to the bookshelf and opened a small cabinet, pulling out a glass decanter of some amber liquor that glittered in the window light.

"Sir," Noam said.

Lehrer's attention was focused on the decanter as he poured two fingers of whisky into a glass. "Just one moment, Noam."

Noam waited.

Replacing the top of the decanter, Lehrer turned to face him properly, leaning against the shelf. "I suspect," he said, "you're starting to wonder why I accepted you into this program in the first place."

Well, he wasn't wrong. Noam shrugged one shoulder. *I figured you'd put too much bourbon in your coffee that morning* probably wasn't appropriate. "I'm sure you had your reasons, sir."

"Certainly I did. I wouldn't have vouched for you with the committee, or sacrificed my personal time to instruct you, if I didn't think you could catch up."

Lehrer was only bringing this up because he had overheard what Sacha said. Noam knew that. He *knew* that.

"I'm too far behind," he said. It was so hard not to fidget; there was a loose thread on the sofa's faded upholstery Noam was dying to pluck free.

"I don't think you are." Lehrer took a sip of his drink. "And you don't strike me as the kind of person to let a challenge go without a fight."

"So, what? I look like I'm stubborn, so you go to bat for me? You don't even know me."

"I know you well enough to see myself in you, Noam," Lehrer said, looking oddly pleased. He moved away from the bookshelf, closer to Noam, until only the seat cushion separated them. When he rested a hand on the sofa's spine, it was right over that loose thread that had so bothered Noam. A cool shiver ran down Noam's spine, something he didn't know how to interpret. "I was twelve when I stopped going to school. Everything I learned, I taught myself by reading books—on my own, the same way you're doing now. It wasn't easy, but I was sufficiently motivated to learn, so 'easy' didn't matter. Now I'm the most powerful witching alive." He said it without arrogance, just a lifted brow. A statement of fact.

"You're . . ." Noam didn't even know what he was going to say. All the words felt wrong.

"Clever?" Lehrer said. "So are you. And you're curious, as I was. You've lost a great deal, as I had. And you believe, as I did, that if you are powerful enough, no one will ever be able to hurt you again."

What Lehrer had gone through was far worse than anything people alive today could even imagine. Probably . . . probably Lehrer only said that to make Noam feel better. And yet . . .

Lehrer stepped around the back of the sofa and sat as well, angled toward Noam—close enough their knees bumped together.

"I understand," Lehrer said. When Noam dared to glance up, Lehrer was watching, those strange eyes like clear lake water. Impossible, then, to look away. "I lost my family too."

Noam didn't want to think about his parents. He didn't want to think about his father's body, what they might've done to it after he died. Burned, probably.

Atlantian tradition was to bury the dead.

He tried to focus instead on the places he and Lehrer touched, small points of heat. On the way Lehrer smelled, like single malt and fabric starch. It was as if, just by asking, Lehrer had ripped off the flimsy bandages Noam had wrapped around his grief.

Lehrer's hand fell away from his shoulder. Noam felt cold in its absence, somehow. He watched as Lehrer folded his fingers together in his lap, staring at the black *X* tattooed on Lehrer's left hand.

"I sensed your strength the moment we met," Lehrer said eventually. "Raw ability isn't something that can be taught. Colonel Swensson tells me you're making fast progress in your lessons with him, and you've learned curriculum far more quickly than expected."

Noam snorted. "I sleep about three hours a night."

"Be careful with that; magic is not an inexhaustible resource. Have you heard of viral intoxication?"

"Going fevermad, you mean."

"That's one word for it. Magic can be addictive, and if used too much, the viral load rises in your blood—and your body produces more antibodies against magic. The inflammation in your brain can make you go quite . . . well, fevermad. Yes." Lehrer paused, gaze skipping toward the window for a moment like he was distracted, although Noam had never thought Lehrer was the sort. Then Lehrer's attention snapped back to Noam with such keen intensity it was jarring. "That's the first sign. But it can get much worse. If the syndrome isn't treated, your body's immune system starts to attack its own tissue. Fevers, fatigue, joint pain, kidney failure—death, if left unchecked."

"I'll be careful, sir."

Fevermadness was incredibly rare, though. Noam couldn't fathom the amount of magic he'd have to expend to get to that point.

"See that you are. I've invested too much in you already to see your talents wasted on insanity." The words came out sharp enough that Noam nearly flinched—but then Lehrer sighed and shook his head. His marked hand curled in a fist against his thigh. "My brother was ill."

Noam startled before he could stop himself. Surely Lehrer didn't mean—

"We had no idea what fevermadness was at the time, of course." Lehrer's expression did not change. "That was Raphael's discovery—one of the doctors in Wolf's militia. It was shocking at the time, of course, to think magic could eat away at a witching, bit by bit, until they lost the very core of who they were. Such a death is not pleasant, to experience or to witness."

No, Noam didn't imagine it was.

But Adalwolf Lehrer died in the final push against DC, the day the United States fell and new nations rose in its stead. Not of madness.

Even Lehrer wasn't powerful enough to rewrite history.

Right?

The look Lehrer gave him then was softer. Considering. He tapped his fingers against the armrest.

"Your presenting power was technopathy, and you've shown strength using electricity as well, which makes sense. The two often go hand in hand. But you haven't mastered telekinesis. Why?"

He said it as if learning telekinesis was as easy as learning multiplication tables.

"I don't know. Colonel Swensson seemed to think I wasn't ready for anything past electricity."

"Electricity," Lehrer echoed. "But you know physics, Noam, don't you? You read the book I gave you and did well on the problem sets. So you know electricity is just one form of electromagnetism. The other form being . . ." He trailed off meaningfully, watching Noam until Noam finished the thought.

"Magnetism."

"Exactly," Lehrer said. "It should be easy for you to manipulate ferromagnetic metals if you've accomplished electricity. And then, once you've mastered that, it's a short step to telekinesis and moving nonmagnetic objects. It merely becomes a matter of force and inertia rather than magnetic fields." He gestured, and a coin floated out of his pocket to hover in the air between them. As it rotated, sunlight glinted off the face of Gemma Yaxley, first chancellor of Carolinia after Lehrer surrendered power. "Try to move this coin toward yourself. Even an inch will do."

Noam fought the urge to give Lehrer a dubious look. Electricity was easy; he felt the static in the air sparking between objects, a force as constant as gravity. Moving the coin was a different matter entirely.

Okay. Think.

He knew how magnetism worked. Opposites attract—simple. If he knew the charge of the coin, he could charge some attracting object, or the air in front of his hand, maybe, to be the opposite charge. And that was just shifting electrons around. Was he capable of that?

Probably not. Besides, he couldn't just change the electron configuration of gas particles and hope a paramagnetic metal would be attracted to it. He needed to create an actual magnetic *field*. Electricity had positive and negative charges, but magnetism had poles. So he needed a positive pole where the coin was and a negative one where his hand was. That was possible, right? At least, theoretically, but as far as Noam knew, no one had ever proved the existence of a magnetic monopole.

No, thinking like that wasn't helpful. If something was theoretically possible, then magic presumably could accomplish it, just so long as Noam understood the theory.

Okay. Okay.

Imagining he could only work with electricity (which was true, at least right now) and not create a magnetic pole just because he felt like it, what would he do?

When you had a current in a straight line, the magnetic field looped around it like a spring. When you had a current in a spiral, the magnetic field was generated inside the coil. And at the ends of the coil, magnetic objects would be pulled into the field and spat out the other end: right into Noam's hand.

Noam blinked, and the room slid back into focus. Lehrer, on the other side of that coin, patiently watched him as he sipped his whisky. Noam realized only now that he'd shifted while distracted, crossing his legs atop the seat cushion. His foot had gone to sleep beneath his shin.

Well, Noam thought, *here goes nothing*. And he activated the electric charge.

The spark that shot through the air was so bright that Noam nearly spilled out of his chair, half-certain something was about to catch fire.

But in that same moment he felt cold metal against the palm of his hand, fingers reflexively closing around the coin.

Lehrer set down his drink, looking startled, or at least as startled as it was possible for Lehrer to look. Then he clapped, mouth curving belatedly into a smile. "Very good, Noam. A bit overenthusiastic, perhaps, but there's nothing wrong with that when you're learning."

Lehrer gazed pointedly over his left shoulder. Noam looked as well; a black mark singed the lovely blue wall.

"Sorry."

But it was hard to feel truly contrite when . . . *he'd done it.* He'd moved an object. With his mind. Using magic.

Lehrer waved his hand. "I think it adds to the decor, don't you?" He leaned forward, looking at Noam like he had just transformed into the most fascinating person in the world. "Do you think the way you accomplished this trick was the best way?"

Noam reached for his coffee. His hand trembled—the one that wasn't clenched around the fifty-cent piece like it might fly away again if he let go. "I'd hoped it would be easier. But I guess that's not how magic works." The prospect of having to think about the physics of everything before he could do magic was exhausting.

"You've gotten much faster at your technopathy, haven't you? It's become intuitive."

"I have an intuitive understanding of magnetism too," Noam argued. "Colonel Swensson said that's how it works. I know how things theoretically move through the air better than I know how words end up on a text document when I type."

"Presenting powers can be anything," Lehrer said dismissively. "After all, how could one learn the science behind telepathy? And yet, we have presenting-power telepaths. Theorists say there must be some sort of natural affinity between the witching and their presenting power, but in truth, it's only learned powers which rely on knowledge of scientific laws."

Well, Noam was willing to bet Lehrer knew a good deal more about magic than Swensson did.

Still. "Am I going to have to think about physics *every* time?"

"Not every time. You just need to have that knowledge accessible somewhere in your memory, or at least more accessible than it currently is. Your mind is like a filing cabinet, Noam. Your accessible memories are the folders on top. If you have knowledge in one of those top files, you can use it instinctively. And the more drawers in your filing cabinet, the more of those types of accessible memories you can have."

Noam hoped Lehrer was right. If Noam was going to be any use to Brennan, he needed to be able to use his powers quickly. Not spend the first five minutes trying to remember old p-sets.

"Let's do that again," Lehrer said, drawing another coin out of his pocket, "and this time, make it happen as quickly as you can."

They spent the next two hours just like that: first with coins, then ball bearings, then moving away from the ferromagnetic metals until Noam was semisuccessfully shifting Lehrer's silver cuff links around the surface of his desk. Lehrer only ended the lesson when his assistant showed up, holding a briefcase, to tell him he was late for a meeting.

"Duty calls," Lehrer said. He surveyed Noam, appraising, as he slipped the cuff links back onto his sleeves. "Practice this tonight, Noam. See if you can't move something nonmetallic before our lesson tomorrow."

A tall order, especially since Lehrer still expected him to do his readings and problem sets. But that evening, Noam shut himself away in the bedroom while the others were watching a movie, sitting on his bed with *A Physics Primer* open at his side. And he didn't give a damn what Dara thought of all-nighters, because by the time the alarm rang on Noam's bedside table for basic training, he hadn't slept, but he'd sent a piece of notebook paper dancing around his pillow. And, in a fit of impulse, he'd rearranged all the books on Dara's shelf without committing the offense of touching a single one.

Encrypted video from a private repository on the Ministry of Defense servers

The film opens on a bare room. Two figures enter the frame, a white-coated man pushing a boy in a wheelchair. He positions the chair in the center of the room, facing the camera. The boy in the chair is as thin and fragile as a baby bird; a metal contraption covers the bottom half of his face, something sharp and lethal affixed by spikes drilled into bone. He is approximately twelve years old.

The doctor adjusts the plastic tubing snaking out from beneath the boy's hospital gown and rolls the IV stand out of the boy's reach. Or what would be out of reach if the boy's arms weren't strapped down.

The boy shifts in his chair, lifting his gaze briefly to the camera. His eyes are unusually pale. He is conscious, if barely.

Off-screen, a VOICE: "Are you ready to begin?"

DOCTOR, after watching the boy's heartbeat on-screen for a second: "Yes."

VOICE: "Patient 103, session 49. December 14, 2012. Drs. Towson and Green presiding. Dr. Green, start with twenty micrograms."

The first doctor injects something into the boy's central line.

It's a few seconds before the boy starts screaming, sound muffled by the contraption on his face.

VOICE: "Another ten."

Dr. Green obeys. The boy's body quivers violently, limbs tugging against the restraints.

VOICE: "Impress us, Calix, and the pain stops."

But nothing happens. The off-screen voice orders the other doctor to increase the dosage again, and again.

VOICE: "I'm losing my patience."

The boy's eyes are wet, but when he glares at the camera, his gaze is hot enough to sear. Dr. Green prepares another injection, but he doesn't get a chance to push it into the boy's central line.

The room explodes in a sudden crash of sound, the camera skidding back several feet, then toppling over. Dust and brick crash down from the ceiling. Several voices are screaming.

VOICE: "Suppressant!"

The whole world—or so it seems—trembles on its axis. The boy's body is barely visible through the debris, his chair still upright and his chin fallen forward onto his chest.

VOICE: "Dr. Green, the suppressant, now!"

A flurry of white coat, someone reaching for a length of plastic tubing with syringe in hand.

The video goes blank.

Chapter Seven

Two more weeks passed before Noam figured out the trick to getting into the government complex.

He checked the security system every day, some part of him still hoping he'd identify a failure in the ward and be able to break through. Knowing he never would.

Actually, in the end, it came down to good old-fashioned cracking.

Everything Noam ever wanted to know about Xerxes Security Systems—the company responsible for creating the biometric reader—was available online. Noam was a good liar, and technopathy could fake caller ID to make it look like he was sitting behind a desk at the National Cybersecurity Bureau. There was some problem with the biometrics, he told them. Signatures kept getting confused. Sometimes Joe Schmoe was getting logged as Jane Doe, and the NCB was fixin' to switch to Safelarm if they didn't quit piddlin' around.

He had tech support on the line five minutes later.

Of course, Noam said, this was the NCB. National security meant Noam needed to have one of his own employees take care of the problem, no contractors. So he needed detailed schematics sent to his account.

Noam might not be able to use technopathy on a government network, but he sure as hell could use it on the NCB director's phone. He had what he wanted within seconds, then deleted the email from the inbox and trash and kept the director's phone from sounding a notification the entire time.

He used the schematics to clone the biometric-reader software and started practicing. He tried a dozen iterations of the same LOG injection before he finally figured out how to make the biometric reader match his print to someone else's approved identity; then he deleted all record of his print being read in the first place.

And that was how he ended up standing outside a service door to the government complex at ten on a Friday, flopcell in hand, staring at the biometric security reader and wondering if he was being incredibly reckless.

It wasn't really that hard; that was the sad part. Noam fed his program into the device, the latch clicked, and Noam pushed the door open with ease. His pulse raced in his chest, and he half expected to find Swensson standing there on the other side: *I thought you might try something like this.*

There was no one. The hall stretched out before him was identical to the ones in the training wing, all hardwood floor and brick walls. This part of the building was original warehouse, lovingly reconstructed; there were visible spots on the walls where someone had daubed over the crumbling mortar, rescuing it.

This was a terrible idea. Noam had a record. If he got caught breaking the law again, who would believe he was reformed?

Actually, no. Worse than that. Noam was pretty sure what he had planned for Sacha's computer counted as espionage.

Planned. He hadn't done it yet. As of right now, he was just a student out of bounds with plenty of plausible deniability. That would stay true right up until Noam plugged the keylogger into Sacha's computer.

There was a distinct possibility he wouldn't even find anything—but if he sat in the barracks one more night, eating expensive meat and doing nothing while kids got deported south, he'd never forgive himself. If he could get proof of political motive for the deportations, prove it wasn't just contamination threat like the government claimed, that would help. Or, hell, some way to blackmail Sacha into shutting down the whole immigration division would do just fine too.

Noam pulled the steel doors shut. The security cameras watched from overhead, but these weren't warded like the network—Noam had checked. He made sure they saw empty air where he stood. And *that* . . . that was a rush. Today Noam wasn't just another student but something greater, stronger and smarter than everyone else.

This same rush always got him into trouble, of course, but damn was it addictive.

Riding that thrill, Noam moved forward. He did his best not to creep like someone with something to hide, tempting as it was to cling to the walls and peer around corners. The plan only worked if he looked like he belonged here, or at least had a good reason to be in this part of the building. That meant shoulders back, head high, *act cool.*

He turned a corner and practically ran into a woman with a clipboard. Noam nearly froze, his blood running to ice when their eyes met. But if he froze he'd get caught, he'd be expelled, never allowed back here again—

Noam smiled instead, bright and cheery. "Heya!"

Heya?

The woman looked startled, but just said *good morning* and brushed past.

Holy shit, that actually worked.

Unbelievable. He had a cadet star right there *on his sleeve.*

Dizzy off his own success, Noam took the next flight of stairs up one floor. This hall was busier, lined with offices and conference rooms. Noam pulled out his phone and pretended to be absorbed by something on the screen—everyone else was doing the same, after all, with their phones and tablets and holoreaders. And all of it, *all of it*, any information not secured by the ward, was there at Noam's fingertips. A tempest of data battered the boundaries of his mind: someone sending an email, an internet search for *hair salon durham main st*, someone flicking through saved photos depicting a happily drooling dog.

This must be what power felt like.

According to the map of the complex posted near the elevators, the executive offices were on the third floor. That's where he'd find Sacha. Lehrer's office wasn't far either, though nowhere near the study where they usually met. How many offices did Lehrer have?

Noam was still scanning the map when the elevator arrived. Two men in suits loitered behind him, arguing about "deliverables." Noam followed them onto the elevator. They, like everyone else in this place, apparently had no desire to confront him—and it was hard to stay afraid when people's eyes skimmed past him like he was inconvenient furniture. This all seemed so . . . easy. Too easy.

But when he got to Sacha's office, it was occupied; he sensed someone's warded cell phone.

Maybe he could try to find Lehrer's office instead. Noam could play off being Lehrer's new student, use that as an excuse to get in and wait for him—only, no, because then Lehrer would figure out Noam snuck into the building with a fake ID.

Of course, standing here would draw the wrong kind of attention. One step at a time: first, an empty office. If he could just get himself in front of a computer, maybe he could hack in the old-fashioned way.

All the other offices on this floor were out. Too many people, judging by the number of phones and wristwatches glinting in his awareness. Upstairs, maybe? But when Noam got to the fifth floor, it was just more offices. He hesitated outside the one located directly above Sacha's. It felt empty. He could just trip the latch and let himself in, the same way he let himself in downstairs, the whole this-fingerprint-totally-matches-your-databases trick. He reached for the flopcell.

"Can I help you?"

Noam spun around, his heart lurching up into his throat. The speaker was a severe-looking white woman, her arms full of folders. She was nearly as tall as Noam.

Shit shit shit shit.

"Um . . ."

"Minister Holloway is in a meeting," the woman went on, clearly disapproving. "He won't be back for two hours at least. Did you have an appointment?" Her gaze dropped down to the cadet star on Noam's sleeve, and her frown deepened. Noam's fist was clenched tight around the flopcell, but she hadn't asked to see what he was holding, hadn't noticed. Not yet.

Noam's mouth was faster than his brain.

"I can wait," he said, giving her a sunny smile. "I brought homework."

"Name?"

Stupid. Stupid, stupid. "Dara Shirazi."

The second he spoke, he worried she might recognize him—or not recognize him, more like. But despite that sharp breath sucked into her lipsticked mouth, she didn't immediately yell for security. Instead she glanced at her watch. If she hoped to reach for her phone, perhaps to text Holloway and ask if he was expecting Lehrer's ward, it was impossible with all the folders she juggled.

"Very well," she said after a sigh. "You can sit in the anteroom."

Hardly believing his luck, Noam trailed after her as she opened the door with her thumbprint and let him into the office. The anteroom was beautiful, elegantly decorated in forest green and mahogany. The woman sat him down on a luxurious chaise and then took her own chair behind the wooden secretary's desk before the door to Holloway's office.

Noam dumped his bag onto the sofa by his hip and dug out his holoreader. Well. He'd made it to an office. But with a chaperone giving him suspicious looks from ten feet away, he wasn't getting on Holloway's computer anytime soon.

He opened up a text editor and started typing, just to have something to do with his hands. The secretary's phone was in her pocket, sleepy pulses of electrical noise . . .

That could work.

It barely took ten seconds. The secretary's phone buzzed. She drew it out of her coat and glanced down at the screen, which Noam knew without looking had a message from her boss—Need you in room 142, urgent.

Thank god for unblocked radio signals.

"Can you keep yourself occupied for ten or fifteen minutes?" the secretary asked, even as she stood up and dusted off her pencil skirt.

"Sure," Noam said brightly.

Still, she gave him one last sharp look before vanishing out into the hall. Noam stayed seated where he was until the door finally fell shut behind her. Then he leaped up, darting across the room to the mahogany door leading back to Holloway's office; the secretary wouldn't need more than five minutes to realize there was no urgent business on the first floor.

The computer was on the desk, asleep. Noam dug a pair of latex gloves out of his bag and snapped them onto his hands before grabbing the mouse to wake the monitor. And, of fucking course, Holloway had it set up for retina-scan verification. Good thing Noam had that flopcell all programmed up, or else he'd be spending forever trying to script his way past the front door.

He stuck the flopcell in its slot and waited five seconds, ten . . . *why is it taking so long?* Only then the screen flickered, and he was in, *he was in.*

He had to move fast; he needed to give himself time to clean up the cache when he was done so Holloway couldn't check his process history later and wonder what he was doing on his desktop at 11:43 on Friday when he was supposed to be in a meeting.

Noam's first instinct was to get on the server—but when he tried to click into that path, he got a password prompt.

No time for that. What else could he look into?

Maybe . . . email? Would that be unlocked?

No harm trying. And—yes, yes, it was, thank god for small blessings. Where was his other flopcell? Ummm . . . left pocket . . . no, *right* pocket, okay. Filter "sender: Harold Sacha."

There.

Oh god. There were over four thousand results. Filter "sender: Harold Sacha, Atlantia."

Noam opened the first message and skimmed past the usual salutations and small-talk nonsense.

> . . . currently houses nine thousand citizens per square mile. Our infrastructure cannot support the additional numbers of Atlantian refugees. The disease threat alone is formidable—the last outbreak killed nearly seven thousand people, and approval ratings are lower every day. People don't feel safe in their own country. The refugees bring sickness, and crime, and antiwitching sentiment—all threats to Carolinian values.
>
> I know Calix has expressed his objections, but I'm overriding them. We're expanding the camps. All incoming immigrants and registered refugees should be relocated. Deport anyone without papers. If you encounter resistance, use necessary force.
>
> Per Calix's suggestion, I've offered Tom Brennan a position as official immigration adviser as a

goodwill gesture. Calix will speak to him. In the unlikely event Calix finds himself less than persuasive, see that Brennan accepts.

H. Sacha
Chancellor of Carolinia

With every word he read, Noam's stomach twisted a little tighter, until by the end of the letter it was a knot of nausea pulsing above his navel. This, *this* was the kind of thing Brennan needed to see.

It was foolish to pretend diplomacy was going to make any difference to someone like Sacha. Oh, he talked around it nicely enough, but Sacha's meaning was clear.

Take all the foreigners to the refugee camps. Deport undocumented immigrants, even though returning to Atlantia is a death sentence. Obey, even if you find my decision morally repulsive.

Fuck him. Fuck him for trying to justify deportation using the same outbreak that killed Noam's father. Atlantia was a viral cesspool. People had to flee to Carolinia if they wanted to survive. And when they got here, Sacha locked them up in camps and crowded slums, then blamed them when they fell sick.

When Carly found out she'd be sent back to Atlantia, they both cried for days because they knew what that meant. Then she shipped off in one of those canvas trucks, vanishing onto the freeway heading south. By the time her first letter made it to Durham, he'd already received the other letter, the one telling him Carly Jacobs was dead.

Noam's anger was a cold shell closing around his skin.

Focus. Save the message to the flopcell. No—save *all* messages . . . ETA twenty minutes—never mind; save first twenty-five messages.

He pulled both flopcells out and stuffed them into his pocket, then opened the command interface and erased all history of what he'd done.

He left before the secretary returned.

The thrill of sneaking into the government complex was gone. It had been replaced by a deep sense of injustice that throbbed through his body like blood.

Noam passed invisibly between the government employees, all of them just as guilty, all of them traitors for letting Sacha stay in power. Noam might as well be a ghost. The cameras didn't see him. The people didn't see him. His fingers dug into the strap of his bag, short nails cutting crescents into the leather.

He almost made it to the end of the corridor before the alarm went off.

Suddenly the halls were full of red lights flashing from bulbs hidden up near the ceiling, a screeching sound blaring from all sides. Bizarrely, Noam felt a rush of . . . something. Something that wasn't fear.

Let them arrest me. Let them try.

Noam looked around, half expecting to find soldiers marching up behind him or to feel cuffs clasp around his wrists. But everyone there looked as startled as Noam felt, lifting hands to their ears and glancing around as if the walls would tell them what to do.

Running would only draw attention. The alarm shrieked in his ears, sickeningly loud. Noam reached out with his power, flinging it far, trying to find the tech that controlled the alarm. But it was out of reach, impossible to program from this distance, so he did the next best thing.

The electricity cut out. The building plunged into darkness.

Screams erupted all around him. Doors flung open, footsteps pounding through the halls. Someone collided with Noam, running fast, and he stumbled.

Fuck, this was a stupid idea, he thought as his knees hit the floor.

A moment ago people wondered if the alarm was broken, but now they all thought this was some kind of terrorist attack.

Noam clutched his bag to his chest as people raced past, more worried about someone trashing his computer than getting trampled himself. He crawled left until he hit a wall and could pull himself up.

He leaned there, cradling his bag as he reached out with his power to fix the electricity. It didn't work.

Emergency lights flickered on a second later, illuminating the faces around him with a sickly green glow and turning them into eerie skulls. Most people went for the other end of the hall, so the stairs Noam took earlier might be empty. But elevators were bound to be shut down, and if the whole building stampeded the main staircase, other people would start taking the service stairs as well.

But he didn't have another option.

West it was, past frantic secretaries and stern-looking officers in military uniforms. He reached the service stairs and pulled the heavy steel door closed behind him, magnetizing it shut. A flimsy defense.

The stairwell was empty, thank god, but he couldn't stay here. Couldn't go out there either. With people looking for someone who didn't belong, Noam would stand out like a fire burning underwater.

Up led nowhere. Down, soldiers swarmed in from their posts.

Still, going down offered a better shot than getting trapped on the top floor. His footsteps were dangerously loud on the steel traction as he clattered down toward floor four. Right when he rounded the corner on the landing, someone grabbed him from behind, clapping a hand over his mouth.

Noam's immediate reaction was to lurch forward against the arm restraining him, but all the good that did was to pull him and his attacker one step closer to toppling down the stairs together. His reflexive gasp was muffled against the restraining hand, but the man yelped when Noam bit his palm.

"*Stop it*," a familiar voice hissed in his ear, and the arms let go.

Noam grabbed for his power, though what he would have done with it, he couldn't say; there was nothing nearby to use as a weapon.

"What the fuck are you doing here?"

Dara wore a soldier's uniform with stripes on the sleeve instead of a cadet star. His eyes were too bright in the emergency lights. "Don't worry about that right now. Can't you fix that?" He gestured toward the green bulb overhead.

"I tried," Noam said. "I think I fried the electrical wires."

"Idiot." Dara dragged a hand back through his already-messy hair, a muscle twitching in his temple. Noam couldn't even waste time being offended; he was pretty sure Dara was right.

Dara exhaled roughly. "Okay. Listen, we have to get out of here. There are soldiers coming down the second-floor corridor, headed for the stairs. We need to go out on the third floor."

Noam's throat was bone dry. "That's—"

"I know what the third floor is, Álvaro. Do you have a better idea?"

"Yeah, actually. They've obviously got us cornered. Let's just go out there and confess and get it over with. Maybe they'll go easy on us if we turn ourselves in."

Dara made a strange guttural sound, something animalistic, and his fingers closed around Noam's wrist. Dara's palm was sweaty, but his grip was bruising hard. He tugged once, pulling Noam off-balance. "Do you have any idea what they'd do to us if they found us here? Come *on*."

"Let go of me," Noam snapped, trying to pull his wrist free, but Dara's hand only tightened.

"Álvaro, I swear to god, if you don't come with me right now, I will *leave you here* for Lehrer to find. Let's go."

At this point, Dara was freaking Noam out more than the soldiers were. He let Dara drag him down the steps, only managing to shake off Dara's hand once they got to the landing. Below, he felt gunmetal outside the door to the stairs on the second floor. On instinct he magnetized that door shut, too, and just in time. A heavy weight collided with the steel, the sound echoing up the stairwell. The door didn't budge.

"Shit," Dara whispered. And—he had a gun in his hand, *what the fuck, what the fuck—*

Only, no, that was an illusion. Noam felt the magic when he looked for it, glittering around the edges of the thing and refracting light in a perfect pattern.

"I don't think that's going to help," Noam said, but Dara ignored him.

Dara's fear was contagious, seeping off him and curdling in Noam's blood. Dara pressed his whole body against the third-floor door.

"Let's—" Noam started, but Dara just said "*Ssh!*" and leaned his brow against the doorframe.

Noam hovered there, useless. They were both breathing heavily, the air gone humid between them. Noam magnetized the rest of the stairwell doors just in case.

At last, after Noam had started to worry they'd simply run out of oxygen in the staircase and suffocate, Dara tucked the fake gun into the back waistband of his drabs. He glanced over his shoulder at Noam, whites of his eyes gleaming in the strange light.

"Now."

Noam demagnetized the door.

The hall outside was pitch black except for the flicker of emergency lights casting weak green pools on the floor every twenty feet. If anyone was in the hall a moment ago they were gone now, scurrying away in the rooms branching off both sides.

This was insane. Noam was trespassing on government property with a flopcell full of treason and a crazy boy wielding a gun. A crazy boy who had *also been trespassing on government property*. Noam hadn't forgotten that Dara neglected to mention what he'd been doing here.

Noam crept in Dara's wake. The doors they passed loomed like great blank eyes, marking the two trespassers even if the blinded cameras couldn't.

"Careful," Dara said, looking back at him, and Noam realized his fingers sparked with electricity.

He balled his hands into fists and nodded, and after a moment, Dara reached over for his wrist again. This time his touch was light, just the barest pressure against Noam's pulse point, guiding him forward. Dara's magic was as palpable as a thousand quivering strings.

Noam never in his life felt so alive.

"You there! Hey—you!"

He and Dara whipped round. A man strode down the hall toward them. He wore a general's uniform, and if the blue ribbon on his button hadn't betrayed him as a witching, the way he held one hand aloft—as if prepared to stun them both with a jolt of magic where they stood—certainly would have.

Noam's mind seared white. He started toward the end of the hall, ready to run, but Dara grabbed his arm at the last second.

The general lowered his hand, crossing those last steps to Dara and Noam with a slow frown settling onto his lips. "What are you doing here?"

He was looking at Dara, not Noam.

"Oh, you know," Dara said. He waved a hand in the air, casual as anything. "Boyish exploration."

Noam expected the general to snap or call for backup. But instead he sighed, as if Dara were a disobedient son and not a trespasser on government property.

"Even you aren't allowed to wander around secure areas without a chaperone, Dara," the general said, folding arms over his broad chest. He looked down his nose at the pair of them. "And who is your friend?"

"That's Noam," Dara said before Noam could introduce himself. "He's new. Needed the grand tour."

"I see."

Noam couldn't stop staring at Dara. He'd never seen him act like this. Gone was the moody boy Noam knew, all traces of his usual sullenness evaporated. There was even something mischievous about the subtle curve of Dara's mouth, the way he tilted his head to the side.

He was magnetic.

"So-*oo*," Dara said, when several seconds had passed without anyone speaking, "are you going to escort us off the premises or not, General Ames?"

Ames? Like the Ames in Level IV?

Only, no—this was *Ames* Ames. General Gordon Ames, home secretary of Carolinia. Of course Dara knew him. If he grew up here, under Lehrer's care, he must know everybody. So how come he hadn't been recognized, wandering around here when he clearly wasn't allowed?

Illusion magic.

Dara must have made himself look like somebody else and dropped the guise when he ran into Noam.

But why? If he had illusion, he could have walked right out of this place amid the throng of government employees flooding the exits.

That meant . . .

Dara only dropped the illusion because of Noam.

He'd done it to save Noam. Because he didn't want to leave Noam behind.

But you hate me, Noam thought as he stared at the side of Dara's face, the elegant lines of his features in profile so beautiful but always so, so cold. *Why would you help me?*

"'Fraid I can't do that, Dara," Ames said, shaking his head. "We're on total lockdown. Someone tried to hack the Ministry of Defense servers, so no one leaves campus until the building's been swept down."

Fuuuuuck. Noam's fingernails dug so hard into his palms he thought he might have split the skin.

Only . . . technopathy wasn't traceable. And he'd been on Holloway's absurdly unsecured personal computer, not cracking Lehrer's department. He shot another tiny sidelong glance at Dara.

"Oh, come on," Dara said. He took a half step closer to the general, that fey smile curving farther along his lips. "You know we're not supposed to be here. We're going to get in trouble. You've known me since I was five. I'm not a spy. Can't this be our little secret?"

It was a long cry from the way Dara acted with Lehrer. If Noam didn't know better, he'd think Dara was flirting, which was ridiculous, but *really*?

But Ames just gave Dara another fond smile. "I'm afraid this is the worst possible time for you to be out of bounds, Dara. I have to call Minister Lehrer. But I'm sure he can sweep this under the rug."

Ames seemed to believe he was doing Dara a favor, but Noam had been around Dara long enough now to realize this was probably the worst outcome Dara could imagine. Dara's face could have been carved from stone.

Noam felt sick too as he fell in step beside him, Ames leading them both down the hall and into his office. Whether or not they'd trace the hack back to him, whether or not it was even his hack that had set off the alarms, Lehrer would immediately suspect Noam. It would be a pretty huge coincidence otherwise. A technopath in the building while someone else fucked around on the MoD servers?

He and Dara sat side by side on one of General Ames's plush burgundy sofas while the general dialed a number on his desk phone.

"Minister? It's Gordon Ames. I found Dara wandering around the third floor. I've got him up here in my office now. He was with another student." A beat. "No, sir, I haven't told anyone else. I thought you should be the one to handle this. Considering how it might look . . . right. Yes, sir. I'll be here."

He hung up. Neither Noam nor Dara moved, both frozen in place. Dara was pale, his fingers digging into his thighs. Of course he was nervous—he'd hacked the MoD. He was the one they were searching for. And Noam or no Noam, Dara must think there was a good chance Lehrer would figure that out, too, or else he wouldn't look like he was about to throw up.

What was he doing? Dara had no reason to hack the MoD. The minister of defense was basically his father. Why would he . . .

An idea splintered through Noam's mind, cold and terrifying—an idea that united Dara's presence here, the hack, Dara's obvious fear.

What if Dara is working against Lehrer?

"It'll be a spell before Minister Lehrer gets here," Ames told them, taking a seat in his desk chair and gazing at them like a benevolent god, oblivious to both of their discomfort. "I'm not sure what else he's got to do given the situation, so y'all go on and get comfortable."

But it was no time at all before Lehrer showed up. He shook Ames's hand at the door, thanked him for looking after Dara and Noam, and barely spared the slightest glance at either boy until he gestured for them to follow him out into the hall.

The electricity hadn't been fixed yet, the emergency lights nauseatingly green on Dara's skin as they followed Lehrer in silence. Lehrer didn't say a word either. His disapproval wound out behind him like a thread that wrapped around Noam, around Dara, tight and digging into flesh.

Lehrer took them to the study. There were no emergency lights here. Lehrer waved his hand, and flame lit the wicks of several lamps and candles scattered throughout the room, cutting the darkness with an incongruous warmth.

He turned to look at Noam and Dara, silhouetted black against the window. "Sit."

They sat.

Lehrer observed them wordlessly for a moment, and although Noam couldn't see his face, he could imagine the look on it. The flopcell in his bag burned in his awareness like a magnesium flare.

"I'm sorry, sir," Noam said at last. Better to seize control of the conversation early before Lehrer could start in on his interrogation. With the way Dara looked right now, Noam didn't trust him to avoid implicating himself. "This is all my fault."

"*Your* fault?" Lehrer said. His voice was dangerously soft. "Explain."

Noam managed a weak smile, trying to look self-deprecating. "I wanted to see what the government complex looked like inside. Atlantians usually aren't allowed in without a cleaner's uniform, you know."

Okay, that last part wasn't so self-deprecating.

Next to him, Dara stared at Noam like he'd never seen him before, his gaze boring a hole in the side of Noam's neck.

Noam kept going. "I kind of talked Dara into coming with me. I was sick of Dara being . . . being *Dara*, so I told him if he didn't sneak into the government building with me, it meant he was a coward." The lie came easier now, pouring out of him like water from a faucet. Noam shrugged, dedicated to the cocky act now. "Didn't use that exact word, though."

Lehrer moved closer, away from the window. Noam could see his face now, Lehrer examining him as if he could peel apart the layers of Noam's skin and peer into his core. "Is that true, Dara?" he said. He still watched Noam.

"Yes, sir."

"Hmm."

Noam had no idea if Lehrer believed them. He didn't seem angry anymore. More . . . bemused. Pinned by his gaze, Noam felt not unlike a butterfly affixed on velvet.

"Very well. Dara, wait for me in the other room. We'll discuss this later. Noam, stay here."

Noam hadn't even realized there was another room, but Dara rose to unsteady feet all the same, crossing over to one of the bookcases. He did something complicated with his hand, and magic rippled through the air. The bookcase swung inward like a door, exposing a short hall carpeted in blue and leading to another shut door. Dara looked back over his shoulder at Noam like he wanted to say something, eyes wide, but then he stepped inside and the bookcase shut behind him seamlessly.

It was just Noam and Lehrer now.

"Empty your satchel," Lehrer said. Noam's bag lifted itself off the floor and deposited itself in his lap.

Noam undid the buckles with shaking hands, his fingers fumbling the clasps twice before he got them open. He drew out the book he was reading, his black notebook, pens. His empty wallet. A pocket-size Ursascript reference book. And, at last, when the bag was completely empty and Noam didn't have any excuses left to delay, he took out his holoreader and flopcells and set them on the coffee table with the rest.

Lehrer's gaze slid over the objects assembled on the table. "Give me your holoreader and the flopcell. Don't change anything. Don't minimize any windows, don't wipe the cell drive, nothing."

Nausea curdled—once again—in the pit of Noam's stomach. Before Noam could hand the holoreader over, it was tugged out of his grasp by Lehrer's power, floating through the air to land neatly in Lehrer's hands. Lehrer selected a flopcell and plugged it in, then examined the screen, frowning.

Just last week, Noam considered putting extra security on his computer. He'd thought about writing a program where, if he entered a certain password on start-up, anything in his encrypted drives would immediately be deleted. It would have been simple, elegant. It would have meant Noam could erase the text file without Lehrer being any the wiser. But he hadn't done it, because he'd thought he was being paranoid, and that was stupid, *stupid stupid*, because any hacktivist worth shit knew there was no such thing as too paranoid.

"I assume you were responsible for the electricity cutting out," Lehrer said.

He glanced at Noam, who swallowed and nodded once.

"That was a bad idea," Lehrer said. "You caused building-wide panic. It would have been better to let the alarm keep going."

No shit. But why was Lehrer going on about that, of all things, when he'd just read what he had? He held evidence of treason in his hands, and he was telling Noam how the crime could've been performed *better*?

Lehrer shut off the holoreader and passed it back to Noam, who gripped it so hard his hands cramped. He was never letting this computer out of his sight again, not without destroying the cell drive beyond recognition, and Lehrer and his order not to use technopathy could both go fuck themselves.

"I can't cover for you like this again," Lehrer said. "You're going to have to do a better job hiding yourself in the future."

"I—what?"

Lehrer picked up a cup of tea from an end table. The drink had been cold a moment before, but by the time he lifted it to his lips, it was steaming hot. Lehrer took a sip, then smiled, as if amused.

"I really don't care that you broke into the government complex," Lehrer went on, swirling the tea round in his cup. "But really, Noam, a cadet's uniform? You couldn't be bothered to change into your civvies?"

Noam flushed. The truth was, the only "civvies" he had were the ones he wore back from the hospital—and after three months, they'd fallen apart.

His mind was muddled with new information, blown expectations whirling like watercolors.

"I didn't have anything better, sir."

Lehrer gave him a faintly incredulous look. *"Improvise."*

The way he said it made Noam want to shrivel up with embarrassment. "Yes, sir."

"Then," Lehrer said, completely unmoved by Noam's anxiety, "there's the matter of your digital trespassing."

Anger resurfaced like a monster from the deep, surging up into the shallows of Noam's mind and subsuming the anxiety of a moment before.

"You read that email," Noam burst out. "You heard what he said. Sacha's *evil,* sir. He's crazy, or he's stupid, or—people *die* in those refugee camps. They're overcrowded, and people get sick, and they never come back. And we all know Atlantia's a death trap."

"I did read the email," Lehrer confirmed. He sat down in his usual chair, perching an elbow on the armrest and cupping his tea between both hands. "And I agree with you, Noam. Sacha's behavior is reprehensible."

"But you aren't going to do anything about it." Noam's voice hurt, like broken glass in his throat. "That makes you just as bad as he is."

Lehrer's oddly transparent eyes did not blink. "I wouldn't say I'm doing nothing."

The words hung in the air between them. They grew there, transformed, spread long limbs into the empty corners and twined around Noam's heart.

"What, then?" he said, when he couldn't stand the silence anymore. "*What* are you doing? Because as far as I can see, you're full of sympathy and promises but not much else." The last word cracked on its way out, Noam's chest seizing painfully.

Lehrer put down his tea and leaned forward, bracing his forearms against his knees and clasping his hands between them. The smile was gone.

"Listen to me, Noam," Lehrer said. "This has happened before. My grandparents were so-called foreigners in their own land. Their German countrymen locked them away in prison camps for the crime of being Jews. And then, in the 2000s, the United States rounded up all witchings and their families and had them killed, allegedly for the safety of the uninfected. I survived not because I was spared, but because I was powerful enough to be studied *before* I was killed. What Sacha is trying to do now is no different. He's afraid of the virus, but fear is just as infectious. This country is paralyzed by it. Sacha believes he is protecting the people from disease by taking a hard line on immigration, but *he is wrong*."

Lehrer said the last part so forcefully that Noam felt it like a blow to the gut. Something shattered on the other side of the room; Noam leaped to his feet before he could stop himself.

The decanter had fallen off the table, heavy crystal in pieces all over the floor and scotch dripping onto the rug.

"My apologies," Lehrer said. "I forget myself."

The decanter repaired itself before Noam's eyes, and the spilled liquor vanished.

Slowly, slowly, Noam sat down.

His heart still raced.

"I didn't know," Noam said, when he could talk without the words coming out raw and bloody. "About your family, that is. I didn't . . ." But then something else occurred to him, and he said, "You're *Jewish*?"

Lehrer lifted a brow. "Do they leave that part out of the history books?" he said, and Noam laughed, surprising himself.

"No, it's not that. But. My mom is—*was*. Jewish. I'm Jewish."

A moment ago Noam had been so—he'd been furious, and he wished he could go back to that feeling, because it felt wrong to just *move on* after what he'd read in Holloway's office, but right now his mind had short-circuited on this one fact, this tiny common thread tied between him and Lehrer. He wanted to weave that thread into a ribbon, a rope. He grinned, and after a moment, Lehrer smiled back. It was a small smile, a quiet smile, but worth so much more for that.

Lehrer's grandparents had survived the Holocaust—had survived a genocide that shipped millions of Jews and other undesirables off to camps to be brutally, efficiently exterminated—only to die sixty-some years later. This time at the ends of a different nation's guns, killed not for being Jewish but for daring to have magic. For having children who had magic. Noam couldn't fathom trauma like that.

But he couldn't forget what he'd read today either.

The same magic that gave Lehrer his power would kill the population of an entire country if Sacha forced Atlantians back down south.

"What can we do?" Noam said. He kept his voice low; no one was there to overhear, but speaking the words felt dangerous. "About Sacha. You've tried to talk him out of it. But you have to do more than that."

Lehrer took in a shallow, audible breath. "These things are . . . complicated. Right now, you will just have to believe me when I tell you I haven't forgotten the refugees. I *am* on your side, Noam—I promise you that much."

A politician's answer. Noam wasn't sure what else he expected.

But then Lehrer's expression softened further. He reached over to place a hand on Noam's wrist, fingertips pressing in against the pulse point.

A strange bird fluttered its wings against the cage of Noam's ribs.

"I won't ask you to stop fighting," Lehrer said, very quietly. "I would never ask you that."

I'll never stop, Noam thought, but thinking wasn't speaking. So at last, he made himself nod, and Lehrer—who seemed to have been waiting for just that—squeezed his wrist and drew away.

"Can I keep the emails?"

"I don't see why not."

Noam blinked. "Wait. Seriously?"

Lehrer leaned back in his chair and reached for his tea. "I meant what I said, didn't I?" His voice was dry, but his lips, when they touched his cup, curved up.

"I would've thought you'd tell me it was illegally obtained evidence or something."

"Ah, yes. Your record. Twelve months in juvenile detention for criminal trespass." His eyes, as they met Noam's over the rim of his teacup, glittered too bright. "I should have known you'd recidivate."

It took Noam a second to realize Lehrer was joking.

When he did, though, relief poured like ice water through his veins. *Lehrer, joking*—the idea was almost obscene, and yet . . .

"They caught me plugged in to the server room at the immigration office," Noam admitted. "Totally red-handed."

"Well then, I'm thrilled to be working alongside such a criminal prodigy," Lehrer said dryly.

It felt like a wall crumbling between them. Like Noam was seeing the real Lehrer for the first time, behind the mask and uniform of defense minister. Like Lehrer could still be the boy who loved his parents and went to shul on Fridays, who probably hated charoset and read novels when he was supposed to be praying.

A boy a lot like Noam, maybe.

Lehrer helped him pack his things back into his satchel, Lehrer's magic floating the notebooks in alongside Noam's holoreader. He offered Noam tea, and Noam declined, still queasy from before. Then Lehrer escorted him to the front door with a hand placed between his shoulder blades. A small gesture, but it knotted warm in Noam's chest.

"One more thing," Lehrer said, standing there with fingers poised above the knob. "Be careful with Mr. Shirazi, Noam. Don't share this conversation with him. He may be clever and charming, but he's . . . troubled. I don't say this as a slight against him, of course; I raised him like my own son. But he will not see things our way. Do you understand?"

No shit. Dara hadn't been checking his social media accounts on the MoD servers, after all.

Did Lehrer know Dara was working against him? If so, why hadn't Lehrer stopped him? Noam couldn't believe Lehrer was oblivious.

But if Dara was against Lehrer, and Lehrer was willing to let Noam hold on to sensitive information that could unravel Sacha's government . . .

Was Lehrer against Sacha?

If so, did that mean Dara *wasn't*?

It was too much to try to hold on to, too many threads tangling worse the more he tried to unravel them.

So Noam just nodded.

Lehrer looked relieved. He opened the door.

"Good. Then I'll see you Monday, at our regular time. Do try not to damage any more government property on your way out, will you?"

He hadn't called for Howard to escort Noam from the study back to the training wing. Impossible not to take note of that, after what Lehrer had just told him. Even so, Noam didn't take any detours—just went straight to the barracks before the others could return from class, where he set himself up in the common room with his books, like he'd been there all along.

Dara didn't get back until late. He let himself into the barracks sometime around eleven. He'd taken the fake lieutenant stripes off his uniform. Such a small thing, but without them Dara looked younger, a quiet shadow with a lowered gaze.

"Hey," Noam said, moving his textbook off his lap and onto the end table. Dara glanced up, their eyes meeting across the common room. "Are you all right? What happened?"

Dara turned the latch. "I'm fine. Lehrer was angry, but I expected that."

"Does he know you . . ."

But when Dara looked at him again, the question died in Noam's throat. Instead he shoved the other books and papers off the sofa, tapped the cushion. He was a little surprised when Dara took the invitation and settled himself down on the other end of the sofa. He drew his legs up onto the seat, like he was trying to make himself small.

"You didn't have to lie for me," Dara said.

"You didn't have to drop your illusion to help me escape."

Dara glanced at Noam out of the corner of his eye, a tiny smile flickering across his face. "You're cleverer than I thought."

"Not like that was a high bar to begin with," Noam said, but Dara shook his head.

"I knew you were smart. That's not the same thing as liking you."

"And why *don't* you?" Noam asked before he could stop himself. Dara arched a brow, but Noam barreled on regardless. "What did I ever do to you?"

Dara twisted around, draping one arm along the back of the sofa and tilting his head against his own shoulder. "I don't like naïveté, I suppose."

"You really think I'm naive?"

"You trust Lehrer."

Noam fought not to roll his eyes. "He hasn't given me any reason not to. I'm sure you know more than I do, considering he raised you or whatever, but I have to make my own opinions about people. That's not naïveté. That's critical thinking."

Dara laughed, but it wasn't cruel. He looked otherworldly like this, watching Noam with steady black eyes and messy hair falling into his face. "Something tells me critical thinking isn't your strong suit, Álvaro."

"I suppose not, if you equate being cynical with being logical."

"Mmm." Dara closed his eyes, and for a moment Noam thought he was going to go to sleep right here in the common room, with his fingertips so nearly brushing Noam's arm. When he opened his eyes again, they were half-lidded, lashes low and dark. "What did Lehrer tell you?"

"He said you were troubled and that I should stay away from you."

"I bet he did." Dara's smile was bladed. He had Noam captured there as thoroughly as if he'd tied him down, because Noam couldn't imagine moving when Dara was looking at him like that. He was sure that if he did, he wouldn't escape unscathed. "And since you're such a rebel now, do you plan on obeying?"

"It's like I told you. I make my own opinions."

Noam didn't flinch, and when Dara exhaled, Noam felt the gust of air against his own brow.

"Look at that," Dara murmured. "Noam Álvaro, interesting after all."

"Don't think I've forgotten you were there, too, Shirazi," Noam said and refused to break Dara's gaze—not even when it sharpened. "Feel like offering some kind of explanation?"

"Not tonight," Dara said. He closed his eyes again, and when Dara wasn't glaring, it was easier to see how unwell he looked—too thin, exhausted, like he hadn't slept in days.

Noam chewed the inside of his cheek. He couldn't just let this go, no matter how pathetic Dara looked. He had to know what Dara was up to, whether it was going to cause problems for Noam's own plans.

But perhaps it could wait. At least until tomorrow.

Dara unfolded himself from the sofa, rising to his feet. Noam was still frozen in place, watching him move.

"I'm going to take a shower," Dara said. "I'll see you tomorrow, I expect."

It felt like a question. Noam nodded.

"Good."

Dara left, and Noam—Noam was drawn up on tenterhooks, poised on edge until he heard the bedroom door shut behind Dara, and the spell broke.

He still stayed away from the bedroom for another hour, staring at his books, until he was sure Dara was asleep.

Chapter Eight

Noam kept expecting Lehrer to change his mind. But no men in anti-witching armor showed up at midnight to demand Noam hand over his flopcell. No MoD soldiers reached for him as he left the government complex that morning and dragged him back behind bars. He stepped out into the snowy December streets with treason burning a hole in his pocket, and Lehrer just *let him*.

Lehrer was playing some kind of game; that much was clear. He'd all but admitted it that night in the courtyard when Noam first joined Level IV—and again, when he taught Noam magnetism.

But what were Lehrer's plans for Noam?

If Lehrer was manipulating him, then Noam was really screwed. He had no idea how the hell he was supposed to outwit the smartest man alive.

True to promise, Noam was allowed to keep his job at the convenience store, which had been spared the firebomb postoutbreak by a scant four hundred yards and opened back up again last week. If anything, Larry, the owner, was desperate for staff since half his people died in fever, and though he must've known that Noam survived the virus—that Noam was a witching now—he didn't ask too many questions.

Noam was dying to go straight to Brennan and hand over the data and watch the look on Brennan's face transform from disgust to delight. Would have, if not for the early shift. He might not have his dad to support anymore, but going to work felt more important than ever. Another way to prove Noam wasn't one of those government soldiers, not really, that his blood still belonged to the west side. To Atlantia.

Level IV covered taxi fare, but Noam took the bus. He liked that better: sitting on a hard plastic seat next to someone's grandmother holding that week's groceries in her lap, the kid in the back blasting music from his phone, the man in a secondhand suit on his way to a job interview. He tipped his head toward the window and watched the familiar buildings slide past. Still his city, even with an empty scar where Ninth used to be. Still his, even if—had he come here wearing his cadet uniform instead of the ill-fitting civvies Howard gave him—*his* city wouldn't want him anymore.

The thought stuck in his chest like a swallowed chicken bone, scratching against the inside of his sternum the rest of the way across town.

Noam sat behind the counter at his corner-store job and rubbed his thumb against the flopcell's outer shell. He found he could actually read the data off it without a computer, just like this. He went over that email so many times he memorized it, every dirty word.

What next? That was the question he kept coming back to. Lehrer wouldn't intervene—he had some mysterious unspecified plan—but that meant it was up to Noam to change things in Carolinia.

This was a start. Atlantians had no voice in government, but Noam could be their ears.

So Noam went straight to the Migrant Center when he got off work.

"He's not here," Linda said when he asked to see Brennan, which was an obvious lie—but at least she didn't try to stop him when he shouldered into the building anyway, heading down the narrow hall to the back rooms.

"Hi," Noam said when he pushed open Brennan's door.

Brennan, at his desk, jerked his head up too quickly to disguise the flicker of guilt that passed over his face. Only then his expression twisted toward anger instead.

"I told you—"

"Yeah, I remember. But you're gonna want to see this."

Noam plunked himself down in the chair opposite Brennan's and slid the flopcell across the desk.

"What's this?"

"Stick it in your computer and find out."

Brennan's eyes narrowed. "Is it malware?"

Noam glared at him, just long enough for Brennan to sigh and take the flopcell.

Noam watched Brennan read the email, both hands gripping the bottom of his seat. He was surprised Brennan managed to keep himself under control, considering what he was reading. Only a slight tic in his jaw betrayed Brennan's true feelings.

"How did you get this?" Brennan asked at last.

"How do you think?"

Brennan looked up. Noam was perversely satisfied to know he had Brennan on the end of a string, that he finally found something Brennan wanted badly enough to forget Noam was a witching.

As if Noam would let him forget.

"My presenting power—you know, my *magic*"—he leaned on the word just to watch Brennan flinch—"gives me power over technology."

"Diplomacy only works so far with Sacha," Brennan muttered at last. "Until now it has been the sole tool in our arsenal. But . . ." He glanced back at the email. "This gives us an advantage. We know what he's planning, and so we can prepare for it. We'll have protests organized and be ready to march the second the news is made public. We'll organize a citywide labor strike, sit-ins . . ."

Noam waited in impatient silence while Brennan reread the email, fingers tapping against the edge of his desk. At last, when he couldn't stand it any longer, Noam burst out:

"I can get more."

Brennan's attention leaped up. Noam wished he didn't need that attention so badly, that it didn't make something warm bloom in his chest, the same feeling he got when Brennan and his father picked him up when he was released from juvie two weeks after his thirteenth birthday, Noam pinned between them with his father's arms around his body and Brennan's hand a solid weight at his nape. That feeling of *finally*.

"I can get around the antitechnopathy wards on the government servers if I have enough time. I can figure out what they're up to." He was at the edge of his seat, all but willing Brennan to listen.

Brennan sighed. "I can't pretend that doesn't sound . . . obviously I'm tempted, Noam. But we can't sink to their level. Your father and I have always disagreed on this, but I do believe peaceful protest is the only way. Besides, I don't want you going back to prison." A beat passed, Brennan's mouth twisting. "Perhaps I was unfair to you before. You must know I have your best interests at heart. How can I live with myself if I let you damn yourself on my behalf?"

"I'm going to do it anyway, whether you sign off or not."

Brennan's fingertips hovered over the screen. Noam wondered if he was about to delete all that hard-gained data, or if he might—perhaps—

"I can't condone this," Brennan said at last.

He didn't say it out loud, but Noam still got the gist.

I can't condone this, but I'll accept whatever you can give me.

Even if you're still a witching.

"I understand," he said.

He wished he didn't.

He wished they could go back to whatever it was they had before.

"I can't believe you didn't get caught," Brennan said after several seconds, shaking his head.

"I kind of did. General Ames found me and . . . found me on the third floor. He got Lehrer."

Brennan's gaze sharpened. "He got Lehrer? What did you say? How did you—"

"Lehrer saw the email." There was no point talking around it. "He made me empty out my bag and give him my computer."

Brennan looked ill. His hands clenched and unclenched atop the desk, impotent. "You should be in jail right now. Executed, more like. Why . . . how are you here?"

Executed? Noam hadn't at all gotten that impression from Lehrer, who'd been angry, of course, but even then Noam assumed he was facing arrest. Not death.

Maybe that was foolish. Treason was treason, and Dara had been terrified.

He swallowed against the uncomfortable lump that had lodged itself in his throat. "Lehrer's sympathetic to the refugees. He said . . ."

No. Whatever happened to Lehrer or Lehrer's grandparents was Lehrer's business.

"He said if we were planning something, he wouldn't stand in our way."

Brennan turned his face toward the ceiling as if in silent prayer. "Thank god. I hate to say it, but without Lehrer on our side, we wouldn't last a week. Lehrer controls the army. If he refuses to aid Sacha . . . well. Sacha will find himself ill equipped to round up immigrants without military enforcement."

Noam couldn't help thinking that Brennan's route to change was woefully underdeveloped. It all hinged on Lehrer refusing to use the army to round up refugees, and Noam wasn't so sure the army would obey Lehrer if the choice was between obedience to a commanding officer and treason. Especially if they feared, like most, that the refugees brought magic with them into Carolinia to infect their families.

He wasn't sure Lehrer would even help Brennan's movement in the first place.

Noam kept ruminating on that well into the afternoon, which he spent volunteering in the Migrant Center's soup kitchen, spooning casserole onto trays for a seemingly never-ending line of refugees. Before Level IV he wouldn't have noticed how gaunt they looked, how shocking the razor edge of a collarbone, the gray tinge to cheeks. It would have seemed normal to the old Noam, the one who grew up in tenement housing and was constantly hungry himself.

Now Noam had everything. Incredible how quickly he had gotten used to a soft bed and a full stomach and a world's worth of knowledge at his fingertips. How foolish to complain about grueling boot camp sessions when all around him people starved to death.

If Sacha's plans succeeded, most of them would be dead this time next year.

"It's nearly six," Linda said when she found him still there hours later, perspiring from kitchen heat and ladling stew into bowls. She started untying his apron strings without even asking, tugging him back away from the food line. "You have to go back to school, Noam. It's Remembrance Day today. Aren't you going to be in trouble if you stay out late?"

Probably. "I'll be fine."

She pulled the apron off over his head and tossed it into the growing pile of laundry. "Don't be ridiculous, sugar. We have plenty of volunteers who can take over from here. You should go home. Get some dinner. Watch the memorial ceremony on TV."

The food served in Level IV was meat and fresh vegetables. The stew the Migrant Center fed the refugees was carefully prepared to be high calorie and low cost: frozen potatoes, soy protein, broth from reconstituted powder.

The thought of going home and eating like a king was repulsive.

Could magic create food? If someone understood molecular biology, would that person be able to piece together the structure of an apple, or a kale plant, or even meat? Could the virus create life just as easily as it snuffed it out?

Think how many lives they could save.

Noam walked back downtown instead of taking the bus, hood tugged up to keep the snow out of his eyes and ungloved hands stuffed deep in both pockets. Without his uniform he was just another teen—in this neighborhood, a refugee—but as soon as he crossed into the government district he'd become the kid of some important minister, waiting for Daddy's car.

He stopped at the Gregson Street intersection and stood there for a second, cheeks stinging in the bitter wind as he gazed down toward the smokestack that landmarked the government complex. People in suits edged around him without saying a word, heading to work in the refurbished tobacco warehouses that made up Brightleaf Square or north to their fancy apartments.

For the first time since he joined Level IV, Noam realized he didn't feel that immediate plunge of nausea when he looked east. The idea of going back to the government complex didn't make him want to lie down on the cracked sidewalk and let himself get trampled to death.

It wasn't that he was happy to go back, but . . .

By the time he got back to the complex, it was late; the guard at the door took down his name with a grim sort of pleasure, meaning Noam would probably be on toilet duty for the next week. When he got upstairs the other students were already eating dinner, all that delicious food designed by nutritionists to help them grow strong, water that didn't have shit floating in it, real silverware.

Noam ate. The meal tasted like wax.

A new strain of resentment grew inside him, a virus spreading from cell to cell. Bethany was from Richmond; her mother was a doctor. Taye's parents were still alive, university professors he visited some weekends. Ames's father was home secretary. None of them could possibly understand where Noam came from.

And then there was Dara, of course, Lehrer's ward. Dara, whom General Ames recognized in the halls. Dara, who got his indiscretions erased from the record without comment, even felony trespassing. Dara, whose name and face had been kept from the media so he could grow up in cloistered, privileged peace.

Dara, who grew up with more of a father than Noam had these past three years but who seemed determined to blow up his life in a fit of teenage disobedience.

Noam watched Dara push his collards around his plate with the tines of his fork, silently dragging them past a little hill of creamed corn but never eating them. He hadn't eaten anything on his plate, actually; he'd just cut it all up and left it there. Because he could afford to be not hungry. Because wasting food was nothing to him.

When Noam was a kid and felt picky about choking down gefilte fish on Pesach, his dad sat him down and told him the story of la pobre viejecita. *Once upon a time, there was an old lady with nothing to eat but meat, fruit, and sweets* . . . and he'd flop another lump of poached fish on Noam's plate and say, "God bless us with the poverty of *that* poor woman."

Noam had a hard time imagining Lehrer guilt-tripping Dara into eating gefilte fish.

"Wait," Noam said, when dinner was finished and Dara went to scrape his plate into the trash. He forced a smile for Dara's benefit and tugged the plate from his hands. "I'll take that. For later."

Dara gave him a strange look, but he let Noam pour his leftovers into a plastic container without conflict. Noam could bring it to the Migrant Center tomorrow; maybe someone would eat it.

Dara was still standing there. Noam kept glancing at him out of the corner of his eye as he rinsed off the dishes, Dara's arms crossed over his chest. Waiting.

Well, fuck him. Dara still might have issues with Noam, but Noam had questions for him too.

"Listen," he said, when he finally set the last plate on the drying rack. "I need to talk to you. Is there anywhere we can go where we won't be overheard?"

"I was starting to think you'd lost your nerve. Let's go down to the courtyard."

"Is that private?"

"Private enough. Get your coat."

They ended up on a bench near the stream that cut through the courtyard, right where it poured over a manufactured outcropping of rocks. The water was loud enough that they wouldn't be overheard, not even by the soldiers patrolling the perimeter or government employees with open windows overhead. Even so, Dara did something complicated with his magic before they sat. A ward muffling their conversation? Noam couldn't tell what it was, but he sensed it, Dara's magic as bright and green as summer.

Noam drew his feet up onto the seat and faced Dara, who kept one leg on the ground as he pulled his satchel onto the bench between them and dug out a bottle of bourbon. He unscrewed the cap and pushed it across the wood to bump against Noam's shin.

It wasn't exactly what Noam had in mind when he asked Dara out here, but he took a swig anyway. The drink burned going down, like swallowing a smoldering silk ribbon.

"Where'd you get this?" he said, looking at the label. He wasn't that familiar with whiskeys, but a double-oaked bourbon sounded like a pretty big deal. At the very least, bourbon tasted better than the shine he and Carly used to share during late nights on the roof of their favorite café —nasty swill, like drinking laundry water, but it did the job.

"It was a gift," Dara said. He reached out a hand, and Noam passed the bottle. "I didn't want to drink it alone. Well, that's a lie, but . . ."

"So you're sharing it with me?"

"If you'll break into the government complex all on your own, you've clearly got the spine for it."

"Speaking of." Noam put the whiskey down on the bench between them and arched a brow.

"Right." Dara reached for the bottle, staring down its open mouth. "You want to know what I was doing there."

"And?"

"You know, I could have asked you the same thing, but I didn't." Dara's mouth twisted into a brief and superficial smile, and he looked up. "How about you don't ask, and I continue to return the favor."

"I already told you and Lehrer what I was up to. I was bored and decided to have a look around. Your turn."

"Oh," Dara said, waving a vague hand. "You know. Same."

"You hacked into the Ministry of Defense."

"Hacking is more your wheelhouse, Álvaro. Guess you need to practice your technopathy more, seeing as you got caught."

Noam made a face. "Alternatively," he said, "you could just tell me what you were looking for. Maybe I can help."

"Nice try. Cute, though."

"Are you trying to undermine Lehrer?"

"Now why would I do a thing like that?" There was something to the lilt of Dara's voice, something almost bitter.

"You tell me. Is it just to get Lehrer's attention?"

That hit a nerve. Dara physically recoiled, knuckles going briefly white around the neck of the bourbon bottle. His mouth was a thin line.

"I'm sorry," Noam said. "I didn't mean that. I just . . ."

"Wanted to get under my skin?" Dara said, voice still strained, even though he smiled before he took a swig of whiskey. "Well, good job. I think you're right. That must be it."

Noam bit his lip to stop himself from asking more questions. "Yeah," he said instead, just to fill the silence. "So. New topic. Um. What do you want to be when you grow up?"

Dara snorted.

"I mean it. Bethany wants to be a healer. Ames wants to keep climbing military ranks. Taye's gonna . . . well, okay, who even knows what Taye wants. But what about you?"

Dara drank again, relaxing back against the bench and turning his face toward the market lights strung overhead. "I don't know," he said, passing the bottle back to Noam.

This time, Noam kept it. He could tell Dara was already starting to feel the liquor—his eyes were glassy-bright, cheeks flushed. He must've been drinking already, before they came out here.

Maybe it wasn't any of Noam's business. Dara would almost certainly say so, that he was allowed to drink if he wanted to drink.

But Noam wanted to get to know him. To really know him, not just the version of Dara that emerged from the bottom of a bourbon bottle.

"Sure you do," Noam said.

"I really don't."

"What about politics? You have the connections for it." Connections to Lehrer. To Sacha, whom Dara didn't even bother to greet in the hall.

It wasn't an entirely innocent question, but Noam kept himself wide eyed and curious all the same.

"Not that," Dara said, screwing up his face and shaking his head. "I always thought . . ." He hesitated for a moment, darting a quick glance at Noam from beneath his lashes. Then: "I'd like to live out on a farm somewhere. With a garden, and maybe some goats. Somewhere I can see the stars."

Oh please.

Whatever. If Dara didn't want to tell him the truth, then fine.

Noam was happy to just drink with him. It was good whiskey. And besides, Noam liked the way the liquor made him feel, his thoughts warm, fat fish swimming through the sea of his mind. He was still better off than Dara, who had finally tugged the bottle back out of Noam's grasp and slung one arm over the railing, his face toward the glittering sky.

"Never had bourbon before," Noam said at last. "No, really. It's all beer and shine in my parts." Or aguardiente, if Noam's dad was feeling nostalgic. "You ever had moonshine?"

"Do you really think Lehrer let me drink moonshine growing up?"

"Lehrer does seem more the vintage imported whisky type," Noam admitted. "Like, he'd probably say we could only enjoy this drink if we had sophisticated adult palates."

"You're right," Dara said, looking back to Noam and holding the bottle out over the brick sidewalk, mischievous. "Maybe we should just pour it out. Better than insulting the distillery by drinking it with our crude palates."

"Don't you dare." Noam lurched forward, grabbing for the bottle, but Dara was quicker, pulling it out of reach and tipping his head back for another swallow, this one long, as if he were luxuriating in it. Dara gave him a considering look when at last he lowered the bottle, fingers toying with the neck. He had transformed, somehow, in the past several minutes—from cold and cautious to something brighter, buoyant.

Dara reminded Noam of a piece of tourmaline he found once, gleaming a different color every time he tilted it to a new angle. He was fascinating.

"We should do this again sometime," Dara said.

Noam fought to ignore the sudden, prickling rush of adrenaline flooding beneath his skin.

"Oh yeah?"

Dara set the bottle down on the bench between them with a clink of glass on wood. "Yeah," he said. "It's not often that I meet someone who shares my taste in liquor."

"Or tastelessness, as it happens."

Dara smirked and put the bourbon away. "Yes, well. We should get inside before Howard sends someone looking for us."

Noam got to his feet, and after a second's hesitation, extended a hand to help Dara up. Dara laughed and ignored him, pushing himself up with far more grace and ease than Noam had expected.

"I'm not as drunk as you think," Dara said.

"You just consumed your body weight in bourbon."

"Well, I did grow up drinking *decent* whiskey instead of your bootleg moonshine, so I suppose I've built up a tolerance." Dara started off toward the training wing, glancing back after three paces to gesture Noam along.

When they got back to the barracks, it was to find the others still awake and crowded into the common room, bowls of popcorn perched on their knees.

"Hey, you're back just in time," Taye said. "Look what we're watching." He gestured toward the television and grinned.

"What am I supposed to be looking at here?" Dara said as Noam dropped into the armchair nearest Ames, who flicked a popcorn kernel at his ear.

"It's the new Lehrer biopic. Released just in time for Remembrance Day."

Dara's expression darkened so immediately it was as if a curtain had pulled shut behind his eyes. "Let's not."

"Too bad, overruled by democratic process." Taye swung his leg where it was hooked over the arm of the sofa, clearly trying to kick Dara in the thigh, but missed. "Besides. You just don't wanna watch 'cause he's your *daddy*."

Dara looked like he wanted to be physically ill. "Don't say that."

"What, don't say the truth?"

"We aren't related."

"Yeah, okay, doesn't make him not your dad. I wish Lehrer was *my* dad."

Ames snorted. "C'mon, Taye, we've all met your dad. Your dad's awesome." She pulled a pack of cigarettes out of her back pocket and tapped them against the end table. "Howard's not here—y'all mind if I smoke?"

"Go for it," Dara muttered, and he spun on his heel, disappearing down the dim hall toward the bedrooms.

He didn't emerge again, not even when Taye paused the movie to pass around obligatory it's-a-national-holiday shots, even though Dara never missed an opportunity to get drunk. Noam was halfway to wasted already, and the shots just made it worse.

Probably inappropriate, all of them trashed on shitty tequila—except Bethany, whom Ames had developed some bizarre sense of protectiveness toward; the older girl snatched every shot passed Bethany's way right out of her hand. For her own part, Bethany just kept giggling about the biceps of the actor playing Lehrer, drunk enough on cherry soda. A part of Noam felt guilty. It was Remembrance Day. They ought to, like, watch the memorial ceremony, or something, where the real Lehrer was speaking on the loss of his brother and everyone murdered during the catastrophe.

Instead he ended up sprawled on the couch, with his head in Bethany's lap and his legs in Taye's, Ames in the chair by the window, where she could blow her smoke into the night air.

The movie was actually good. Noam had read the book, of course—it'd been one of his first self-prescribed assignments after he started Level IV. Lehrer had been Noam's age when he was liberated from the hospital, but even at sixteen he'd been more legend than teenage boy.

Lehrer's brother died when Lehrer was nineteen, and Lehrer was crowned king less than a year later. Then he'd spent years fighting off Canada and Mexico and half of Europe when they all tried to bomb Carolinia off the map. They'd claimed they couldn't let someone as powerful as Lehrer rule a country, but everyone knew the truth: Lehrer declared Carolinia a witching state, and that was something the mundane world would never allow.

Meanwhile, Noam had done . . . what, exactly?

He'd hacked a few websites. Gone to some protests.

Hadn't made a bit of difference.

Brennan would've said he was too young to change the world on his own, but Lehrer was proof that age was no excuse.

He noticed Ames was gone an hour or so into the movie, right after the part where Lehrer closed Carolinian borders for the last time. Her cigarette was a cold butt abandoned on the windowsill, popcorn bowl empty.

"Be right back," he murmured.

He slipped down the hall to where a sliver of amber light glowed from the door to the boys' bedroom, left ajar. Noam didn't mean to eavesdrop, not really, but there was no other excuse for the way he started to step softly as soon as he heard the low murmur of voices from within.

" . . . let it get to you," Ames said, and when Noam moved closer, he could see her through the half-open door. She had her hands on Dara's narrow hips, head leaned in so her brow rested against his. She hadn't seen Noam, but Dara did almost immediately.

Their gazes met. Dara's eyes were coals gleaming in the lamplight, the expression that flitted across his face nearly inhuman in the moment before he grasped Ames's arms and pushed her back. She looked over her shoulder. When she saw Noam, her mouth twisted.

"Sorry," Noam said, lifting both hands. "Just looking for Ames."

She glanced at Dara, who said nothing.

"Be right back," Ames said, after the silence had stretched on just a beat too long. She moved away from Dara and out into the hall with Noam, pulling the door shut behind her. "What's up?" she asked.

"Is he all right?" Noam kept it just above a whisper.

Ames exhaled softly, then said, "C'mon" and tugged him after her across the hall into the girls' bedroom. She didn't bother turning on the light, just shut them in, the room lit only by the gray moonlight from outside the window. "Listen," she said, keeping one hand on the doorknob. "It's not a big deal. It's just . . . complicated. Dara and Lehrer don't have a great relationship, and Taye can be kind of oblivious."

"What happened?" Noam asked.

Ames made a strange, abortive little gesture toward her pocket, then muttered, "Damn, left my cigarettes" and dropped her head back. Sighed. "You'd have to ask him," she said eventually. "It's not something he'd want me to share around, you know? Anyway, just . . ." She waved one hand. "Just keep it in mind. Not all of us had a great, loving fatherly relationship."

Noam bit his cheek over what he could have said in response to that. Instead: "Clearly it goes a little past that." Shitty father-son relationships didn't make people try to hack the Ministry of Defense.

"I don't know what to tell you," Ames said. "I know Dara gives you a hard time, but he doesn't usually hate people for no reason. That includes Lehrer." She opened the door and stepped out into the hall again. "I'm gonna make sure Dara hasn't finished a whole bottle of gin on his own, okay? I'll be out later. Hold down the fort."

She clapped Noam on the shoulder and flashed one of those fake smiles that didn't reach her eyes. He watched her disappear back into the other room, to Dara and Dara's gin and Dara's secrets. To whatever else they'd been doing, Ames with her hands on Dara's body and their lips so, so close.

Bethany and Taye were still watching the movie, popcorn bowl lodged between their legs and Bethany's head against Taye's arm. Noam took Ames's seat by the window instead. He didn't smoke, but he lit one of Ames's cigarettes and took a few drags anyway.

An hour later, Ames returned to claim her chair and cigarettes, and in another hour, Dara emerged from the bedroom wearing something black that clung to his body like it was painted on. He didn't say a word. Just walked past the chairs and the movie screen, the edge of his coat grazing Noam's thigh as he stepped over a forgotten glass on the floor.

He smelled like liquor and left through the front door. He didn't come back till morning.

Chapter Nine

Monday, Lehrer was making coffee when Noam and Dara showed up for their lessons, seemingly having forgotten all about the incident at the government complex. As he shook ground beans into a filter and Noam and Dara dumped their satchels onto the floor, he spoke.

"Dara, at the table, please."

Dara only made it two feet before he came to an abrupt stop.

Noam looked.

On the table was a small iron cage. In the cage lay the body of a dead goldfinch.

"I thought we'd try this again," Lehrer said to Dara, watching him as he poured water over the coffee grounds. "You've had plenty of time to study."

"You know I can't."

"Not with that attitude, surely."

One of the chairs at the table pulled out by telekinesis. After several moments, Dara sat.

Noam opened his book and held it up just high enough so he could still see over the pages. Dara stared at the dead bird like it was something horribly contagious.

Lehrer took the seat opposite Dara, crossing long legs and balancing his coffee cup on his knee. "Whenever you're ready," he said, and Dara's cheeks were bloodless.

Noam turned a page in his book, just for show.

"I don't even know healing," Dara said, clearly stalling.

Lehrer said nothing.

Dara exhaled and lifted both hands, fingers hovering over the iron bars of the cage. He trembled, very slightly, with the effort.

And then—

—the bird's still body shuddered once and flopped onto its stomach. Noam muffled a gasp against the pages of his book as the bird rose on unsteady legs, wings twitching spasmodically.

He did it, he *really did it*, Dara—what the *fuck*, how could someone possibly . . . that bird was dead. *Dead* dead. Noam had never heard of anyone doing anything like this, not ever, not even in legends from the turn of the millennium when magic was still young.

If Dara could perform resurrection, he was . . .

A cold shiver went down Noam's spine, because if Dara could do this, there was nothing he couldn't do.

"No," Lehrer said.

The bird vanished.

The corpse lay on the floor of the cage, had never moved.

An illusion.

"That," Lehrer said, and Noam didn't think he'd ever heard Lehrer's voice with quite so sharp an edge, "was beneath you."

Lehrer set his cup on the table with a click of ceramic on wood. There was something too slow and precise about the way he moved, an intent that carved through silence.

A spark of gold lit the air.

The bird burst into flight.

The sudden violence of it seared straight through Noam's veins, and he startled, book toppling off his lap onto the floor.

The bird flung itself against the bars of its cage, a horrible screeching noise ripping from its throat. Its frantic wings beat too hard, too fast, feathers already gone bloody.

This was *wrong*—completely, fundamentally wrong in a way that set Noam's teeth on edge.

"Stop it," Dara hissed.

The bird kept screaming. Lehrer watched Dara with mild interest, as if cataloging his reaction for future study.

God . . . *god*, the bird collided with the cage again, its bones snapping like fine twigs. Bile flooded Noam's mouth.

"*Stop*," Dara pleaded again.

This time, at last, Lehrer nodded. The bird dropped like a stone, instantly and perfectly dead.

Lehrer picked up his coffee cup again and took a sip. Dara was breathless, his hands in fists and his magic a green and quivering aura. The whole thing was disturbing, yes, but Dara was ashen.

For the first time, Noam thought he understood why Dara hated Lehrer so much.

Noam stared at the bird's corpse, which lay in a lump of red-and-gold feathers, open beak pointed skyward. For a brief moment, he remembered the girl from the red ward, her face frozen in a death mask.

"It felt no pain, Dara," Lehrer said, with the impatient tone of a man who has said this many times before. "It didn't have a mind. Just reflexes."

Dara's next inhale shuddered audibly. "Even if I could resurrect it," he said, clearly forcing the words past clenched teeth, "it would still be mindless. It would still be *nothing*, and nobody."

"Perhaps . . . very well. Take Noam's seat. Read Hirschel's *Practical Virology, Volume 4*."

Dara frowned. "That's elementary stuff. You had me read Hirschel when I was twelve."

Complaining was a mistake. Lehrer's gaze narrowed, and he tapped his fingers on the arm of his chair. "Do as I say. Tomorrow, I expect you to come to our lesson prepared. Noam, move to the red chair."

Shit.

If Lehrer could be that frustrated with Dara for being unable to do something so clearly impossible for everyone but Lehrer himself, what would he think when he turned his attention to Noam? Noam hadn't read a goddamn word since he walked in.

Still, he rose to his feet and collected his book and satchel from the floor. He met Dara's eyes as they passed each other; Dara's mouth was pressed into a thin line, a muscle twitching in his jaw.

Dara's gaze darted away from Noam just as quickly, back toward Lehrer. This glance was more furtive—but he headed for the bookshelves without argument, leaving Noam with no choice but to sink down into the burgundy-upholstered armchair Dara sat in moments ago.

Noam watched, hardly daring to breathe, as Lehrer removed the birdcage and placed it under the table, out of sight.

But when Lehrer turned that calm attention to Noam, it wasn't to demand he perform impossible magic. He just had Noam run through a mind-expansion exercise, memorizing strings of numbers and then reciting them back after a filler task. As Lehrer put it, "Your antibodies to the virus keep it from killing you, but the more antibodies you have, the less magic is free to be wielded. Quite aside from the risk of inflammation, of course. Lower antibodies mean a more powerful witching. You have room in your body for lots of magic, so let's make sure there's plenty of room in your head too."

Noam recited the numbers without complaint, keenly aware of Dara watching him from across the room and of the dead bird under the table, his foot bumping the metal cage when he crossed his legs. Lehrer didn't relent, not until the clock hand approached the hour—and then, before Noam could get up, Lehrer said:

"No, stay here. Dara, you may return to the barracks and prepare for your next class."

Dara caught Noam's gaze, one of his brows flicking upward. Noam couldn't shrug, not with Lehrer watching, so he hoped the look on his face made it clear enough that he had no idea what Lehrer could want.

Still, Dara took his sweet time packing his satchel. When he eventually left, it was without comment.

Lehrer finished his coffee in one last swallow. When he got to his feet, it gave the impression of something unfolding, Lehrer's height making the chair look diminutive by comparison. He gestured toward one of the bookshelves. "I need to take Wolf out, do you mind? That's my dog." He pronounced it like "vulf."

"Oh. No. Of course not. I can just wait here until you're done."

"Don't be ridiculous. You'll come with us," Lehrer said. "You like dogs, don't you?" Noam nodded. "Then it's not a problem."

He gestured for Noam to follow as he crossed the room to one of the bookshelves and reached in above the spines of *To the Lighthouse* and *Jeeves and Wooster* to flick something metal. Noam sensed something deeper moving in the walls, a complicated set of steel mechanisms shifting and latching, completely unconnected to the lever, which Noam realized now wasn't actually connected to anything at all. The apparatus was driven by magic, Lehrer's magic, the switch just there for show. A panel of the wall directly to the right clicked and swung inward, exposing a carpeted hall. It was the same hall Dara disappeared down before, after General Ames caught them in the government complex.

Lehrer stepped inside with the confidence of a man who'd done this many times. When Noam didn't immediately follow, he looked back, motioning again with his hand until Noam followed after him. The hall was lit from overhead by little golden lights casting pools against the beige walls and blue rug, all soft colors and warmth. Was this where Lehrer lived? Would Lehrer really bring him home?

Even with Lehrer in front, right where Noam could see him, Noam couldn't stop thinking how easily Lehrer had quenched the life from the resurrected bird. He could do the same thing to Noam, here in the dim secrecy of his home. Noam would be dead before he hit the floor.

"I'll warn you," Lehrer told Noam. "Wolf isn't used to company."

He led them into a foyer of some kind, open doors branching out into other rooms. Noam caught glimpses from here: a sitting room, a library, the telltale electromagnetic hum of cutlery from what must be the kitchen. There was no tech at all. Nothing, not even a microwave, in this entire apartment.

Noam didn't have much time to stare, though, before there was the click of nails on hardwood floor, and Lehrer said, "Here, Wolf!"

The dog bolted out of the sitting room, tail wagging so hard Noam was surprised it kept its balance. He could see where Wolf got the name: it had pale eyes and a clever lupine face, with the sleek body of a wild animal. Its thick coat gleamed, nothing like the mangy strays that wandered through the west side, and when Lehrer knelt down to scratch Wolf behind an ear, it made every effort to lick his cheek.

"Good boy," Lehrer murmured, smiling at Wolf. "You can pet him, if you like."

Noam moved forward, feeling a little awkward acting like this in Lehrer's house, like he belonged here, could stand so close to Lehrer with Lehrer still in his dress grays and bend over to stroke Lehrer's dog. He did it anyway. Wolf's attention latched on to him almost immediately, hot tongue lapping at the underside of Noam's wrist.

Bizarre, to know Lehrer had killed that bird—twice, just to teach Dara a lesson—and yet he could be so gentle with Wolf. So affectionate.

"He's beautiful," Noam said, glancing over at Lehrer, who watched with those silver eyes. Noam always felt uneasy to discover himself directly in Lehrer's focus when he didn't realize he was being observed.

"Yes," Lehrer said, "he is. And he likes you. He doesn't like everyone." Lehrer pushed off the floor, rising back to his full height. He held out a hand, palm up, and before Noam could blink, a leash and collar were in his grasp that hadn't been just a second earlier. "Sit, Wolf," he said. The collar attached itself around the dog's neck, aluminum tags clinking as Wolf shook his head.

"Let's go," Lehrer said, to Noam as much as to the dog.

They headed back through the outer study, Wolf trotting happily at Lehrer's side all the way out into the main corridor. It was empty, as Noam had come to expect, but there was life downstairs once they'd exited the stairwell out onto the ground floor. People kept giving Noam these looks, like they thought he wasn't important enough to walk with the defense minister.

"Courtyard?" Lehrer suggested, and Noam nodded.

The courtyard was every bit as lovely as it had been that night with Dara and the bourbon. The spring air was a cool rush on Noam's face as soon as they stepped out onto the flagstones, chilling the nape of his neck and ruffling through his hair. Beside him, Lehrer turned his face toward the sky.

"I prefer winter," Lehrer mused. Wolf walked at a measured pace by Lehrer's heel, not trying to rush ahead the way Noam had seen other dogs do. "Summer's too humid and muggy. Before the catastrophe it was far worse than it is now. Say what you will about the nuclear option, but it certainly improved the weather forecast."

The history books had always seemed remarkably sparse on foreign relations details, unless you counted making it clear the US had been evil. Lehrer was the only person left who could answer any question Noam threw at him.

"Why didn't the rest of the world keep bombing North America after the catastrophe was over?" Noam asked Lehrer. "Surely they were motivated to wipe out Carolinia before it was even founded. They hated you."

"Oh yes," Lehrer said, shooting Noam an amused glance. "They tried. I deflected the first bomb into the Atlantic and told them the next would find its way back where it came from."

Deflected a nuclear bomb.

Lehrer, at age nineteen, *deflected* a *nuclear bomb.*

It shouldn't be shocking, not after what Noam saw Lehrer do today. Resurrection, even if partial resurrection, was completely unfathomable.

In fact, Noam was pretty sure his theory books had said it was outside the ability of magic.

Someone really did need to update those books.

They meandered along the perimeter of the courtyard under the trees, still bare from winter. The chill settled into Noam's bones the longer they stayed outside. For his part, Lehrer barely seemed to notice the unseasonable cold; his bare hand only loosely grasped the handle of Wolf's leash, skin unmottled.

"You're doing well," Lehrer said at last, after Noam started wondering if Lehrer planned to say anything at all. "Your progress in our lessons has been exponential, and Colonel Swensson tells me you are succeeding in your classes with him. Starting tomorrow, you'll join your peers in regular course work."

Noam ought to have been relieved—finally, he was good enough to be done with remedial lessons—but he felt like something heavy had dropped into his stomach.

No more lessons with Lehrer. That was what this meant.

He was normal now, no different from any of the rest. He'd go to basic training, then lectures on engineering and war strategy and law, then do his homework in the common room next to Bethany and Taye and Ames, and graduate when he turned eighteen. Then he'd join the army or be filed into some bureaucratic position to serve his country from behind a desk.

And this connection to Lehrer, this opportunity to find out if Lehrer might sympathize with Brennan, might aid the cause, would disintegrate.

"Of course," Lehrer went on, "you'll still have your private lessons with me."

Noam startled, jerking his head up to look at Lehrer so fast it earned a low laugh on Lehrer's part.

"Oh yes. I have no intention of abandoning our sessions. In fact, I think we should start sparring soon. You have such impressive dynamics,

Noam—and, like me, you are remarkably intelligent despite a paucity of formal education. It would be criminal not to take advantage."

A wave of heat lit Noam's cheeks. He shouldn't be so thrilled by Lehrer's attention. Lehrer was the means to an end, nothing more.

And then there was the matter of whatever Lehrer had planned for Noam, those secrets he kept cryptically hinting at. Was it connected to Dara and what Dara had been up to in the government complex? Only it hadn't seemed like Lehrer and Dara were working together.

But then there was the way Lehrer watched Dara beg earlier today, Lehrer's expression as placid as calm water. As if Dara's pain was a moderately interesting academic observation.

"I won't disappoint you," Noam said. "But I need to know why I'm here. Why are you training me?"

Lehrer turned them onto a fresh path, crossing the stream that cut through the courtyard. For a moment, Noam thought he wasn't going to answer. But then—

"You and I have a lot in common," Lehrer said again. "More than just being Jewish and uneducated, I think. But it appears patience is not one of those shared virtues."

Noam flushed, but he didn't get a chance to respond.

Lehrer's hand caught Noam's for the briefest moment, long fingers curving in against Noam's and pressing something into his palm. Noam grasped it on reflex, and Lehrer withdrew, shifting Wolf's leash over to that hand as if nothing happened. Noam's heart pounded in his throat, and Lehrer glanced toward the sky like he could divine the time from the orientation of stars and said, "Let's head back."

The note was folded four times over. Later, when Noam was alone in the barracks, he unfolded it by the light of his phone screen and read the single word written there in Lehrer's neat, slanted script:

Faraday.

Brief audio recording, stolen from C. Lehrer's personal collection.

MAN 1: Okay, it's recording.

MAN 2 (a softer voice): This is stupid.

MAN 1: You don't know till you try, Calix. Come on.

MAN 2/CALIX: It doesn't work this way. Turn it off, Wolf, we're going to be late.

MAN 1/ADALWOLF: They can't start the meeting without us. Pretty please?

CALIX: I said no. Stop asking.

ADALWOLF: Don't you dare—

CALIX: I didn't!

ADALWOLF: Okay. Okay, but, just once. For me.

CALIX: Fine. Turn this thing off.

ADALWOLF: *Thank* you.

[The recording ends.]

Chapter Ten

Faraday.

There was only one thing that could mean, of course—Faraday, as in Faraday shield, as in a conductive material that blocked electromagnetic waves.

Why Lehrer was passing him notes about this was harder to understand.

Noam stayed up late thinking about it almost every night that week, turning the word over and over in his mind until it lost all meaning.

Faraday.

How was that supposed to help the refugees? Was Sacha planning some kind of electromagnetic attack against them? Was Noam meant to use his newfound power over electromagnetism to build a Faraday shield and protect them?

Noam lingered after lessons every day, hoping Lehrer would give another hint (or another note, or another several notes), but Lehrer seemed to have said all he planned to on the matter. As if oblivious to how much mental energy Noam spent trying to decrypt his code, Lehrer even gave him just as much homework as usual—on top of everything his new regular teachers assigned.

A week later, there was another outbreak of the virus.

Magic hit a refugee camp near the coast, piling up so many bodies that the local authorities couldn't burn them quickly enough. Without any safe way to transport patients to the major hospitals in Richmond or Raleigh, Sacha declared a state of emergency. That meant resources pouring east, and those resources included as many witching students and soldiers as Lehrer could spare.

After the plane landed, the cadets were ushered into army trucks that carried them over broken roads, every pothole jostling them against the fabric walls and adding salt to the nausea that swelled up in Noam's stomach, bilious and thick. He was grateful when they finally came to a shuddering stop. Or, he was grateful until he took a breath and his lungs filled with the stench of blood and vomit and rotting flesh.

Next to him, a Charleston cadet retched, lurching forward over his knees. Luckily, nothing came out. Noam pressed a hand over his nose and mouth, breathing in shallow little gulps of his own humid air.

"What the hell is that?" someone said in a thin voice.

The driver drew back the curtain at the rear of the truck, and they found out.

The dirt streets of the camp were crowded with huge white tents constructed of some material thicker than canvas, each tent opening on to a little courtyard filled with tables and chairs and soldiers milling about. The source of the smell was obvious. At the rear of each pair of tents, piles of black body bags awaited incineration, buzzing with flies.

"God," Bethany said from just over Noam's shoulder as they jumped out of the truck. "What *is* this? Where are the red wards?"

"Not enough room," Dara said. Noam hadn't even noticed him coming up, and now he stood just to Noam's right, looking out at the street and its tents stretching as far as the eye could see. "Backwater places like this, they run out of space in the red wards fast, especially in a bad outbreak."

"And especially when the patients are refugees," Noam added, heart a stone in his chest. "Better save space for the people you actually want to survive."

Dara and Bethany exchanged looks, but Noam didn't care if they thought he was militant. They hadn't read those emails. They hadn't grown up in places like this.

He couldn't imagine a worse place for an outbreak than a refugee camp. Close quarters and high population, poor access to health care or hygiene facilities. The tents probably made things even worse. Even though they made volunteers shower when they entered the wards and when they left—even when they sprayed them all with decontamination fluid—those seemed like half measures compared to what was possible in an actual hospital. Here, they couldn't even filter the airflow.

The soldiers split the cadets up into platoons, assigning three platoons per tent. Noam's group was under Colonel Swensson's command, which was just Noam's luck because Swensson hated him.

"Listen up!" Swensson said. He didn't even have to raise his voice to get their attention. "You might be immune to the virus, but you still have to follow hygiene protocol. That means washing your hands before and after each patient. Use full decontamination procedure when entering and leaving the ward. Wear gloves and a face mask, always. You might not be able to get sick, but you can still get other people sick if you're carrying virus particles around on your skin and hair and clothing. Understand?"

He waited for them all to shout, "Yes, sir!" before going on.

"Good. You'd better. Now, the staff tell you to do something, you do it. No questions asked. These people are risking their lives to help in this crisis, and they know more than you. Respect that."

With that, he funneled them past the gate, through decontamination, then across the courtyard toward their assigned tents. Stepping through that door was like stepping onto another planet. Noam would never have thought they could cram so many beds into such a small area, except they did, just enough room left between the mattresses to stand. A couple soldiers milled about carrying linens or jugs of water. Amid them drifted doctors and nurses wearing what looked like space suits. The smell was stronger here, reeking of the latrine buckets and the sick, sweaty bodies of the patients on their cots, interspersed with the chlorine scent of bleach.

The ground underfoot sprouted with flowers: magical little buds of gold and silver that moved without breeze, glittering petals spiraling up into the air. They weren't real—when he reached out to touch them, they dissolved in a shower of sparks. When Noam inhaled, their magic was spun sugar on his tongue.

He was assigned to Dr. Halsing, as were Bethany and Taye. It was impossible to tell what kind of woman Dr. Halsing was behind all that protective gear: her eyes were the only thing visible, glinting above her paper face mask and shielded by the lenses of her plastic goggles. She'd never been infected.

"You'll be helping me with patient care today," she said, voice muffled. "Have you been through training?"

The others nodded, but Noam shook his head. Halsing muttered something behind her mask, possibly a curse.

"I know we're shorthanded, but . . . well, you're what we've got, and it's better than nothing. Come on. I'll show you our patients."

There were six. Noam repeated their names over and over in his mind so he wouldn't forget: *Martha, Shaqwan, Lola, Amy, William, Beatriz.* Most were too sick for it to matter, drifting deep in comatose waters. He dabbed the crusted blood from the corners of their mouths and moved sharp objects out of the way when they had seizures, kept an eye out for rogue magic with a habit of setting bedsheets ablaze.

The little girl was the best off. Beatriz King. Bea. She still hovered on the knife-edge of consciousness, tipping over to one side or the other from time to time. When they first met her, she was sitting up in bed, hair damp with sweat and pulled back from her face, a bucket between her knees and a book resting against her thighs. She put the book down when the doctor needed to check her heart and lungs, though no one needed a stethoscope to hear the way air rattled in her chest.

"How are you feeling?" Bethany asked, sitting on the edge of the bed.

"All right," Bea said. Even her voice was weak, like watered-down tea. "Who are you?"

"I'm Bethany. This is Noam and Taye. We're helping Dr. Halsing today."

"You don't have those big space suits," she said, pointing at Bethany. "You're going to get sick."

"We've already been sick," Taye reassured her. He angled his body away from her all the same.

"Oh. Can you do magic, then?"

"Sure can," Noam said. "Want to see?"

She nodded, perhaps not as enthusiastically as she might have had she been well. Noam rubbed his gloved fingertips together, capturing the static and letting it spark into seed lightning, sizzling white against his palm.

"Be careful!" Taye said from somewhere over his left shoulder, but Noam ignored him. Bea's face lit up, a smile spreading her cracked lips.

"Does it hurt?" she asked, leaning forward a little, and Noam shook his head.

"Not me. I wouldn't touch it, though, if I were you." He clenched his hand into a fist, and the lightning quenched. Bea pressed her fingers to the middle of his hand, as if testing to see if it was still warm. To her, maybe it was. Her skin was dry and cracked, fragile as paper.

"What else can you do?" she said.

"I can make things bigger and smaller," Taye said. It was the kind of confession that made Noam twist round to look at him—Taye'd never talked about his presenting power before, at least not where Noam could hear.

"What kinds of things?" Noam said.

"You know. Whatever. Anything. Could do this table. Could do myself, even."

Noam frowned. "Isn't that complicated? I mean, you'd have to concentrate on . . . a lot of organs."

Taye just smiled at him and said, "Nah, man. It's just, like, exponents." As if to demonstrate, a pen on the table by Bea's cot expanded to almost six times its original size, then shrank just as easily.

"Exponents."

"Yeah."

"Exponents as in . . . math."

Taye picked up the pen and twirled it between his fingers, completely unfazed by the flabbergasted look on Noam's face. "Yeah, like math. If you think about cells and atoms and shit as numbers and then just raise them to whatever power, it's easy."

Easy if you were a goddamn math prodigy.

Still, Bea found Taye's tricks delightful—so they spent the next five or ten minutes showing some of the more interesting applications of both their powers until at last Halsing swept down to demand they go and see to other patients.

Bea seems to be doing well, Noam thought as he sponged down an older man who was hours into the coma stage. She was alert, even if she wasn't strong, and she was reading. Maybe she would be like them. Maybe she'd be a witching, and one day she'd be showing off magic tricks of her very own.

The idea stuck with him, a warm kernel of hope he returned to later when one of the other patients died and he and Dara carried the body out wrapped in a sheet—they ran out of body bags ages ago—and tossed it onto a pile with the others to be burned. Dara's cheeks were pink, a few curls stuck to his forehead; with all those feverish bodies crammed inside, the tent was sweltering.

"Do you remember this?" he asked Noam before they went back in, the pair of them sharing a bottle of water near the entrance. "Being sick."

"Not really. I was unconscious most of the time."

"So you had it bad, then. You didn't know you were going to survive." He passed Noam the bottle, and Noam took a sip; the water was lukewarm.

"They left me there, actually. In the red ward. I woke up alone."

Dara stared. "They *left* you there?"

"They probably assumed I was going to die either way. When you can't afford to pay for all those fancy experimental drugs, survival odds kinda go down a bit. There were cameras, though. When they realized I survived, they had people there in minutes. Even Lehrer came."

Noam gave Dara back the water, but Dara just stood there, holding it in one hand without drinking. At last Dara shook his head and said, "Fine. Fine, I shouldn't be surprised."

Right. Because Dara had the luxury of finding such things *surprising*.

Some of that must have shown on Noam's face, because Dara sighed. "I know." He dragged his fingers back through his hair. "All right, come on. Let's go back inside."

The cadets were housed in barracks, unused now that most of the soldiers were down south "reconstructing" Atlantia. The barracks faced the sea; when the wind rolled in off the ocean, it whistled through the cracks in the walls and tasted like salt. All their clothes smelled like death, sinking into fibers and bruising itself on skin.

Noam didn't sleep well that night.

The next day was worse. Four patients died, but six more were brought in to take their place, spreading the ranks of doctors and cadets even thinner.

Bea, at least, still lived. She woke up for a little while around noon and managed to drink some soup, spooned into her mouth by Taye, but she vomited it up an hour later. Noam tried doing more magic tricks, but she couldn't stay awake for them. Noam's stomach cramped; she'd smiled the day before, if weakly. Yesterday's hope had dried up overnight, leaving a crawling feeling in its wake.

Noam touched Bea's forehead with the back of his hand, and Taye said, "She's really hot, isn't she? I think her fever's getting worse."

Her skin burned. Noam drew his hand away and sat down in one of the empty chairs.

His entire body felt heavy.

This was how his father died. In a red ward, leaking blood and magic from every orifice. He'd read that the symptoms of magic were what they were because it wasn't like a regular virus at all. People's bodies just weren't meant to host magic. And if his mother hadn't hanged herself, she would've died this way too.

Only maybe not. Maybe, just maybe, Rivka Mendel would have survived. And she'd never been as antigovernment as Brennan or his father—she might have stayed by Noam's side the way no one else had.

"Is she okay?" Taye said abruptly.

Noam turned to look. Bea's whole body had gone rigid, spine arced off the bed. Her eyes were open but rolled back, exposing glazed whites. "Shit," Noam whispered, just as Bea's body relaxed, then seized again, rhythmic contractions that rocked the cot back against the canvas and threatened to spill her thin body onto the floor.

"Wait—" Taye started, but Noam was already on his feet, dragging the IV stand out of the way so Bea wouldn't hit it as she flailed.

"Bethany!" Noam shouted, casting his gaze out, hoping it would land on Bethany but unable to spare more than a second looking. On the bed, Bea shook violently, her jaw clenched and hands clawlike.

"Should I hold her down?" Taye asked.

"No. I mean, I don't know, maybe . . . no, no, actually, that won't help. Um. Make sure she doesn't hurt herself on anything?"

And then Bethany was there, kneeling on the floor next to Bea's bed, face bloodless. Her hands didn't shake, though, as she pushed a syringe of clear fluid into Bea's IV line.

"I sent someone for Halsing. It'll be a while. She's outside the air lock," Bethany said. Her free hand twisted around a fistful of bedsheets. "But. I don't think . . . It doesn't look good."

"Don't talk like that," Taye yelped. "She'll be fine. We just need to wait for the doctor."

Bethany didn't look convinced, but she shut her mouth.

They hovered there, useless, as Bea shook and choked for air. She sounded awful, like her throat was convulsing the same way as the rest of her body, horrible fleshy noises, her mouth gaping open and lips rolling inward. Bethany turned Bea on her side at one point, in case she vomited, but nothing came out except spit.

Bea was still seizing when Halsing arrived, Noam crouched down at her bedside and holding on to her sweaty little palm. He could barely bring himself to look at her.

"How long has she been like this?" Halsing said.

Bethany shook her head. "Too long. Fifteen minutes, at least."

Halsing's mouth was a straight line.

"Is she going to be all right?" Taye asked. His tone seemed forcibly even, like he was trying hard to seem unaffected.

"I doubt it," Halsing said. No sugarcoating.

"Can't you do something?" Noam retorted. "Where the hell have you been, anyway? A *child* is dying, and you're off doing what? *Help her!*"

Halsing brushed her gloved fingertips against Bea's temple, wiping away a bead of perspiration. "I wish I could, but it's regulation. I have to spend my resources on those who might survive."

Painfully, perfectly logical. After all, this place couldn't support mechanical ventilation. Noam knew that. Bethany knew it too; Noam saw it in the lines between her brows and the set of her shoulders as she leaned in over the bed, like she thought proximity might keep Bea alive.

"Her IV bag is empty," Noam said. His voice sounded like it came from far away, hard and angry. "I'll get her a new one. We can at least spare fluids, right?"

Halsing hesitated, but then she nodded. When Noam returned from the supply closet, she and Taye had both moved on to other patients, leaving Noam and Bethany to watch Bea.

Bea's body was so still. So . . .

"It's okay," he told her.

Bea made a strident noise in the back of her throat, wrists jerking awkwardly. Noam fumbled with her hand for a second, staring down at Bea's pale face and wishing . . . he wished he knew healing magic, even though it wouldn't work on something like this. Even if he knew how, the magic he would use to heal her was the same magic that was killing her. The thing that made Noam a witching would ensure Bea never was.

He brushed damp hair from her forehead, sweeping it behind her hot ear. "It's okay to let go," he whispered. He chose to believe she understood.

A nurse took over eventually and sent Noam to hang fluids and bathe sweaty brows. He kept checking on Bea every chance he could, even when nothing changed, until at last, late in the afternoon, when the setting sun cast red light into the tents, he looked over, and her bed was empty.

Dara found him that night out by the boardwalk. The wind had picked up sometime in the dusk hours, and it whipped sea-smell off the ocean, briny and fishy, tangling Noam's hair and blowing sand up the back of his shirt. Off duty, Dara had changed out of his greens into something gray and fitted, the whites of his eyes flashing in the lights from the pier.

"I thought I'd find you out here," Dara said when he reached Noam's side. He was close enough their shoulders almost touched.

"I've never seen the ocean before."

Noam gazed out at the black water, the moonlight glancing off the crests of waves as they crashed into shore. And past that, where the sea blurred into starless sky.

Dara kicked at a few broken shells in the sand, scattering them toward the dune grasses. Silence unspooled between them, Dara's tension drawn in his posture and the wordless line of his lips. Noam felt it too; he'd been feeling it ever since Bea died.

"This is Lehrer's fault," Dara said.

Noam looked at him, heart stumbling over a beat, but Dara was focused on the horizon, as if he'd temporarily forgotten Noam was there.

"And how do you figure that?"

As Dara turned away from the sea, his hair blew across his face, dark and wild. "If Lehrer cared about stopping the virus, don't you think he'd send *real* doctors? Don't you think he'd spend tax money on vaccine research and supportive care, not . . . not these pointless wars in Atlantia, fighting for territory that was never ours to begin with?"

"Don't get me wrong—I think the Atlantian occupation is fucked up, and of course I support vaccine research," Noam said. "But Sacha's the one running this country, not Lehrer."

Even saying Sacha's name made him feel like he'd been poisoned.

Dara's face twisted in disdain. "Sacha doesn't have any actual power. He does exactly what Lehrer wants him to do."

Noam knew that wasn't true, having read Sacha's emails and witnessed him disregard Lehrer's wishes to commit horrible crimes. But Dara didn't want to hear that. Dara didn't want to hear anything that wasn't what he already believed.

"Why do you hate Lehrer so much?" Noam said, exhaling heavily even as he glanced back toward the barracks; if they were having this conversation, he didn't want to be interrupted. Dara made a face, and Noam rolled his eyes. "I mean it. You can barely look at him. Do you really think there's some conspiracy? Or do you just hate him for personal reasons?"

Dara snorted and dropped down onto the sand, his legs stretched out toward the sea, heels digging into the bank of shells rolled in by the last tide. After a moment Noam joined him. The sand was cold beneath his elbows and uncomfortably damp.

"There are a lot of reasons," Dara said. He'd lowered his voice even though no one was nearby; maybe he thought the wind would carry it back to the barracks. "You're right, many of them personal. I've been his ward a long time. I know him. And as soon as I would feel close to him, he'd pull away. Every time I thought he could be like a father, he proved he wasn't. I don't know what you've been imagining about our relationship—I suppose you think we had Shabbos dinner every Friday night, and he helped me with my biology homework and told me about his childhood. Well. You have no idea what our relationship was like. And, of course, it makes no difference to you."

Noam opened his mouth to argue, but Dara shook his head, cutting him off.

"I know it doesn't. You wouldn't understand. But I doubt Lehrer's capable of loving anyone—and especially not me."

Noam chewed his lip, quiet. *I'm not sure my father loved me either, toward the end.* The words scratched at the inside of Noam's chest. He didn't dare say them out loud.

Dara might know Lehrer, but he didn't understand him. He'd never experienced the kind of loss that Lehrer had.

He'd never experienced much loss at all, as far as Noam could tell.

"For the rest of it, I know you'll think this is me being evasive, but I can't tell you. Not because I don't want to, but because I *can't.*" Dara held Noam's gaze. "For one, you wouldn't believe me—don't give me that look; I know you wouldn't. But even if you would, I still couldn't tell you. For your own safety."

"This isn't Stalinist Russia, Dara. You're not going to get arrested for criticizing the defense minister."

"Who said anything about arrested? But suffice to say, things are going to change in this country, Noam. Sooner than you think. You don't have to take my word for it. Ask one of the soldiers. They'll tell you just how often they have to fend off riots. These won't stay skirmishes for long, and Lehrer knows it."

"No shit," Noam burst out. "Because Sacha is rounding everyone up and throwing them into refugee camps, where they're pretty much damned to *die* just like we saw today. How can you be so fucking blind? How can you stand there and talk about how bad Lehrer is when Sacha's doing *this*?"

"What else is he supposed to do? Really, Noam, I'd love to know. We don't have resources to support the entire population of Atlantia—"

"The entire—*Jesus*. You are so fucking privileged, Dara, it makes me fucking sick."

"Privileged?" Dara barked out a laugh, something raw and strangled. He hunched over, pressing a hand to his chest, and from the manic grimace on his face it was impossible to tell if he was amused or in pain. "You have no idea what you're talking about."

"I grew up starving," Noam hissed. "I grew up hiding my father from the people who would take him away. I watched my mother kill herself and my father hide from the real world. I went to *prison* because I did what was necessary to protect my family. You grew up . . . you had Lehrer. You had everything."

Dara's eyes were bright obsidian stones in his face, gaze sharp enough to cut. "No. What I *had* was—" He cut off abruptly, like he'd thought better of what he'd been about to say. Dara exhaled, a brittle smile twisting his mouth. After a moment, he said, "I don't know what to tell you. I don't know what I *can* tell you, or how much I even want to. You've put me in an interesting position, Noam Álvaro. In that way, I suppose Lehrer's already won."

Noam had no idea what Dara was talking about.

Dara lifted his face up toward the darkened sky, exposing the long line of his throat. Noam wanted to reach for him. He dug his fingers into the sand so he couldn't.

"What do you mean, he's won?" Noam asked. "Won what? Dara . . ."

But Dara's expression had fallen back into the same placid mask of normalcy Noam had come to expect.

But it *was* a mask. How had Noam never noticed before?

Another wave crashed onto the sand, this one creeping up far enough that the foam slipped over the toes of Noam's boots. He bent his knees to draw his feet out of range.

It was one thing for Dara to hate Lehrer, or even work against him. But if Dara was with Sacha, then Noam would never forgive him.

"You're right," he said. "I trust Lehrer. I'm not going to tell you you're wrong or that I don't believe you, but I don't have to agree just because we're friends."

"Oh, we're friends now? I hadn't realized."

"Fuck off, Dara," Noam said, but Dara just smiled and tossed a broken piece of shell toward the ocean.

The salty sea wind was what burned his cheeks, Noam told himself. It had nothing to do with the unsteady patter of his heart.

After a moment, Dara leaned back again. That smile was gone, replaced by the same old unreadable expression.

The void from earlier was back, yawning wide in Noam's chest. Dara felt it, too, he thought. Dara might not have lost his family, but he had that same hole inside him. They matched.

There was so much more to Dara than the cold, bitter façade he'd presented. He was that, too, but he was also Dara: the effortless genius, the political critic and poker cheat, the boy who analyzed everything he read according to poststructuralist theory and kept fresh flowers in a vase on his bedside table. Dara, who claimed he hated everything but secretly dreamed of counting the stars.

Noam needed a moment to get up the nerve.

"Dara . . ." Noam started, but he didn't know how to finish. He reached over instead and touched Dara's arm.

Dara flinched away so violently that it felt like being struck himself, Dara's entire body recoiling as if Noam had branded him with a hot coal. His eyes snapped to meet Noam's, wide and overly bright as he shoved himself up again.

"I'm sorry," Noam said quickly, holding his hands up. Surrender.

"No . . . you're all right. I'm sorry." Dara looked away, gaze skittering out toward the ocean, the barracks, then finally settling somewhere in the vicinity of Noam's shoulder. "It's . . . been a long day. We should go inside."

Noam's gut shriveled. Still, he nodded and followed a half step behind Dara back up to the barracks.

Dara seemed normal the next day, smiling at jokes and doing his work with the swift single-mindedness that he was known for. And maybe Dara was right—they weren't friends. Better if Noam remembered that from now on, instead of . . . instead of whatever he'd been thinking lately. But sometimes Noam caught Dara looking at him from across the room with a thoughtful expression, and Noam wondered if he really understood Dara at all.

Scanned analog file stored on encrypted MoD server.

FEDERAL BUREAU OF INVESTIGATION
To: Counterterrorism **From:** Chicago
Re: 10-29 Witching Militant Attack
Precedence: IMMEDIATE
Date: 11-01-2016
Title: RESULTS OF INITIAL INVESTIGATION INTO 10-29 ATTACK
Synopsis: To provide results of the initial investigation into the witching militia "Avenging Angels" attack in Chicago.

Details: On 10/29/2016 a bomb threat was received, stating the Avenging Angels intended to detonate a fuse bomb in the vicinity of Hyde Park. Initial reports suggested this threat was both credible and imminent. Evacuation commenced immediately, redirecting civilians to a presumed safe location.

On 10/29/2016 at 11:42 AM, 18 fuse bombs detonated in the Chicago metro area, particularly

Millennium Park, where many evacuees were being detained. Subsequent attacks targeted first responders and paramedics. At the time this memorandum was drafted, there were 339 confirmed deaths and 192 missing.

The Avenging Angels released a video broadcast on all major news networks claiming responsibility for the attack.

Intelligence confirms the Avenging Angels still operate under the leadership of Adalwolf Lehrer, a.k.a. Uriel [see Appendix A], former army private first class, witching with presenting power pyromancy (ability level 3). Additional reports suggest A. Lehrer has suffered from unexplained illness for some months. Intelligence officers now believe the primary strategic force among the Avenging Angels is A. Lehrer's 18-year-old brother, Calix Lehrer, a.k.a. Azriel [see attached]. C. Lehrer is a former patient of St. George's Hospital, a witching with numerous extramagical abilities. Officers, be advised: C. Lehrer's presenting power is—*file damage, illegible*—(ability level 4). Take appropriate precautions [see Appendix B for recommendations].

Chapter Eleven

He dreamed Bea stood in that ocean just off the boardwalk, salt water around her ankles and blood on her dress. Magic was her electric crown.

"I'm sorry," Noam told her. "I tried. There wasn't anything I could do. I'm sorry."

Then he was in the ocean at her side, her wet fingers cold as they slid along his cheek and pulled him down.

The waves crashed against Noam's legs.

Into his ear she whispered:

"Faraday."

The dream cracked like an egg.

Noam lurched upright in his bed, sheets a damp tangle around his feet and pulse hot in his mouth. The clock on his bedside table read 2:03—another three hours till his alarm. Noam was certain if he closed his eyes again, that dream would pick up right where it left off, with the smell of gore and death on the sea breeze.

He slipped out of bed, grabbing a coat from the back of the door and toeing on shoes. The government complex was so quiet at this hour it felt like a moment trapped in amber, as if the real world might still spin on outside these walls, but here—here would never change.

He still tasted magic, sour and sharp on his tongue as he headed downstairs. He needed fresh air, that was all. Just . . . somewhere to sit and breathe where he wasn't suffocating.

The guards at the door to the courtyard recognized him well enough now not to say anything as he went past; they opened the door and let him step out into the chilly spring night.

He missed the days Lehrer talked about, when Carolinian spring was still warm. The thin coat wasn't enough to keep the wind from burning into his bones. He tugged it closer round his shoulders, realizing only when he caught the scent of smoke and spilled bourbon that this wasn't even his coat. It was Dara's.

He headed toward the stream, which had frozen over during the night. Now it was a white scar cutting through the brick underfoot. The courtyard was so utterly silent, the cicadas still in hibernation.

Noam should never have given those emails to Brennan. He should've released them to the public and exposed Sacha's moral rot for the world to see.

He'd spent so much time waiting, hoping Brennan might come around, understand that now they were all each other had. That Brennan would let Noam take his father's place at Brennan's side, and together they would repair the world.

Only he kept waiting, and hoping, and Brennan did nothing.

All Noam did these days was *wait*. He was waiting right now, even: on Lehrer. Lehrer, who had a plan. Lehrer, passing cryptic notes in empty courtyards.

Maybe it was childish to keep wishing someone—Brennan, or Lehrer, or his father—would come along and tell him what to do next.

He ought to fight, whether he had help or not.

When the European Federation found out what the US was doing to witchings, it had intervened. The whole country was nuked half to hell by the time Adalwolf and Calix Lehrer's militia started gaining ground. Maybe Europe would intervene now, too, on behalf of the refugees.

Or maybe not.

Still, Noam could have done something. And then there would be no refugee camps where Sacha could condemn people to grisly death by infection and magic.

Whatever Brennan was planning, it wasn't enough. It hadn't stopped Bea from dying, and it wouldn't stop the next outbreak either.

But if Noam acted on his own and failed, could he live with himself?

Noam turned to head toward the smokestack, and when he looked up, he saw him: a shadowed figure on a balcony dimly illuminated by the lamplight. Lehrer leaned against a wrought iron railing, the red coal of his cigarette glowing as he brought it to his mouth and inhaled. His attention was fixed out toward the distant horizon.

It wasn't the Lehrer Noam knew from lessons or press conferences. This Lehrer had shed his military uniform, shirtsleeves rolled up to his elbows and his collar left undone. The look on his face was softer than Noam expected. Pensive. Lehrer draped his wrist over the rail, cigarette smoke drifting through the frozen air like fog.

Lehrer hadn't noticed Noam's presence. There was something strange and intimate about Noam watching Lehrer and Lehrer watching the sky—like sharing a secret.

Eventually Lehrer put his cigarette out on the iron, the burning coal a sudden bright blaze in Noam's sense of the metal, and turned to disappear back inside.

Noam stayed, staring up at the gold light still visible through that open door. With Lehrer's antitechnopathy wards temporarily unraveled, Noam could sense the movement of his wristwatch within the apartment, Lehrer's body heat against the gold as real as if Noam were to feel it against his own skin. Then the door fell shut, and Noam's sense of him cut off with the close of the latch.

Faraday.

Lehrer said they were alike, and what he'd meant was Noam couldn't wait to grow up or gain power to make a difference in Carolinia. If

Noam wanted things to change, he had to change them. At sixteen, Calix Lehrer incited a war.

Noam had his own war to win.

And Faraday was the key.

Brennan was waiting when Noam arrived at the Migrant Center that next Saturday, standing in the office where Noam usually did his database tasks and wearing his government suit. He looked uncomfortable, like the expensive cotton was abrasive on his skin. Noam couldn't imagine what Lehrer said to make Brennan take on the liaison position. He knew better than anyone what Brennan thought of people who aligned themselves with the feds, even for the greater good.

"I heard about the outbreak," Brennan started, and when Noam's gaze met Brennan's, it was suddenly difficult to breathe.

He took a step forward, then another, and then Brennan was reaching for him, Brennan's arms closing around Noam's shoulders. Noam pressed his face against the fine collar of Brennan's shirt and sucked in shallow gulps of detergent-scented air.

Brennan's hand was a steady pressure on Noam's spine. "I'm so sorry," he murmured. His breath on Noam's neck was warm. "I can't . . . I can't even imagine."

Noam was shaking, he realized belatedly, a tremor that got worse when he noticed it. Brennan's fingers twisted into the fabric of Noam's sweater, like he thought that might keep him still.

"Everyone died," Noam whispered. "Everyone."

Only that wasn't true, was it? There were four survivors out of four hundred, or so Noam heard. They were witchings now. They were going to Charleston.

Their magic was paid for with other people's lives.

"We have to do something," Noam said. This time he pushed Brennan back, hating the way his cheeks felt damp but needing to see

Brennan for this. To look him in the eye and *make* him understand they couldn't keep quiet anymore, couldn't keep pushing papers around a desk and hoping for change. "How many more people will die if Sacha starts mass deportations?" He pushed against Brennan's shoulders with both hands, knocking him back a half step. Anger twisted up his spine like a rope soaked in poison. "*Do* something!"

Do anything.

Do what Lehrer would have done a hundred years ago.

"I know," Brennan said. His voice was soft but stricken.

"I mean it," Noam said.

"I—"

"Tom, *please*!"

Brennan still had hold of Noam, one hand on each arm. That grip tightened now. "Listen to me, Noam. The recent outbreak has only made Sacha more determined to initiate deportations—I met with him this morning. He thinks what happened in the camp is a harbinger of what would happen in the cities if he let the refugees stay."

"But that's not true," Noam burst out. "The outbreaks are worse for refugees because we don't have the papers to get proper jobs, so we can't buy proper houses, so we live in tenements or get kicked into refugee camps—and how the hell does Sacha think this works, anyway? That's how disease *spreads*."

Brennan nodded slowly. "It is . . . but that's precisely why Sacha and the Republican Democrats want mass deportation. They claim if the refugees were gone, the outbreaks would stop."

"People would still die. But maybe they don't give a shit about that, so long as it's Atlantian corpses in the ground and not Carolinian."

"They believe they have an obligation to protect Carolinians first." Brennan's face twisted in a grimace. "Or at least that's what they're chanting down at the catastrophe memorial right now. 'Carolinia First.'"

"I'm going to fucking kill them."

"Noam—"

At the catastrophe memorial. In front of the statue of Adalwolf Lehrer. In front of the monument labeled with the names of all those innocent people killed for their magic in the 2010s.

That was where Sacha's bullies went to crow about nationalism and call for the passive extermination of an entire nation.

This new young Carolinian upper class hated the refugees because they didn't want to be infected—didn't want to become witchings themselves—but they were perfectly fine tolerating the witchings who maintained border control and kept Atlantians out. Fucked up. It was so *fucking*—

He pushed past Brennan and out the door, ignoring Brennan calling his name. He barely heard anything but the pound of his own blood in his ears and traffic roaring past as he stepped out of the building and onto the sidewalk.

The catastrophe memorial was halfway between here and the government complex, although the bus line Noam took to get to the Migrant Center hadn't gone anywhere near it—probably the only reason Noam hadn't known what was going on.

He didn't take the bus this time. He just ran.

When he first joined Level IV, he'd struggled with a nine-minute mile. Now, on the other side of recovery and three months of grueling training, Noam barely felt tired as he sprinted past Brightleaf toward central downtown.

He heard the protest before he saw it. He knew the sound of hate, knew it down to his bones. It was the comments Carolinian kids used to make at school before he stopped going. It was the high-pressure spray of tear gas grenades. It was voices like these shouting "We come first" and "Carolinia for Carolinians."

Noam's father used to organize counterprotests. He'd be one of those people yelling at the assholes with the banners, the one getting up in some fascist's face and daring him to do more than talk.

And thank god, they were still here. He knew who they were, even with their faces obscured by masks and bandannas. Knew how Grace walked and the shape of DeShawn's body under those black clothes. But they weren't enough, too few of them against all those protesters carrying Carolinian flags with violence in their eyes. The protesters had surrounded the monument—Adalwolf Lehrer cast in bronze, towering over these people screaming in his name. Like Adalwolf would have wanted this, like he hadn't died fighting this same virophobia. The police were already there, of course—fucking Sacha fascists must've gotten permits—standing by with riot shields and hands on their guns, eyeing the counterprotesters as though they might, if they were lucky, get the chance to shoot a few Atlantian kids dead.

"Noam!" one of the counterprotesters—Sam, he was pretty sure—shouted.

Noam darted over to join them, taking the black bandanna someone passed him and tying it tight over his nose and mouth, tugging up his hoodie to conceal his hair.

"And here I thought you were a witching now," one of them said, his voice unidentifiable behind his bandanna. But Noam didn't have time to snap back, because whoever it was just clapped Noam on the shoulder like they were old friends and said, "C'mon. Let's fuck up the fash."

Someone thrust a sign into Noam's hand—**IMPEACH SACHA**—and he spun around to face the protesters and the memorial and a hundred years of forgotten history and held the sign high overhead.

Fuck you, fuck you, fuck you, he thought at the protesters and willed them to hear it—and when that didn't happen, he just shouted it at them instead, meaningless words that fed the rage that seethed inside him.

All of them were so very proud an accident of birth made them Carolinian and bought them a lifetime of safety and privilege instead of fear and poverty and death. They ought to walk into that camp with the ground soaked in blood and magic and look Bea King in the face as she died alone and frightened at eight years old, at *eight years old*, and tell her she didn't deserve to stay in their country because her parents brought her here illegally. Because she was a refugee.

"Impeach Sacha!" Noam shouted, one of a dozen voices all shouting the exact same thing, and the angry white man in front of him twisted up his face and spat at him.

"Go home," the man said. His eyes were black beads in his reddened face, his spit soaking through the bandanna to stick damp against Noam's cheek. "Go home and fucking die there."

And he punched Noam in the face.

Pain burst like fireworks behind Noam's cheekbone, scintillating and bright. And he reacted without thinking, action provoking reaction, and he hit the man back so hard he felt cartilage snap under the force of his fist. He sensed iron searing the air—blood.

The satisfaction he felt seeing the man stagger back, blood flooding from his broken nose and dripping onto the concrete, was short lived.

It didn't matter who threw the first blow. As far as Sacha would be concerned, Atlantians just incited a riot.

Fuck. Fuck—Noam's cheek throbbed, the pain sending him staggering into the waiting hands of the counterprotesters. Someone grabbed his arm, yanking him back behind the lines before the fash could retaliate.

The invisible, thin ribbons holding people back all snapped at once. Sacha's protesters surged forward, and the counterprotesters were there to meet them, people shouting, one of the fascists breaking a signpost over his knee and waving it in front of him like a sword. The police moved in, trying to get bodies and riot shields between Sacha's people and Noam's.

To protect Carolinians, of course. Not because they were concerned about keeping the peace.

"Disperse!" The police megaphone was loud enough to be heard over the chanting and the screams. "Disperse now!"

"Like fuck we will," Noam shouted back, and a fresh wave of agony rippled from his eye socket down to his mouth. He didn't care. He didn't give a single shit about anything but the fire burning white hot down to his very last nerve.

The person next to him roared a wordless noise and punched the air, the other arm looped around Noam's neck and tugging him into a rough embrace.

The protest was fast becoming something else, rage claiming a life of its own as it swept through the crowd. Someone shouted, and Noam sensed metal careening toward them—*tear gas*. On reflex, his power latched on to the grenade and sent it hurtling toward the fascists instead.

Shit.

The knowledge that there was a witching with the Atlantians rippled through the crowd. It grew as it spread, a fresh tide of anger and fear. Older Carolinians might respect witchings, in memory of the catastrophe, but this new generation didn't care. To them, the catastrophe was ancient history, and witchings were just dangerous creatures afforded far too much power by the government.

He sensed, too, when the police called for an antiwitching unit, but he couldn't use his power to shut off comms without giving away his technopathy and, by extension, making it obvious exactly which witching hid under the antifascist masks.

"We gotta get out of here," he shouted at the nearest guy he could grab—Sam, he was pretty sure. "They just called in backup!"

"Fuck their backup!" Sam yelled back and made a violent gesture toward the statue.

Noam looked. A knot of Carolinia First protesters had managed to get one of the Atlantians away from the group—Grace, on the ground, her mask fallen, someone dragging her by the hair while another guy kicked her in the gut over and over. The police stood five feet away and did nothing. *Nothing.*

"Come on!" Noam and Sam ran forward, ducking under someone's swinging sign and sprinting toward the statue of Adalwolf Lehrer.

The police saw them coming and rounded with plastic shields thrust out, someone tugging the pin out of another tear gas grenade. Grace was screaming. Noam and Sam dodged right and let themselves get swallowed by the roiling crowd, out of sight.

"This way," Sam said. He and Noam elbowed their way through all the nameless and faceless bodies until they somehow slid around the police line before the perimeter closed.

Noam's power was all instinct, an ungrounded electric current. He wanted to use it to burn the life out of the men beating Grace. Instead he sent it unfurling through the square, mapping metal until he sensed something familiar and yanked it toward himself. Police-issue 9 mm handgun, with a plastic casing that felt cold when Noam's fingers closed around the grip. Not far off from the model they used in Level IV basic training.

Grace remained on the ground, coiled in on herself to protect vital organs, but Noam could still see the blood on her face.

"Leave her alone," Noam yelled, and twin smirks curled round the mouths of the two guys holding her.

The one with his hand twisted in her hair said, "Fuck off, kid. Go home to Mommy."

But then he saw the gun in Noam's hand, and his skin went the color of fish meat. "You don't know how to use that."

Noam raised the pistol and pointed it at him. "Don't fucking try me."

The two guys exchanged looks and immediately released Grace. Hands up in the air, they backed away two steps—three—then turned tail and ran.

Sam darted forward, kneeling on the ground at Grace's side. Her blood was all over the pavement. Noam's hands were shaking, the gun suddenly impossibly hot in his grasp. He dropped it and kicked it away.

"Shit," he whispered, nausea crawling up his throat. "Shit."

"You'd better get out of here," Sam advised.

Yeah.

Noam ran.

The air was thick with tear gas to the east, so he went west, stumbling over a broken section of sidewalk and scraping his palms. He pushed himself up, had to keep going, because once antiwitching units got here, it would be fifty times harder to break perimeter.

Fuck.

The cavalry had already arrived. The antiwitching armor gleamed like abalone shell in the afternoon sun. Noam's power slid off them, oil on wet asphalt.

"Okay," he told himself, ignoring the fear prickling like heat at the nape of his neck. "Okay—think, *think*—"

He spun around, prepared to dart back into the crowd, and nearly collided with the broad armored chest of an antiwitching soldier. The man's hand closed around Noam's arm with inhuman strength, and maybe he wasn't human, maybe there was nothing behind that black-glazed mask but technology and magic. A faceless voice spoke.

"You're under arrest."

The city jail was next to the government complex, right across the street from where Dara and Bethany and Taye and Ames were probably sitting down for dinner.

The officer who booked Noam was a heavyset man with bushy eyebrows. He didn't even meet Noam's gaze as he demanded, "Papers."

"Don't have any," Noam lied.

The man huffed. "Figures. All right, gimme your hand. Fingerprints."

The gun.

The gun, on the sidewalk, that Noam had stolen from a police officer with magic. The gun with Noam's prints all over it.

When Noam didn't immediately react, the man just grabbed at his wrist himself, pressing Noam's hand against a screen. Noam felt the machine scan his prints and couldn't do a damn thing about it, couldn't wipe himself from the system without getting caught using technopathy and giving himself away.

Whatever. If Noam went to juvie again because he was fighting fascism on behalf of Atlantians, he was okay with that.

"Name?" the man asked.

Noam didn't answer, just to be contrary. Instead he tried to track whether the system immediately told the police his identity, but the data packet with his fingerprints uploaded instantly to federal servers. Servers which were, of course, concealed by antitechnopathy wards. Great.

They crowded Noam and all the other refugees—the Carolinia First contingent was notably absent from the arrestees—into a holding cell guarded by antiwitching soldiers. A man in a suit stood on the other side of the cell bars and said, "Listen up. We know one of you is an unregistered witching. If you own up to it, maybe we go a little easier on you."

Silence answered. Noam and the others all avoided looking at each other, as if making eye contact might be taken as evidence.

The man waited patiently, seconds stretching out into minutes.

"Very well," he said at last. "Then let me put it this way. Anyone who tells me who the witching is gets to walk out of here today. No charges. No questions. No deportation." His cool gaze surveying each of them in turn. When he looked at Noam, Noam stood.

"We're entitled to legal defense," he said.

"As illegal immigrants, you aren't entitled to anything."

Noam was pretty sure he was more familiar with Carolinian law at this point than the man in the suit. He'd read quite a bit of it in the free library at juvie. "Carolinian law states every person is entitled to a public defender against federal charges. Every *person*, not just every citizen."

The man looked at him. "Let me rephrase: illegals are not entitled to government-funded lawyers for immigration-related charges." His smile was thin, mean. "After all, who said anything about charging you with *federal* crimes?"

Right—because why bother wasting resources charging them with incitement when they could just deport everyone in this room to Atlantia on immigration charges and save the trouble? They'd figure out who Noam was sooner or later, and that he was a Carolinian citizen, but for everyone else . . .

Noam sat back down.

The man in the suit was still smiling as he turned toward the room again, hands on his hips. "I'll say it one more time. Who wants to walk out of here?"

Noam stole a glance at Sam, who still had Grace's blood on his shirt. At DeShawn, with his left eye swollen shut. At the others, people Noam didn't even know but who might know him, who had no reason to defend a Level IV witching when they could save their own skin in trade.

No one spoke up.

Noam should have been terrified, but warmth bloomed in his chest too.

He nudged Sam's ankle. Sam didn't react. So Noam found the wedding ring on his finger and warmed it up until Sam flinched and finally glared over at him, hand flexing. Noam stared back, brows lifted.

Do it, you idiot.

Sam exhaled a heavy breath. And at last he said, "It's him," and jerked his thumb toward Noam. "But joke's on you, assholes. He's not unregistered; he's Level IV."

The man in the suit looked back at Noam with narrowed eyes.

Noam smirked, even though it made his bruised cheekbone hurt like fuck. "I can see the headline now: 'Level IV–trained witching arrested at anti-Sacha protest.' Ouch. Hope you have a good PR department."

He relished the look on that man's face: hatred, resentment. Apprehension.

The man looked to one of the uniformed officers. "Call the Ministry of Defense and figure out how they want to handle it. You." He pointed at Noam. "Get up. You're coming with me."

Noam got up—what else was he going to do?—and crossed the small space between the bench and the bars. They didn't bother trying to cuff him this time, just opened the door and tugged him out by the arm. The door slammed shut after him, an officer twisting his key in the lock.

"Wait," Noam said, gesturing to Sam. "What about him?"

The man in the suit tapped his tongue against the backs of his teeth. "Too bad," he said. "Shoulda got it in writing."

The holding cell erupted in a cacophony of shouts and threats, Sam lurching off the bench to bang his wrist against the bars so hard it probably bruised. But Noam wasn't surprised. Not anymore.

The man walked away; Noam and the officers followed in his wake until the refugees' anger was just an echo at the end of a long hall, cutting to silence as steel double doors fell shut.

No. Noam wasn't surprised.

But this wasn't over—because ever since the guy with the eyebrows pressed Noam's hand against the fingerprint scanner, an idea had been taking shape in his mind. Formless at first, its blurry lines had become bold edges.

They locked him in a room and told him to wait. They didn't say for how long.

Good. Noam needed time to work.

He knew what Faraday meant.

CHAPTER TWELVE

Noam spent two hours in that cell, staring at the wall opposite his chair without really seeing it. His awareness of the room faded to a gray blur, punctuated by the occasional buzz of a fly whirring past his ear. He only knew how long he was there because he felt the second hand of his watch tick-ticking along, a metronome beating out of rhythm with his heart.

The antitechnopathy wards were a Faraday shield.

A magical one, sure, but a *Faraday shield*—that was why Noam's electric power couldn't penetrate them. But that meant he just had to find the right wavelength of electromagnetic radiation to penetrate the shield.

That took the first hour and a half. The rest of the time was spent extracting data from the government servers by transmitting them at the same frequency as the shield to the flopcell Noam habitually kept in his jeans pocket, filling it up with anything and everything he could get his metaphorical hands on.

Ablaze with information, that flopcell glittered in his awareness like a thousand concentrated fireflies.

Two hours. The door opened. Lehrer stepped in.

Noam blinked, and the holding room slid back into focus. Lehrer was too tall for this place, Noam observed, his thoughts slippery and hard to hold on to. That or the ceiling was low. Lehrer had to bend his head to one side to keep from hitting it.

"What happened here?" Lehrer said and touched his own cheek.

"Fascism."

"Hmm." Lehrer stepped forward, claiming the seat opposite Noam's. The interrogation table looked child sized when Lehrer placed his elbows atop its surface and surveyed Noam over the bridge of his hands. "Why don't you tell me what happened, in your own words?"

"There was an antirefugee protest at the catastrophe memorial," Noam said. "Carolinia First was there."

If Lehrer had a reaction to the idea of Sacha's followers using Lehrer's own trauma as a vehicle for their message of hatred and intolerance, it didn't show. His face was as impassive as always—like stone worn smooth, thousands of years of water flowing over its surface and blunting sharp edges.

At last the silence was unbearable enough that Noam had to say something to break it. "Things escalated. Sacha's people started beating a girl, one of the refugees. I stole a police officer's gun and threatened them with it, and they stopped. Then antiwitching units showed up, and I got arrested. And here I am."

Lehrer lowered his hands to the table, tapping his thumb against its edge. "I notice you call them 'Sacha's people.'"

"That's what they are. Sacha is responsible for them. He *creates* them, by creating a public environment where people fear refugees instead of empathizing with them. Everything Carolinia First does, they do in Sacha's name." He exhaled, very slowly. "I'm not going to apologize for what I did. If you're going to kick me out of Level IV or throw me in jail, just do it."

"I'm going to do no such thing," Lehrer said.

Noam frowned. "Okay. What?"

"I've taken care of the situation. Your friends have been released, the record of your fingerprints on that gun has been erased, and I've ensured the officers will keep their silence on the matter. There's nothing for you to worry about."

Noam gritted his teeth so hard it hurt. "I can't believe you," he snapped, and he shoved his chair back, on his feet before Lehrer could react. "You're powerful enough to just—to wipe the slate clean like that, to clear my guilt for crimes *I actually committed*, but you aren't powerful enough to do anything real that might actually *save lives*?"

"Noam—"

Noam slapped his hand against the table, its legs rattling against the floor. "No. Shut up. I don't want to hear whatever excuse you've come up with—it's good to know just how bad the corruption in the Carolinian government really is, I guess." He felt like he had a fever, like his blood had risen beneath the surface of his skin. "Back in 2018 you were willing to do whatever it took to overthrow the US and get justice for witchings. But if it's Atlantians, suddenly it's all mild sympathies and cryptic notes and cleaning up my messes. So I guess while you will *literally* lift a finger on behalf of refugees, that's about the extent of it." His mouth twisted around the bitter taste on his tongue, mimicking Lehrer's raised-brow disapproval. "Go on. Prove me wrong."

Lehrer sighed, but instead of telling Noam to sit down, he rose to his feet as well in a single graceful movement. "Let's continue this discussion elsewhere. I hate to impose on the officers' time."

"Fuck the officers."

Lehrer reached into his pocket and passed Noam a blank two-terabyte flopcell.

Noam opened his mouth, but the look Lehrer gave him in response killed the words on his lips.

"I thought you might need an extra," Lehrer said.

Noam fumbled for something to say, gripping the flopcell in his fist. "How did you know I—"

"Later," Lehrer interrupted. He gestured toward the door. "After you."

Noam slipped the flopcell into his back pocket to join its mate and preceded Lehrer out.

Lehrer didn't speak as they left, not to Noam and not to the police officers—not that he had to. They got out of his way the second they saw him coming, doors opening the moment Noam and Lehrer reached them.

To Noam's surprise, Lehrer didn't lead him up to his study or even to the government complex. They took a sharp left on the street, away from the city and toward residential areas. Noam trailed at Lehrer's heel, questions crowding his mouth, but Lehrer didn't say a word. Just walked, hands slipped in his uniform pockets, casual as anything.

Noam wondered if he was being tested. If all these times when Noam questioned Lehrer and Lehrer fed him just enough crumbs to keep Noam on his side—if this was all being calculated and tallied up as points for and against. Like if Noam was just patient enough, Lehrer might eventually tell him the truth.

Fuck that.

"Where are we going? Sir."

"I don't want to be overheard." Lehrer's tone didn't leave room for questions.

Out of downtown, trees sprouted from the ground lining the sidewalk. In winter their branches would reach like bony fingers toward a slate-gray sky—but in spring their broad leaves cast dappled shadows on the path. Somehow they managed to grow, despite the cold spell that had persisted into late spring. Noam shivered; they'd taken his coat at the jail and never given it back.

Lehrer glanced at him as they turned onto a new street. "Are you cold?"

"A little."

Lehrer's jacket buttons unclasped themselves—this close, Noam felt Lehrer's gold-thread magic looping round each one in turn—and Lehrer shrugged off his coat, passing it to Noam. The wool was heavy in his hands, laden with all the sewn patches and stripes of Lehrer's various honors and awards. Noam put it on anyway, sliding his arms through the sleeves.

"Thanks," he said, and Lehrer nodded once.

Without his jacket, Lehrer looked far more human. He was still impossibly tall, broad shouldered, but the tailored dress shirt he wore betrayed a deceptively narrow waist. If it weren't for the magic Noam still sensed on his skin, or the way Lehrer didn't shiver in the icy air, he might have forgotten Lehrer was dangerous.

"I brought you here because I couldn't discuss this where we might be overheard," Lehrer said finally. When Noam looked, Lehrer was watching him.

"Your note?"

"I sensed it when you took the wards down."

When Noam gave him a confused look, Lehrer just shrugged and said, "I made them. Very few witchings are capable of creating sustained magical shields, but I am one."

"Okay," Noam said, and at last he rounded on Lehrer, stopping there in the middle of the sidewalk. "But then why couldn't you just take it down in the first place? You knew I was trying to expose Sacha. That day you caught me and Dara in the government complex and read the email off my computer, you could've just taken the wards down right then and there. Why didn't you?"

"I had to know you could be trusted. If you weren't serious about this—if you wouldn't risk everything to take down Sacha—then I had no use for you."

Noam's chest went tight. This was it. This was what Lehrer had been up to, the whole reason he'd kept Noam on.

"Use for me?"

"I gave you a note instead of telling you the secret outright because I suspect Sacha has my study and my apartment bugged. I've looked, of course, but I'm no technopath—and I couldn't risk being overheard plotting treason."

The silence that followed was punctuated only by the dead leaves that rustled underfoot, caught up in a breeze.

"I don't understand," Noam said.

"These things are delicate." Lehrer stood as still as calm water. "We cannot simply depose Sacha and declare power. Our rise must appear necessary and inevitable."

Realization cut through Noam's core.

Calix Lehrer hadn't gone soft in the years since the catastrophe. Beneath that military uniform and the careful trappings of a government man, he was the same revolutionary who forged a new nation from the wreckage of genocide. And he'd witnessed Sacha assault the very foundations of that utopia.

Lehrer gave up the crown because he feared the corruption of absolute power, but corruption crept into Carolinia regardless.

"You're planning a coup."

A beat, then Lehrer nodded.

Maybe it was just the magic Noam had spent downloading two terabytes of classified government data, but his skin felt as if a current ran through it, blue and electric.

"Your ability is valuable and untraceable. You've already proved you know how to use it as a weapon." Lehrer gestured toward the flopcell in Noam's hand. "I assume you planned to leak that to the press."

"I don't trust the press. I was going to publish it on an independent website."

"Good. Do that."

They stood there, encapsulated in the soft grayness of their mutual secret, a quiet world that existed just in that moment, floating outside of time.

Noam had the strange urge to reach out and touch Lehrer, to put a hand on his arm and squeeze. He had the even stranger feeling that Lehrer would let him.

At last, Lehrer broke that gentle silence. "Thank you, Noam. I can't tell you how much it means to have an ally in this."

"Of course."

"It will be dangerous."

"I know."

"Do you?" Lehrer said it with a slight leftward slant of his head.

Noam met Lehrer's pale gaze. The real Lehrer looked back at him, the man beneath all these layers of diplomacy and politics, the one who shattered a nation.

"I would rather die than do nothing."

"Hopefully it won't come to that." Lehrer touched the back of Noam's arm, guiding him down the sidewalk toward the government complex. Noam went, and it was several seconds before Lehrer's hand fell away, but even then Noam felt the residual heat from his touch.

"There is one thing, though. You will need to stop working with Tom Brennan."

"What?" Noam frowned. "Why?"

"He means well, but diplomatic methods will achieve nothing. With him you're invested in a losing battle. Besides, public opinion is divided on the issue of the Atlantian occupation—not to mention immigration—and we can't appear to take sides. Your actions reflect upon me now, and I can't publicly ally myself with Brennan."

"Politics, then," Noam translated flatly. "Somehow I think Carolinia will support you no matter what I do. You're a war hero. You could declare yourself dictator tomorrow morning, and people would still love you."

The look Lehrer gave him was half a warning. Still, Noam thought he detected a light curve to one corner of Lehrer's mouth. A secret smile, for the secret they shared.

No one else would hesitate to obey. And yet here Noam stood, remembering what Dara told him: *I don't like naïveté.*

"Brennan's the only person I have left from my old life," Noam managed to say. The words caught in his throat like small stones.

"I know."

Brennan was there when they took Noam's mother's body down. He sat with Noam in the Russian literature section and read *The Brothers Karamazov* out loud until Noam's father got home. He offered to let Noam stay with him for a while, but Noam said no, because if Noam left—if Noam abandoned his father the same way his mom had—he didn't think Jaime would ever crawl out of the grave he'd dug for himself.

Still, Brennan had offered, and now he could barely stand to be in the same room as Noam.

Noam pressed the heel of one hand to his brow and closed his eyes, taking in an unsteady breath. Yeah, Brennan wasn't exactly doing anything to foment *real* change, but could Noam cut him off entirely?

When he looked again, Lehrer still watched patiently, his ageless face blank and unreadable.

Maybe he was right. Maybe Noam was wasting his time trying to talk Brennan into seeing a truth that was, to Lehrer, already clear.

"All right. I'll stop."

Lehrer inclined his head, a slow nod Noam found hard to interpret. Could he tell Noam was lying? If so, he didn't make accusations. "Thank you, Noam. I know it's a lot to ask. But if you value the migrant cause as you claim, you'll see the logic in being circumspect."

Right. Noam swallowed against an uneasy stomach. "What happens if we fail?"

"We won't fail."

Lehrer touched chilly fingers to Noam's cheek, turning his face toward the streetlamp. His thumb skimmed the throbbing skin just below Noam's eye. Noam shivered. It still hurt.

"Would you like me to heal this?" Lehrer asked.

"I think I'd rather keep it," Noam said and caught Lehrer's gaze. "I earned it."

Lehrer laughed, and after a beat, his hand fell away. "Stubborn youth."

Doubt crept back in only when Noam was back in the barracks, sitting next to Dara on the sofa and trying to concentrate while Dara lounged about, reading *Pale Fire* and being consummately distracting. Was it a mistake to uncritically trust Lehrer? Even if Lehrer was telling the truth about his coup, who said he wouldn't try to pin the blame on Noam if things went sour?

No. No more excuses. It was time to act, the way Noam had promised himself he would, back when he first started Level IV.

Noam watched Dara lick his thumb and turn the page, right in rhythm.

Dara would tell Noam to choose a direction headed away from Lehrer, to start running and never look back.

But Dara wasn't a refugee, and Dara didn't have anything to lose.

Noam slid his holoreader out of his satchel and opened it on his knees. He'd finished downloading the contents of the government servers on his way back from Lehrer's, two flopcells full of damning emails and violent memos.

Four terabytes of Sacha's evil.

Noam plugged the first flopcell into his computer and uploaded its contents to a public repository.

Time for Carolinia to learn the truth.

Time for a real revolution.

Encrypted video recording, April 2017, from Calix Lehrer's personal archives

The camera displays a therapist's office: two armchairs facing a sofa, a desk by a window, bookshelves. A man, Dr. Gleeson, is visible on the right edge of the frame. He stands in an open doorway, facing away from the camera and speaking to someone in the waiting room (off-screen).

GLEESON: "You must be Calix. Would you like to come on back now?"

[inaudible response]

Gleeson moves away from the door, retreating deeper into the room. He is followed by a tall boy, nineteen years old, attractive with light hair and lighter eyes. The boy, Calix Lehrer, carries a book. He scans the room, as if assessing for quick exits.

GLEESON: "Take a seat wherever you like."

Calix sits in the chair nearest the door. His body is too long for it, knees bent at a sharp angle and elbows tucked in close. He opens his book on his thigh and begins reading again.

Gleeson takes the seat opposite.

GLEESON: "Schopenhauer. *The World as Will and Representation*?"

Calix tilts the book to show him the spine.

GLEESON: "Interesting philosophy. The world, and humans as part of it, are mere manifestations of a metaphysical Will. Depressing, I always thought. Since we don't understand others are composed of the same Will, we are doomed to perpetual violence and suffering."

CALIX (without looking up): "That's about the whole of it."

GLEESON: "Tell me about yourself, Calix."

CALIX: "You know everything there is to know."

GLEESON: "Tell me something I couldn't read in the papers."

Calix eyes him without lifting his head. Frowns. The desk drawer opens and a bottle of scotch emerges by telekinesis, accompanied by a snifter. The bottle uncaps itself, fills the glass.

CALIX: "I think I'll just read, if you don't mind. Analyze that however you like. Or you're welcome to just sit there and think whatever baseline humans think about when left idle."

GLEESON: "That's not very nice."

CALIX: "Did Wolf tell you I was nice?"

Calix licks his thumb, turns the page. The scotch arrives and rests on his knee.

Silence. Then Gleeson reaches for a pen and begins writing.

Calix looks up, handsome mouth in a dissatisfied moue.

CALIX: "What are you doing?"

GLEESON: "Taking notes. Tell me more about your relationship with Adalwolf."

CALIX (confused): "Why are you—"

Gleeson looks up, then smiles. He puts down his pen.

GLEESON: "Your power doesn't seem to work on me, does it?"

CALIX: "I beg your pardon?"

GLEESON: "Your power. It isn't working."

Calix stares. He's forgotten his book entirely, the pages falling shut and losing his place.

GLEESON: "Of course, I'm not an expert or anything, but I'm guessing it has something to do with my telepathy."

CALIX: "*What?*" (His expression shifts, a calm sea roused to anger.) "You can't—you—get out of my head!"

Gleeson is still smiling.

Calix pushes himself up so violently the glass topples off his knee, spilling expensive liquor on Gleeson's carpet.

CALIX: "I'm leaving. Tell Adalwolf whatever you want, but I'm not sitting through this. No."

He's halfway to the door, flinging it open by telekinesis, before Gleeson speaks.

GLEESON: "I should have thought you'd jump at the chance to speak to someone who understands you."

Calix turns, fixes him with a narrowed gaze.

Gleeson uncaps and recaps his pen.

CALIX: "Just because you can read my mind doesn't mean you *understand* me."

GLEESON: "Not that. Think about it, Calix. Pyromancy, telekinesis, healing . . . those powers are all very impressive, yes, but they aren't like ours. We're something else. Something not quite human."

Calix hovers there in the doorway. At last he closes the door and returns, this time sitting on the sofa. His face is impassive, but one gets the sense of something else, movement beneath dark waters.

CALIX: "All right, I'll bite. When did you learn telepathy?"

GLEESON: "It was my presenting power. I woke up with it after the fever. I was twenty. But you survived the virus quite young—two, yes? This ability is all you can remember. Your view of other people is completely shaped by it . . ."

Calix says nothing. He sits there, holding Gleeson's gaze until Gleeson sighs.

GLEESON: "That's a tangent, of course. My real question is, how long have you been having these nightmares?"

CALIX: "We're not talking about me."

GLEESON (laughing): "My boy, of course we're talking about you. If you want me to answer your questions, you'll have to answer a few of my own. It's only fair."

Silence.

GLEESON (as if in response to something unspoken but overheard): "Yes. But I'd still like to discuss them with you. So, I'll ask again. How long have you been having the nightmares?"

CALIX (eventually): "Since the hospital."

GLEESON: "Every night?"

CALIX: "Just about. Wolf got me some sleeping pills, but they don't help . . . if you write a word of this down, I'm leaving."

Gleeson puts down the pen.

GLEESON: "What are the dreams about?"

CALIX: "No, it's my turn. You made the rules, remember?"

GLEESON: "By all means."

CALIX: "Have you met any other telepaths?"

Gleeson pauses for several seconds, perhaps considering if he intends to lie.

GLEESON: "Yes. But it was not their presenting power."

Calix's strange eyes are too bright now, fixed on Gleeson.

Gleeson shifts in his seat, uncomfortable.

GLEESON: "My turn. What are the dreams about, Calix?"

CALIX: "They're about what happened to me in the hospitals." (pause) "They tortured me to inspire new powers. They thought if they put my body under enough stress, it would be forced to defend itself. It worked. I was useful because I was powerful, and the more powerful they made me, the more useful I became. If they could suppress me, they could suppress anyone."

Calix pauses, then shrugs.

CALIX: "They were trying to invent a vaccine for the virus when I was liberated."

GLEESON: "Did they succeed?"

CALIX (shaking his head): "They were able to make suppression work on me, though, if only for an hour per dose. My question, now."

GLEESON: "Not so fast. You still haven't said what the dreams were about. Not specifically."

CALIX: "I told you, they're about what happened to me in—"

GLEESON: "They tortured you, yes. So you said. But how?"

Calix's hands clutch the sofa cushions. When he swallows, his throat bobs visibly.

CALIX: "They . . . anything they could think of to induce pain. Cutting into me, breaking bones. Capsaicin injections. They . . ."

Calix shudders, eyes fluttering shut.

GLEESON (gently): "It's all right, Calix. That's enough."

Calix doesn't appear to hear. He drops his head back, his voice thin and shaking.

CALIX: "They had me gagged. I couldn't . . ."

GLEESON (urgent, his expression nauseated): "I know."

At last Calix opens his eyes. He's pale. Gleeson removes his spectacles with trembling fingers and scrubs the heel of his other hand against his face.

GLEESON: "Go ahead and ask what you were going to ask me."

A long moment passes. Gleeson puts his glasses back on.

CALIX: "Can you learn telepathy?"

GLEESON: "I don't know. It would seem so, although the only other telepath I knew could never quite define how she acquired the ability. But she couldn't read *every* mind, as I can. Her ability was limited, perhaps because it wasn't her presenting power. She could only read the minds of people she had a close, personal connection to. She spent years trying to cultivate telepathy but never got past this limitation. She could read the minds of people she understood on a deep and intimate level, and only if they felt a close connection to her in return. But no one else."

Calix says nothing.

GLEESON: "I advise against it. Telepathy is a curse as much as a blessing. Far worse when you use it on a loved one and realize all the nasty things they think about you but would never say out loud."

CALIX: "I want to help him."

GLEESON: "I know you do." (He drags his hand through his hair again.) "I know, Calix. But reading Adalwolf's mind won't help you help him. Believe me."

CALIX: "You think I could learn, though."

GLEESON: "I think . . . I think that would be a very bad idea."

Calix is still looking at him, his face lean and hungry. He opens his mouth to speak again.

The video ends here.

Chapter Thirteen

Noam was sprawled across his bed on Friday afternoon, halfway through *Oryx and Crake*, chewing on one of Taye's red lollipops, when Dara and Ames cornered him with demands that Noam attend some dinner party Ames's dad was throwing. It wasn't the kind of thing Noam was into, hanging out with old rich people and playing sycophant. He was about to make his excuses, but then Dara said, "You should come."

And that decided it, really.

That night, Dara and Noam took a cab out of downtown toward Forest Hills and the massive mansions belonging to the rich and famous and government employed. Noam watched the houses slide past, each more ostentatious than the last. Some were larger than the entire training wing. Dara, smiling down at something on his phone, didn't seem to notice.

"So glad you could make it," Ames said. She met them at the door to the home secretary's residence, drabs replaced by tight black trousers and a well-fitted men's blazer. A glass of brandy dangled from one hand. "Go home, Dara; I'm sure Noam and I can find some way to entertain ourselves without you here."

Dara laughed. "Consider me his chaperone." He plucked the brandy out of Ames's hand, finishing the rest of it in a single long swallow. "I'm here to make sure you don't take advantage."

"Me? Take advantage? Never."

They followed her into the mansion—and it was exactly that: a mansion, with a white board façade and an interior constructed of hardwood floors and fleur-de-lis patterned wallpaper, fine art framed on the walls or featured as centerpieces. Noam had read in the bookstore history section that traditional Carolinian architecture was considered unpretentious by contemporaries. Still, he couldn't help comparing it to what he'd seen of Lehrer's apartment. Here there were no faded rugs or worn-down upholstery. Everything was restored and polished to gleaming perfection, down to the silver candlesticks.

If Noam stole one of those candlesticks, he'd feed a whole tenement for three months.

Maybe he was morally obligated to do just that.

General Ames met them in the sitting room along with three other guests—Major General Amelia García, chair of the Joint Chiefs of Staff; a handsome black man Noam recognized as James Attwood, a famous actor; and a blonde woman who was probably Attwood's wife. Noam saluted on reflex; Major General García smiled and told him "at ease," but Ames Sr. just laughed.

Noam realized why a second later as Dara swept past him, all smiles, to shake the general's hand like they were equals.

And maybe they were. Lehrer was General Ames's commanding officer, and Dara was Lehrer's ward. Perhaps in the home secretary's eyes, Dara wasn't a cadet—he was political royalty.

"So glad you could make it, Dara," General Ames said, tugging Dara in by the shoulder for a one-armed embrace. "And you brought your friend, too, I see—that's good. Very good."

Ames had joined Noam in the doorway; she pressed two fingers to Noam's spine, nudging him forward. Noam went, feeling too aware now of his ill-fitting sweater and battered old shoes creaking against the floorboards. All gazes lingered on the bruise at Noam's eye.

"Nice to meet you again, sir," Noam said, trying to be careful of the way he said it, to emphasize the right syllables and drawl the right vowels. Great. Here he was, worried about whether he sounded Carolinian enough to impress a rich white man.

The general paused, clearly not remembering having met Noam before, and Dara said, "This is Noam Álvaro. Lehrer's new student."

"Ah!" General Ames's affect brightened considerably at that. "Yes, I remember Calix saying something to that effect. You do some mess with computers, isn't that right?"

"Yes, sir. Technopathy."

"Impressive," García said, shaking Noam's hand as well. "Minister Lehrer has many good things to say about your abilities, Cadet."

"Really?" Noam said, hoping she'd elaborate, but General Ames barreled on before García could answer.

"If we're lucky, Calix will join us later on. He's stuck in some meeting or another, but I told him I wasn't going to tolerate any more excuses." He laughed. "They're fixin' to serve dinner, at any rate. Shall we get started?"

As it turned out, rich people didn't just eat one dinner. They ate several. One course was even beef—real beef, not synthetic. It wasn't until the dessert course that the general turned his attention to Noam, swirling his wine in his glass. "Who were your parents, my boy? I don't believe Carter said."

Wait, was Ames's first name *Carter*?

Noam had just put his fork in his mouth, which meant he had to sit there and finish chewing while the home secretary looked on with his watery eyes, his daughter tapping the tabletop the way she did when she craved a cigarette. Next to him, Dara was carefully disassembling his dessert into its component parts and eating none of it; no one but Noam seemed to notice.

"Um," Noam said at last, once he'd forced down a bite and chased it with a sip of water. Attwood watched with polite interest; even García seemed to await Noam's answer. He got the sense they weren't expecting *Jaime Álvaro and Rivka Mendel.*

"Noam's father died three months ago," Dara said before Noam had to figure out what to say, looking up from his deconstructed cake. "I don't think he wants to talk about it."

Noam didn't know how to thank Dara, not right now. He settled for nudging Dara's ankle with the side of his foot and received a tiny smile in response.

"Minister Lehrer has arrived, sir," a footman announced, half a breath before Lehrer stepped into the room.

Everyone present immediately rose to their feet—everyone except Noam, who fumbled out of his chair a beat too late, and Dara, who was busy examining his fork prongs.

Lehrer was in a suit, not his military uniform, but that did little to undermine the way all these powerful people stared at him, like his presence sucked all the air from the room.

"Please," Lehrer said with a small smile. "Continue."

"I'm glad you could make it, Minister," Attwood said as they all resumed their seats. "I know it's a nightmare right now."

General Ames snorted. "You don't know the half of it. This whole scandal with the leaks, with the whole damn network being posted online bit by bit, for the world to see . . ."

"Can't you just shut down the site?" Attwood's wife asked. "Call the domain provider?"

Lehrer didn't look at Noam. It felt like a calculated decision. "The domain is registered in Texas."

Noam took a hasty swallow of water, hiding his smile behind the glass.

"Twice the treason, if you ask me," Ames Sr. muttered. "Texans hate witchings more than anyone. This is a matter of national security."

Yeah. That was the whole point. Governments didn't have to listen to the people until the people made it hurt *not* to listen. Right now, or so Lehrer had told him earlier that afternoon during their lesson, after sending Dara home—right now, everyone in the Ministry of Defense was terrified that Texas or England or York or another enemy nation would glean some precious detail from something Noam had leaked and use it to demolish Carolinian defenses.

That wouldn't happen, of course. Lehrer had gone over the data Noam drained from the networks. They weren't releasing anything that might cost lives. Only enough to make it clear that Sacha wasn't just too incompetent to prevent the leak—he was actually evil. In a few days, Lehrer would miraculously discover the responsible party and shore up the leak, and all would be well. They were framing one of Sacha's most trusted advisers, someone known to be antithetical to Lehrer on almost every single policy issue. All the better to position Lehrer in opposition to both Sacha and the hack.

All the better to make Lehrer electable.

Of course, to General Ames, the hack was just punk kids trying to make a statement and a public relations nightmare.

"And I'm sure," Ames Sr. went on, gesturing with his wine, "you've all seen that mess Sacha's wearing on his head these days."

"What's that?" Noam said, sitting straighter.

"Looks like a damn crown," the general went on. "Tasteless. Utterly tasteless. You should talk to him, Calix."

The weak light here made Lehrer's face look smooth as polished stone. "I would, but I'm afraid Harold doesn't find my company appealing of late."

Dara, next to Noam, seemed far too pleased with himself.

The general muttered, "Should tell him he's no king. Damn disrespectful, if you ask me."

Lehrer nodded once, his expression shuttered, no doubt making comparisons to the gold circlet he'd worn before abdicating as king. All those speeches he'd made about the corruption of power.

The footman drifted forward to refill Lehrer's scotch. Bowing, even, like he thought Lehrer was still royal.

There was enough power in this room to turn the tide for the refugees, but with the exception of Lehrer, everyone here used that power to make things worse. Perhaps they did it on Sacha's orders, perhaps not. Noam didn't care. Major General García helped organize the military intervention in Atlantia. General Ames was responsible for writing immigration policy, including the policies restricting how many legal refugees Carolinia accepted from Atlantia. The Attwoods were socialites whose money fed into the system, buying campaigns, votes, laws.

What would they do, he wondered, *if they knew I was Atlantian?*

He was dying to just say it, the words weighing on his tongue as the guests finished dinner and went into a new room, one the general called *the drawing room.*

Everything about the general rubbed Noam the wrong way—how he smacked his lips after he sipped his wine, the oddly paternal way he squeezed Dara's shoulder as he pushed him down into an armchair, how he didn't make eye contact with the footman who served his coffee.

Yeah, Noam needed to take a break.

He joined Ames on the sofa. She'd gotten out a new cigarette, though she hadn't lit it yet.

"Hey," Noam said.

"Hey."

"So, where's the bathroom?"

After a pause, one corner of her mouth quirked up. "I'll show you."

She abandoned the cigarette on the end table and got to her feet, tugging Noam up after her with one hand around his wrist. The general scarcely seemed to notice them go, too invested in his conversation with Dara—but Dara caught Noam's eye just as he and Ames slipped out the door. He looked awful jealous for someone who at least had a whiskey in hand.

Ames and Noam headed down a dim hall, lit only by lamplight glowing odd colors from behind stained-glass shades. The shadows it cast beneath her vertebrae made her neck look thin and vulnerable.

"How do you not get lost in this house?" Noam murmured after what felt like the fifth turn into a new corridor and a set of stairs.

"My presenting power is a keen navigational sense."

"Wait, really?"

"Nope."

Ames pushed open a door on the second floor. "Here you go," she said with an elaborate gesture across the threshold.

It wasn't a bathroom.

"Is this . . . ?"

"Where the magic happens, yep."

If the rest of the house was a museum of Carolinian history and architecture, Ames's bedroom was an exhibit on teenage squalor. Noam was fairly certain the carpet was blue under all the discarded chip bags and T-shirts.

"I thought for sure y'all had maids."

A comment Ames chose to ignore.

"Bathroom's through here." Ames made her way through the maze of debris with the delicate elegance of a dancer to kick open another door. This one actually did lead to a bathroom, one that was bigger than Noam's entire apartment growing up.

"Are you serious?" he asked, staring at the marble counters. *Marble.*

"Dead serious. Do you have to pee or not?"

"Not, actually."

He wandered in anyway, mostly to examine the gold taps. Ames followed.

"Want some?" she asked and pulled a bag of white powder from her trouser pocket.

"Don't tempt me." Noam hitched himself up onto the counter, legs dangling in midair and shoes bumping against the mahogany cabinets. "But I think if I took an upper right now, I'd end up trying to fistfight your dad over Marxist-Leninism."

It was the least judgmental thing he could think to say. And he *was* judging her—but only a little, and only because rich people had no need to use drugs. The people Noam knew who used had lives that weren't worth living sober. Ames's family was too rich to have problems.

"Oh, my dad's a card-carrying capitalist all right," Ames said and shook a tiny pile of coke out onto the counter. "Don't know how he and Lehrer can stand each other. Mutual interests, I guess."

"Only your father pushed through a whole lot of anti-Atlantian legislation last year," Noam said. "Not exactly Lehrer's style."

"I suppose you'd know," Ames said.

"What the hell does that mean?"

"Nothing." She drew a couple short lines—with her fingers, not a razor. "Anyway. Dara thinks you're cool, which means I think you're cool. So be cool and do a line with me."

"Dara thinks I'm cool?"

Ames rolled her eyes dramatically and hunched forward. The first line disappeared up an elegant metal straw she seemed to have produced from thin air. "Oh Jesus. Don't go all pathetic. I know Dara can't help it—he just *transforms* gay boys into these drooling stalkers by existing in proximity, but I don't want to start puking this early."

"Okay, well, I'm not gay. Must be your lucky night."

"Noam. Come on."

He kicked his heels against the cabinets and smiled at her.

Of course, now he wanted to know about these pathetic gay boys. He wanted to know who all Dara had been kissing. If Dara kissed a lot of men. If Dara kissed *only* men.

"Dara and I aren't together, in case you were wondering," Ames said, straightening up. When she met Noam's gaze, arms crossed over her chest, it felt like a challenge.

Noam pushed himself back to his feet. He moved closer to Ames, one step, then another, until he could lift his hand and brush a bit of white powder off the tip of her nose. A part of him braced for her to flinch the way Dara had, as if Noam carried some deadly disease.

"And I meant it when I said I wasn't gay," Noam said.

Ames looked disbelieving, but she didn't pull away.

Noam smirked. "Bisexual isn't gay."

At last Ames laughed. Her hand came to rest on Noam's hip, and his fingers skimmed over the line of her cheekbone, past her ear and into short-cropped hair. She had brown eyes the calm color of cedarwood and smelled like cigarette smoke.

She was beautiful, but she wasn't who Noam wanted. Not at all.

"Hope I'm not interrupting."

Noam took a sharp step back, blood turned to ice water.

Reflected in the mirror, a bladed smile cut across Dara's mouth. He lifted a glass of whiskey and took a sip.

"Don't you knock?" Ames snapped.

Noam twisted around to meet Dara's gaze properly, but Dara wasn't looking at him anymore. He'd fixed Ames with that same strange expression on his face, head tilted toward the doorframe.

"I can't believe," Dara enunciated slowly, but his words slurred all the same, "you would leave me alone down there."

Ames looked a little guiltier than was strictly warranted, in Noam's opinion. She snatched the whiskey out of Dara's hand and set it on the sink, then grasped both his shoulders, propelling him out the bathroom door and into her room. Noam trailed behind them like an afterthought.

"Sit," Ames demanded.

Dara dropped back on Ames's bed and stared up at the ceiling. Noam sat next to him, a bit gingerly; his weight dipped the mattress so that Dara's hip leaned against Noam's. For a moment that single warm point of contact was all Noam could think about.

"Are you okay?" he asked Dara, bracing a hand against the headboard.

"I'm fine."

He didn't look fine. He closed his eyes, lips parting as he exhaled. His lashes were like a smudge of charcoal against his cheek—Noam wanted to touch him. If he did, he imagined Dara's skin would be fever hot.

"Do you need to puke and rally?" Ames asked him.

"No."

"Want to do a line, then?"

"I'm all right." Dara opened his eyes again and pushed himself up, that brief vulnerability so thoroughly erased that Noam might've thought he'd imagined it. Would have, if not for the way Ames still looked at Dara with her brow knit, like she thought Dara was two heartbeats from breaking apart.

Noam got the distinct sense Dara had swallowed something else with all that whiskey. His pupils were dilated.

But no matter how fucked up Dara already was, it didn't stop him and Ames from digging out the tequila hidden in her underwear drawer. Somehow, over the next fifteen minutes, they all ended up sprawled over Ames's unmade bed—Noam's legs slung up against the wall, Dara's head on his stomach, Ames's feet hitched over Dara's knees. Noam lost count of how many rounds that bottle of tequila had made in their little circle, but he knew it was a lot. His whole body was pleasantly overwarm, the bottle was half-empty, and Dara's head was practically *in his lap*, oh god. Noam never wanted this moment to end.

"How many blow jobs do you think my dad's managed to give Lehrer by now?" Ames asked between swigs, and Dara laughed.

"I'm just imagining Lehrer down there, on his seventh bottle of scotch, wishing he could actually still get drunk enough to make it through this evening."

"Lehrer can't get drunk?" Noam asked, propping himself up on his elbows and sending Dara's head shifting a few inches lower on his torso.

"Nope, utterly incapable. Spends all his magic keeping himself young and alive. Of course, that means fast alcohol metabolism. Drinking doesn't affect him at all."

Ames passed Noam the bottle when Noam reached for it. "Kind of surprised he hasn't given himself that viral intoxication syndrome thingy by now, if it takes that much work to keep himself looking pretty."

"Not likely," Dara said.

"I know." Ames kicked her feet up in the air above her head. "He's, like, immortal."

"Immortal to fevermadness?" Noam asked.

"Immortal."

Noam sighed. Ames and Dara were both cracking up again over whatever-it-was, but Dara's hand was on Noam's thigh, fingers tracing odd little circles against Noam's hip, Noam slowly sinking through a dark and starry sea. His eyelids were heavy.

Eventually, Ames shifted—or Noam thought it must be Ames, because Dara's head was still on his stomach—and another weight settled down on the bed next to him, someone's breath warm on the side of his neck.

"I wish my dad would try something like that. Use too much magic, kill himself trying to stay young."

Noam snorted.

"I'm serious," Ames said. "I wish he'd die."

Noam opened his eyes. It was a struggle to draw Ames's face back into focus, even though she was so close. "You don't mean that."

"Oh, but I do."

"Be careful what you wish for." Dara shifted, arching his back like a cat. Noam stared at him, at the way that movement dragged the hem of his shirt up just enough to expose a swath of flat brown skin, Dara's trousers tugged taut against his thighs. Dara cracked open his eyes to look back at the pair of them, black irises barely visible beneath his lowered lashes. "I suspect there are plenty of people who'd love to see your father dead."

"Good. I hope they assassinate him."

Ames said it with a viciousness that cut through the haze of Noam's intoxication. He blinked, twice, and looked back to her.

"He doesn't seem that bad. I mean, he's like . . . bougie, I guess . . . but not *that* bad."

"He killed my mother."

Noam sat upright, quickly enough that Dara had to flinch out of the way of Noam's elbows. "What?"

Ames hadn't moved from where she lay, one arm flung overhead with fingers dangling off the edge of the mattress. Her eyes glinted in the lamplight. "You heard me. He brought me and my brother and our mom into the quarantined zone when I was, like, six. Got us all sick. Mom and brother died, but I lived. Obviously."

Noam couldn't—he didn't want to believe it. Who would do something like that? Nobody was that crazy. Right?

Ames's other hand was on his side, toying with the hem of his shirt. She said, "Guess he didn't want to bother with a family if we weren't gonna be witchings."

He stared at Ames's profile, her elegant features so incongruous with the half-shaved head and tattoos, her gaze fixed on her hand and Noam's shirt.

"Did you tell anyone?" Noam asked, his voice barely audible even to his own ears. Surely Lehrer hadn't known. "Before now?"

Ames shrugged. "Told Dara. Hard not to tell Dara."

"What do you mean?"

A strange smile curled round her lips. "Don't you know? Dara—"

"Shut up, Ames," Dara snapped.

Noam looked. Dara was sitting up now, too, but he didn't seem drunk anymore; his shoulders rose and fell with quick, shallow breaths.

"Jesus, fine, *fine*," Ames said and rolled onto her stomach, pushing herself up. She made a face at the pair of them. "The point I'm trying to make is that I fucking hate him. Yeah?"

"Yeah," Noam said. He kind of hated the general now too.

"Great. Okay. I think I'm gonna be sick."

Dara grabbed at a nearby wastebasket, getting it under Ames's head just in time for her to puke dinner and tequila into the liner bag. Dara had one hand on Ames's back, rubbing circles and murmuring quiet words of reassurance, and Noam—

Noam tipped his head back and closed his eyes and tried to keep his own stomach where it belonged. Six years old. Six, and General Ames had taken his daughter—his wife, his son, his *whole family*—out where magic was endemic. Knowing they'd get sick. Knowing they'd rot from the inside just like Bea King, knowing they had a 90 percent chance of dying. Finding those odds favorable.

Ames was right. Someone ought to kill him.

"Noam." Dara's hand was on his knee, Dara's voice murmuring in his ear. "Look at me."

Noam looked.

Dara was close, close enough that Noam could've counted each eyelash were he sober enough to see straight. Ames still hunched over the trash, shivering.

"We need to go back downstairs," Dara said.

"Why?"

"Because Lehrer's going to send someone looking for us if we don't. We've been gone a long time."

Noam couldn't look away from Ames, the damp back of her neck where her collar stuck to her skin. "What about—"

"She'll be okay," Dara said. "Promise. You'll be okay, right, Ames?"

Ames managed a weak thumbs-up.

"She's fine. Can you make it downstairs?"

"I'm drunk, not incapacitated."

Dara smiled and crawled back off the bed. He offered Noam a hand, pulling him up to his feet. The room swayed, then settled. "Good?"

"Good."

They made it downstairs without breaking any bones, but it was a near thing. Dara could barely stand upright half the time, stumbling into Noam and knocking him against the wall. Dara's body was too hot, his waist firm when Noam grabbed at it to keep Dara from tripping down the last few stairs. Dara laughed, and Noam was dizzy, bright.

In the drawing room, General Ames lounged in one of his overstuffed, claw-foot armchairs, puffing away at a cigar.

All that rage crashed back in at once, quenching the dazed euphoria of a second before. Noam glared, wishing one of his abilities was the kind where you could cause someone incredible pain just by looking. He wanted to see the general writhing on the floor like a fish out of water, skin purpling in agony.

Next to him, Dara finally let go from where he'd been clinging to Noam with both hands. He wavered on his feet, and for a second Noam thought he might have to grab the back of Dara's shirt to keep him from tipping over.

Lehrer stood by the lit fireplace with James Attwood. He'd discarded his suit jacket to wear just his shirt and waistcoat, a cigarette held between his fingers. "You look pale, Noam. Are you feeling all right?"

Your friend is batshit fucking crazy, Noam thought in Lehrer's general direction and wished Lehrer could hear him. God. Someone had to tell Lehrer. *Someone* had to.

Noam opened his mouth to answer, but Dara got there first. He sidled up to Lehrer and Attwood, stumbling just a little as he hooked his arm through Attwood's elbow.

"Do you mind if I . . . ?" he asked and took Attwood's drink out of his hand.

Attwood stared at Dara in shocked silence as Dara sipped his scotch and leaned a little farther into Attwood's side. When Dara finally lowered the glass and looked at Lehrer, he smiled.

"Where were you?" Lehrer said, too calmly.

Dara's smile chilled. "Don't you know?" he said. He tapped one finger against the rim of Attwood's glass. "You and Noam are very close now, aren't you, Calix? What with all the time you've spent together lately. *Bonding*."

It was the first time Noam'd ever heard Dara call Lehrer by his actual name.

Lehrer was expressionless. "Perhaps you should stop drinking."

"Where's the fun in that?" Dara lifted the scotch to his mouth again, but Lehrer moved inhumanly fast. He plucked the glass from Dara's hand.

Attwood diplomatically chose that moment to disentangle himself from Dara's grasp.

"Excuse me—" Dara started, but Lehrer shook his head.

"You've had enough."

Dara sneered like he was about to actually argue with Lehrer on that point—but he didn't, thank god. Maybe this was why he and Ames both wanted Noam to come along so badly—to stop them all from killing each other.

"You know what," Dara said. Lehrer still stood there, near enough to touch, but Dara hadn't flinched. Noam couldn't name the look on his face, Dara's eyes glittering like black basalt and his chin pointed toward Lehrer. "I have, actually."

Noam swore he tasted magic in the air, sharp as spilled blood.

Lehrer set the scotch glass on the mantel above the fireplace. "It's late. We should be getting home."

Thank fuck, thank fuck, *thank fuck*.

Noam tried to steady himself from the tequila haze, wishing he had Dara close enough again to keep himself upright.

"You boys can stay here if you like," General Ames said without getting up. Smoke puffed out from his mouth as he spoke. "We have plenty of guest rooms. What do you say, Dara?"

"Dara will be coming home with me tonight, I think," Lehrer interrupted smoothly. He put out his cigarette on an ashtray and raised a brow in Dara's direction.

"Actually . . ." Dara said, but Lehrer shook his head.

"It's been a while since we've spent time together. I feel I've been remiss in my duties as your guardian. You'll spend the weekend."

Dara looked like he would rather break each of his fingers individually than spend any alone time with Lehrer, but he didn't argue. A muscle twitched in his cheek as he glanced at Noam instead. "Well, you'll still ride with us, right, Noam? No point wasting taxi fare."

"Sure," Noam said, because the alternative was loitering around here with the general until his car came, and yeah, *no*.

Dara and Lehrer were both silent on the ride back to the government complex, Dara sitting to Noam's right and twisted so he could look out the window and not at either of them, Lehrer opposite them reading emails on his phone.

Eventually, and without looking up from his phone, Lehrer spoke. "You will not embarrass me again."

Something in the pit of Noam's stomach shriveled, his cheeks going hot. Lehrer couldn't just be talking to Dara; he had to mean Noam too.

Noam kept staring at them both, waiting for one or the other to speak again, but Lehrer appeared to have said his piece. Dara had his brow pressed against the window now, both hands fisted in his lap.

Noam shut his eyes and tried very hard to concentrate on not puking.

He did eventually, anyway, once he made it back to the barracks—when he had an empty bathroom and what felt like years' worth of disgust and anger to vomit up.

The general, with all those medals glittering on his uniform.

Ames's face when she said *he killed my mother*.

He kept telling himself this was Sacha's Carolinia, this was what Lehrer's coup would overthrow.

It didn't make him feel any better.

Chapter Fourteen

The day following the dinner party dragged past like molasses. Everything Noam wanted to say about the general stuck in his throat like wet sugar when he met Ames's gaze. If he told Lehrer, Ames would kill him. But how the hell was Noam supposed to ally with Lehrer, plotting Sacha's downfall and Lehrer's subsequent rise to power, when Lehrer's rule came with a man like *that* at his side?

Noam walked himself through each option Saturday afternoon, sitting behind the store counter. He chewed his way through three moon pies before he remembered they were coming out of his paycheck and made himself do a round of price stickering instead.

He had to tell Lehrer.

At least Dara will be there, he thought as he headed across the atrium late that night. Dara could back him up.

He evaded the antitechnopathy wards easily this time, letting himself into the west wing as deftly as if he'd had a pass card of his very own. Not that anyone was around to appreciate the feat—it was past ten o'clock. The halls were empty of anyone who might look twice at a young cadet wandering the government complex alone.

He knocked at the door to Lehrer's study, then hung back, waiting. Could Lehrer hear knocks at the study door from inside his apartment? Maybe Noam should text him or something. Or text Dara.

Only then the door opened, and Lehrer was there—not wearing his uniform or a suit. Just trousers and a cable-knit sweater, looking more like he belonged in someone's private library than in the Ministry of Defense.

"Noam," he said, and it was perhaps the first time Noam had ever seen Lehrer caught off guard. "What are you doing here? Is everything all right?"

"Sort of. Can I come in?"

A part of him wondered if Lehrer was still angry after last night—he still cringed every time he remembered the softness with which Lehrer had spoken in the car, words like ice in his veins.

But Lehrer just stepped aside, gesturing Noam into the darkened study. "Of course. Please."

This late at night, the room was lit only by a few odd lamps, elongated shadows stretching out on the floor and obscuring Lehrer's face. He moved through those shadows with the ease of someone who'd had a hundred years to learn the topography of the room. This time Noam paid attention when Lehrer unlocked the wards to his apartment, watching the glitter-gold threads quaver beneath Lehrer's touch and then dissolve. Even now Noam couldn't make sense of it. What type of scientific knowledge allowed someone to construct something like this? The ward seemed like it was crafted out of raw magic, not theory.

"How did you do that?" Noam asked. It came out more accusatory than he'd intended. "That, and the antitechnopathy . . . I'm sorry, sir, but—I can't figure it out."

Lehrer stepped through the door to his apartment, Noam following bemusedly and trailing his own magic against the withdrawn wards as if that could tell him how they were built. It was only once he was past the doorway, toeing off his shoes in Lehrer's foyer, that he realized he forgot to touch the mezuzah.

"Telling you would defeat the purpose of having wards, don't you think?"

You told Dara. Noam bit his cheek over that one.

"In theory," he insisted.

"In theory," Lehrer said, "you could build a ward of your own. Imagine an electromagnetic field you maintained around your person like an invisible shield to deflect bullets. Creating it takes magic, but so does releasing it. When you get very good, you can release one part of such a shield while maintaining the rest."

Wolf scampered out from the other room, skidding a little when he leaped off the rug and onto the hardwood floor. Noam crouched to scratch behind his ears. "That wasn't electromagnetism, though," he said, glancing up toward Lehrer.

"No. But you must let me keep *some* secrets."

Although Noam had been in Lehrer's apartment once before, it felt different now that he was here with the intent of staying longer than a few seconds. He drank in the shapes and colors as he followed Lehrer into a sitting room. The whole place was surprisingly simple; what furniture Lehrer did have was clearly antique, the exposed floorboards half-covered with Persian carpets worn along what must be familiar paths. Noam didn't have to be an expert to know quality when he saw it, even when that quality was likely older than Noam and Lehrer put together.

Lehrer turned to face him, standing there with one hand resting on the back of a sofa. "Now, tell me what's going on."

"Noam?" Dara emerged from the hallway, sleep tousled and tugging a sweater down over his short-sleeved shirt. He scowled, arms folding over his chest. His gaze flicked from Noam to Lehrer, then back.

"Hey, Dara," Noam said and tried to look casual.

"Hey, yourself. Why are you here?"

"Dara, you shouldn't be out of bed," Lehrer said. "You need to rest."

Noam frowned. "Are you sick?"

"I'm fine. I'll ask again. Why are you *here*?"

"Let's not be rude," Lehrer chided. He touched Noam's arm instead, just below the elbow. "Please, Noam, make yourself at home. Can I get you something to drink?"

"I'll take hot tea," Dara said before Noam could answer.

Lehrer just kept looking at Noam, though, until at last Noam shrugged and said, "Sure. Thanks. Um. Tea for me too."

Lehrer allowed them both a cursory smile, then disappeared through a door into a room where Noam sensed metal cutlery and saucepans. There weren't, he noticed, any tiny hidden circuit boards. If Sacha had bugged Lehrer's apartment, as Lehrer suspected, he did it without using technology.

"*Are* you sick?" he asked Dara, moving closer.

Dara shrugged one shoulder. "Not really. Just tired." His fingers kept picking at the cuffs of his sweater sleeves, pulling at loose threads.

"Have you eaten anything today?" Noam asked suspiciously, but Dara made a face at him.

"Doesn't matter. You haven't answered my question."

"I'm here about General Ames," Noam said. "About what Ames told us about him. Or told *me*, rather, since you apparently already knew." Knew and hadn't told anyone. Noam tapped his fingers against the seat cushion. "Which, what the hell, Dara?"

Dara stepped closer—though when he spoke, his voice was so low that Noam still had to lean in to hear properly. He was near enough that Noam could smell Dara's shampoo clinging to his hair. "There's a reason I didn't tell anyone, Noam. And you shouldn't either. Okay?"

"No, *not* okay! He killed people, Dara, he would have killed Ames too if she hadn't gotten lucky—"

"I mean it, Noam," Dara hissed. He grabbed on to Noam's wrist, fingers pressing in hard. "I know it's difficult for you to let things go sometimes, but you need to *let this go*. I will tell the people who need to know, but I'll tell them in the right way and at the right time. Please just let me handle it."

"He needs to be punished." Noam's eyes prickled with a painful heat, and he wanted to look away, but he couldn't—he couldn't just let it go. "He can't just get away with this."

"He won't," Dara promised.

Noam would kill General Ames himself if he had to. He'd never hated anyone this much. Never mind a fair trial; the general deserved to be in the ground.

"Trust me," Dara said, and Noam didn't get a chance to respond, because then Lehrer emerged from the kitchen with a tea tray balanced in hand. Dara took a quick step back, releasing Noam and staring at the floor instead.

"Everything all right in here?" Lehrer asked, glancing dubiously at Noam's reddened wrist.

"We're good," Noam said. He blinked back those furious tears—if he cried in front of Lehrer, he'd fucking shoot himself. "Thanks for the tea."

"It's no trouble at all," Lehrer said. He set the tray down on the coffee table, gesturing for Noam and Dara to come sit.

They did, one on each side of the sofa with an ocean's space between them. Lehrer took the armchair, surveying them both through the steam drifting up from his tea.

"Did you have something you wanted to tell me, Noam?" Lehrer said at last.

"Yeah, but it . . ." Noam glanced at Dara, who stared back with narrowed eyes. "I . . . should probably tell you some other time. In private."

Let Lehrer think it had to do with the coup.

Lehrer frowned, tapping one finger against the curve of his mug. "Dara, would you . . . ?"

"No, no, it's fine, it's not urgent," Noam said quickly. "We can talk later."

"After we spar on Monday, perhaps?"

Noam nodded.

Still, he stayed for half an hour and drank the tea just to be polite, making small conversation about classwork and his part-time job until he could justify excusing himself.

Back in the barracks, he couldn't meet Ames's gaze. He stayed out in the common room with Bethany, sharing a bag of Taye's cinnamon candies until Bethany trailed off to bed. That meant getting cornered by Ames after all, who'd unearthed another bottle of vodka and was making noises about going out to Raleigh.

She'd settled herself on Noam's lap, legs slung over the arm of the chair and her head against his shoulder. Her breath was hot on the side of his neck. Her hand was on his thigh.

If Noam went with her, he knew what would happen: he'd get drunk, they'd dance, they'd fuck in a dirty bar bathroom.

That wasn't unappealing, per se; it just . . .

He went to bed early.

Dara returned from his weekend with Lehrer around five Sunday night. He went straight back to the bedroom and didn't come out for dinner. Noam gathered the whole parental bonding thing didn't go well.

And then on Monday, Lehrer dismissed Dara from lessons early, leaving him and Noam alone in the study with the last few remnants of Noam's constructed starlight glittering just below the ceiling. Lehrer reached up and trailed his fingers through them, navigating the constellations.

"How have you been feeling lately?" Lehrer asked, then clarified: "With your magic."

"Fine. What do you mean?"

Lehrer's gaze skipped away from the lights, fixing on Noam. "No fevers, no chills, no aches and pains?"

"No."

"And nothing else either?"

"I haven't gone crazy yet, if that's what you mean," Noam said. He'd been examining the bruise left on his wrist from sparring with Lehrer earlier, a purpling mark that Lehrer hadn't offered to heal. He rolled his sleeve down now, to look at Lehrer instead. "I'm playing by the rules. Magic only on special occasions."

Lehrer gave him a crooked smile. "Now why don't I believe that?"

He didn't give Noam a chance to respond. Instead he leaned back against the edge of his desk and crossed his arms, surveying Noam with an even expression.

"So. What was it you had to talk to me about? We can go for another walk through the city. Perhaps the fresh air would do us both good."

It took Noam a second to catch what Lehrer was getting at.

"Oh," Noam said. "No. I checked. There aren't any bugs here or in your apartment."

"I'm relieved to hear it. Very well, we'll speak freely. Have you given our plan some thought?"

Noam nodded slowly. Hard not to think about it when he'd spent half his evenings sitting at the store register watching Atlantian parents fumble through change on the counter and come up short. *Lisa, sugar, go put those canned peas back on the shelf.*

"You're right about Brennan," Noam said after a second. "He's not going to do anything big. Now that he's got that liaison job, he thinks he can make Sacha see reason."

"That," Lehrer said, "will never happen."

"Yeah, no shit," Noam said, then flushed, because *Lehrer*—but Lehrer didn't say a word. "So . . . so, I was thinking that if we want something to happen, we need to make it happen. Things are shitty right now, but they've been shitty for a long time. People are used to it." He smiled, a quick upward flick of his mouth. "Let's make things worse."

That got a reaction. Lehrer's arms uncrossed, hands grasping the edge of his desk. The way he looked at Noam now, it was like he was trying to see past his face and right into his mind. "What do you mean by that?"

"I mean, you need an excuse to take power, right? We can't let people get complacent. If we make Sacha seem terrible enough . . . tensions are high already. It wouldn't take a lot to push that over the edge." Noam caught himself fidgeting with the sleeve of his shirt and pressed his palms against his thighs. God, Lehrer was still looking at him like that, like . . . was this too far? Surely not. Lehrer and his brother did a lot worse during the catastrophe. Maybe the situations weren't comparable, but Lehrer was no saint.

Still, he didn't speak, so Noam had no choice but to keep going. "When people get angry enough, they'll protest. Not little skirmishes like what happened with Carolinia First, but massive, organized marches. Sit-ins. Strikes. Last time that happened—I was eight, but I still remember all the soldiers out on the street. Trying to prevent riots, right?"

Lehrer said nothing.

"But those are *your* men," Noam went on. "They're all Ministry of Defense. Shit gets bad, people protest, the army goes out to keep the peace, then—"

"Then things get even worse," Lehrer finished for him, his voice soft. "Bad enough to incite a riot. With my men already on the streets, we're positioned to isolate Sacha and his loyalists completely. We will deliver him to the people's justice."

Noam nodded. "And when you offer the Atlantians citizenship rights, they'll beg you to run for office." He couldn't help sliding that in there, but Lehrer didn't disagree, just grinned and straightened away from the desk.

"Very good," he said. "You have an intellect for politics, Noam. That will serve you well." He moved closer now, and closer again. Noam felt Lehrer's magic like this, a constant golden static.

"Tell me," Lehrer said, "what do you think we should do first?"

Noam told him.

And only after Lehrer drew Noam's holoreader out from his satchel and watched Noam put their plan into motion did Noam wonder if this is how it happened, how Lehrer won Carolinia the first time. If this was Lehrer's particular brand of utilitarianism: the first of many sins committed in the name of the greater good.

They had the battery fan up and running by the time Noam got to work the next weekend.

"It's hotter than Satan's house cat up in here," the girl on the previous shift said as she passed Noam the door keys, still waving a folded-up magazine toward her face. Her skin was as red as her hair. "Lord. They still got AC downtown?"

"Power's on everywhere east of the university."

"I swear they're fucking with us." She slapped the edge of the counter with the magazine and shook her head. "Look, I'm fixin' to take one of them water bottles—you won't tell Larry, right? He won't know better. Camera's dead."

"Go ahead," Noam said, and when she grabbed a bottle out of the cooler, she tossed him one too.

He usually liked to play around with scripts during his shifts at the store, mostly writing little games for himself—internet in the city wasn't good enough for activism—but for once he found himself adrift in this new analog sea. He had a book, but it was too hot to concentrate. His shirt plastered against his skin, and every time he moved, it dragged against his shoulder blades, waves of humidity swimming over his nape.

He held the water bottle to the side of his face, but that only felt cold for a second. His mind circled round and round its imaginary map of the slums. What if someone got sick? There were elderly here, children. If they weren't citizens, that meant they didn't have insurance.

How were they supposed to get medical care at a proper hospital? The tent clinics wouldn't have power, so there'd be no help there.

If people died, it was Noam's fault. He wasn't stupid enough to pretend he hadn't thought about this when he came up with the plan. He *was* responsible. Telling himself those victims were only hypothetical was lying.

Noam preferred the lie.

Two days. Just two days, then Lehrer would publicly denounce Sacha for failing to fix the problem in good time, would personally supply free generators to those in need.

Of course, generators wouldn't bring the internet back. That was the real endgame here. No email, no messaging, and most importantly, no news.

He picked up one of the pamphlets left behind by the girl who had the shift before him, although he had every word memorized.

THE TYRANNY OF HAROLD SACHA.

He and Lehrer spent a while making sure the wording was perfect. Lehrer had a hundred years' experience in rhetoric, so he knew what worked. Noam paid street kids ten argents to plaster these all over the city, and it'd been worth the price. Folks were talking. On his way in, Noam had spotted the pamphlets tucked into back pockets, stacked on the edges of food carts for customers to take, scattered in the gutters.

He'd also seen the immigration officials rounding up people two streets over, tagging them for deportation.

Right now, these pamphlets were the only link the refugees had to the outside world. Without internet, print *was* communication. Noam and Lehrer controlled the flow of information. And when that information said exactly what people wanted to hear, it could be very effective indeed.

The door opened and a fresh wave of heat poured into the store, bearing Brennan on its crest.

"I got your note," Brennan said.

Noam slid off the plastic desk chair. Standing upright put him a couple inches taller than Brennan, though it didn't feel like it when he was behind this counter. "I didn't mean to be cryptic," he said. "I just didn't think I could talk about this at the center."

And Lehrer would probably notice Noam going over there to meet with Brennan. There was that.

Then again, in his government suit, hair all gelled back, Brennan wasn't exactly flying under the radar coming here either.

"Yes, you haven't been to the Center in a while, have you? Linda mentioned it."

"I know. I'm sorry, things have been—" Noam waved his hand and made a face. "Never mind. Listen. I looked into the power outages. I read that people thought Sacha might be behind it, and . . . well, with my ability, that's an answerable question."

"Ah, yes." Brennan drummed his fingers atop the pamphlet on the counter. "I saw these. Noam, you shouldn't believe everything you read. They're just propaganda. There's no evidence Sacha had anything to do with the outages."

"That's what I wanted to talk to you about." Noam fiddled with the unscrewed cap of his water bottle. It wasn't real anxiety, just an affectation. He didn't want to come across too scripted, but he had to make sure Brennan walked away from this with the right ideas. Noam needed him pushing the refugees toward reaction, not acceptance. "It looked like failing circuit breakers. And there *was* a problem with the breakers, but it was caused by a rootkit installed in the electrical system mainframe. Somebody hacked the power grid and scheduled a massive blackout. *Then* the rootkit executed a script that made it look like a circuit breaker issue."

"I don't speak hacker, Noam."

"The point is," Noam insisted, clenching the water bottle cap in his free hand, "someone made the power go out on purpose. And they made it so it only affected the refugee zone."

Brennan frowned, gaze slipping down to the pamphlet, although he didn't pick it up. At first Noam thought he wasn't going to speak at all—like maybe Noam wasn't convincing enough, or Brennan just didn't *want* to believe him—but then he said, "Plenty of people don't like the refugees. How do you know it was Sacha?"

"Hacktivists sign their work. If you have a message, you want that message to get conveyed, right? So you take credit for whatever you did, either writing your name into the script or claiming it on social media or something. But not this. There's nothing on the rootkit about who wrote it or why, and no one's come out online taking responsibility."

"That's a stretch, Noam."

"It's *not* a stretch!" Noam slapped the bottle cap down onto the counter. "What other evidence do you want? Am I supposed to have traced it back to Sacha's home computer or something? I know he did it. Or more likely paid someone to do it. But he did it."

Brennan didn't so much as blink. "Even if that's true, I'm afraid there's nothing we can do. We're guests in this country, Noam. Fighting for better treatment is one thing. Fighting against the occupation, for better pay, for health insurance, even for citizenship—fine. But we can't depose a sitting chancellor."

I don't see why the hell not. "Fine," Noam snapped. Beneath his hand the bottle cap contorted, losing its shape to conform to the hills and valleys of his palm. Almost hot enough to blister. "Fight, then. You're the one among us with any kind of influence. Why aren't you doing something?"

For the briefest moment, Brennan looked pained. The expression was gone so quickly Noam might have imagined it. "There are rules. We have to work within those boundaries if we want to be taken seriously. I'll organize a protest. We'll march on the government complex.

This is how progress happens, Noam. It's slow and frustrating, but this is reality."

"Since when?" Sweat cut a slick line down the back of Noam's neck. Heat was a living thing pulsing beneath his skin like a second heartbeat. He sucked in a sharp breath, and the pen he'd been chewing on earlier rolled off the counter. The sound it made when it hit the floor was too loud. Violent. "The last time this country saw real change was in 2018, but I don't recall it taking all that long."

"A different time."

"Not that different. The Lehrer brothers' militia didn't do much peaceful protesting either."

Brennan's gaze went sharp. "Do I look like Calix Lehrer to you?"

"No. More's the pity."

Silence followed. It stretched out like saltwater taffy, until all Noam could hear was his own rage buzzing between his ears.

At long last, Brennan slid the pamphlet off the side of the counter and folded it along neat lines. It was wet; it had gotten caught in the puddle of condensation from Noam's water bottle.

"You're angry. I understand. We're all angry, Noam. But you should take care that anger doesn't blind you to reason." He paused, glancing down at the pamphlet even though the text was nearly unreadable now. "You've always been a bright boy. What happened to your parents was criminal, but now you have a chance to go back to school and make something of yourself. With the cards in your deck, one day you could effect real and lasting change in this country. Don't be shortsighted."

Brennan tucked the pamphlet into his jacket pocket. In its place he set down a few coins.

"For a water bottle."

After he left, it was several seconds before Noam could think to sit down. And then several more before he could concentrate to sharpen his power enough to cut the mutated plastic bottle cap off his palm.

Chapter Fifteen

A note, signed with Lehrer's name, waited for Noam after he finished field training one Saturday evening.

It wasn't in code, but it didn't have to be. Noam knew exactly what this was about, because yesterday he'd cut power to the west side again.

People were incandescent with rage. By the time Noam arrived and Lehrer was opening the study door, Noam'd read through the past six hours' worth of live updates on social media.

"Did you tell anyone you were coming?"

"No," Noam said. "Of course not."

Lehrer nodded once, then allowed Noam a small smile. "Then you'd better come in," he said, "before people start asking why I have teenage boys visiting my apartment in the middle of the night."

He gestured Noam into the study. Noam paid attention, again, when Lehrer undid the wards to his apartment, but they were as opaque as ever. *One day*, Noam thought, trailing his own bluish magic through Lehrer's characteristic gold. *One day I'll figure it out.*

Lehrer's apartment was cool tonight, the windows all thrown open to let the summer breeze ripple in past the curtains.

"How are people reacting to the power outage?" Lehrer asked him.

"As you might expect." Noam leaned to give Wolf the scratch behind the ears he demanded, Wolf's tail happily knocking against

Noam's leg. "They're furious. They'll be even angrier once they read the new pamphlets."

"Good. Would you like a drink?"

This time, Noam felt the magic in the air before Lehrer even gestured; a cabinet unlocked, and two glasses plus a bottle flew to hover in the air between them.

Interesting. So Lehrer really didn't need the gestures at all; they were just habit. Or perhaps not even that. A farce? If opponents thought Lehrer needed hand movements to perform magic, then they'd be watching for them, giving Lehrer the advantage.

"Have you tried scotch before?" Lehrer asked, pouring both glasses.

Noam shook his head.

"Well then, you're in for a treat. This is an Islay single malt—very peaty and very good. Smell it first."

Noam did. It felt like breathing in campfire smoke.

"Drink," Lehrer said.

The taste was much the same, a hot streak burning its way down the back of Noam's throat as he swallowed. Lehrer was watching; he wouldn't miss the heat that bloomed in Noam's cheeks.

"It takes some getting used to," Lehrer said, though when he took a sip it was with his characteristic control. "Please, sit. Relax. Can I get you anything else? Something to eat, perhaps, before we discuss our next move?"

"No. Thank you."

Noam wasn't the sort of person who ought to be holding a glass of expensive scotch and sitting on the defense minister's sofa. The friction between his world and Lehrer's scratched against his every nerve.

"Thank you, by the way," Lehrer said, claiming the armchair opposite. "For everything you're doing to help with this. I can't tell you how much I appreciate it."

"Oh—no, I'm happy to help." Wait, that sounded wrong. "I want Sacha gone as much as you do, I mean." Noam took a hasty sip of scotch to cover his embarrassment. It didn't burn so badly this time.

"Mmm. Adalwolf would have hated this whole plan. He never wanted me to take power."

The blood went still in Noam's veins. Lehrer so rarely talked about his brother. Noam felt like if he moved too suddenly, the moment would shatter.

Lehrer sipped his drink, eyes falling shut. He didn't seem like he was going to elaborate, so after a while, Noam said, "He was . . . wouldn't he be happy, though? To see what you've made of Carolinia." It felt false to say *he would have been proud* when Noam had never known him.

Lehrer made a vague gesture. "Adalwolf didn't live to see Carolinia established. A witching state . . . yes, he would have wanted that. But now? Overcrowded with the disenfranchised and headed by a baseline like Sacha? I don't think he would have liked that much at all."

"But he wouldn't like you ruling any better?" Noam asked, feeling oddly like he was questioning Lehrer's own past and half expecting Lehrer to scold him for it. "You'll return Carolinia to the way it was meant to be."

"Adalwolf was of the belief," Lehrer said, "that what I experienced in the hospital made me ill suited for leadership. He believed the trauma did irreparable damage to my mind."

Noam nearly recoiled, but Lehrer was perfectly calm, swirling scotch in his glass and swinging one foot idly.

"You don't do things by half measures," Noam said, battering down the anger that smoldered below his breastbone. Adalwolf Lehrer had been dead for a hundred years. "That's all."

When Lehrer smiled this time, it didn't reach his eyes. "Quite."

Noam didn't like that look on Lehrer's face. It was too strange, too—*mechanical.* As if it had been pieced together as carefully as the wards around this room.

He fumbled for something to say, anything else. He didn't want Lehrer to change the subject to the coup, not just yet, even if that's why Lehrer had brought him here. It felt like, in this moment, Lehrer had chosen to let Noam past the shields he had drawn around his private life. Noam didn't want that to end. "My . . . I don't think my parents would have liked me being here, actually. Not the coup; they'd have loved that. Being a witching, though."

"Really?"

Noam rubbed the edge of his thumb against the lip of his glass. "I don't know. I guess I'm not exactly part of the revolutionary proletariat anymore, am I?"

Lehrer's expression eased, something more human softening the edges of his mouth again. "I don't know if I'd say that," he said. "Consider yourself part of the proletariat vanguard in the Leninist sense. A professional revolutionary." He nodded at the room surrounding them, the faded wallpaper and worn curtains. "All this . . . it's ephemera. When I take power, it won't be for myself. I might be one man, but I represent a dictatorship of the proletariat."

"You know, I've read Lenin and I still think that sounds bad," Noam said, grinning.

"Have you?" Lehrer gave him an arch look. "Then you know the quote. 'Dictatorship does not necessarily mean the abolition of democracy for the class that exercises the dictatorship over other classes, but for the class over which the dictatorship is exercised.' The dictatorship of the proletariat is true social democracy."

Noam watched Lehrer over the rim of his glass. "Sacha was democratically elected, you mean," he said eventually. "But he's still a dictator because his power disenfranchises refugees and the working poor."

"Very good." Lehrer tipped his drink in Noam's direction. "Knowing that, how could your parents have been anything but proud? You are creating a future for this world, Noam. For refugees, for witchings, for anyone who has ever been oppressed by a system that saw them as tools or weapons but never people."

Noam's chest convulsed in a way that made him feel abruptly short of breath; he put the scotch down on the coffee table.

"You should have talked to my mom," he said after a second. "She was so passionate about Marxist theory. I couldn't keep up with her half the time, her mind moved so fast."

"And your father?"

"He was brilliant, but he wasn't into philosophy. 'Too much talking,' he'd say. 'Not enough doing.'"

Lehrer laughed. "Oh, Adalwolf would have said the same. He gave me such a hard time for reading books instead of spending extra time at the range. That I was a telekinetic who could *make* the bullet hit my target never seemed to factor into the argument."

Another hint from Lehrer's past. Noam seized upon it, like catching fireflies in the dark. "Was that your presenting power? Telekinesis?"

"Oh, no. I learned it early, though. I drove my parents mad sending the saltshaker dancing round the dinner table."

The image was comical, for all Noam had no mental image whatsoever of Lehrer as a child.

He tried picturing Lehrer his own age instead, sixteen, surviving what Lehrer had survived. Leading a coup. Sitting on a couch just like this one, with *State and Revolution* open on his knee and a cigarette held between his fingers.

Noam had the sudden urge to reach over and press his hand to Lehrer's wrist. He wondered what Lehrer would do if he did.

There was no chance to find out. Lehrer's smile faltered, and a moment later he set his drink aside and stood, narrowed eyes fixed on the door.

"What is it?" Noam asked.

"Sacha's outside."

The shell of that soft moment they'd shared cracked. Noam straightened, tension a sudden ache in his neck.

"You shouldn't be here," Lehrer said.

"It's eleven at night!"

"Chancellors don't abide by good manners." There was a cold set to Lehrer's expression that Noam didn't like one bit. Lehrer nodded toward another hall, this one heading away from the study and toward a darkened warren of rooms. "Second door on the right is Dara's room. Go in there and shut the door. Take your glass with you. Don't come out until I say."

Noam wasn't about to disobey. Even so, he couldn't resist looking back over his shoulder as he headed down the hall; Lehrer, in the middle of the room, stood as still and perfect as a black-and-white photograph.

The interior of the bedroom was dark, but even so, Noam could tell it was devoid of any of Dara's personal effects—Dara's room in name only, it seemed. Noam didn't dare turn on the lights. He just closed his eyes and leaned against the inside of the shut door, rebreathing his own humid air. Out there he sensed the movement of Lehrer's wristwatch across the floor and down the hall toward the study. Then Sacha's voice, with its gratingly perfect enunciation.

"Don't look at me like that, Calix. Aren't you going to invite me in?"

"It's very late, Chancellor."

Sacha chuckled. "And you've been trying to catch me alone for weeks now. Surely you won't pass up this opportunity."

Silence stretched out. Then at last: "Please. Come in."

Two pairs of footsteps headed down the hall this time. Sacha was wearing that crown of his; Noam sensed it. This time he let his power skim the curve of what felt to be a steel-and-copper circlet. There was magic there, too, oddly enough, green and glimmering.

Probably to keep the metal shiny.

Lehrer and Sacha headed for the sitting room. Lehrer's power sparked gold in the darkness behind Noam's shut eyelids as he conjured a flame.

"Cigarette?" said Lehrer.

"I don't smoke. As you know."

"Ah, that's right. Well, please, have a seat. Shall I offer you a drink?"

"How considerate of you. Gin and tonic."

Noam's own glass was slippery in his grasp; he caught it with telekinesis instead and sent it floating off somewhere into the room behind him. Did Lehrer know Noam could hear everything they were saying from here?

Heat flared from the other room, Lehrer taking a drag from his cigarette. "To what do I owe this rare pleasure?"

"I'm here on business, I'm afraid," Sacha said. "We were just informed that Atlantian workers are protesting the power outages, beginning tomorrow at eight. Apparently there's been some . . . incitement."

The pamphlets.

Noam's power hovered over Sacha's phone. How much trouble would Lehrer give him, he wondered, if he just wiped Sacha's data? Fused all the circuits, turned his phone into an expensive mess of metal?

He opened his eyes, but the darkness in the room was as heavy as ever.

"That's a problem for the Ministry of Labor," Lehrer said, milk-mild.

"Well, it's about to be your problem," Sacha said. "I've told your man Brennan that we'll have zero tolerance for further violence. If these strikes lead to any kind of problem, which I'm sure they will, I'll see the law enforced."

"And what does that entail?"

"I want a Ministry of Defense presence at all protests and assemblies. These people aren't citizens—if they disturb Carolinian peace, we can deport them to Atlantia. I'll institute a curfew, if necessary."

"Hmm. Imposing martial law over a few disgruntled refugees? Surely the situation isn't yet so dire."

"No more weakness, Calix. You've been trying to undermine my administration for years, but that ends now." Sacha made a harsh noise, like air being forced through a tight space. Uncharacteristic—he'd always struck Noam as the consummate politician, but now . . . "You can't control me anymore."

Lehrer crushed his cigarette coal into a metal tray and laughed. "That's right. You have a crown now, don't you?"

Sacha didn't respond to that. Noam's magic seethed just under the surface of his skin, and he clenched his hands, worried the static might escape into the ambient air. That Sacha might feel it.

After a moment, Lehrer said, "I believe some of my orders should still be in effect. You *do* remember them, don't you?"

"Doesn't matter. Not with this."

Lehrer's sigh was audible even from the bedroom. Noam twisted round in the dark and held out his hand for the scotch glass, finishing what was left of it in a single hard swallow.

This could only be a good thing. If Sacha started making mass arrests, it wouldn't be long before Brennan's restraint over the refugees fractured. Last time that happened, rioters burned a path halfway down Broad Street. Even the university shut down temporarily, all those bourgeois parents afraid to let their kids go to school near such hooliganism. Noam had been too young to join the protesters, but his father went.

"It's beautiful craftsmanship," Lehrer said at last, and for a moment, Noam didn't know what he was talking about. But then he felt fingertips—likely Sacha's, as he couldn't imagine the chancellor letting Lehrer get so close—touching the steel rim of the circlet. Noam could picture the look on Lehrer's face so clearly, the small smile and the emotionless eyes. "I recognize the handiwork."

The sofa shifted: Sacha, standing up. Noam felt him put down his glass on the end table as well, the click of crystal on wood. His voice, when he spoke, was incredibly calm, such a departure from just a few moments ago that Noam got mental whiplash.

"You know, Lehrer," Sacha said, "if you treated your toys better, maybe they wouldn't break so badly."

The silence that followed was lethal.

"You should leave."

"Yes, I think perhaps you're right. Thanks for the drink."

Noam didn't breathe until he heard Sacha's footsteps retreat down the other hall and the study door open—then shut—behind him. Even then he didn't move. In the sitting room, Lehrer stood. The nails in the soles of his shoes paced toward the window, then back again. Stopped.

Noam clutched the empty glass between both hands and shut his eyes.

"You can come out," Lehrer's voice said.

Noam sucked in a breath and opened the door with his power. His gaze met Lehrer's as he stepped out into the hall, Lehrer silhouetted against the sitting room with his hands in his pockets.

Words tumbled in the back of Noam's throat, but none felt right enough to say aloud. He put his glass down the first chance he got, Lehrer turning to allow Noam to move past him into the room.

"Sir," Noam said, when he couldn't stand it any longer.

"It won't be long now," Lehrer said. The tips of his fingers pressed against Noam's back, right between his shoulder blades, propelling him the last few feet farther into the sitting room. Even that small contact was a rush akin to standing on a high peak, looking down. Noam shivered and hoped to god Lehrer didn't notice. "We need to be prepared."

"Brennan won't let them riot," Noam said.

"We'll see about that."

Lehrer's hand fell away. In the absence of his touch, Noam felt both relieved and strangely bereft.

Noam turned to look at him, and Lehrer nodded. "Go on back to the barracks. I've kept you very late already, and you have basic in the morning."

He said it like an apology. For that, Noam gave him a smile. "All right. Good night, then, sir."

Dara was still awake when Noam got back. He sat alone in the den by the window, the book on his knee tilted toward the light. He looked up when Noam came in, folding down the corner of his page and slipping his feet off the seat cushion.

"Hey," he said.

"Hey." Noam toed off his shoes by the door. "You're up late for a weeknight."

"Couldn't sleep."

Noam edged around the coffee table so he could sit on the arm of the sofa nearest Dara's chair. The corner of Dara's lower lip was flushed, like he'd been chewing on it. "You have this problem a lot," he said. "You should talk to Howard. She could get you some kind of prescription."

"I have one," Dara said dryly. "But thanks for the suggestion."

Noam couldn't stop looking at that spot on Dara's lip. He wanted to lean over and kiss it, find out for himself if the flesh was as warm and swollen as it looked.

Concentrate.

Dara glanced away from him, turning his face toward the window. "I don't mind being up," he said. "It's a nice night. No clouds. You can even see Mars—look."

There was no way to look without sliding off his armrest and moving into Dara's space. But Dara seemed to want that. His hand caught Noam's wrist and tugged him closer, until Noam was leaning over him with his free hand braced against the windowsill, Dara's left thigh perilously close to Noam's groin, and, *fuck*.

Dara shifted in his seat, perhaps oblivious—but then again, perhaps not. His shoulder bumped Noam's, Dara squirming in the narrow space left between Noam's body and the armchair to face the window properly. Only then did he let go of Noam's hand.

Noam wanted to place it right there, at the small of Dara's back where his shirt rode up to expose a slice of naked skin.

"Do you see it?" Dara said.

Noam put his hand on the back of the chair instead. Just behind Dara's head, close enough that one of Dara's curls grazed the underside of Noam's wrist.

"No. Where?"

"East of the Lucky Strike tower. The reddish-looking star."

That wasn't what Noam wanted to look at. He looked anyway. And there it was—tiny, only slightly ruddier than its fellows, glinting like a dropped garnet in a field of diamonds.

"Now?"

"I see it," Noam said. His voice came out rougher than usual.

Dara smiled. The book slid off the seat of his chair and fell on the floor, and neither he nor Noam moved to retrieve it.

"It's strange," Dara murmured. He was still looking up at the sky, eyes overbright. "Any one of those stars could be dead now. And we'd never know."

Noam followed his gaze back out into the night. "Wouldn't we?"

"No. Not until it was too late. It takes thousands of years for light to travel from those stars to Earth." He exhaled softly, breath fogging the window glass. He looked so . . . happy, as if he'd swallowed one of those stars and it illuminated him from within. Noam was struck with the urge to capture this moment somehow, so Dara could relive it.

Noam slid one knee onto the seat cushion next to Dara's, half expecting Dara to push him away. He didn't. His hip was feverish hot against Noam's leg; his throat shifted as he swallowed—but he didn't move.

"Do you ever think about . . ." Dara started, then broke off. His hand tightened on the armrest, fingertips digging into the upholstery. "All of it—it's all random chance. The universe. Us. An infinite cascade of chaos. A series of impossible accidents is the only reason we even exist."

Noam hadn't thought about it. That was the sort of thing he'd known, on some level, but never *felt.* Not before Dara said it to him, like that, soft as a secret.

Dara had a way of making even the mundane extraordinary.

If he spoke, the moment might break. In the window light, Dara's face was glazed with silver. Juxtaposed with the amber lamplight on his hair, he was . . .

Noam had thought Dara was beautiful that night on the beach. That was nothing compared to this.

Dara looked at him, turning his head just enough that Noam could see the curve of his opposite cheek, the glint of both eyes.

If Noam kissed him right now, Dara would think Noam was just like everyone else.

And maybe Noam wasn't special, but he wanted to be. He had to be more than the next in line of a hundred men who wanted to have sex with Dara Shirazi.

"I'm glad you exist," he said.

Dara smiled. Looking at that mouth didn't help Noam's cause.

Noam forced himself to turn back to the window, staring at Mars glimmering from so very far away and not—*not*—at Dara.

"I'd better go to bed," he said, still looking out. He could see Dara, though, a blurry figure in his peripheral vision. "If I don't now, I never will."

"Go on, then," Dara said, not unkindly, and nudged Noam off the chair.

The room felt much colder than it had earlier, now that Dara wasn't pressed up against him.

Dara's legs unfolded into the space Noam had opened up, and he leaned forward to pick his book up off the floor, tucking it between his thigh and the armrest. When he met Noam's eyes, his face was perfectly unreadable.

"I'll still be here," Dara said, "if you change your mind."

Noam didn't—for better or worse.

Chapter Sixteen

From time to time, Lehrer brought Noam to his official office for lessons instead of the study. Those days, Dara wasn't invited, and they didn't spar—though Noam still had bruises from all the times Lehrer's magic threw him to the ground like it was nothing. Lehrer worked on business of state and Noam sat with his holoreader open atop crossed legs, uploading everything he could reach from Sacha's computer two offices down. He didn't bother sending them to Brennan anymore.

"People are angry," Linda told Noam as they scooped shepherd's pie onto dinner trays one Monday. "It's not in the papers, obviously, but people are furious about Sacha declaring martial law."

"How angry?" Noam murmured back. "Angry enough to fight back?"

"They do, sugar. We have protests every day now. But it's hard to protest properly when Sacha's got his soldiers out on the street keeping the peace and enforcing curfew." She slapped another dollop of shepherd's pie onto a plate. "I declare, I don't know what got into those kids last week, attacking a cop like that. It was supposed to be a peaceful demonstration."

Good thing they did, though, or else they might've been waiting forever for Sacha to find an excuse to declare martial law. Noam was sick of waiting. If they didn't do something, and soon, people would get complacent.

And it would be Brennan's goddamn fault when they died for it.

"Speaking of martial law," Noam said as he shoved his spoon back into the casserole dish. "Does Brennan have some kind of plan, or is he enjoying his cushy new job as government liaison too much to risk losing it?"

Linda shot him a look of disapproval. "Don't you start with that sass, Noam Álvaro. All of us have our roles to play."

And Noam's, apparently, was to take all the risks.

Linda's sharp elbow bumped against his ribs. "I think you have a visitor," she said and winked.

Noam looked up. Dara stood by the entrance, leaning back against the wall with his hands in his pockets, eyes fixed on Noam. Dara wore his cadet uniform, and the refugees gave him a wide berth—as if he might demand to see papers. After a moment, Dara drew one hand out of his pocket and waved.

"Friend of yours?" Linda asked.

"Sort of."

For Noam, seeing Dara here, outside the context of Level IV and firmly in Noam's world, was like suddenly losing balance. When he ladled the next serving of pie onto a plate, his hand shook.

Linda nudged him again. "He's cute."

Dara was too far away to see Noam's cheeks flush. But he nodded his head in Noam's direction before slipping out the door.

"I have to go," Noam muttered, and Linda didn't fight him on it as he stripped his apron off and ran out onto the street. He expected to find Dara leaning against the brick wall, cigarette in hand and something sharp to say, but he wasn't. Noam floundered for a moment, looking up the road past the bums with their change cups and the kids chasing a deflated soccer ball down the snowy gutter. And—there, a glimpse of Dara's uniform turning the corner up ahead.

Noam started after him, half jogging, and he broke onto the main street just in time to see Dara's head disappear into a cab. The car peeled away from the curb and left Noam standing there right as it started raining. The water soaked through Noam's shirt and crystallized cold in Noam's bones. He hugged his arms around his waist.

Why was Dara here?

Had he come to see Noam? If so, why hadn't he stayed or said something? Had Lehrer sent Dara to find him? Or was this something to do with whatever Dara got up to those nights he didn't come back to the barracks? Noam had always assumed he was out, in bed with some gorgeous stranger. But lately he'd started imagining Dara sitting in Sacha's office far past midnight, the pair of them plotting just as Noam and Lehrer did, Dara leaning over Sacha's desk with pen in hand, sketching the outline of Lehrer's demise.

It was a cold, wet walk back to the government complex; back in the barracks, Bethany and Taye and Ames were watching some old movie.

"Where's Dara?"

"I think he went up to the roof," Bethany mumbled through a mouth full of popcorn.

It's too wet to be on the roof, Noam almost said. Didn't, though, because then they'd all get caught up debating the merits of drowning to death, and he wasn't going to let Dara run off again.

The rain was falling more heavily by the time Noam got to the roof, as if the storm had been waiting for dusk to fall before it really hit.

Dara stood at the far end, leaning against the black iron railing, a dark smudge against the gray landscape. He wasn't wearing a raincoat. With his back to Noam he was a slim figure frozen in time, storm whirling around him unseen. He didn't look back when Noam started across the roof toward him.

The stone was perilously slippery beneath Noam's boots. He hugged his jacket tight around him, tugging the hood up to keep out the rain—for what little good it did. The market lights strung over the courtyard looked like blurry fireflies caught in a thunderstorm.

It was only when he reached Dara's side that Dara looked at him.

"Don't you think the weather's a little bad to be out here like this?" Noam said.

Dara was soaked through, hair plastered against his forehead and rainwater slick on his skin.

"I don't mind it," Dara said. His voice was soft, barely audible even though they were close. "We can go inside, if you'd rather."

Noam shrugged and grasped the railing, the steel cold beneath his palms as he looked out over the courtyard below. Four stories down, the stream cut through the flagstones, running faster with all the extra water. A lone soldier made his rounds, hunched over against the elements.

"You came to the Migrant Center today."

"Yes."

"You left pretty quickly." Noam glanced at Dara. "I don't suppose you were looking for a volunteer position."

Silence for a moment. Then: "No."

Noam waited, but more information didn't seem to be forthcoming. At last he gave up. "Well? Why were you there?"

Dara's hands visibly tightened around the railing, his body a straight line from his hips to the back of his neck. For a second Noam thought he might not answer at all, but then: "I knew you worked there sometimes," Dara said. "I . . . keep thinking about what you'd said, that night on the beach. About me being lucky."

Noam stayed silent.

"I wanted to see if you were right."

Noam's chest kept clenching uselessly, a dull pain humming beneath his sternum. The humid air felt suffocating even when he breathed it in. "And was I?"

Dara's mouth turned to a small and humorless smile. He looked at Noam again, raindrops glittering on his lashes, falling onto his cheeks when he blinked.

"I don't want you to think I don't sympathize with the refugees," Dara said.

"But you still support Sacha."

"Over Lehrer, yes." Dara sighed. "There are more than two sides to this story, Noam. What would you say if I told you Sacha didn't make these decisions on his own recognizance? What if he was just a character in someone else's play, and all this suffering and death was smoke and special effects distracting you from the real agenda?"

"I'd tell you those are *actual people* whose suffering and death you're talking about."

"Of course they're real," Dara said. There was an edge of sincere passion to his voice this time, his body turning to face Noam more fully even though his hands stayed frozen in place. "That makes it worse! Lehrer doesn't care about the refugees. He just wants Sacha as a convenient scapegoat so he can seize power."

Noam frowned. Dara didn't know about Lehrer's coup—right?

"Dara . . . if Lehrer wanted to seize power, don't you think he'd just do it? He controls the whole army. He wouldn't need a scapegoat."

"That depends," Dara said. "I think I know Lehrer somewhat better than you do, having had the past fourteen years to make his intimate acquaintance. He won't want power he has to take by force. He wants it *given* to him, the way it was when Carolinia was founded. He wants people to beg him to take over."

"Lehrer gave up the crown because he wanted to return power to the people. That's why we have a social democracy, Dara. I hate Sacha as much as anyone, but even I have to admit he was elected fair and square."

"No," Dara said flatly. "Sacha is a figurehead. Lehrer is in power now, just as he has *always* been in power. Absolute power."

Noam looked back down at the courtyard, which was empty now, even the soldier presumably having gone inside in search of shelter.

What if Dara was right?

What if all Lehrer cared about was control?

"That doesn't make any sense," he said eventually. "Why bother trying to be chancellor himself, in that case? If he already had absolute power as minister of defense, according to you, then he wouldn't need the title. Seems pointless to go through all this trouble."

Dara just shrugged.

"I take it you don't have a good answer to that, then."

"No. I have no idea why he'd want the title now. Maybe he feels like people don't appreciate him enough anymore. Maybe he hopes he'll finally figure out resurrection magic and bring his brother back and make him king instead. I don't know. It doesn't matter. It's still true."

Dara's words reached into the heart of Noam's last lingering doubts, twisting them into something larger: *What if Dara's right? What if Lehrer's just power hungry? What if we lose and the refugees are no better off and Lehrer blames it all on me?*

Dara leaned forward as though he was thinking about letting his body weight pull him over the railing and into the rain. Noam glimpsed the base of Dara's neck, where his skin vanished beneath the collar of his sweater, and swallowed.

"I'm glad you came, anyway."

Dara's weight dropped back onto his heels. "Why's that?"

Noam chewed his cheek, wishing he'd thought before he spoke. That he wasn't having to admit now, quiet and half expecting Dara to laugh in his face: "Because I'm always glad to see you."

He heard Dara's soft inhale, and for a moment time stood still, stretching out around them. The world had condensed down to the two of them, the patter-fall of water muffling everything else, and Noam was too aware of how close Dara was. If he leaned in just a few inches, their noses would touch. Dara's would be cold from being out here so long. But Noam imagined his lips would be warm.

Dara's eyes lowered—*looking at my mouth*, Noam realized with a shudder of exhilaration. Slowly, slowly, as if moving too quickly might shatter it all, Noam edged his hand closer to Dara's along the railing, until the edges of their fingers touched. It was perfect. The wind tugging them together, everything cold outside the two of them, golden market lights shimmering through the downpour. He'd never have a better moment, Noam knew, his pulse pounding in his temples. This was it. Noam should—

"We should go inside," Dara said, and just like that, the moment unraveled. Dara turned away, a small step taking him outside the circle they'd built around themselves.

"Oh," Noam said. His voice sounded stretched and surreal to his own ears. That warmth was gone, the aching chill in its place like poison darting through Noam's veins. "Sure. All right."

Dara started off across the roof, feet sure even on wet stone, leaving Noam to falter after him.

It was a silent descent down to the barracks, Dara two steps ahead of Noam on the stairs, the back of his neck wet and flushed. Noam tried to think about nothing at all. Not the shape of Dara's body beneath those sodden clothes, not how badly Noam wanted him, not how much Noam hated himself right now for being such an idiot.

Inside felt too hot. His clothes were freezing against his skin. Dara smiled as if nothing was wrong, laughing when someone made a comment about the trail of water they'd left behind them on the floor and heading off toward the showers.

Noam didn't want to follow him. He wanted to go into the bedroom and curl up still-soaked in his bed and sink through the mattress, through the floor, into the center of the earth.

He waited until he heard the bathroom door shut before he opened the door to the bedroom. For a moment he just stood there, staring at all the artifacts of their lives that he never paid attention to normally—Taye's rumpled sheets, the book on the floor by the head of Noam's bed, the bourbon he knew was hidden in a slit beneath Dara's mattress.

Had Noam imagined it? Was there no substance to the way Dara looked at him, no secret to his smiles?

He unlaced his boots using telekinesis and peeled them off, kicking them into a corner. His squelching socks joined them a moment later.

Ridiculous to think that Dara would be interested in someone like Noam when he could have anyone he wanted. *Had* anyone he wanted, from what Noam could tell.

Don't think about him. But Dara always found a way of creeping back in, like a persistent virus.

Noam had just started in on the buttons of his shirt when the bathroom door opened.

He spun around. His head pounded with too much blood, skin hot.

Dara stood in the open doorway, a watercolor painting with clothes plastered to his skin like streaked paint, the blur of his eyes beneath wet lashes. He was—angry, Noam thought, because why else would his mouth knot like that, or his pupils glint so brightly.

"What is it now?" he snapped.

Dara didn't answer. He stepped forward, water dripping in his wake, closer and closer until Noam moved back—but nowhere to go, nothing but the window glass pressing against his spine, freezing through his thin shirt.

When Dara touched him, his cold fingertips sliding over Noam's damp cheek, Noam shivered.

"Dara," he started.

Dara kissed him.

It—Dara's mouth, that was *Dara's mouth*, Dara's teeth catching his lower lip, Dara's hands twining in his hair, Dara's body, Dara's heartbeat against his chest.

The shape of him was both familiar and new. Familiar because he'd studied it in sidelong glances, in fantasies. New because none of Noam's fantasies did justice to the topography of Dara's ribs beneath his palms or the smooth plane at the small of his back, his body shifting muscle and shallow breathing, short nails digging into Noam's skull.

"Wait," Noam said—gasped, really, against Dara's open mouth, because what if this—he wanted Dara to *mean it*, for this to mean something, not just . . . not . . .

Dara drew back a fraction of an inch, just enough that Noam could see him properly. A bead of water cut a quick path down Dara's cheek. "You don't want me to wait," he said.

He was right.

This time Noam kissed him, surging forward and clasping Dara's perfect face between both hands, keeping him there where Noam could feel every part of him—including *that* part of him, which was hard and pressing against Noam's hip. Jesus.

Dara's fingers found the last of Noam's shirt buttons, pushing them free with expert efficiency. The cotton fabric stuck to Noam's skin—Dara had to peel it off him.

This was happening. This was really happening.

The window latch dug into Noam's back. He didn't care. He didn't care about anything but the way Dara touched him like he couldn't get enough, his mouth at Noam's neck and kissing its way toward his collarbone. Noam dragged the hem of Dara's shirt up, off, over his head. Dara's hair was a mess now, looked like he'd already had someone twist their fingers into the curls, like he'd already done unspeakable things.

Noam made a soft, desperate sound, and Dara smiled, a sharp little expression that suggested he knew exactly what he was doing.

"Come on," Dara murmured. His thumbs hooked into Noam's belt loops, tugging him forward one step, another.

Belatedly, Noam locked the door. It was a distracted, careless bit of magic that probably melted the latch. Whatever. That was a problem for later, when Dara wasn't half-naked in front of him saying things like *come on* and pushing Noam back onto one of the beds and shoving down his trousers and, and . . .

"The light?" Noam murmured against Dara's mouth, once Dara crawled onto the bed after him and straddled his hips. He held Noam there with his hand on his chest, thumb pressing into the hollow of Noam's throat. It was ever-so-slightly uncomfortable, each breath pushing back against the weight of Dara's hand.

"No," Dara said and nipped at Noam's lip before he drew back, hands finding Noam's belt buckle.

"What?" Noam smirked. "Are you afraid of the dark?"

Dara glanced up, raised a brow. "Something like that."

Any other day, Noam would never let him live that down. Today, he had Dara's bare skin beneath his palms. He wasn't saying anything to put that in jeopardy.

Noam grasped him by the hips and pushed him over onto his back instead.

Dara was born to lie on mussed bedsheets with wet hair spilling like an ink stain onto white pillows, flush cheeked. Noam could use his power to undo Dara's fly, but he didn't want to, wanted to use his hands, rubbing the pad of his thumb against the brass buttons and pressing his palm against what was underneath that fabric.

"I don't want you to think I'm just like all the others," Noam said, hesitating there with his hand in Dara's lap and Dara frowning expectantly up at him, Dara's fingers loosely curled round Noam's wrist.

"I know you're not," Dara said.

"I'm not going to fuck you and then just—"

"I know."

"I like you, and I want . . . I need to make sure you know that, because—"

"Noam."

Noam stopped talking.

Dara arched up to kiss his chest, and Noam pushed the last button free on his fly. He tugged Dara's trousers down, then off, and smoothed his hands over Dara's skin. He kissed the inside of Dara's knee, the dusky bruises on his thigh where some other lover held him a little too hard—Dara shivered when Noam did that—his hip bone, the flat plane beneath his navel. Dara was warm, still rain-damp, and smelled like bourbon and boy.

"Just fucking *do* it," Dara gasped, and it was the first time Noam had ever heard Dara say the word *fuck*, and he didn't have it in him to disobey.

Afterward, Dara kissed him openmouthed and hot and messy, grasping at Noam with both hands like he'd die if he didn't have more—more of that, of Noam.

And as it turned out, Dara's mouth was good at more than just talking.

Later, when their hair was nearly dry, they lay tangled up in the narrow twin bed, Noam's fingers laced into Dara's curls. Dara tracked a trail of languid kisses along Noam's sternum.

Noam had been with boys before, but Dara was definitely the most experienced. A part of Noam felt awkward in comparison, like a child pretending to be grown up.

"Don't," Dara murmured and bit him just beneath the collarbone.

"Don't what?"

"You're overthinking things," Dara said. He lifted his head, propping his chin against Noam's chest. "I can tell."

Noam made a face at him, but there was no point denying it. Dara's forefinger traced little patterns on his skin, as if oblivious to the way that made Noam's heart stumble.

"All right. I won't overthink things." He skimmed his hand down Dara's side instead, again incredulous that Dara's skin could be so smooth. "You have been with a lot more people than I have, though."

"So?"

"So . . ." Noam turned the words over on his tongue, not sure how to phrase this. They felt unwieldy, like holding stones in his mouth. He looked at Dara and bit the inside of his lip until it hurt. "I know this doesn't mean we're together. I know you're not really a relationship person."

Dara's mouth flattened. "What is that supposed to mean?"

"I just mean . . . I mean, you like to . . . I don't know, Dara. It's pretty clear you're not into relationships. That's all."

But Dara had already pushed himself upright, twisting one hand in the bedsheets.

"I can fuck whomever I want."

"Of course you can," Noam said, baffled. "I'm not saying you can't."

He ignored the part of himself that felt like it was withering just saying so, hearing Dara talk about *wanting* to fuck other people—it wasn't like Noam thought he and Dara were, would be . . .

Dara wasn't a monogamous person, maybe, which was fine. But.

"I can't not say something, Dara. I'm sorry. But you have bruises on your leg, and on your ribs, and here . . ." He reached for Dara's arm, to brush fingertips against the yellowing marks just above the elbow, the ones Noam hadn't noticed until Dara had his head down between Noam's thighs.

Dara jerked his arm out of reach.

Noam put his hand back on his own knee, safe. "I'm not going to be a shitty friend and pretend not to notice."

"Maybe you'd rather whisper sweet nothings in someone's ear and have boring, predictable sex, but not all of us aspire to such bland heights."

Wait. Did Dara think Noam was boring?

Noam bit the inside of his lip, suddenly adrift in an uneasy sea. He didn't know how to respond to that. "Okay. So someone gave you those bruises during sex?"

Dara's cheeks flushed darker than Noam had ever seen them before. For a moment Noam was so sure Dara was going to—hit him? Curse at him? *Something*. But Dara swung his legs off the edge of the bed and grabbed for his trousers instead, movements jerky and inhuman.

Noam sat up, abruptly conscious of his own nakedness. "*Dara.* Please just talk to me."

Dara rounded on him again with flashing eyes and his shirt gripped between both hands. "I *do* talk to you. I talk to you all the time, Álvaro, but you never listen."

"Okay, like when? You don't say *shit*, Dara. I feel like I barely fucking know you sometimes, and that's not for lack of trying."

Dara jabbed one finger at Noam's chest. "I try to tell you about Lehrer."

"That's such bullshit, Dara, and you know it. Just because I don't agree with you—"

Dara hurled the shirt onto the floor so violently that Noam startled where he sat, knocking back against the headboard. "Shut the *fuck* up. If I have to listen to you justify your own willful ignorance one more time—you—" He dragged a hand back through his hair too roughly, fingers tugging at the messy curls. "I try to tell you, but I *don't* tell you, do you understand? You think you know everything, but you know nothing, you know absolutely nothing. It's not about you agreeing with me. Lehrer—"

"I don't want to hear it, Dara. I swear to god. I don't want to hear it."

"Oh, believe me," Dara snapped, "*I know.*"

Okay. Okay, fine—*fine*. Noam shoved the bedsheets aside and got to his feet, heat flooding his whole body in an unexpected wave.

"You wanna talk about some fucked-up shit? All right. Yeah. Let's talk about that, because you've known about Ames's dad for I don't even know how long, and you haven't done shit about it."

Noam was taller than Dara when they were both standing straight, and right now he needed that. He needed the way Dara took a half step back when Noam crossed his arms over his chest, that brief retreat like a victory, fuel for Noam's anger.

"You won't shut up about Lehrer and his hypothetical corruption or *whatever*, but there's somebody in government we both know is corrupt. You made me keep quiet about it. You said you'd handle it. Well? What have you done, Dara? Because as far as I can see, you're content to let a murderer sit as home secretary and do nothing."

"I told you I'd handle Gordon Ames, and I will. That's not the point, Noam!"

"You have a point? Well, thank god for that."

The noise Dara made was wild, derisive and deranged all at once. He spun on his heel, striding toward the door—but as soon as he reached the other end of the room, he just turned round and paced back again. If Noam weren't so furious he might be worried, because Dara . . . Dara didn't look well. He looked like someone who hadn't slept in a week, manic and fevered.

"You—god, you're so stubborn, and I—that's what I love about you, it *is*, but it's the *worst* thing about you, because now I can't. If I, if you know, and he knows—knows you know—there're some things I just can't say, Noam. There—I won't be the reason you die!" The last part burst out of him like a dam breaking, and Dara pressed both hands to his face, nails digging into his brow.

"Dara . . ."

Noam moved toward him, carefully this time—like Dara might bolt if he moved too quickly. Dara was shivering. Noam reached out, his hand hovering there, uncertain. When he finally touched him, Dara's skin was hot and dry.

"It's okay," Noam said slowly. He let his hand settle more firmly where it was, palm against the sharp wing of Dara's collarbone where it met his shoulder.

Dara slapped at his wrist, knocking Noam's hand away. This time when he looked at Noam, his eyes gleamed with something more than just anger. Dara rubbed the heel of his palm against his damp cheeks, not that it did any good. "It's not."

"All right. It's not. Do you want to . . . we can talk about it. I promise I'll listen."

Dara laughed, low and bitter. "No. It's fine. I'm going to shower."

It felt like his chest was caving in, organs crushed, even if Dara hadn't said anything worse than what he already had. It wasn't what Dara said, anyway. It was that Dara didn't think there was anything he *could* say. That Dara was picking his shirt back up off the floor and walking away. That Noam stood there, naked in the middle of this room, and watched him go and didn't stop him.

Noam took a shower in the girls' bathroom with permission from Bethany and Ames, changing into dry clothes and waiting out in the common room for twenty minutes, thirty, just in case Dara needed the time alone.

But when he finally returned to the bedroom, Dara was already gone.

Chapter Seventeen

Noam saw the headline before anyone else. He'd been reading the news while he waited for his coffee to brew, print paper in one hand and the other reaching into a box of salted crackers. The front page was taken up by a story about an anti-Sacha attack down south in Charleston, twelve confirmed dead.

A terrorist attack meant the other story was pushed to the second page, as otherwise it would have been the top headline in every paper. A small banner on the first page declared the news:

HOME SECRETARY ASSASSINATED. Turn to p. 2.

Noam tore the paper open so quickly he nearly ripped the corner off.

A color photograph of the man took up half the second page; Gordon Ames wore his military uniform, the medal awarded for bravery pinned to his breast.

Noam put down his half-eaten cracker.

> . . . Ames, 49, is survived by his brother Henry
> Ames and his daughter, Carter Ames . . .

"Have you seen this?" Noam said when Bethany emerged from the hallway, already wearing her drabs and boots.

Bethany held out a hand, beckoning. Noam passed her the paper. "Oh no," Bethany murmured as she scanned the article. "Poor Ames. I guess that explains why she wasn't here this morning."

Never mind that. Ames was probably thrilled.

Noam did his best to look dismayed, but he had to keep biting back the twitch at the corners of his lips.

General Ames was dead.

That lying, murdering son of a bitch was *dead.*

It was a pity Noam wasn't the one who killed him, but whatever, the outcome was the same. That's what mattered.

"I'm gonna check on Dara," Noam said.

Noam left Bethany with the paper, skipping a little on the off step as he headed down the hall toward the bedrooms. The door to the bathroom was shut, thankfully. From the sound of it, Taye was taking a shower. Dara was a lump beneath his bedsheets, face turned to the wall and his hair a dark halo against the sheets.

Dara would forgive Noam for waking him when it was news like this.

He crouched on the floor by Dara's bed and set a hand on his shoulder, shaking him as lightly as he could. "Dara," he whispered. Dara didn't move. *"Dara."*

Dara mumbled something indistinct and swatted at Noam's hand.

"What?"

"Let me sleep," Dara said, curling tighter beneath the covers.

It was Sunday, but it wasn't like Dara to sleep in. He'd come back late last night, long after Noam had gone to bed. They hadn't talked about what had happened in this same room, bare skin on skin, all those soft little noises muffled against each other's mouths.

Or what came after that.

Noam frowned. "It's eight thirty."

"I don't feel well."

Noam couldn't see Dara's face from here. Just his hair, a messy tangle on the pillow. Noam wanted to twist one of those loose curls around his finger. *Inappropriate. You're supposed to be announcing a murder.* And Dara was possibly—probably—still angry.

"You need to get up anyway," Noam said after a moment and squeezed his arm. "I have to talk to you. It's important."

Dara rolled over, eyes opening to narrow slits. Noam could just barely see the glimmer of black irises. He *looked* sick, or maybe just exhausted, green-tinged with both hands clutching the bedsheets.

For a moment, Noam thought about Lehrer's brother—about Adalwolf, gone fevermad.

Only Lehrer wouldn't let that happen to another person he loved. Right?

Noam was thinking that maybe he'd better let Dara sleep awhile longer and evade another fight when Dara finally sighed and opened his eyes all the way, shoving down the duvet and sitting up.

"Okay," Dara said. He patted the bed next to him, and Noam . . . he hesitated for a second, heart doing something painful. Yesterday Dara said *shut the fuck up* and left and didn't come back. But Noam couldn't keep squatting on the floor either, so he took the invitation for what it was and sat with one knee pulled up onto the mattress, body angled toward Dara. The bed was still warm.

"I read in the paper this morning . . . ," Noam started, but that felt so impersonal. He tried again, unsure if he should seem pleased about this or if Dara might . . . be upset, perhaps, because he and the general had been close. "Dara, Ames's father was assassinated last night."

Dara just kept staring at him, slim fingers braided together in his lap.

"He's . . . dead," Noam said. Just in case that hadn't been clear.

Dara closed his eyes. He was trembling. Noam couldn't see it, but, sitting this close, he could feel it. "Did the paper say how it happened?"

"It . . . well. They say he was stabbed to death."

He watched Dara carefully, marking each minute shift in expression. Dara ducked his head, and Noam couldn't see his face anymore. One unsteady hand dragged through his hair.

The reaction didn't seem faked. But it sure was a mighty big coincidence—that last night Noam accused Dara of doing nothing, and now the general was dead.

But did Noam think Dara could really commit *murder*?

If the papers were true, then Dara went into that house, where Ames Sr. thought he was safe, and he stabbed the general sixteen times.

Noam edged closer, his touch drifting to Dara's knee. He wanted to reassure him, somehow—but that was all it took to push Dara over the edge. Dara leaned against Noam's shoulder, whole body shuddering now as he . . .

He was crying, Noam realized. Dara was crying.

Very carefully, Noam wrapped his arms around Dara's body and just . . . held him there, while both of Dara's hands took fistfuls of his shirt and clung on tight. He was feverish hot; Noam could feel it even through the sweater Dara wore. It was like holding on to a live coal.

"It's going to be all right," Noam murmured against Dara's ear, even though he had no way of knowing that was true. "He deserved it. You know that. I would have killed him myself, if you had let me."

Dara didn't tell him to fuck off, though, and didn't pull away. His weight leaned against Noam's chest, one of Dara's hands abandoning Noam's shirt to press against the base of his skull instead. Gently, so gently, Noam stroked Dara's back and wished he was better at this. He had no idea what he was doing, if he was comforting Dara in his grief, or if Dara just . . .

"Is there anything you need?" Noam asked eventually. His shoulder was damp, Dara still curled in against him and smelling like stale cigarette smoke. "Can I get you something?"

Dara lifted his head slowly. His eyes were so bright, almost glassy. Then he kissed Noam, soft lips pressing against Noam's mouth, his hand on Noam's hip. It was—Noam nearly lost his balance, but Dara's power caught him, some invisible telekinetic force pressing up on the small of Noam's back. He . . . he . . .

He kissed back. What else could he do? He slipped his fingers into Dara's sleep-tangled hair, keeping him close. Softer, it was *softer* than Noam had remembered. Dara climbed into his lap, Dara's firm thighs straddling Noam's hips, his tongue in Noam's mouth.

"Dara," Noam started, though he couldn't think what he was going to say.

It was . . . fast. *Too fast*, Noam thought. Too much. He tasted salt on his tongue, Dara's tears.

"Stop," he said, gasping.

Dara didn't stop. He just kissed Noam again, body moving against Noam's like he wanted everything Noam had to give. Noam hated himself in that moment, but he reached for Dara's wrists anyway, pushing his hands away and pulling back from the kiss.

"I'm sorry," Noam said. "But you . . . not now. I can't. I'm sorry."

He couldn't have sex with Dara when Dara was like this. Not when Dara had been so eager to avoid him last night. How did he know Dara wanted *him*, and not just distraction?

Dara wet his lips, wide eyed and staring at Noam like he'd never seen him before. Noam still held on to his wrists, but Dara didn't try to draw them away.

"You're in shock," Noam said when it was clear Dara wasn't going to speak.

A small, tremulous smile flitted over Dara's mouth, something almost self-deprecating. "I thought you wanted me."

"Dara—"

Noam had never seen Dara lost before, but that was the only word for the way he looked in this moment. His hands were limp where Noam held on to his wrists, and the longer Noam kept touching him, the more uncomfortable he felt. He let go.

Dara looked down, where he still sat splayed across Noam's lap. He made a soft noise in the back of his throat, half a snort. "I guess this is why you're a good person."

Enough of this.

"Dara," Noam said again, quieter this time. He placed both hands on Dara's thighs, because if he touched his face, Dara might flinch. "You didn't come back last night."

Dara said nothing. His damp cheeks were flushed.

"We argued, and I told you—you said you'd take care of General Ames, and then you left, and you didn't come back, and now he's dead."

Dara lifted one hand, slid his fingertips along the backs of Noam's. Noam kept his hand still, so still.

His heart beat a strange rhythm, lungs tightening when he tried to inhale.

"Dara, tell me."

Dara's gaze flickered up at last. He was so—he was *so* close, his weight atop Noam's lap, lips still red and kiss bitten. "I think it's better if I don't say anything at all."

Noam squeezed Dara's thighs—he couldn't not, a reflex gesture that made Dara tremble.

He did it. He really did it.

Dara killed General Ames.

That knowledge thumped in Noam's chest like a second heartbeat, arrhythmic and sickening. For a moment, when he shut his eyes, all he could see was the general's body lying in a pool of his own blood.

But then Noam looked back to Dara, whose cheeks were as ashen as a magic victim's.

"Good," Noam said, surprising himself with the viciousness of it. "He deserved it."

"Noam . . . please."

"I mean it. You did the right thing."

Dara looked stricken. And maybe Dara felt guilty for killing a man, but Noam refused to reinforce that. The general deserved it. (He deserved it. *He deserved* it.) Noam smiled at Dara and turned his hand palm up on Dara's leg, twining their fingers together.

"You did clean up after yourself, right?" Noam thought to ask after a second, because, god, the last thing they needed was Lehrer's department finding Dara's prints all over the crime scene.

"I told you I don't want to talk about it." Dara disentangled his hand and, after a moment, slid off Noam's lap. He retreated to the corner of the bed, back against the wall and knees drawn up to his chest. He watched Noam from that safe distance, wary, like Noam might lurch forward at any moment.

"Fine," Noam said, holding both hands up in surrender. He started rebuttoning his shirt, telekinesis clumsy on the metal button backs. Dara sat in silence the whole time, expression closed off. "I'll leave you alone, if that's what you want."

Dara nodded once.

The mattress creaked as Noam's weight shifted off. He glanced back at Dara, who hadn't moved.

He wanted to say something else.

There was nothing else to say.

So he did what Dara wanted: he left.

Chapter Eighteen

Dara slept the rest of the day, emerging only to steal toast around three before retreating to his self-imposed isolation. Noam avoided the bedroom as much as possible. The one time he went in to get a book, Dara was sitting on the bed in his drabs, and the way he'd looked at Noam when Noam came in, it was—

Well. It made Noam want to do inappropriate things to Dara, situation be damned.

But if Noam hoped to talk to Dara the next day, those hopes were dashed when Lehrer rescheduled his meeting with Noam for early morning. He didn't invite Dara, because it wasn't a lesson. Not this time.

Lehrer looked like he hadn't slept. There was a gauntness to his face, like his bones were finer than before—a hunger. He had a mug of black coffee in one hand as he paced the length of his study. Noam sensed the sparking threads of magic that kept the coffee from spilling out of its cup and onto Lehrer's uniform, thin live wires enmeshed over the ceramic rim.

"I'm sorry for your loss," Noam said when Lehrer was on his eighth lap and showing no signs of slowing down, or indeed acknowledging Noam at all. "General Ames was your friend, right?"

"Yes," Lehrer said, finally. He stopped at the end of the ninth pace, turning to face Noam and setting the coffee down. "He was. A close friend, in fact. I'd known him since he was a child."

Noam nodded as if he understood. "I'm sorry," he said again. "Please tell me if there's anything I can . . . do."

Lehrer watched him with cool eyes.

For a single reeling moment, Noam had the sense that Lehrer *knew*, somehow—that he knew just by looking that Noam wasn't sorry at all.

Lehrer said, "Actually, there is. Gordon's funeral is this afternoon. I want you to attend."

So soon? General Ames had just been murdered—why were they rushing him into the ground?

"I didn't . . ." Noam started to say, *I didn't really know him* but thought better of it at the last second. "Of course. I'll go."

"Good. You'll be my second set of eyes. Report anything and anyone suspicious; Gordon's killer will be there."

Yeah, no kidding. Of course Dara would be there—General Ames had doted on him, practically saw him like his own son, to hear Ames tell it. But what was Noam supposed to report back to Lehrer? *Yeah, I paid attention, but no one was acting weird; sorry I can't be of more help?*

"How do you know?"

"It would have been someone he knew. He was killed in his own bed. If not his daughter, then perhaps a lover." Lehrer tapped his fingers on the edge of the table where he'd put his coffee, *one-two-three*. "We arrested Carter this morning. I spent some time interrogating her personally, but I'm convinced of her innocence. Her alibi is solid, and she told me she wasn't involved in the murder. She couldn't have lied to me."

Lehrer sounded far more confident about that than Noam thought was warranted, but then again, Noam didn't want to imagine what was involved in Ministry of Defense interrogations.

There was no warning Dara. He was gone when Noam got back to the barracks. Noam waited around, sitting at the common room table, shuffling and reshuffling the same deck of cards as if setting up a poker game might somehow summon Dara. But then it was past three, Dara wasn't back, and Noam had to go meet Lehrer for the funeral.

Lehrer had another coffee as he slid into the car, this one in a thermos, but he looked like he'd pulled himself together sometime between their lesson that morning and now. The circles under his eyes were gone, hair combed in its usual neat style. Only the tension between his shoulders betrayed the truth.

"Are you all right, sir?" Noam asked eventually, when they were stuck in traffic.

"I know about as much as I did this morning."

Noam tugged at the cuff of his sleeve, pressing it against the side of his thumb hard enough it blanched the skin. "So it could be half the people in Carolinian high society."

Lehrer shook his head. "I have my ideas," he said, "but I can't prove them. Not yet."

He reached over with one hand and grasped the corner of Noam's collar between thumb and forefinger, adjusting its angle. Noam stayed still, let him, and wished desperately that he could peer inside Lehrer's mind in this moment and see—what was he thinking? He'd been talking about lovers, but he hadn't said anything about the obvious alternative: a surrogate son, who would easily have been allowed anywhere in the home secretary's mansion.

Was Lehrer so blinded by his affection for Dara that he couldn't guess?

Noam swallowed against the sudden queasiness in his stomach and turned his face toward the window as the car drew up in front of the house. Attendees had spilled onto the back lawn, their cell phones and wristwatches a low hum to Noam's magic.

He followed Lehrer out of the car and up the drive. In the foyer, the mahogany display tables lining the walls bore antique vases overflowing with anemones and lilies. The smell was sickly sweet.

"Sign the guest book," Lehrer instructed, gesturing to one of the tables. Noam added his name below those of major generals and ministers, and Lehrer signed beneath that, bracketing him in.

It wasn't difficult to figure out where they were meant to go; they followed the sound of voices. Even with their chatter muted, out of respect for the dead, there were enough people present that Noam could hear them all the way out at the entrance. Noam spotted Ames, almost immediately, in the sitting room. Mourners clustered around her like iron filings to a magnet.

Lehrer conveyed his condolences. Noam waited just behind him, not quite able to see Ames's face given Lehrer's height but able to hear her voice responding, soft and low. And, if Noam wasn't mistaken, with the faintest edge; Ames probably still smarted from her arrest by Lehrer's department. It was only after Lehrer moved away, drawn into conversation by one of the other well-wishers, that Ames saw him.

"Oh," Ames said. "Hi." She sounded tired. Looked it too.

"I was sorry to hear about your father."

Ames snorted. "Don't give me that bullshit, Noam."

"Okay, I won't. But I didn't think you wanted me saying, 'Oh, what a relief your dad's dead now' when you just got done being accused of his murder."

"Thanks," Ames said and actually laughed a little. "Hey. Do me a favor and stay here and pretend you're talking to me for a while? I can't stand playing polite with these obsequious old fucks anymore."

"Sure," he said, following when Ames gestured for him to sit in one of the empty armchairs.

Ames took the seat next to it, stretching her legs out along the floor and resting her head back. For a moment she was silent, long enough that Noam wondered if she was actually going to say anything or if his presence here was enough. Then: "I didn't do it, for the record."

"Do what?"

"I didn't kill my father." She glanced over at Noam. "God knows he deserved it, though," Ames went on, earning a carefully blank stare from Noam. "Can't say I'm surprised someone finally did him in."

"Who?" Noam said, widening his eyes just a little. Innocent. "Do you think it was political?"

Ames's lips twisted. "It was probably someone sympathetic to the refugees, considering all the legislation my dad helped enact against Atlantian citizenship. Anyone who might want to undermine Lehrer's government."

The undermining Lehrer part sounded about right. Where was Dara, anyway? Noam was afraid to look around too obviously; Lehrer had a way of seeing everything that happened in his vicinity.

Ames sat upright, her mouth white around the edges. "It wasn't me. You believe me, right?"

"Of course I believe you. And so does Lehrer, or he wouldn't have let you go."

Ames didn't look convinced, but she didn't argue. "Whatever. Fuck 'em—I don't care." She reached into her jacket pocket and pulled something out—a flask. She unscrewed the top and took a long swallow, then offered it to Noam. "Want some?"

Noam shook his head, and Ames drank again, more this time. Noam was surprised the flask wasn't empty when Ames finally lowered it.

"I think your dad's looking for you."

Noam must have seemed confused—he *was* confused—but Ames pointed, and he saw Lehrer standing on the other side of the room, watching them. Lehrer didn't beckon, just inclined his head slightly before turning back to his conversation with Major General García.

Right. Noam should be talking to other people, not just Ames, especially since Lehrer already believed she was innocent. He had to at least *act* like he was looking for a killer.

"See you, then."

The funeral itself was at four thirty, which meant a long time lingering around these ornamental rooms. Noam occupied himself with the refreshment table, eating bite-size tartlets and fresh fruit. *Maybe*, he thought as he munched on a miniature quiche, *I ought to slip off to the private parts of the house and make sure Dara hasn't left any evidence*. The Ministry of Defense would have been through here already, of course, but they wouldn't all be witchings. There might be something they missed. Something they might come back and find.

He waited until Ames came into the room, attention shifting to focus on the bereaved, then stepped over the velvet rope blocking off the hall.

The house was empty and dark, now that Noam had put some distance between him and the wake. The light streaming in through the windows insufficiently illuminated the portraits of austere white men in military uniforms and priceless landscape paintings. On the second floor Noam opened the doors one by one to look inside, using his power so he wouldn't leave fingerprints on the knobs. He didn't waste much time on the guest bedrooms or Ames's room, just kept going until he found the master suite.

The bed, king size and white, was neatly made, the dresser tops all swept clean of dust and personal effects alike. At first Noam just stared at it, because . . . well, if reports were to be believed, this was where Ames Sr. was killed.

Sixteen times.

There was no blood. Someone did a very thorough job cleaning up. Still, it felt like the scene of an assassination ought to be more dramatic.

A small bookcase sat near the vanity: mostly pulp novels, which was surprising, but Noam supposed that explained why they were kept here and not on display downstairs in the library. In the bedside table he found a carton of cigarettes, a strip of condoms, and lube.

There was no computer in the bedroom, but Noam sensed one down the hall, its circuit boards quiet now, powered down. He found it in the general's study, a smaller room with drawn curtains and an oak desk, an iron poker leaning against the cold hearth.

He seriously doubted Dara had taken a second after killing General Ames to check his email, but he couldn't pass up this opportunity with the general's computer right there. The cell drive was probably full of shit Noam could leak on the site.

If Noam was extra lucky, maybe he could even find a way to pin the general's murder on Sacha's supporters.

Noam told the computer to turn itself on and took a seat in the comfortable leather chair behind the desk, feeling the processor work as it loaded the desktop and programs.

An empty flopcell was stuffed away in one of the drawers. Noam plugged it into the drive and told the computer to start copying the documents folder to the chip, then open the folder on-screen for Noam to view. He had to do all the work via technopathy, since he hadn't brought gloves and couldn't risk touching the keyboard.

He went through General Ames's financial records first. Pretty normal: food expenses, salaries for the household staff. But then there was the money he spent at the liquor store, nice restaurants, expensive hotels. *Local* hotels—maybe Lehrer had been right about the general having a lover, if nothing else.

But this was looking more and more like a personal computer; Noam found very few documents relevant to the general's job as home secretary. A few memos here and there, things he obviously intended to take care of back at the office. Reports from Swensson about his daughter's bad behavior.

The clock on the bottom right-hand corner of the screen said it was just past three thirty. Noam had spent too much time here. He needed to move on. But if there was going to be something here . . . something actually *useful* . . . it might not be on the desktop. You didn't get to be home secretary by being an idiot, after all. Anything good would be hidden.

Noam let the flopcell continue downloading desktop files, but he turned his attention deeper. There were some pretty thorough ways of deleting files, but when Noam had worked in the computer repair shop, half the customers came in for disk recovery. Some stuff was more difficult to recover, and the shop commensurately charged a lot more for it, but at the end of the day, the only way to really get rid of a file was to destroy the cell drive completely.

The general hadn't done that.

And . . . *yes*.

General Ames had covered his tracks—that was for sure. He'd not only deleted files; he'd also reformatted a whole partition of the drive and then overwritten it. That partition was full of bogus temp files and multiple large .mp3s with nothing on them. Amateur. The .mp3s stood out like bloody handprints.

If he'd had to rely on software or even the command line, it would have taken next to forever to recover anything from that kind of damage. But with technopathy it took five minutes, Noam's power quicker than a program at flipping through the metadata and absorbing it. And metadata was the thing that stood out, in a folder entitled *Software Updates*. Not unusual itself, but its original path had been from the desktop, not applications.

It was full of video files.

Noam opened it on-screen. Dozens of thumbnails popped up in the window, moments frozen in time. Even just from the preview images, Noam could tell what kind of videos they were—a blur of skin and hair, naked bodies tangled up in sheets and trapped in ecstasy.

Noam's heart pounded as he told the computer to open one of the videos and play, palms sweaty where he pressed them flat against his thighs to resist the urge to reach for the mouse. The general was instantly recognizable; he or his lover must have held the camera with telekinesis to get them both in the frame at once. For what it was, the cinematography was exquisitely composed. The candlelight gave everything a warmer glow, easing the contrast between the general's pale skin and the brown flesh of his lover, like snow against maple wood.

He really is beautiful, Noam thought, gazing at Dara's face. He was everything Noam had ever wanted.

Noam's body remembered Dara's heat, as if Dara had branded himself on Noam's skin when he touched him. He felt sick.

Everything—everything took on new meaning now. The way the general had looked at Dara, touched Dara, tried to get Dara to stay with him after the dinner party. Did Lehrer know? Is that why he'd insisted Dara come home with him instead?

Fuck—did Lehrer suspect Dara killed Ames Sr.?

Noam felt like all his guts had been torn out, leaving him empty of anything except this knowledge.

He checked the dates in properties. The videos were from all different times. Some were recent, taken last month. Some years old. Noam didn't want to calculate Dara's age, didn't want his mind to start automatically ticking down the years from age eighteen, seventeen, sixteen, fifteen . . . Noam tasted bile, no matter how many times he tried to swallow.

The videos uploaded to the flopcell. Noam pulled it out of the port and slipped it into his pocket, then cleared the last few minutes from the computer's memory. He floated back out into the hall and down the stairs to the ground floor. The low hum of conversation from the wake sounded far away.

Noam couldn't stop thinking about those bruises on Dara's skin, where someone's fingers had pressed in. And he couldn't get those videos out of his head.

God.

Noam's pulse was so loud in his ears it was a miracle he heard them at all: soft voices, in a room to the right. Or maybe it was because he was thinking about Dara, a kind of psychic self-fulfilling prophecy—*speak of the devil and he shall appear*.

Only, no, of course Dara had come. The home secretary had been like a father to him (*some father*). So here he was, returned to the scene of the crime.

But why was he talking to Lehrer?

Noam drew closer. His chest felt tighter than it had just a moment ago because—*Lehrer*. Lehrer must have figured it out. Somehow, without saying a word, Lehrer knew Dara was a killer, would arrest Dara here and now—

"Well?" Dara's voice said. He was barely audible. "Is this it, then? The final step in your master plan?"

A moment of silence, broken only by the rustle of cloth. It stretched on and on, long enough it felt like Noam's nerves were being dragged over razor wire. He wasn't thinking clearly, Noam decided later; he was still in shock from what he'd seen upstairs. That was why he crept toward the door, close enough that he could press his face to where it was held ajar and peer within. Out of pure bloody luck neither Lehrer nor Dara saw him. Lehrer stood just two feet from Dara with his back to Noam, close enough to be heard while speaking quietly. Lehrer had one hand on Dara's shoulder. There was something paternalistic in the way he squeezed it, like he was giving reassurance.

Dara didn't seem reassured. In fact, Noam had never seen Dara this on edge. Tension practically rolled off him in poisonous waves, his gaze so fixed on Lehrer that he didn't notice Noam watching.

The wood of the doorframe was cold against Noam's brow, Noam's own anxiety a fever inside him.

"With your remarkable gift, Dara, surely you must know the answer to that question," Lehrer said, far too calmly.

Noam gripped the flopcell in one hand, tightly enough it dug into his palm. *What gift?*

His stomach was full of hot tar.

"You know I don't," Dara said. "You're stronger than I am. You'll always *be* stronger."

Noam didn't have to see Lehrer's face to know he was smiling. "And don't you forget it."

His hand fell from Dara's shoulder back to his side. Dara, both hands pressed to his own stomach, was visibly relieved.

"I do wish you would trust me more," Lehrer said, sounding genuinely disappointed. "I taught you better than this. Such accusations should not be made lightly."

"I'm sorry, sir," Dara said, and when Lehrer moved, he flinched, even though all Lehrer was doing was lifting a hand to adjust his own tie. Lehrer laughed softly.

"Relax. You're a nervous mess today, really. And you should be out there with your friend, who is mourning her father. We'll speak again later."

Dara didn't need to be told a second time. It took Noam a moment to realize—*shit*—and dart back: one, two steps, reaching behind him with his power for the knob to another door. He shut himself inside the hall closet not a second too soon. Dara's footsteps echoed off the hardwood floor as he walked past. Noam waited there, holding his breath, until he heard the other door open and shut again and Lehrer's own steps passing by, slower than Dara's.

What the hell had Noam just overheard?

Lehrer and Dara's creepy-ass relationship was a problem for another day, though. Right now there were bigger issues—like what Ames did to Dara. Like Lehrer possibly knowing Dara killed the general.

Several minutes passed before Noam was able to make himself open the door again. He half expected to find someone waiting there in the hall outside, standing silently between Noam and where Noam was supposed to be, but the corridor was empty.

Noam didn't want to go back. He wanted to stand in this dim light until he learned to stop feeling, because right now everything hurt.

Only someone would find him eventually, and Noam couldn't be caught here.

No one noticed him stepping over the velvet rope and rejoining the guests. He looked for Dara first and found him by the windows with Ames, touching Ames's wrist with his head slanted toward her; backlit, he looked like he came from another world. Noam's heart ached.

"We should go," Lehrer's voice said from behind Noam's left shoulder. "The service will be starting soon; people are already leaving."

Noam managed to exhale, then looked back at him, hoping none of what he felt showed on his face. "I'm ready."

He followed Lehrer out to the car. The thought of driving to the church, then sitting for the service, the funeral procession, the burial . . . it was a weight crushing Noam's chest.

But he didn't want to go home either. Home was the barracks, close quarters. Dara.

The driver shut the car door. Lehrer turned to him, expectant. "Any luck?"

"Ames—Carter Ames—still insists she's innocent," Noam said as normally as he could. "I believe her, for what that's worth."

"As do I," Lehrer said. "Which means the killer is still out there. Did you have the opportunity to search the house?"

The flopcell in Noam's pocket smoldered against his thigh. "Yes. I didn't find anything, though. Nothing useful."

"Really?"

Noam had always been a good liar. But his lips still felt foreign when he spoke again. "Really."

Lehrer made a quiet noise. He reached out and touched Noam's temple with just the tips of his fingers. Noam's skin tingled, an electric current darting up his spine as Lehrer brushed his hand back to sweep a lock of hair out of Noam's face. "All right," he said.

Noam sat frozen in place while Lehrer turned to look out the window at the city sliding by. The sky outside was the same color as the steel watch around Lehrer's wrist. Strange detail to notice, but Noam couldn't stop staring at it the rest of the way to the service, its mechanical insides ticking away the seconds like a heartbeat.

Newspaper clipping, carefully preserved between the pages of a book in the apartment of C. Lehrer.

THE TORONTO STAR
Tuesday, May 8, 2019

CALIX LEHRER CROWNED KING IN CAROLINIA

DURHAM—Following a unanimous committee vote, Carolinia crowned Calix Lehrer its first king yesterday in a small ceremony.

Lehrer is the twenty-year-old major general of the Avenging Angels, the militia founded by his brother, Adalwolf Lehrer, and labeled a domestic terrorist organisation by the former United States. A survivor of the US-attempted genocide against so-called witchings, Lehrer was once notorious for his role as strategist with the Avenging Angels. That infamy has been overshadowed, however, by recent events: Reports suggest Lehrer is the official who gave the order to detonate a weaponised form of the magic virus across multiple locations in Washington, DC, an attack that killed millions of civilians and effectively ended the United States. Lehrer is also implicated in a number of specific actions taken against foreign military troops.

Lehrer delivered a press conference last week, which was broadcast internationally. In his speech, he directly addressed Canadian, British, and French leadership. "I wish to state clearly," Lehrer said, "that any retaliatory measures taken by foreign powers against Carolinia will be met with the full force of our extensive military resources, both magical and nuclear," a pronouncement praised by Carolinian civilians. Intelligence reports corroborate Lehrer's claims that he possesses a large proportion of the US nuclear arsenal, along with the weaponised virus. Officials believe Lehrer's threats are not idle. Canadian diplomats meet with Lehrer this week to discuss a treaty.

As king, Lehrer's first act was closure of Carolinian borders, ostensibly to prevent further spread of the virus.

Chapter Nineteen

Noam didn't go to the barracks after Lehrer dropped him off. He spent what felt like hours walking in circles around the government complex, trying to drag his thoughts into some semblance of order. It was late when he got back, but everyone was still up. Dara, Taye, and Bethany sat at the kitchen table, the two boys teaching Bethany the basics of poker. A half-gone bottle of whiskey sat on the empty chair.

Dara tensed as he met Noam's gaze. The movement was almost imperceptible, an unhappy ripple that Dara quickly wiped away.

"Hi," Noam said, careful to sound casual. Normal. "Who's winning?"

"Dara, as always," Taye said with a dramatic sigh, tossing his cards onto the table. "I don't know why I bother. I'm just hemorrhaging argents at this point."

Bethany giggled, burying her pink-flushed face in her hands.

Noam pointed his finger down at the crown of her head and raised a brow.

"Oh yeah," Taye confirmed. "Wasted."

"Ames is gonna kill you for corrupting a fourteen-year-old."

"What Ames doesn't know won't hurt her."

Dara picked up the cards and started shuffling. He hadn't said a word.

"Dara," Noam said. "Can I talk to you for a second?"

Dara did something complicated with the cards, the kind of elaborate shuffling trick Noam used to watch gamblers perform at card tables crammed onto sidewalks and in the back rooms of stores. "What is it?"

Great. Dara had apparently decided to revert to old habits. Like he'd forgotten all about the way he moaned Noam's name, fingers all tangled up in Noam's hair.

Now it was back to how it was when they first met. Dara certainly had a flair for timing.

"Alone," Noam said. He tried not to sound snappish; he didn't want to give Dara an excuse to say no.

"I can finish shuffling," Taye piped up.

Still, Dara hesitated for a long moment before he sighed and put the cards down. His chair legs scraped against the floor when he pushed back from the table, an obnoxious sound that grated Noam's last nerve. His stomach was a mess of buzzing insects. He didn't know how Dara was gonna react when Noam told him what he saw. But he couldn't . . . he had to say *something*. Dara shouldn't have to carry this secret alone.

Noam led the way down the hall, glancing back once to make sure Dara still followed. He was there, a featureless shadow in the dim light, but Noam didn't need to see his face to know the expression on it. He sensed Dara's magic, a dark-green glitter barely restrained, as if Dara thought he might have to use it.

Dara didn't shut the bedroom door behind them, so Noam did it himself, a twist of telekinesis flipping the latch. He turned on the light.

"I'd rather not have this conversation," Dara said.

"I'm not here to talk to you about the general. Well. I am, actually, but not . . . not the murder." Noam forced himself to flex his fingers.

Dara stayed by the door, one hand resting on the knob.

"Do you . . . want to sit down?"

"I'm good, thanks." Dara's face was so deliberately blank. Only Dara couldn't hide from Noam anymore. Noam knew him too well.

He was afraid.

But afraid of what?

"Okay," Noam said. "Okay. I don't know how to put this, so . . . I'm just gonna say it? I went upstairs during the wake. I wanted to make sure there wasn't anything left behind that might tie you to the assassination, but then I found the general's computer, and I . . ."—*wanted to dig up anti-Sacha shit for Lehrer*—"I don't know, I'm nosy, I guess, so I looked through it. And he had these . . . videos."

He spoke the word so carefully, the syllables like poison on the tip of his tongue, but Dara was perfectly unaffected, as if Noam had said nothing at all.

Did he not realize the general filmed them together?

He had to. Someone had tried to erase those files, and whoever it was did it the same night the general died. It had to be Dara.

"Dara, are you listening to me?" Noam pressed, and he took a half step closer. "I saw the videos. I know what he did to you."

"I told you I didn't want to talk about this."

Untrue, as Dara had no way of knowing this was what Noam wanted to talk about. But Noam kept that particular comment to himself.

"We don't have to," Noam said quickly, because even though he already—ugh—knew all the dirty details, he didn't want to discuss them with Dara either.

"But," Dara finished for him, tone flat.

"*But*," Noam said, "Dara, have you . . . told anyone?" Someone who could put a stop to the abuse. Someone who could be a support for Dara when he needed it. Obviously Lehrer and Dara had problems, but Lehrer still cared. If he knew Dara was in trouble, he'd intervene. Even so, Noam sucked in a steadying breath before he could make himself say, "At the very least, you have to tell Lehrer."

"Tell him what, exactly?" Dara snapped. All at once the pretense of insouciance vanished, replaced by a savage anger. "That I fucked his friend? Lehrer wouldn't *care*. He'd say, 'I should have known you'd throw yourself at him eventually' and laugh." Dara moved forward, his eyes gleaming like black glass in the lamplight. "Because, as you've astutely pointed out, that's what I do. I'd fuck absolutely *anyone*."

Noam swallowed. It shouldn't hurt; Dara hadn't said it like that to—to cut. But it did anyway. Because that was Noam. Noam was *absolutely anyone*.

"This is different," Noam said, once he was sure he could speak. Dara was too close. He'd been drinking again; Noam could smell the alcohol. "General Ames raped you."

It was the wrong word. Dara recoiled, cheeks flushing dark. "No. He didn't."

"You were fifteen, Dara, and he's . . . it can't have been consensual."

"Well, it was." Dara's shoulders shook with each shallow breath. "Not only was it consensual, but I liked it. I *loved* it." He hurled the word toward Noam like a live grenade. "There's something so much better about being with someone older, isn't there? Someone *experienced*."

It was Noam's turn to flinch. *Don't react. Don't react.*

The sharp curl to Dara's lips suggested he knew exactly what he'd said and how Noam felt when he said it. He took a step toward the door.

"Dara," Noam started, but Dara ignored him.

No, fuck that, he couldn't just walk away from this—

Noam grasped Dara's arm. It was like touching white-hot iron. He yelped and stumbled back, Dara's magic sparking over skin.

"Don't you touch me," Dara hissed, and he shoved Noam so hard he nearly knocked him off his feet. "Don't you *fucking* touch me."

"I'm sorry," Noam said. "I didn't—"

"You should mind your own goddamn business, Álvaro."

Dara pushed Noam again, rougher this time. Noam's head slammed into the wall. Silver stars burst behind his eyes, a searing pain that made him gasp. Dara's face swam before him, blood-drained and furious.

This time, when Dara left, Noam didn't bother chasing him.

Noam spent over an hour in the bathroom with the door locked and the water on, huddled under the heat with steam filling his lungs. His argument with Dara played on an unending loop in the back of his mind.

He should have let it go. Dara was right. It was none of Noam's goddamn business, and if Dara wasn't ready to talk about it, well, that was that.

He sat down on the tile floor and stared at his arms resting atop his knees. Training bruises he got sparring with Lehrer blossomed beneath his skin, all ages and colors. A sudden sickness knotted in his stomach—Dara killed Lehrer's best friend. What would Lehrer do when he learned Noam was hiding Dara's betrayal from him?

And Lehrer *would* find out. Sooner or later.

Noam stayed until the water went cold. It was only when he had turned off the shower and started toweling himself off that a knock came at the door.

"Noam?" Dara's soft voice said. "Are you all right in there?"

Noam froze where he stood in the middle of the bathroom, towel around his waist and comb halfway through his hair.

"I'm fine."

A heavy sound, perhaps Dara leaning against the shut door. Noam imagined him in his drabs with the sleeves rolled up, one hand on the doorframe.

"Let me in?" Dara asked.

He could have let himself in, of course. But he didn't. Surely that was a good sign. Noam clenched his hands against the sink counter and made himself exhale, nice and slow. "We'll talk after I get dressed. All right?"

"All right," Dara said. His footsteps retreated into the bedroom and then away, the bedroom door clicking shut.

It wouldn't look good to rush to obey the second Dara wanted to talk. Still, Noam barely managed to wait about ten seconds before he stepped out into the bedroom, scrambling to grab civvies out of his dresser drawer. He heard voices down at the end of the hall as soon as he opened the door, Bethany's and Taye's, but not Dara's. Even so, Noam sensed Dara's wristwatch and the buttons on his uniform, warm against his skin. Noam entered the common room, where Dara was sitting in an armchair.

"You ready?" Noam asked.

Dara nodded, pushing up to his feet. "Want to go for a walk?"

He meant outside, of course; you couldn't talk treason in the barracks like it was just any Wednesday.

"Sure."

Dara trailed after him out into the corridor and down the stairs to the ground floor. The street was quiet this time of night, just a few cars idling beneath the black sky and glittering streetlights. It was hot even for June, humid air clouding his lungs.

The farther they got from the complex, the more Noam thought he ought to say something—*I'm sorry* or *I'm glad you want to talk*—but nothing came. His throat was too dry to speak.

"We should keep walking," Dara said when Noam slowed. "The more distance between us and those guards, the longer we'll have before someone comes to retrieve us." A beat. "Don't worry—I'm not going to hurt you."

Noam wondered if this was what passed for an apology in Dara-land.

"I know you're not," Noam said.

"That's not what it looks like."

"I can't help my face, Dara."

"It's not just your face," Dara said. "You think I'm unstable. That I might get violent."

"Not really. Maybe you've been a little moody lately, sure."

A lot moody.

Sixteen times.

"You said you wanted to talk," Noam said.

"Yes." Dara exhaled long and heavy, glancing at Noam like he thought Noam might have changed his mind about listening. "I think there're some things I ought to tell you. Things I should have told you a long time ago."

"Okay," Noam said, but Dara didn't speak again, at least not immediately.

After several silent moments, Dara unearthed a flask from his back pocket and took a long pull.

"Okay," Dara echoed at last. "So. I was fifteen the first time I slept with Gordon."

He hesitated again, fidgeting with the flask.

"How did it start?" Noam nudged gently.

"That doesn't matter. But it did, and we . . . it wasn't the way you're thinking." Dara drank again. "I know it was stupid, getting involved with high command like that. I think I hoped it would get back to Lehrer somehow, and he'd have to . . . I don't know. Pay attention to me, for once. I wanted him to be angry."

Maybe it wasn't a good idea to make Dara talk about this. Dara was . . . Noam had never seen him so on edge, not if you didn't count the time after they had sex. He kept fiddling with the flask, kept reaching up to tug at his hair. His temples glimmered with sweat.

"It's okay," Noam said, reaching over to touch Dara's wrist, only just remembering not to grasp. Dara's skin was summer-hot. Dara let his hand drop from his hair and, after a beat, he laced his fingers together with Noam's.

"Not really," Dara whispered.

"General Ames is dead. You never have to see him again."

Dara's grip tightened, and he laughed, a low bitter sound.

"You don't have to call it rape if you don't want—but Dara, he *hurt* you. That's . . . is that why you killed him? The real reason?"

"He didn't hurt me."

"Dara, *someone* did that to you. The bruises—"

"It wasn't him," Dara insisted. He yanked his hand out of Noam's grasp, face pale and eyes dark; he looked like a ghost. "I killed Gordon because of what he did to Ames, and because Chancellor Sacha asked me to."

The relief was short lived.

Noam felt like he'd been stabbed in the stomach, acid burning on the back of his tongue. He didn't want to believe it. He couldn't. But Dara wasn't lying. Noam should have known this a long time ago, but he hadn't wanted to believe it.

Dara didn't just sympathize with Sacha. He *killed* for him.

For the same man who spent four years undermining and oppressing people like Noam.

The back of his throat was dry. Noam swallowed against it twice, three times. It felt like gagging.

"You . . . you're working for him."

"Yes. I have been for a while." Dara's gaze was fixed on a spot on the ground some inches ahead of them.

"How?" Noam demanded. "*How* did this happen?"

Dara's expression did something complicated. "Someone approached me several years ago, around the time Lehrer . . . around the time I realized the truth about Lehrer. I was planning to do something stupid, but they talked me out of it. You can imagine what a boon it was, to have Lehrer's ward as your spy. I was able to steal all kinds of old files from Lehrer's apartment and the MoD servers. We'd hoped some of it might undermine Lehrer's legacy in the court of public opinion, when we moved against him." He waved a hand, dismissive. Noam felt motion sick just watching him. "But I'm about to graduate now, so I've outlived my utility."

"That's why you killed the home secretary. Because it doesn't matter anymore if you get caught and executed for it." Noam's nails dug into his palms. He wished he could walk fast enough to leave Dara behind. "Fucking hell, Dara."

"You should talk," Dara snapped. "Everything you're doing with Lehrer—you know that's why Sacha had me kill Gordon, right? Because Lehrer's planning to overthrow Sacha. Texas is practically salivating for the chance to jump on a weakened Carolinia. Sacha thinks maybe, *maybe* Lehrer won't usurp him if the political situation is destabilized by an assassination. Of course," Dara said with a snort, "that just goes to show Sacha doesn't understand Lehrer at all."

Noam stopped in the middle of the sidewalk. "How do you even—how do you *know* about that?"

"It doesn't matter," Dara said. "But I'm not going to apologize. I don't regret what I did."

"Of course you don't. You're a fucking white knight, galloping in on your mighty steed to save the world. And who cares what you have to do or who you have to hurt?"

Noam said it as cruelly as possible, wanting Dara to feel pain, to feel as cold and hollowed out as Noam did. And from the look on Dara's face, he was succeeding.

Dara dragged his fingers through his hair, the gesture rough and the curls catching against his knuckles. "I don't expect you to forgive me—"

"Oh, I don't," Noam snarled. "And now you'll ask me to keep your dirty little secret, won't you? Do you really think I won't tell Lehrer?"

"It doesn't matter," Dara said. "You'll do what you think is right." A moment passed, then Dara abruptly turned his face away. His spine was too straight, head bowed like he was waiting for the blade to fall.

"Dara," Noam started.

Dara looked at him. Noam was shocked to see his eyes were wet. "I'm sorry," Dara said. "I . . . I had planned to tell you when we came out here. But now I don't know what I *can* tell you without putting you in danger. I don't know how close you are to Lehrer. You might be too close, in which case, the less you know the better."

Noam frowned. "I don't understand. If there's something you can tell me that would explain all of this, I think you'd better just fucking tell me. Let me make my own decisions, Dara."

The sound Dara made was like a laugh, but not. "No. No. I can defend myself, but you . . ." He shook his head, letting out a rough sigh, then turned his face up toward the streetlamp. "Tell Lehrer whatever you want."

"I don't know what you're *talking* about. Jesus, Dara, if you could stop being so obtuse for just one second—" Words failed him. Noam's rage was a living thing inside him, clawing up the ladder of his rib cage and scratching at his sternum. He growled out an exasperated noise. "And you—I don't understand how you *knew*. About the coup. Or . . ."

Or when Noam came back from the funeral and Dara didn't want to talk to him, as if he'd predicted what Noam was going to say.

No.

Lehrer, in that room: *With your remarkable gift, Dara, surely you must already know the answer . . .*

Noam's pulse roared in his ears, that sudden realization crashing down on him like a massive wave.

Impossible. There would have been signs.

Only there were signs; Noam just hadn't been paying attention.

Fuck. *Fuck.* The frigid night suddenly felt crushingly hot.

"You're a telepath," Noam croaked out.

Dara stared determinedly at the streetlamp, a muscle pulsing in his jaw.

"You're a—you can *read my mind*?" Noam was going to throw up, he was sure of it. His thoughts were nothing but white noise. "You didn't . . . you didn't *tell* me—you didn't—Jesus. This whole time? This whole time, you knew what I was doing with Lehrer. You knew how I . . ."

How I felt about you.

"I'm sorry," Dara whispered.

"And Lehrer? Have you been reading his mind too?" Noam only knew some details about the coup. If Dara read his mind and reported back to Sacha, the plan might be safe. But if he'd read Lehrer's mind . . . Noam felt dizzy.

"No. Not Lehrer. I can't read Lehrer's mind."

"Why not?"

Dara exhaled. "I just can't. I suppose if you get to his age, you pick up on a few tricks. Either way, I can't read his mind any more than you can."

Noam didn't believe him. He had to imagine Dara would say anything to help him and Sacha achieve their ends and bring down Lehrer, but . . .

But Lehrer would have known Dara's presenting power too. It was probably the reason he took such a personal interest when Dara first survived the virus. Lehrer wouldn't risk having Dara so close if he thought Dara could read all Carolinia's secrets from his mind like words on a page. He must have safeguards in place.

Safeguards Noam definitely didn't have.

That must be why Lehrer had always been so cryptic with Noam before, only told Noam his plans on a need-to-know basis. He knew that anything he told Noam, he might as well be telling Dara.

And Sacha.

"Why?" he said. "Why didn't you tell me? Because you didn't trust me to trust *you*? Because you can't read Lehrer, and you figured the closer I got to him, the more you could know what's going on in his head?" Every breath was broken glass. "Or was it because you liked having access to my private thoughts without me knowing?"

Noam hated the hot lump that swelled in his throat. He felt too tight, skin stretched over bone, vision blurry.

"You're right," Dara said. "I should have told you. I'm sorry."

"I hope it was worth it."

Noam started walking again, still away from the complex, even though he was starting to wish he could turn around and go back. Dara followed, his steps a beat slower than Noam's, just out of sight, though Noam felt his gaze on the back of his head. Felt Dara, slipping between his thoughts.

"Noam," Dara said eventually. Noam didn't turn around. He knew what he'd see. "Noam, please."

"What."

"Noam, please look at me."

Dara's fingertips touched the back of Noam's arm, and Noam whirled around, yanking himself out of reach. God, he fucking hated the heat prickling at his eyes right now. Dara would be in his mind, too, reading exactly how Noam felt, every last sickening beat of his emotions on vivid display.

And a part of Noam didn't mind that. Some fucked-up part of him still *wanted* Dara there, twining their minds together. Like he craved being near Dara even now, after everything.

"I love you, Noam," Dara said. It was almost pleading. "I know you don't believe me, but it's true. I know you better than anyone. I've had almost a year in your mind—I know what you've been through. I know what you want, what you're afraid of, all those secret thoughts you'd never tell anyone—I *know you*. And I love you."

Two weeks ago, Noam would have been the happiest person in the world. Now those words were poison. Noam tasted venom like heat on his tongue.

"So read my mind," Noam said, brandishing a hand toward his own temple. "I believe you, Dara. I just don't care."

He relished the look on Dara's face, as if Noam had torn out his guts with his bare hand. And he left him there, standing alone on the sidewalk as Noam walked away and didn't look back.

Chapter Twenty

As it turned out, Noam didn't have to avoid Dara over the next week. Dara avoided him instead.

If Noam came into the room, Dara found an excuse to go out. He only returned to the bedroom late at night, presumably so he wouldn't have to undress for bed while avoiding making eye contact. They were forced together for meals, which neither could finish. Noam respected food, he *did*, but his stomach rebelled against every bite of porridge. Everything he ate congealed in his gut.

It wasn't that he was oblivious to the effect all this had on Dara. More than once he came into the bedroom only to catch Dara scrambling to hide a liquor bottle under his mattress or lying alone and quiet on his bed at midday.

Guilty conscience, Noam thought cruelly and half hoped Dara overheard it. For all he'd said, "I believe you" to Dara, he knew Dara didn't love him at all. Dara would have said anything.

And yet Noam hadn't told Lehrer the truth either. He carried that flopcell in his pocket everywhere he went, feeling out its shape with technopathy even as he pretended to listen to Lehrer's instructions during lessons. He knew he needed to turn Dara in. But turning Dara in was tantamount to signing his execution warrant, and Noam—that was something Noam wouldn't do.

"I need you to pay attention now," Lehrer said one day, just as Noam had been fiddling with the flopcell again. Noam startled, a little guiltily, and sat up straighter. Lehrer looked back steadily, and for a brief, reeling moment of panic Noam thought, *He knows.*

"I'm sorry, sir."

The expression on Lehrer's face was wry, as if to say: *I doubt that very much.* Lehrer shifted in his seat to put down his coffee cup, but when he turned back, it was with that same intensity of focus. "You've been following the news," he said. Not a question.

Noam nodded. And then, because he knew Lehrer liked it when Noam provided his own interpretation of current events, he added, "Between martial law and General Ames's assassination, I'm surprised there hasn't been a riot."

"Exactly." Lehrer tapped his fingers against the armrest of his chair. "It's time to start one."

Noam's pulse stumbled over the next beat. He leaned forward, hardly daring to breathe. It brought him into Lehrer's space, but he didn't care.

"It's time, Noam," Lehrer said. "There's no point in drawing this out any longer. Conditions will never be better. Half the world is itching to attack us while we're down—and they will, if we don't move fast. But if I'm in charge, they won't touch us. The European Federation learned their lesson back in the 2010s; they know exactly how far I'm willing to go to protect this country. Sacha's government is fatally wounded. We need to strike the killing blow."

It felt . . . too soon, somehow. Like there was something else they ought to have done, some preparations left unfinished. But Lehrer was right. Both refugees and Carolinians were fed up with the current system; they were desperate to accept any replacement, even a military junta. Lehrer had planned this for years.

And Dara saw it coming a mile away.

"It sounds like you already have something in mind."

"I do," Lehrer said slowly, as if tasting each word. "But you're not going to like it."

"Tell me."

"We need a large gesture, something we could easily pin on Sacha, that would catapult people into action. It needs to destabilize the refugee population and put them in a position where revolt is their best option." Lehrer had both hands clasped in his lap, like he was discussing an assigned chapter. "The most efficient way of accomplishing this is to assassinate Tom Brennan."

Noam stared at him. Just hearing Lehrer say it was enough to make his stomach churn so violently he almost thought he was going to throw up.

"You're right," Noam managed. "I don't like it. There's another way."

Right?

"I'm afraid not," Lehrer said, nearly apologetic. "Killing Brennan will catalyze refugee anger without sacrificing many more innocent lives. It's better than cutting off food or medical supplies or introducing some sort of disease threat. This way, only one person has to die, and we get an immediate reaction. With Brennan gone, there will be no one in a centralized position of authority to prevent riots. Brennan's a pacifist; we'll never see violent revolution while he's alive."

It was so . . . so brutally *logical.* This was almost worse than if Lehrer had given him no reason at all. Noam could have railed against the shapeless enemy of Lehrer's undisclosed reasons and felt like he wasn't so fucking . . . complicit.

Instead Noam hated himself, because his first thought was *Yes, that makes sense.*

Noam's head hurt. Like a goddamn vise was being slowly tightened around his skull. He gritted his teeth, which of course only made it worse—

This was all Dara's fault. If Dara hadn't killed Gordon Ames, if Dara hadn't been fighting Lehrer every step of the way, they might not be in this position. They wouldn't need to make a move before England or Texas did. They'd have time.

Lehrer was wrong, had to be wrong. He only chose killing Brennan because it was convenient.

On the other hand, it was convenient for a reason. Brennan was the last thread holding back the cause.

It felt wrong that Noam should be so easily persuaded they should kill someone he'd once loved like an uncle.

"I'm sorry. I know you were close," Lehrer said. He touched Noam's knee very lightly, just a brush of fingertips Noam barely felt through his trousers.

Were being the operative word. Had they ever been *close*?

Even before, they'd never had something like what Noam had with Lehrer. Lehrer was ten times as powerful as Brennan, was minister of defense, but he still found time to teach Noam personally.

Lehrer had saved the world a dozen times over—and he'd done it using tactics just like this.

"I need to think," Noam said. He lifted both hands to his head, thumbs pressing against his temples.

"We don't have time for that," Lehrer said. "We have to move quickly, before the rage dies down and people become complacent under martial law. I need you to say that you will help me in this."

The headache kept getting worse.

It was impossible to think of anything else but that pain. Pain and the awful decision that coalesced in his mind like dark fog—yes. Yes, Noam would help Lehrer.

Yes, of course.

Yes, yes, yes, *yes*.

He loathed himself, because he didn't even bother trying to fight it.

"God," Noam dropped his head back, face toward the ceiling. "Fuck. Okay. Okay. I'll help you. Jesus."

He was selling his fucking soul.

"Thank you," Lehrer murmured. His hand curled around one of Noam's wrists, fingers cool against skin. "Noam, this is what I've been training you for all this time. I'd planned to use Dara, of course, but that isn't going to be possible now. You have the skill and the knowledge. And most importantly, you have my trust. You are, perhaps, the only person I *can* trust."

Noam knew where this was heading. He was so stupid; he should have realized, of course, of *course*. His gut sloshed, full of salt water.

"I can't be anywhere near this. You know that," Lehrer said, hand tightening slightly on Noam's wrist. "It has to be you."

"Surely you have people for this," Noam said, lowering his head to look at Lehrer again, struggling to keep the tension out of his voice. "You're minister of defense. Don't you have some kind of personal assassin you can use?"

"Most of those people are on government payroll. I can't be sure they'll be loyal to me over Sacha, in the end. If caught, they might betray me."

"And if I'm caught, I won't? Even if I refuse to say a word, everyone knows I'm your student."

"Don't get caught." Lehrer said it too evenly, like it was that easy. But then, after a beat, he added, "If you do, I trust you'll do what's necessary to keep this quiet."

Noam got the gist.

He tipped forward, bracing his forehead against the fingertips of one hand and staring at the other lying there in his lap, Lehrer's fingers still curled around its wrist. That other presence in Noam's mind, that shadow version of himself, twined its way through his every thought. Was this who Noam really was?

Maybe. Maybe he'd known the truth for a while: that he'd do just about anything to win this war.

"How long do I have to plan?"

"Two weeks."

Noam and his first girlfriend, back before the virus, used to sit and plot out what they called the "perfect murder." He had a feeling the real thing took a bit longer than a few hours in Carly's tenement to plan.

Noam touched his throbbing temple very, very gingerly.

"All right." Just thinking about this made him want to go to sleep for a year. "But what about Dara? He's a telepath. He'll know what I'm planning."

And tell Sacha, because he's a traitor.

Shit. He shouldn't have mentioned Dara's telepathy. Lehrer already knew, of course, but Noam probably wasn't supposed to.

"Speaking of Mr. Shirazi . . . ," Lehrer said. Although he must have noticed Noam's slip, he didn't mention it. "I don't know if you've noticed, but he hasn't been well lately."

Noam had noticed. "He's stressed."

Murder tends to have that effect on people.

"It's not stress. I've seen this before. I should have done something sooner, but . . ." Lehrer ran his fingers through his hair, a few fair strands falling loose over his forehead. All of a sudden he looked older. Tired. His attention dipped away from Noam's for a moment, grasp finally dropping from Noam's wrist. "I told you about Wolf."

It took Noam several seconds to realize Lehrer meant his brother, not the dog.

And then his own heartbeat was all he could hear.

"You don't think . . ." He swallowed against the rawness in his throat.

The manic glint in Dara's eyes as he'd paced back and forth across their narrow bedroom. The dry-desert heat of his skin. His wild theories, his paranoia. *I won't be the one that kills you.*

Noam's nails dug into the meat of his palm, but the pain didn't chase this away.

"I'm afraid so. I've had my concerns for a while now. I thought perhaps—Dara's always been high strung, and with his drinking problem . . ."

Lehrer looked positively anguished. Noam didn't have time to care about that.

"Are you sure it's not just—Dara *hates* you. Maybe he just—"

"Dara's fevermad, Noam."

Was he? Noam struggled to sift through all his memories of the past several months, stringing them together like beads on a thread. It fit. It . . . fit.

And a part of Noam felt as if he'd already known that.

Lehrer squeezed his knee. Noam barely felt it. "It's the early stages," Lehrer told him. "He can be treated. It will take a few months. But it's possible, if I keep him safe."

Noam thought about saying, *Convenient, how "keeping him safe" also keeps him out of our way.*

As if he knew what Noam was thinking, Lehrer sighed. "I know none of this is ideal, Noam, but you're going to have to trust me."

"I will. I . . . do."

What the hell had this come to? How had he ended up here?

"Remember what I've taught you," Lehrer's voice said. Noam couldn't see him, had closed his eyes. "The life of one is worth nothing compared to the lives of many. This is why I chose you as my student. You're capable of things that others are not. You're intelligent enough to understand why such things are necessary, and strong enough to pursue what's right. Don't disappoint me now."

Noam floated back to the barracks in an odd haze, his mind drifting far above his body. He took the long way back. He needed time to think.

Think about what? There was nothing to think about.

Just Brennan, who would die.

Dara, who might be dying.

He was walking in circles, had passed the same security camera five times. Somewhere on the other end, a guard was probably wondering what the hell Noam was doing. Noam really couldn't afford to get caught loitering in the government complex a second time.

And that was another thing. Security cameras. He'd have to remember to take care of those when the time came to kill Brennan.

His feet dragged as he turned into the hall toward the barracks. He considered turning around and doing another loop of the training wing, but . . . but. He needed to get this over with.

He had to face Dara.

He opened the door and stepped inside. Bethany launched out of her chair the second she laid eyes on him, face white. On the sofa, Taye and Ames sat in silence, both of them staring at the TV, although Noam got the sense they weren't really watching.

He dropped his satchel by the door and said slowly, "Where's Dara?"

"He's gone," Bethany said, every word agonized. "Soldiers from the Ministry of Defense came by just a few minutes ago. They took Dara. We don't know where he went."

Stolen from C. Lehrer's personal collection

Wolf,

Here are the files you wanted from Azriel.

I need to talk to you when you get a chance. It's about your brother.

Let's put it this way: there's something I can't tell you. I hope you understand what that means.

—Raphael

Chapter Twenty-One

"They have to say what they're arresting you for," Bethany said over breakfast, which none of them ate. "That's Carolinian law. They didn't tell Dara anything. Just, 'Mr. Shirazi, you need to come with us,' and Dara went." She twisted her napkin between her hands, tighter and tighter. None of them could come up with a good reason why Dara hadn't asked questions.

Except Noam, of course. Noam knew.

"He's fine," Lehrer assured him during their meeting the next day, as he pressed a warm cup of coffee into Noam's hands. "He's sedated and on a steroid drip. He'll feel better in no time."

"Can I see him?"

That was all Noam had thought about all night. Dara, locked away in Lehrer's apartment like some damsel in a fairy tale.

Dara was no damsel, perhaps, but the thought still nauseated Noam. Maybe Dara only thought he hated Lehrer because he was sick. But even so, until he was better, Dara would loathe being alone with him.

And what if it wasn't just fevermadness? What if Lehrer had figured out Dara worked for Sacha? What if this was all part of Lehrer's ploy to take Dara out of the game at the crucial moment?

It couldn't be. Right? If Lehrer knew Dara was a traitor, Dara wouldn't still be alive.

Was Dara still alive?

"I'm afraid not," Lehrer said. "He needs to rest. He's probably sleeping."

Probably.

But what happened if the madness got worse before it got better? If Dara lost control and told Lehrer everything—confessed to working with Sacha, to killing General Ames—

"Can't I just—"

"I told you he's safe. Now stop asking." Lehrer turned away, toward the cabinet, pulling down a bottle of scotch and pouring himself a dram. "You have better things to worry about."

Lehrer put Noam through his paces, the same as every other day, sparring first with magic and then with fists. He didn't seem concerned about conserving Noam's energy for Brennan. Just about making sure Noam was still as powerful as he'd been last week.

Back in the barracks, the other three cadets accosted him as soon as he stepped inside.

"What did Lehrer say?" Ames asked, blocking Noam's path to the showers with her body. "You asked about Dara, right?"

"The same thing we all figured," Noam said, trying to edge around. "Dara's been taken into protective custody. There was some kind of death threat. I don't know the details."

"Who would want to kill *Dara*?"

"Isn't it obvious?" Taye said. "Someone who thinks they can get to Lehrer through him. I mean, it makes sense. Lehrer kept Dara's face and identity as secret as he could, but even when you've got PR handling information flow, shit still gets out. You can't keep something as interesting as Calix Lehrer adopting a child private."

Noam hadn't known Dara was actually adopted by Lehrer. He'd just assumed Lehrer took a special interest in Dara from a young age, like he did Noam. He frowned. "Lehrer *adopted* him? How come I didn't hear about this?"

Ames and Taye exchanged glances, and then Bethany said, almost gently, "You didn't exactly grow up knowing the kinds of people who were privy to this information. Maybe it's not surprising you hadn't heard."

"My mom thought it was nuts," Taye said. "She used to work in the government complex, you know, so she was pretty up to date on the gossip. She thought there was no way Lehrer had the time to deal with a kid that age. Of course, Dara lived in Level IV since the start, so I guess Lehrer didn't have to do much."

Dara never talked about it. Then again, maybe he didn't want to. Noam had only ever known him to hate Lehrer.

But what if that hadn't always been true?

"I need to shower," Noam muttered, finally pushing past Ames.

Noam slid down the shower wall the moment he was under the spray, sitting on the tile floor with his arms crossed over his knees. He stared at his hands, imagining how they might look covered in blood.

How red Dara's must have been after stabbing the general so many times.

Only . . . Dara couldn't have killed the general and covered his tracks so efficiently if he hadn't had experience. Dara was more powerful than Noam. He was a telepath. He knew illusion magic.

Was that it, then?

Noam knew how Lehrer's mind worked. Lehrer would have viewed Dara as a natural-born assassin. Had Lehrer asked Dara to make a similar sacrifice as he asked of Noam now?

Then, when Dara realized Lehrer had only taken him in so he could train him to be a killer, he rebelled and defected to Sacha.

Dara must have seen this as the perfect vengeance, using what Lehrer taught him to kill Lehrer's friend—the one who had infected his own children with magic. *This is what happens when you try to turn children into witchings and witching children into tools.*

Did Dara feel sick when the general's blood spurted over his hands? When he felt flesh give way and watched Ames Sr. take his last liquid breaths, did he feel guilty? Or had Lehrer trained that out of him?

What would Noam feel, when the time came?

He closed his eyes and stayed until the water ran cold.

It was Noam who identified the perfect patsy: Fred Hornsby, a former soldier who'd retired after an injury sustained in the war against Atlantia and had been complaining about refugees ever since. He was a custodian in the government complex, which meant his access card could get him pretty much anywhere. Even better, he'd been Sacha's friend at university. As far as Noam could tell from trawling through Hornsby's emails, Hornsby and the chancellor lost contact years ago, but the connection was close enough. Any closer and whomever they framed for Brennan's murder would be an obvious ruse.

He and Lehrer agreed it was too complicated to convince the security cameras that Noam was Hornsby in real time. Noam would have to get the appearance perfect, the mannerisms. No. Better if Noam had the cameras see nothing at all, then erase the tapes later. It would look like Sacha tried to hide the evidence.

"And you're sure this won't hurt him permanently?" Noam asked, dubiously examining the vial of clear liquid Lehrer passed him.

Lehrer arched a brow. "Noam, you're already framing Hornsby for Brennan's murder. As someone who's willing to let a man get executed in your place, I can't understand why you're having qualms now."

Noam stared at Lehrer, waiting. Finally, Lehrer sighed.

"Yes, I'm sure it won't kill him," Lehrer said. "It wouldn't do us any good if he died in his home while he was supposed to be assassinating Tom Brennan, after all."

"And what about this?" Noam picked up the gun from the seat cushion next to him, balancing it in his palm. It was a .22, Texan made and more advanced than what Noam was used to. "What if I miss?"

"You are a trained soldier, Mr. Álvaro."

"I've shot targets. I've never shot people."

Lehrer beckoned, and Noam handed him the gun. Lehrer picked up the silencer from the end table, screwing it onto the barrel with quick, efficient movements. "It isn't difficult," Lehrer said. He pressed the gun's cold snout to Noam's temple. Knowing the gun wasn't loaded made no difference; Noam's heart pounded bloody in his mouth. Lehrer's lips formed a dry smile. "Point and shoot."

Point and shoot. Those words beat like an anthem in Noam's head as he pressed his hand to the scanning screen at the entrance to the government complex and the computer read in Fred Hornsby's biometrics. *Point and shoot.*

Lehrer made sure the antitechnopathy wards were inactive for the next four hours. It was the very rare witching, Lehrer told him, who could sense magic. The only one aside from Noam and Lehrer who might be able to tell the wards were down was Dara, and Dara wasn't going to be warning anyone from MoD custody. Still, Noam was sick to his stomach waiting there, watching the door watch him as it processed the image of Hornsby's retina. But then the lock clicked, and the door swung open to reveal a cramped service stairwell.

Fourth floor, Noam told himself. It helped when he thought it in the harsh tone Sergeant Li might've used during a drill. *Fourth floor, soldier.*

The red exit signs glowed so brightly they gave him a headache; he squinted every time he rounded the corner to take the next flight up. He stood at the door to the fourth floor for a long while, brow pressed against the cold metal frame, tracking the movement of people's bodies up and down the hall beyond. Overhead the security camera droned blindly on. Noam wondered if Lehrer was watching, if he had some way of bypassing Noam's technopathy.

Probably not. Lehrer didn't have any technopathy of his own. If he did, he wouldn't need Noam.

The gun tucked into the waist of Noam's civilian trousers felt large and obvious, even though Noam knew it wasn't visible beneath his loose shirt. They should've done this at nighttime, sneaked into Brennan's house and killed him while he slept. It would've been easier. Kinder too. But Lehrer kept insisting it happen today, in broad daylight. Brennan was due to give a press conference at three, but he would never show up. People crowded the square outside for a scheduled protest in support of Brennan's speech; they'd been audible even from the barracks, but the only word Noam could make out was *down*.

Down. Down, down, down.

A door shut, and the hall was empty. Noam pushed those questions aside and seized his chance—he didn't know how long it would last or when he'd get another one.

The hall he stepped into was short, maybe forty feet. That was a good thing: Noam wouldn't have far to run, if he had to run. The closest office to the stairwell was W402, four doors to go. Mouth dry, Noam walked at a steady pace, his power threading out in all directions. It webbed through the electrical wires, the computers on desks in the rooms he passed. It was strange, Noam thought, that his heart beat so fast when he felt nothing at all.

He paused outside Brennan's door. His head throbbed.

He could leave. Tell Lehrer he changed his mind, wasn't interested in doing this kind of work. That when he'd said he was willing to kill for the greater good, he hadn't meant it.

Brennan would finish up and go home. Fred Hornsby would be sick for twelve hours, then recover and come to work tomorrow, confused why his emailed sick note never reached his supervisor. Everything would proceed as usual.

The refugees would keep screaming for freedom, like always. And like always, they'd be ignored.

Behind him and two doors down, someone's chair slid back from a desk. The person moved toward the door. Noam had to get out of the hall before he was seen, one way or another. He knocked.

Two doors down was four paces away, three, two—a wristwatch approached the knob. Bile surged up in the back of Noam's throat.

"Enter," said a voice within Brennan's office.

Noam stepped out of the hall just in time, the other door swinging open even as Brennan's slammed shut.

Brennan sat behind his desk, still typing. Just looking at him made Noam's heart ache. Those furrows on Brennan's brow were new. They hadn't been there when Brennan used to come with Noam's father to pick Noam up from school, when he'd go home with them to peruse the shelves of the bookshop—*Rivka, can I borrow . . . ?*

Brennan looked up. "Noam." Brennan sounded surprised. He shut off his holoreader immediately. Why? Did he think Noam would spy on him too? Noam was here to do far worse. "What are you doing here?"

Point and shoot. That simple. Noam would pull out the gun and aim it at Brennan's head and shoot him and blood and brain would spatter the wallpaper behind his desk and he'd be dead.

Noam pressed damp palms against his thighs. Carefully, so carefully, his power latched the door. "I have private lessons in the building. You remember. With Minister Lehrer?"

"And you thought you'd drop by to see where I spend my time these days?" Brennan asked, clasping his hands together atop his computer. He didn't believe him. "You shouldn't be here. It looks suspicious enough, you volunteering at the Migrant Center. You don't want to be accused of conspiring with the enemy."

Oh.

It would have been so much better, easier, if Brennan had said almost anything else. Because now all Noam could think was how he was conspiring with Lehrer. Had been conspiring, for weeks now, to murder. And here sat Brennan, wanting Noam to go home and stay safe.

And, a voice added cruelly, *to not get involved in things you don't understand.*

Noam took in a steadying breath. "I'm not really . . . worried about that," he said.

Brennan sighed. "I know you want to help, but you really need to stay far away from this. Bad enough I was responsible for one black mark on your record already."

"Lehrer's on our side," Noam said abruptly. That got Brennan's attention; he sat up a little straighter in his chair, frowning. Noam's brain was all wordless static. "We're working together. He's trying to bring down Sacha."

Brennan pushed back his chair and stood. For a moment he hovered there, fingertips pressed atop the surface of his desk, but then he moved, stepping away and toward the window. There was something about his posture that was . . . off. His spine was stiff, shoulders squared as he glanced out between the curtains. The protesters outside kept shouting.

Down.

Brennan dragged his fingers back through his hair, and Noam realized with a jolt that his hand was shaking. "Listen to me," Brennan said, although he didn't look at Noam. He was still staring out at the protesters in the square. "The last time Lehrer overthrew a government—"

"The last time Lehrer overthrew a government, we got Carolinia," Noam said.

"I don't doubt his ability. Just his methods."

The gun was white hot against Noam's back. "He did what was necessary. I've read the history books too."

"History is written by the victors." Brennan turned, his narrowed gaze holding Noam in place. Brennan's mouth was thin. "You look nervous, boy."

Did he? Sweat prickled the back of Noam's neck.

God, his head felt like it was about to explode.

"I'm not," Noam said.

Brennan frowned, like he saw right through the lie and into Noam's quivering core. There was a certain weakness to the way he grasped the arms of his chair as he sat again. When he spoke, it was with surprising gentleness.

"Why don't you tell me why you're really here?"

He knows. Brennan knows.

Noam hadn't realized, a moment ago, how comforting it was to feel he still had a choice. But with those words, Brennan had just slammed shut the door of escape. If he tried to leave now, he'd have to kill his way out of here once Brennan called for help. Everyone would know the truth—that Noam came to kill someone and that Lehrer had sent him. In one moment of cowardice, Noam would demolish half of Carolinia's government. He'd damn the refugees. He'd reinforce Sacha's authority.

He couldn't just walk away.

"I don't know what you mean, sir," Noam said, trying to buy himself time, but there wasn't any. It had leaked away, all of it, while Noam wasn't looking.

Brennan shook his head. "You do." He breathed in. Noam could see the tension in his neck from here. "You're sixteen. You've never killed a man."

Noam shook his head and wondered if this was it, if this was the moment he was supposed to *do* something. He stood there silently and watched it slide by.

"Don't be in such a rush to get started."

Brennan looked past Noam, toward the shut door, and a shadow crossed his face—something almost like pain, deepening at the end toward regret. Noam understood why a split second later when he felt Brennan's hand close around the handgun strapped to the underside of the desk.

Noam had sparred too often with Lehrer to hesitate. He yanked the gun out of Brennan's hand before Brennan could pull back the hammer. The grip was slippery in Noam's palm when he caught it out of the air, and he shifted his posture to a steadier stance. Aimed the gun at Brennan's head.

"Don't move!"

Brennan, on his feet, stopped, both hands slowly lifting to shoulder height.

"Noam," he said, very carefully, "think about this. You don't have to do this. I know you think you're doing the right thing, but there are other ways. Let . . . we can talk about them. Sit down. Please."

"Be quiet," Noam said. If he thought his headache was bad before, that was nothing compared to the way it felt now.

Brennan shut up. His gaze flicked around the room, looking for another exit.

There wasn't one. Noam had checked.

Noam squeezed his eyes shut. Fuck. Maybe he could just knock Brennan out. Maybe if he hit hard enough, Brennan wouldn't remember what had happened when he woke up.

Red sparks flashed against his eyelids.

He was so fucking stupid. He never should have come here. He should have stayed in the barracks where he belonged. He wasn't Dara, and he sure as hell wasn't Lehrer—no matter how much he might like to be. What was he *doing* here?

Brennan's wristwatch moved.

"Stay where you are," Noam snapped and opened his eyes. Brennan had made it to the side of his desk, hands still in the air. "I mean it. Stay right there, or I'll shoot."

"You won't," Brennan said. He took another tiny step forward. "You can't. You're too afraid."

"That makes me more likely to shoot you, not less." Noam's hands were so sweaty he felt like he was going to drop the gun, but they didn't shake.

He and Brennan stared at each other across the scant five feet between them. Brennan's eyes were so wide Noam could see white all around his irises.

"Put the gun down."

Noam's power burned through the chamber. "I told you to be quiet."

Another step closer. "Please, son. It's all right. It's all right."

Brennan was so close now, close enough that Noam saw the sheen of perspiration on his brow.

"I'm not your fucking son!" Noam's voice cracked on the last word.

Electricity snapped visibly in the air now, wild and dangerous. Noam's head pounded; it felt like an earthquake shuddering in the ground beneath him, through him.

I'm going to shoot him, Noam thought. *I'm going to have to shoot him; he's giving me no other choice—*

Brennan grasped the barrel of the gun.

And Noam . . .

Noam let it go.

The gun fell into Brennan's waiting hand, Brennan's relief a thick fog dipping between them.

Brennan exhaled.

"Good," he said, "good." And he reached for Noam's arm.

It wasn't quite reflex, but it wasn't quite intentional either. It was a cascade of light, searing down Noam's spine and hurling Brennan back. He hit the floor eight feet away. He twitched once, twice, and went still.

Electricity still sparked across the surface of Noam's skin and in the ambient air. His thoughts were white, formless, the room stretching dizzily around him as he knelt on the floor beside Brennan's body.

Those brown eyes gazed blankly up at him, cold now and seeing nothing.

He was dead. He was dead, but Noam checked for a pulse anyway, because what if—*what if?*

Oh god.

It was an accident, Noam thought, his mind finally surging up on a rising tide of panic. *It was . . .*

He had to walk away. Right now, he had to stand up and walk out of here. Brennan was supposed to give a speech soon—in, fuck, in twenty minutes. Someone was going to come here for him, and when they found the body, Noam had to be gone.

The room tilted dangerously when Noam stood, sliding so far sideways that he had to catch himself on the edge of Brennan's desk. And then, with another jolt of adrenaline, Noam tugged his sleeve down over his hand to rub his fingerprints away.

Fuck. Fuck, this was all wrong. Brennan was dead. Electrocuted. Fred Hornsby couldn't . . . Brennan was supposed to get shot, the way a baseline would have done it.

Noam fumbled for the second gun, the one tucked into his waistband. Only after it was in his hand and pointed at Brennan's head did he think, *No, no, why would Hornsby shoot him if he was already lying down?*

Noam dropped the gun on the desk and crouched down by Brennan's body, reaching—fuck, don't think about it, *don't think about it*—and grabbing him under both arms. God, he was heavy, nothing but limp muscle and bone as Noam struggled to drag him back toward the desk chair. *Dead weight.* Noam wanted to laugh, the urge insane, almost overpowering.

Don't look at Brennan's face. Don't look at his eyes.

Brennan's head lolled forward as Noam hitched him up off the ground and into the chair, grunting with the effort.

His body was still warm. Jesus, he was *still warm.*

In that chair, Brennan looked like a marionette with its strings cut.

Noam picked up the gun again and pressed the silencer's barrel to Brennan's forehead. Then he took two steps back, trying to keep the gun steady. He only wanted to do this once. His hands shook.

Remember your training.

Inhale. Good. Exhale. Relax. Aim.

Fire.

Blood and brain matter exploded against the blue wallpaper behind the desk.

Noam stood there, watching the blood drip down toward the wood floor. He felt nothing. That shadow-self had its hands on his shoulders, cold comfort.

He edged closer, crouching down just enough to get a good look at the entrance wound. It was small, a round void surrounded by black powder residue. There was hardly any blood on Brennan's face.

Shouldn't he be horrified? All Noam could think about was training.

He and Lehrer had talked about this.

Leave the bullet and shell wherever they are, because they'll trace to this gun, which we'll plant in Hornsby's house. Wipe your hands on your pants to get rid of powder residue. Hide the gun, not in Brennan's office, and someone from the Ministry of Defense will retrieve it later.

Noam's face was still too close to Brennan's. Blood trickled from Brennan's nose, his ears.

Reality crashed back in like a summer storm.

Noam stumbled back and turned roughly away, gulping in several breaths of air. *Don't puke at the goddamn crime scene.*

Get out of here. Right now.

Brennan's gun got kicked under the desk somehow while Noam was dragging the body around. He tugged it out with telekinesis, wiped it with a microfiber cloth, then put it on the desk again. Just to be safe, he wiped down the spot he'd grabbed the desk earlier one more time.

Then the . . . the murder weapon. *Unscrew the silencer. Clean the prints; drop it in a plastic bag. Tie the bag off; tuck it back into trousers.*

Through it all, Brennan's eyes watched him with glassy interest. Noam couldn't stop thinking about that, or the tick of the clock on the wall. He kept glancing over his shoulder to be sure Brennan was really dead, half-certain each time that he'd find the corpse hovering there with its hollowed-out skull.

The last moments, standing there looking at that scene and trying to make sure he hadn't forgotten anything, were the longest in Noam's life. There could be fibers. Hair. Noam had no way of being sure. Lehrer said he'd make sure any such evidence got buried in the investigation, but that assumed Lehrer had power after this to bury anything at all.

Couldn't worry about it now.

Noam waited at Brennan's door, listening to the movements in the hall outside. Cell phones. Tablets. Wristwatches. As soon as the hall was clear, he reached out and plunged his power into the security cameras again.

It was clumsy. The wires fried. *Fuck.* Someone was gonna notice that.

Noam darted into the hall, shutting Brennan's door and heading toward the staircase as fast as he could without outright running. Fear was a constant fire at his back. He couldn't think straight. He knew he'd forgotten something—he must have. His blood roared in his ears.

He made it three steps before a door at the end of the hall swung open.

Shit, shit—

Noam spun on his heel and started walking in the opposite direction. He ducked his head, eyes trained on the ground five feet in front of him and hoping the most anyone saw of him was the back of his neck.

"—talk to Barbara about getting those papers signed before the end of the day," a female voice said behind him.

"She should still be in her office," someone replied. They were at least a few yards behind Noam but between him and the way he came in.

Any second now, he thought. Any second someone would call out to him, and he'd have to choose between showing his face and running.

An exit sign glowed over a door at the end of the hall. Alarmed, though, emergency exit only. There wasn't a biometric reader, not that Noam could sense, no way to tag Hornsby's presence here a second time. No turning around either. This had to be good enough.

Noam cut the alarm signal as he shouldered the door open. The stairs were dimly lit and narrow, concrete walls bowing in on either side. When the door slammed shut, that first gasp of air gusted into his lungs so fast and cold his chest ached.

Of course, he wasn't free yet. These stairs seemed to stretch on forever.

Fuck it. Noam looped magnetism around the handrails for balance and swung himself over, dropping into the void. Three floors shot past, Noam's power dragging against metal to slow his fall.

His knees buckled when he landed, pain shooting up the outside of his right ankle, but Noam didn't stop. He clinched off the wiring in the final door and pushed out into the brilliant white sunlight.

The alley was, thankfully, deserted, drain water splashing underfoot as Noam ran toward the street. The square in front of the government complex teemed with people, with more dashing up the road to join them waving flags bearing the red star of Atlantia.

Right. That's right, Brennan was meant to speak; these people were here for him. All refugees?

Didn't matter. They were good cover. Noam ducked his head and pushed into the throng, weaving through the shouting voices and sharp elbows.

They were still chanting, he realized as he struggled past all these unfamiliar bodies, one word that rose above the stamping of feet and shouting of orphan children: Brennan's name.

Noam's body felt too hot, burning ash consuming him from the inside out. Nausea sloshing in his throat, he grabbed on to the arm of a stranger as the world tilted off its axis.

What had he done?

Everyone stared, their eyes all whites. *Brennan, Brennan.* It pounded through the ground and throbbed in the air.

Noam lurched forward and vomited. There wasn't much to get up, just bile and foam, but it got on someone's shoes, and the man whose arm Noam grasped pushed him roughly away.

He stumbled to the right and bumped into someone else, nowhere to go that wasn't already taken. Noam's mouth tasted like blood, and he felt blood, too, against the back of his hand. Only he looked and, no, it was just a quarter, someone's lost change magnetized to his skin.

The gun. He had to get rid of the gun.

Noam cast his gaze wildly about, but all he saw were people. More people. An endless throng.

No. There.

He followed the scent of metal, tracking it to a garbage bin on a street corner. It was crowded enough that no one noticed Noam stuff the plastic bag in with the rest of the refuse. Or he hoped no one noticed. This was . . . this was . . . Blackwell and Vivian. Don't forget. Blackwell and Vivian, trash can on the corner.

Noam wiped his mouth on his sleeve and took in a steadying breath, turning to look back toward the government complex again. Soon they'd set up a perimeter. They'd search everyone and strip every last shred of evidence. They'd find Noam.

What time was it? How long until Brennan was supposed to give his press conference?

Lehrer's people were here, too, interspersed through the crowd in their green uniforms. He felt their guns, their witching magic.

Noam couldn't be on the street when the riots began.

After it's done, Lehrer had told him, *come to my study. I'll be your alibi . . . though hopefully you won't need one.*

Noam headed back toward the government complex, shouldering his way through the shouting crowd and keeping his head down. Only . . . the entrance guards. They'd recognize him. Idiot, he never should have left the building. He could've gone down the hall on some other floor and made it back to Lehrer's study with time to spare. It was probably a matter of minutes before they found the body.

If they hadn't already.

He couldn't use Hornsby's biometrics again and get caught reentering the government complex, not when Hornsby was supposed to get arrested at home. Another emergency exit, then? Where the hell would he find one?

No time to search. He'd have to go back the way he came. If he was fast, he could dart through and into a first- or second-floor hallway before they put everything on lockdown.

Not a great plan, but better than being trapped out here with no alibi and rioting refugees when they started hunting for a killer.

Noam took a sharp left and got an elbow in the ribs when he nearly tripped over a man wearing red face paint. "Sorry," Noam muttered and kept going.

Every fiber of him was desperate to run, anxiety clawing up his spine like a live thing. What if one of the soldiers out here recognized him?

Don't think about that. Keep going.

The alley was still deserted. Finally, Noam gave in to instinct and broke into a sprint.

Please, please, don't sound the alarm, not yet, please . . .

Noam yanked the door open with his power and tumbled into the dark stairwell for a second time. His legs trembled as he dashed up the steps two at a time. Hall was empty. Good. Noam let himself in.

His heart pounded so hard in his chest he felt like he might be dying. Could sixteen-year-olds have heart attacks?

Noam rubbed his hands against his sweaty face, pushing his hair back into something resembling order. Okay. Just a regular person with a totally good reason to be here, walking down the hall. Just walking.

The door at the other end of the hall opened. Three soldiers, headed this way.

They wore antiwitching armor.

Noam's stomach convulsed. *Act normal, act normal, act normal. They don't care about you. They don't care. Don't do anything stupid.*

He should run. He should get the fuck out of here while he still could.

The three soldiers were still walking. They hadn't drawn their weapons.

You're safe. Go. Keep going.

Twenty feet away. Ten feet. Noam kept his gaze trained on the floor. *Don't recognize me, don't recognize me, please, fuck, please don't even look at me—*

The three soldiers walked past and didn't give Noam a second glance.

Noam felt like he was going to shatter into a million pieces. Fuck, okay, fuck, almost there. Five minutes.

The door opened again, and out spilled six soldiers in iridescent armor—another antiwitching unit. Every one of them had a gun. Every gun was aimed at Noam.

"Stop!"

A hot flare burst in Noam's gut. He spun around, but those three soldiers he'd passed blocked him in from behind, two with guns drawn and the third holding up hands that sizzled with magic.

Witchings, they have witchings.

"Wait," Noam gasped out. He held up his arms, fingers spread wide. "I think . . . there's been some kind of mistake."

"No mistake."

Noam knew that voice. Noam *knew that voice.*

He turned, slowly, slowly, back to face the six soldiers at the door. A seventh man had joined their number, this one clothed in a neat black suit. A silvery circlet perched upon his head. His face was a twisted mask of satisfaction.

Noam's insides turned to stone, and Sacha smiled.

"Arrest him."

Chapter Twenty-Two

They took him to the fifth floor, far away from the Ministry of Defense and, presumably, Lehrer's influence.

The soldier to Noam's right had a bruising grip on his arm even though Noam wasn't struggling, pulling at him every three steps and nearly knocking Noam off his feet. People they passed in the hall stared, government workers and soldiers alike.

Surely at least one of these people will recognize me, Noam thought. Someone would tell Lehrer. Right? But then, he wasn't in his cadet uniform. In his worn-out civvies he could've been anyone—a refugee kid dragged in off the street for incitement.

Noam spent the whole trip asking what he'd done, insisting something was wrong because he didn't belong here—he was just trespassing, he swears, he *swears*. He knew it was useless but kept talking anyway. Just in case.

They got on the elevator, and Noam opened his mind to the web of technology glimmering out of normal sight, quivering little waves and wires connecting people to machine. Lehrer didn't have a computer, as if he thought owning something made after 1965 would throw off his aesthetic. But he had a phone. Noam bypassed the wards and made the message show up on Lehrer's screen:

Arrested. With Sacha now.—N

He didn't dare say anything about Brennan or the mission. His attention hovered over that phone like a finger over the screen, waiting for some kind of confirmation that Lehrer had seen it, but there was no way to know. Lehrer might be busy dealing with the fallout from Brennan's murder. He might be orchestrating a riot. What if he didn't check his phone for hours? What if Sacha decided to have Noam executed before then? He'd killed a government official. They could decide he was a threat to national security and sentence him without a trial.

Could Sacha make that kind of determination without Lehrer signing off on it? Noam had no idea.

He sensed the Faraday cage as soon as they stepped out of the elevator. It was hidden behind an unlabeled white door, metal glittering in Noam's awareness like the outline of a weapon.

Sacha turned to look at him, his expression something that could have been amusement, but wasn't quite.

"That's right," Sacha said, as if he could tell what Noam was thinking. "Pure copper. I had it made specially. In there, you can't use your power to influence anything outside that room, and no one else's power can reach you. Still. Better to be cautious."

He gestured, and something sharp jabbed into Noam's neck.

"Suppressant," Sacha said as the soldier to Noam's left put the plastic cap back on his syringe. Noam clapped a hand to his neck, as if that would make a difference. "Developed by the old US government during the catastrophe. Illegal now, of course. Our mutual friend made sure of that. But there are always loopholes."

The soldier on Noam's right entered a code on the keypad next to the door, and when the door slid open, he shoved Noam inside. By the time Noam caught his balance, the door had shut, trapping him within that perfect copper net.

Immediately he reached out with his power—or tried to. It was like grasping at someone's soapy hand, grip slipping every time he clenched his fingers.

"Fuck!" Noam shouted, kicking the table hard enough it skidded two feet across the concrete floor.

Calm the fuck down, he told himself, his toe throbbing and breaths coming in shallow little gasps. *That wall's a one-way mirror. Sacha's out there. You have to be calm.*

All right. Okay.

Single table, two folding chairs. One door, locked. Observation mirror. Suppressants. Faraday cage.

Well, Noam could presumably use the chairs as weapons if he had to, but even if he knocked out whomever was in the room with him, he wouldn't get far. There was no keypad to unlock the door from inside, for one. And if he got into the hall, he'd have to deal with the other soldiers. They'd have guns, and he didn't have magic.

How long did the shit in that syringe last, anyway? Was there a chance it could wear off before they remembered to re-up him? Noam scanned the room but couldn't see cameras or any other tech.

I had it made specially, Sacha had said.

Noam got the feeling he wasn't the one this room was built to contain.

That's it, then. He was fucked. If this room was strong enough to keep Lehrer in, no way was Noam breaking out.

Single table, two folding chairs. One door, locked. Observation mirror. Suppressants. Faraday cage. No cameras. What else?

People. There were people out there, presumably watching right now. Could they hear him?

That tech could be fucking flawless, but Noam was a programmer. He knew all about human error.

"Hello?" Noam said, turning to face the one-way mirror. His reflection peered back, wide eyed and pale. "Can you hear me?"

Nothing.

"Listen," Noam said anyway, hugging his arms round his waist and trying to look harmless. Just a scared kid caught in something too big for him to understand. "I think there's been a misunderstanding. Can we talk? Please?"

He moved closer to the mirror, imagining Sacha standing on the other side. Even though he was probably staring somewhere over Sacha's shoulder or something, Noam met his own gaze in the reflection and held it.

"Please. I just . . . I'm sorry. I know I was out of bounds. It was stupid. I won't do it again. But really, isn't this"—he waved his hand at the room—"overkill?"

Silence answered.

"Can I at least get a lawyer?"

He ought to stop talking. He had no idea what Sacha's people knew. He could be damning himself with every word.

He spun away from the mirror so they couldn't see his face. He was so fucked. Sacha knew Noam was Lehrer's protégé. Sacha had little to no chance of ever getting Lehrer in this position with good reason to detain him and strip away his rights, so Noam was the next best thing.

Noam dragged one of the folding chairs out from behind the table and dropped into the seat. Okay. Eventually, Sacha would send somebody in. They'd ask about Brennan. About Lehrer. They'd probably torture him.

Let them, Noam thought. He knew how to keep his mouth shut.

They'd probably try to turn him against Lehrer. They'd use Dara, their ally, in any way they could.

But if he was careful . . . he could survive this. Lehrer's coup would succeed, and he'd get Noam out of here.

Noam just had to live that long.

The door slid open. Noam was up on his feet before he realized he was moving. He didn't know what he'd expected—some masked man in black with a tray of knives, maybe—but it was Chancellor Sacha. He was alone.

"Before you think about bashing my skull in with that chair," Sacha said, "recall there are eight highly trained killers standing right behind that mirror just waiting for an excuse to shoot you the way you shot Tom Brennan."

Stick to the story.

"*What?*" Noam choked out, grabbing on to the edge of the table for balance. It wasn't even hard to fake that horrified edge to his voice. Noam *was* horrified. "What the fu—what are you talking about? Brennan, is he—is he okay?"

Blank eyes staring at the ceiling. Blood on the wall.

Sacha's gaze narrowed. "That's right," he said, stepping farther into the room. "I nearly forgot. You were close with him, yes? We know you spent a lot of time at that center of his, both before and after your feverwake." A pause. "Did that make it easier or harder to kill him?"

Noam shook his head, violently enough that it sent a fresh dart of pain shooting through his skull. "No, *no*, I—what do you mean? He's *dead*?"

"Oh yes." Sacha dragged out the other chair and sat down. He crossed his legs neatly at the knees and looked at Noam, overhead light glittering off his steel circlet. He gave Noam a humorless smile. "Very *thoroughly* dead. I'm sure Lehrer would be proud, were he here." Sacha paused. "Or maybe not. You did get caught, after all."

Noam stared, fighting to keep his heart from leaping into his throat. "I'm not . . . I didn't do it. I didn't. You have to believe me." He lurched up out of his chair and turned away from Sacha to pace along the wall of the cell. "Fuck."

Why was Sacha *here*? Why was he interrogating Noam personally when he had an impending coup to contend with? What was his game?

"We know it was you, Noam," Sacha said from behind him. "Anonymous tip, an hour ago. Everything all tied up in a neat little package. Location, approximate time, victim, villain. Mechanism of death, just in case we doubted its validity. It arrived a little too late for us to save Brennan, but at least we got you."

Noam faltered midstep. He didn't recover quickly enough; he knew Sacha saw.

But there were only three people who had that information. Noam himself, obviously. Dara, locked up in isolation.

And Lehrer.

Noam inhaled sharply and turned to pace back the way he came. That didn't make sense. Why would Lehrer turn Noam in? This was *his* plan! Noam getting caught assassinating someone would undermine Lehrer's whole coup. Everyone would know Noam did it on Lehrer's orders.

Wouldn't be the first anonymous tip he's sent lately, a little voice whispered in the back of Noam's mind.

"Well," Noam said, fumbling to reclaim his anger. His ears rang. "They're lying, obviously. Because I *didn't fucking kill anyone*!"

Sacha watched him with interest, tracking Noam's progress back across the room to the opposite corner.

No. Lehrer was a lot of things, but he was ultimately rational. He liked risks, but only when he was sure he could control the outcome.

Surely it wasn't him.

Surely.

"You know," Sacha said as Noam reached the other wall and spun around again, "if you hadn't doubled back into the building, you might have gotten away."

"I didn't do it," Noam recited, stomach writhing.

"Mmm. Yes, you said. Please sit. You're making even me nervous."

Which . . . actually, Sacha *did* look nervous. Sweat beaded his brow; his tie was knotted askew like he'd thrown it on last minute.

Of course. Noam was down here getting interrogated for murder, but to Sacha he was a weapon—perhaps the only one Sacha had left to resist Lehrer's coup. This whole time Sacha had been a step behind, realizing Lehrer had a plan only after he'd already carried it out. But now he was in the middle of it, Lehrer's plot unfurling around him like a black flag. That's why he was down here, with Noam, instead of out there amid the chaos.

Noam was it. Either Sacha got him to turn on Lehrer, or Sacha went down.

Noam sat.

"Thank you," Sacha said. He exhaled, then twisted in his seat to face Noam directly. He kept his hands folded atop the table, like they were in a goddamn business meeting.

"Noam, where is Dara Shirazi?"

Not the question Noam expected. "Why are you asking me about Dara when I'm being accused of *murder*?"

Sacha gave him an arch look. "Answer the question."

"I don't know. Protective custody, I think."

"That's convenient," Sacha said. "A threat to Mr. Shirazi's life arrives right before Lehrer plans to make his final gambit. The telepathic spy is off the chessboard."

"I don't know what you're talking about."

"Of course you do. You're friends, aren't you? And we all know you, Mr. Álvaro, are not as stupid as your test scores would have you appear." Sacha's mouth twitched up, like it was some mutual joke. "So I'll ask again. Where is Dara?"

"I don't *know*. Probably the Ministry of Defense. I'd tell you to ask Lehrer, but I know you won't." Noam crossed his arms over his chest, glaring at Sacha with all the hatred he'd stored up these past years. *Fuck you. Fuck you. You're a fucking murderer.* "You already decided what you think happened. So fuck the truth, am I right?"

"He's not in the Ministry," Sacha said. "I checked. I even asked Calix, but he told me Dara's safety depended on his location staying a secret."

"Yeah. It probably does. So why are you still asking?"

"Because there's no *death threat*, Noam. Not unless you count whatever Calix plans to do to Dara when this is all over."

"You're crazy," Noam said, but that did nothing for the cold that laced down the back of his neck.

"I'm trying to protect him."

"Yeah. You have a great track record protecting the people who live in your country." He gritted his teeth so hard it hurt. "*Fuck you*. I can say that, right? Or is that treason now too?"

"Of course," Sacha murmured, unclasping his hands. He leaned back in his seat. "You consider yourself one of the refugees, don't you? You were born here in Carolinia, but your parents weren't."

Noam glared in silence.

"Undocumented too. I looked them up. We never managed to get our hands on your father, but he had quite the unofficial record himself. Is that how you got involved with Brennan's people in the first place? Your dad?"

"How dare you talk about my dad," Noam snapped. "You have no right."

"Should we talk about you instead?" Sacha was unmoving. "After your mother killed herself, you filled her shoes well enough. You got two jobs and dropped out of school. You took care of Daddy when he couldn't take care of himself."

"Shut. Up." Noam couldn't quite breathe. The air in his lungs felt like acid. He was drowning in it.

Sacha gazed back at him dispassionately. "Then let's change the subject. Tell me what Lehrer is *really* after—because I know he doesn't care about being king again."

Noam imagined Sacha with his neck on a guillotine. That was how Lehrer had dealt with traitors after the catastrophe, after all.

A pretty thought. Noam exhaled, long and slow. *Steady. Calm.*

This headache was fucking stunning.

"I don't know," Noam said.

Sacha was grasping at straws, trying to make Noam angry enough to give something away. That meant he was almost out of time.

Good.

Sacha rubbed his temple with two fingers. Was Noam imagining it, or did he look paler now than he had a moment ago?

At last, Sacha sighed again and met Noam's eyes, his mouth drawn into a thin line. He gestured toward the crown on his head. "Do you know why I wear this thing?" he asked.

"Because you're an asshole?"

"It's a Faraday cage. Just like the one you're sitting in right now." Sacha reached up and lifted the circlet from his head, placing it on the table between them. It was plain, no ornamentation, just a seamless steel-and-copper band.

Of course. Noam had sensed the copper worked into the circlet that time in Lehrer's apartment. It didn't seem like a Faraday cage then, but now that Sacha said it, that was obviously what the crown really was.

"Plus a few magical additions, courtesy of your friend Mr. Shirazi," Sacha said. "It's always nice to have a telepath on your side when you're up against someone like Minister Lehrer."

Noam frowned and crossed his arms again. "Yeah, I can tell you and Dara have a lot in common. Why don't you stop being cryptic and just say what you're trying to say?"

Sacha gave him an appraising look. "All right," he said. He picked up the circlet, rubbing one thumb against its steely curve. "I had this made so that no one could use magic to influence the electrical signals in my brain. I spent weeks avoiding Calix while it was being built. Didn't want to risk hearing even one word from that silver tongue of his."

Noam's throat felt strange, constricted. Sacha laughed softly.

"Calix can convince you to do anything. Absolutely anything. He might have to tell you verbally, and as far as I can tell, he can only influence a few people at a time, but it's a remarkable power."

Noam . . . he wasn't hearing this.

Sacha was lying again. Right?

"Wait," he started, but Sacha overrode him.

"It's subtle. He doesn't even have to tell you to do something outright. He'll *persuade* you, piece by piece, until you can't tell which thoughts are your own and which are ones he put there." Sacha leaned forward abruptly, close enough that Noam reflexively jerked back. "Who are you, Noam Álvaro? How much of you is still you, and how much is him?"

It was a trick, had to be.

Noam knew this would happen. Sacha was just trying to sow the seeds of doubt. Make Noam distrust Lehrer, or at least doubt him. He *knew* that.

And it was working.

Was that kind of thing even possible? Magic was . . . you had to understand whatever you were trying to do. Like physics. But mind control? What the hell would that even involve? An understanding of . . . of human psychology?

Lehrer had said presenting powers were different. Unpredictable. That they could be anything.

Sacha was looking at him with grim satisfaction on his face, like he thought he'd just made his play and won the game.

Sick. This was fucking sick.

Do I even trust Lehrer? Or do I just think I do?

"Who else knows about this?" Noam said, words coming out tight and aggressive. "If you were telling the truth, someone else would have figured it out too. Abilities have to go on record. You can't keep something like this secret."

Sacha snorted. "My boy," he said, "how many people who know about his power do you think Calix has left alive?"

The question hung in the air, gas waiting for a flame.

Beneath the table, Noam's hands gripped his knees, nails digging in. "You, for one."

"Those in the Defense Ministry loyal to Calix are seizing the city as we speak. Even inside this building, his witchings have turned on us. Oh, my people are putting up a good fight, but we'll soon be surrounded. I suspect my days are numbered."

Noam was going to throw up. For a reeling moment he was so sure of it, was half-out of his chair before the sickness ebbed.

"So you have no proof," Noam insisted, swallowing hard. "You could be making this up. How do I know Lehrer's even staging a coup?"

"I don't need proof," Sacha said evenly. "You already know I'm telling the truth."

Sacha placed the circlet over his brow once more and stood. He lingered there a moment, fingertips brushing the back of his chair. "Your friend Dara knows Lehrer better than anyone. I'm given to understand his telepathy makes him one of the only people Calix can't influence. So why do you think Dara turned on him?" A thin smile. "Consider that, Noam, while you decide how much you'd like to tell me."

Sacha left. The door slid shut behind him, and Noam sat there, staring at his own white-faced reflection in the one-way mirror.

This wasn't something he could dismiss out of hand—he had to . . .

He had to at least consider Sacha might be telling the truth.

But what would that mean? Just how deep did this go? Had Lehrer forced Noam to agree to kill Brennan?

What about the coup, or how easily Noam discarded Dara's warnings in favor of trusting Lehrer?

No one does anything in this country that Lehrer doesn't want them to.

Dara said that, up on the roof. Was it possible—Sacha, with the Faraday cage . . . all those horrible things Sacha did. Was Lehrer responsible for that too? Was it just a play to undermine Sacha's power and pose Lehrer as his heroic opponent?

Noam pressed his brow against the heels of his hands, hunching forward to brace his elbows on the table.

Fuck. No. That wasn't right. Sacha had worn that crown for ages now. So even if Lehrer could have controlled him once, he hadn't for a while. And in that time, Sacha made no moves to dismantle the refugee camps. He'd even declared martial law—goaded by Noam and Lehrer's machinations, sure, but that was still *Sacha's* decision. Sacha wasn't some lily-white victim.

But part of Noam believed him anyway.

Jesus.

How was Noam supposed to untangle this shit? Impossible to tell how much was another layer of Lehrer's game and how much was a ploy on Sacha's part to twist Noam's loyalty. If Noam still trusted Lehrer, was *that* real? Had Lehrer ever ordered Noam to trust him?

He couldn't remember.

Noam exhaled roughly, lifting his head and looking up toward the ceiling. He had to choose. He had to pick a side and hope to hell he wasn't making a mistake.

Either way, he was probably being manipulated.

The door opened again. But it wasn't Sacha this time. It was some man Noam only recognized from photographs, General Ames's replacement: the new home secretary.

Noam frowned. "Minister Holloway?"

"Oh, right," Holloway said and waved his hand.

The illusion dissipated, there one second and gone the next. Noam leaped to his feet, adrenaline burning through his veins. The sudden change in position made him light headed, Noam grabbing on to the table for balance.

Dara was pale, skin stained by the circles beneath his eyes and his clothes disheveled—but it was him. It was *him*.

"Come on," Dara said. "I'm getting you out of here."

Chapter Twenty-Three

Dara. Dara, still flushed with fevermadness. Dara, who could read minds and hated Lehrer and spied for Sacha's government. Dara was *here*. Breaking Noam out of jail.

"We have to hurry," Dara said when Noam didn't move, glancing over his shoulder toward the anteroom.

"What are you doing here? Where's Sacha?" Noam said. "You . . ."

Dara didn't look well. Whatever else, Lehrer was right about that much: Dara was definitely sick.

Dara's face contorted into a brief, complicated expression. "Don't worry about it. Please, Noam, we need to *go*."

He held out his hand, and somehow that broke the fragile ice that had frozen Noam's feet to the floor. Noam lurched forward, and Dara's hand closed around his, firm and overhot and pulling him out the cell door.

The anteroom was filled with bodies.

"Fuck," Noam gasped, stumbling to avoid tripping over the leg of one of those black-clothed soldiers. The man's face was slack and open-mouthed. No blood. "Dara, what did you do?"

All of them, Dara had killed *all of them*. Sacha's body lay twisted near the door, the circlet still lodged atop his head.

Noam's heart convulsed.

God. God, Dara was . . . he was crazy. That was the only explanation. Never mind utilitarianism. Never mind assassinating General Ames for a cause.

Killing six people was *crazy*.

"I did what I had to. Do you really think Sacha would let you walk out alive? Now *come on*."

Dara's grip tightened on Noam's hand, and Noam looked at him, Dara's wide eyes and tousled hair, his fear so out of place he was almost unrecognizable.

Noam sucked in a sharp breath. Sacha's body was visible out of the corner of his eye, limp as a discarded rag. He nodded.

Dara shouldered open the other door, Noam a half step behind as they tumbled into the hall. It was empty, and Noam figured out why a second later. Gunshots, from the east wing.

"I can get us out of here," Dara promised, tugging Noam toward the left.

Noam wasn't sure he ought to trust him. But he didn't have a choice.

He dashed at Dara's side down the hall toward a staircase. His mind was stuck on the same searing note.

Sacha was dead.

They clattered down the stairs, footfalls obscenely loud to Noam's ears. Dara hesitated for a second at the landing, then said, "There are people heading this way. We have to go right. Wait—*fuck*. In here!"

Dara pulled Noam to one side, his power throwing open a random door. They darted inside, and Dara stood there with his forehead pressed against the frame, hand still grasping the knob.

"Dara," Noam whispered. It came out hoarse and odd. "How—"

Glancing at Noam, Dara's eyes gleamed in the light from the cracks between the window blinds. "Lehrer had me locked up in his apartment. He said I was fevermad—can you believe it? After the riots started and Lehrer found out you'd been arrested, he told me where to find you and let me go."

You are *fevermad*, Noam wanted to say.

He didn't have to, of course. Dara heard it anyway, judging by that grimace. In this light, his skin was a delicate, sickly hue. It was like someone had drained the color out of him, leaving a sepia imprint behind.

"Don't believe everything Lehrer tells you," Dara said. "He's the one who got you arrested in the first place. He sent in that tip. You were just a loose end Lehrer had to tie up."

Noam swallowed. If he was honest, he'd known that on some level already.

He reached for Dara's arm, regretting it only a split second after he'd already done it. But for once, Dara didn't flinch. "Sacha . . . Sacha was trying to convince me Lehrer could control people's minds." He made a face, like, *Isn't that ridiculous?* and battered down the lump in his throat.

Dara nodded. "It's true."

Sacha was right. Sacha was right. Sacha was *right.*

"Fuck." Noam let go of Dara's arm to grab at the back of his own neck instead, a compulsion that did little to quell his writhing insides.

Dara rubbed his sweat-glazed brow. "That's one of the things I didn't want to tell you." He almost sounded apologetic. "He doesn't use it all the time, but often enough. For obvious reasons, Lehrer doesn't want that knowledge getting around. If he thought you knew, he'd . . ." Dara bit his lip, letting his words hang in the air.

Noam got the sense he knew exactly what Dara was suggesting Lehrer'd do.

"So why did you just murder Sacha? You're supposed to be on his side!"

"I think it's fair to say I just defected," Dara said dryly, and Noam thought about those bodies again. Sacha's blank eyes.

It was hard to breathe.

"Why?"

Dara gave him an odd look, the shadows softening his features into something strange and inhuman. "I couldn't leave you there." A moment passed, Noam's chest tightening around each exhale. Dara tilted his head to one side. "I suppose Lehrer knows me better than I'd like to admit. Now be quiet. I've got a lot of minds to read."

Dara turned his face back toward the door, eyes closed, and Noam . . . Noam didn't know what to think. It was too much. Sacha dead, Lehrer . . . complicated. And then there was Dara, whom Noam was starting to think he didn't know at all.

And Brennan.

Don't think about that.

Noam scrubbed his hand against his face and turned away from Dara, toward the empty office. There was an uncapped pen on the desk and paperwork strewn over the floor. Someone had left in a hurry.

He sensed the pen cap, he realized, a tiny shock sparking beneath his skin. It had rolled under the floor lamp. Whatever Sacha's people had injected him with was wearing off.

Of course, even if he and Dara got out of here, they had an entire battlefield between them and safety.

Safety being Lehrer—and Lehrer's mind control.

He turned back toward Dara, who was half-slumped against the door, skin gone disturbingly pallid. "Are you okay?"

"Fine," Dara said. He opened his eyes and pushed away from the door. He wavered for a moment, then balanced himself with a hand against the wall. "But Lehrer's about to seize control of this country, and we don't want to be caught up in it when he does." He gestured toward the window. "We need to run. Is your electromagnetism quick enough to deflect bullets?"

"Do you know how fast bullets are?"

Dara sighed. "I figured. Still, better to ask."

"They injected me with suppressant. When it wears off, maybe I can keep a shield up," Noam said. "Once we're out on the streets. That way I don't have to think about it, bullets will just . . ." He waved, and Dara managed a weak smile.

"Perfect," Dara said. "We should leave now. I'll have Holloway escort you; that's safer until we're outside, but then we'll have to be ourselves. The home secretary makes too good a hostage for the refugee block."

Noam almost asked if that was such a good idea—if fevermad people ought to keep using magic—but already Dara was gone, replaced by the same black-haired man from before. The illusion was absolute: Dara had even thought to wrinkle Holloway's collar, the way someone dealing with an ongoing riot might look. Noam saw the threads of magic sewing it all together when he looked closely enough, but no one else would notice.

"Are you ready?" Dara said in Holloway's voice.

Noam wasn't ready. He nodded anyway.

The hall was clear, but Dara didn't break character. He guided Noam down to the left with one hand pressed to Noam's back right between his shoulder blades, a gesture that could appear either paternalistic or authoritarian, depending on what someone expected to see. *A nice touch*, Noam thought, then almost laughed. They were running for their lives, and Noam was assessing Dara's acting ability.

"We're about to run into some people," Dara murmured after a moment, not slowing down. "Hard to say if they know Sacha arrested you; they're not thinking about it right now."

"Can't you cast an illusion on me too?" Noam whispered back.

"I'm good, but I'm not omnipotent. Act natural, and follow my lead."

Noam sucked in a sharp breath. There was just enough time to worry whether his expression looked natural before they turned the corner. A platoon of soldiers held the hall, five covering each end of the corridor. Their CO shouted, five guns snapping up to point right at him and Dara. Noam reached frantically for his power, but all he managed to achieve was an odd little shiver through the metal of the nearest pistol.

Thank god for small mercies. If it weren't for suppressants, Noam would've just given them away.

"I need you to let us through," Dara said. He captured the stern tone of high command so perfectly that Noam could have believed he was listening to Lehrer himself.

Of course, Lehrer was probably exactly whom Dara was trying to emulate.

"Minister Holloway," the lieutenant said. "All members of the administration are supposed to be in the bunker. We'll escort you there immediately."

Dara's hand moved up to Noam's shoulder, squeezing once. "I'm afraid not. I need to deal with this one."

"We'll bring you both to the bunker. It's safer. You shouldn't be out here when—"

"Lieutenant," Dara interrupted, "tell your men to get their guns out of my face."

The man's cheeks darkened. He looked for a moment like he was struggling to get his mouth to cooperate. Then: "Stand down."

The guns lowered.

"Thank you," Dara said, a sardonic edge sharp on his voice. "Now. Let us pass."

"Sir—"

"I don't need to explain my orders to you," Dara said, Holloway's mouth wrinkling with dissatisfaction. "If you like, you may take this up with the chancellor when this is all over. Right now, I don't have time."

"I think perhaps I should radio the captain . . ."

"Lieutenant."

The lieutenant straightened. And, after a beat, faltered into an awkward half bow. "Yes, sir. Of course. Carry on."

Dara's hand tightened on Noam's shoulder, and he nudged him forward through the gathered platoon. Noam kept expecting it to be a trick. What if they'd found Sacha's body? What if they knew someone looking like Minister Holloway had been there, that Noam had been in custody and was now missing?

But no guns rose to meet them. They passed without interference, Holloway and his nameless civilian teenager progressing at measured pace through all that firepower.

"Almost there," Dara whispered when they were out of earshot. "Lehrer's men cover the west exits. We'll have a better chance slipping out there; they trust me since I'm Lehrer's ward. This way."

They managed to avoid other soldiers before reaching the west wing service exit. It took twice as long as it should have—good for Noam's power but less so for his nerves. Dara led them through winding back halls and up and down several sets of stairs, occasionally still shoving him into a shadowy office to stay out of sight while a unit trampled past.

But they made it.

Dara dropped his Holloway illusion at the exit door, stern features fading to reveal Dara's wan face.

"Are you sure you're okay?" Noam said, gingerly touching Dara's elbow. "You look—"

"I said I'm fine," Dara snapped. "Sorry. All this switching sides is making me motion sick."

"It's going to be all right," Noam said. He willed Dara to believe him, feeding confidence into his expression. "I promise. It's almost over, and then we can . . . we'll figure it out. Okay?"

Dara just said, "You should put up that electromagnetic field now."

Noam obeyed, drawing up a thin bubble of charge all around them, strong enough the hairs on his arms stood on end. And then, on Dara's cue, he opened the door.

"Freeze!"

Noam and Dara stumbled to a halt right there on the doorstep, the metal service door clanging shut. At least twenty soldiers surrounded the exit, all with guns pointed at Noam's and Dara's heads. Noam practically tasted his heart in his mouth as he threw his hands up.

Be Lehrer's men—God, fuck, please be Lehrer's men—

The force of Noam's electromagnetic field pushed against the metal guns; the soldiers struggled to keep them steady as the barrels tilted toward the sky. Noam couldn't spare focus to appreciate their confusion. Next to him, Dara was visibly trembling.

"Don't shoot," Noam managed to get out through a tight throat. "We're unarmed. Please don't shoot."

"Sir!" one of the soldiers shouted. "Sir, that's Dara Shirazi."

"Lower your weapons."

The guns went down, if maladroitly, and a beat later so did Noam's hands. The unit leader edged his way between the gathered men. Noam saw, now, that he had a ribbon of ripped blue cloth tied around his upper arm—Carolinian blue. His face was beaded with sweat.

"Dara Shirazi," the man said, pointing at Dara. "And you must be Noam Álvaro, right? Lehrer's new student?"

Noam nodded.

"Hi, Evan," Dara said in a strained voice.

The man, Evan, sighed. "What the hell're you two doing here? You oughta be in the training wing. It ain't safe."

"We need to get to Lehrer," Noam said. It was obvious Dara wasn't going to be able to speak again without throwing up all over Evan's military-issue boots. Dara did manage to send a little burst of static electricity against Noam's shoulder, though, which Noam ignored. Of course Dara wouldn't be happy about going to Lehrer, but he wasn't exactly in a state to be making life-and-death decisions. "Where is he?"

Evan shook his head. "Y'all got about a quarter mile of angry protesters between here and there. I can't recommend it."

"We're both Level IV. We can defend ourselves."

"You think so, do you?" Evan folded his arms over his chest and lifted grizzled gray brows. "This shit's messy as it gets, boy. We're soldiers, and even we can barely tell the difference between us and them. Hard to know who's on which side with everyone wearin' the same uniform. If the rioters don't trample you to death, one side of the Ministry or the other'll shoot you, thinking you're rioting. Not good."

"Please," Noam insisted, knowing that wasn't exactly a good argument, but what was he supposed to say? He couldn't tell what Evan was thinking, had no idea what might convince him. "We can't go back to the training wing; Sacha's got the whole complex covered."

"Y'all can stay here with us."

"And if you get attacked? You're right at the government complex. This isn't exactly a secure position. Dara and I are wearing civvies. We'll blend in with the refugees, so they won't attack us. We've already got an electro—a magic shield up. We'll head straight for Lehrer. He . . ." Noam fumbled for something else to say. Something persuasive. "He told us to come find him. It was a direct order. He's minister of defense, he's our commanding officer, so we *have* to go."

"That what he said, is it?" Evan tapped his fingers against his arm.

"Yes, sir."

Evan looked like he was prepared to argue some more, but at last he just blew out a hard gust of air and said, "Fine. But your shield stays up. *Always*, you got me? Always. Don't you talk to anyone; don't get involved in any skirmishes. And I know y'all're witchings, but you're still gonna take a weapon with you." He snapped his fingers. "Hardy. Give 'em your handgun."

One of the privates unholstered his pistol and passed it to Evan, who handed it to Noam. "Keep that out of sight."

Noam tucked the gun into his jeans, pressed flat against his back and hidden by the hem of his shirt. The cold metal burned his skin.

Blackwell and Vivian.

"Yes, sir," Noam said again and didn't think about that, didn't think about it.

Focus on Dara. His palm was clammy when Noam reached for his hand, but his grasp was strong.

"Get on out of here." Evan gestured toward the mouth of the alley. "Left up there. Keep heading north toward warehouse twelve. Lehrer's commanding a unit roundabout there. And *be careful*."

"We will. Thank you," Noam said, tugging at Dara's hand before Evan could think better of letting them go.

The square teemed with bodies, thousands of faceless people united in a roar of sound. Impossible to tell the difference between chanting and screaming now. Noam gripped Dara's hand, looking back to meet his wide eyes. Glass shattered ten feet to their right, and an answering voice yelled something incoherent and enraged.

"This way," Noam shouted, though it was hard to tell if Dara could hear him. There were too many people, all headed in different directions and bleeding together like paint. Somewhere toward the east, a black cloud of smoke billowed overhead. A pop-pop-pop of gunshots. Noam's pulse stumbled clumsily against his ribs.

"Burn them!" someone yelled behind him, a raw and rough voice that scraped the marrow from Noam's bones. "Burn the rats in their nest—"

North, north, Noam told himself, *just keep going north*. But the crowd was an endless sea stretching over the horizon, no shore in sight.

More screams, closer. Noam didn't look. He didn't want to see. Noam's nails dug into the back of Dara's hand, and they would have been swept underfoot if it weren't for Noam's power pushing people away, and—when that failed—his elbows.

The buildings on the north side of the square were close now; just twenty more feet and they could duck down an alley. He could see warehouse twelve.

More gunshots peppered the air somewhere behind him, the bullets glinting like falling stars to Noam's magic, though none of them met flesh, not yet. Just soldiers shooting deadly warnings toward the sky.

The tide shifted. Suddenly the crowd was all moving in one direction—east, away from the government buildings, as if propelled by some terrible force. Noam's power battered uselessly against the wave of people crushing in from the west. They were like cattle, Noam realized frantically as he found himself swept up in the mad dash. Cattle with wolves biting at their heels.

A blockade was up; it must be. The army had them pinned into this square like an enraged bull crowded into a pen before a fight, chased by guns at their backs to beat themselves bloody against the barricade. Noam learned about this in Swensson's class, remembered the diagrams Swensson drew on the chalkboard, white flaking lines to show troop movements: *barricade here, then hammer nail.*

The crowd roiled against the blockade, burning with a rage that had nowhere to go. Magic sizzled all around. Witchings. Lehrer's soldiers or Sacha's? Not a risk Noam was willing to take.

Warehouse twelve. Just get to warehouse twelve.

Dara yanked on his arm and yelled something.

"What?"

"Noam!"

Noam shoved a stranger out of the way and tugged Dara closer, until they were pressed chest to chest by the seething mob, Dara's breath hot on Noam's neck and his hair a tangled mess.

"What is it?"

"We have to run!"

"We *are* running."

But Dara pulled back against Noam's grip on his wrist. When Noam got a proper look at his face this time, it was . . . changed. Paler than before, if such a thing were even possible.

"No, we have to—into the quarantined zone," Dara said. "I can . . . there are people. I can find people. But I'm not going back."

The mob washed round them like a writhing sea.

"Dara—*no*. You're sick."

"But Lehrer—"

"We'll figure out what to do about Lehrer later. Right now he's our best chance at staying alive."

Noam pulled Dara's arm again, and this time Dara tipped off-balance, knocking against Noam. He was weak, so weak.

"Quarantined zone," Dara murmured against Noam's collarbone, audible only because he was so near. "Go there. I'll go. Safe. They have a vaccine."

But he wasn't fighting Noam's grip on his waist either. Noam hitched his grasp a little higher, under Dara's arms, and took an experimental step forward. Dara stumbled along with him.

"Noam," Dara said. His voice was oddly urgent. Tight, like violin wire.

"It's okay," Noam said.

But Dara jerked his arm hard enough that Noam was the one who nearly toppled off-balance this time. Noam looked at him. It was astonishing that Dara was still standing on his own two feet, for all he clung to Noam with both hands.

"I have to go now."

"Dara, don't—"

Dara glanced over his shoulder, wild and jumpy as cornered prey. "Listen," Dara said. "Listen, you have to—listen, now, believe me."

"No, you listen. You're sick," Noam told Dara, clasping his face between both hands so he could hold Dara's gaze. Dara's pupils were shot wide. "You don't know what you're saying. You can't go into the quarantined zone—for fuck's sake, Dara. You'd die there."

Dara made an agonized noise in the back of his throat, inhuman. His fingers dug into Noam's arms.

"It's Lehrer, he, listen—are you? Listening? Noam. Lehrer, he . . . the virus. Do you understand?"

What the hell was Dara going on about? He was starting to wish Dara had never broken free of Lehrer's apartment. Yeah, Noam would still be under arrest, but at least Dara would be safe: a steroid drip in his arm, a doctor on call.

"There's a . . . they have . . . vaccine. In the quarantined zone. Understand? Lehrer doesn't want . . . he said, told me, *witching state*."

Dara twisted his fingers into Noam's hair and yanked him down again, hard enough Noam had to bite back a yelp of pain. Dara held him there with impossible strength. His eyes were so bright, like something feral, something hungry.

Dara said, "Lehrer did it. The virus. Released it. Himself. On his own people. Infected, to make *witchings.*"

The way he said it was . . . not what Noam expected, somehow. It was low and intense, Dara enunciating every syllable so carefully, like he worried his words would get away from him if he didn't say them deliberately.

An uneasy wave pitched in Noam's stomach. "What . . . Dara, what are you saying?"

"Lehrer . . . causes, he causes them. The outbreaks."

Fevermadness. Wasn't it?

"He's a—telepath. Noam. Reads your mind." Dara gestured violently toward his own temple. He was talking faster now, all of it pouring out of him at once. His cheeks glowed with fever. "Learned it. But only if—only if he—knows you, or something . . . I don't. *Listen to me.* He'll kill me. He, already, he . . ." Dara's voice cracked.

"It's okay," Noam said, but he wasn't sure he even believed that anymore. His voice sounded like it was coming from very far away, blood moving too fast beneath his skin. Where was Lehrer now? How close? Noam imagined the glittering threads of Lehrer's magic twining through his every thought, tightening in a hundred impossible knots.

"*No*, no, now you *listen*—you—this *whole time*. The bruises—it was Lehrer. Not Gordon. Lehrer. He—I was fourteen, Noam! I was . . . but he . . . and I couldn't *tell* anyone because, god, didn't even need his power!" Dara laughed, a mad sound, and he wasn't touching Noam anymore, had both hands pressed up against his own skull. "No one *believed* me."

Those words caught between them, butterflies pinned on velvet. There, where Noam had no choice but to look at them. To *really* look, to see—

All this time. All of it. Everyone Noam knew had burned up in fever because of Lehrer. This whole damn country. And Dara, clutching that secret, afraid to tell Noam in case Lehrer could read his mind and *know*. Dara's hatred, which had never been hate at all.

It had been fear.

Oh god.

Noam had trusted him. Noam had trusted this man, the same one who had murdered all those millions of people. Noam's own father.

There were words for what Lehrer did to Dara too.

Noam's stomach knotted in on itself. Dara was still laughing bizarrely. Or maybe he was crying.

Noam made the decision between one half-choked breath and the next. He reached for Dara, hand faltering in the moment before it touched Dara's arm—*all those times Dara flinched away*—before he pressed just the tips of his fingers against flesh. Dara didn't look like he was breathing, shoulders quivering with the effort of holding in his air.

"I . . ." The word broke as it fell out of Noam's lips.

The next ones, still in his mouth, were as jagged as shattered glass. He didn't want to think about it—didn't want it to be true, but Dara was here, right now, looking at him like Noam had plunged his hand into Dara's chest, past ribs and muscle and sinew to close his fingers around Dara's still-beating heart.

"I believe you, Dara."

Dara made a strange, animalistic sound. "I tried to tell you."

"I know. I . . ." What could he even say? There was nothing that would make this better. Nothing to undo what Lehrer had done: to his own people, his own *child*.

And if they didn't leave now, Lehrer would be the one who found them here. He'd lock Dara up again, and it would be Noam's fault for being so damn naive.

"I'm so sorry, Dara." And that was grotesquely insufficient, of course. Noam felt sick with himself for it. "But you're right, we have to—we need to go. Now, before Lehrer manages to quell the riot."

"The . . . QZ?" Dara's voice was only slightly unsteady.

Noam still hated the idea. If Dara really was fevermad, how could he survive out there, with magic in the soil and water and air? Only—only Lehrer could have lied about that too. He could have made Dara sick somehow, called him fevermad just to make sure Noam would never believe anything Dara told him—

"Yeah," Noam said. "Yeah. If we can get past the barricade, if we move fast . . ."

Dara clenched his jaw, a muscle visibly tensing in his cheek, and nodded.

Lehrer'd had men on the street ever since Sacha's martial law order—Sacha hadn't seen the coup coming. The barricades must be Lehrer's men. But that meant Dara's name would be twice as useful, just so long as no one tried calling it in.

Then again, if Lehrer was listening to Noam's thoughts right now, they were fucked either way.

Noam tried to keep Dara close as they started pushing toward the barricade. The crowds were crammed in so close Noam had to turn sideways to press between them—but they made it.

The barricade was just barbed wire, roll upon roll of it stacked chest high over a metal blockade. Still, few seemed willing to go within five feet of it. Those who did were quickly shocked back by the soldiers' magic.

Soldiers wearing blue ribbons.

Noam broke free of the mob and dashed toward the barricade, half dragging Dara in tow. He didn't dare let go of Dara, just held his free arm up in the air: surrender. He knew what they looked like: two kids in civvies running out of a riot and right at the barricade. The soldiers on the other hand: monolithic, well armed, glaring with flat eyes, resentment setting their jaws. And Noam might pass for white, but Dara sure as hell didn't, which, yeah. *We're gonna get shot.*

Noam opened his mouth to speak, and one of the soldiers lashed out with his power instantly. Noam felt the snap of burning magic in the air a split second before he reacted, dashing it aside with a shield. It sparked and flared against the asphalt, a white firecracker quickly extinguished.

"Don't shoot," Noam shouted, power latching on to the guns before the soldiers could point them at their heads. Noam held his ground. "Don't shoot—just let us through."

Let me handle this, he thought toward Dara as loudly as he could. Dara's silence was answer enough.

Noam didn't let himself entertain other reasons Dara might be incapable of speech.

The two soldiers nearest Noam glanced at each other. One of them spat dip, strings of brown juice dribbling down his chin. "You're a threat, and I'm authorized to shoot threats."

"Yeah? Just try it." Noam had jammed the bullets in their chambers.

He stepped forward again, fighting back nausea and the pounding in his head. One man pulled his trigger, then swore when nothing happened and tossed his gun aside, lifting a hand to use his power instead.

But it was too late. Noam grabbed his wrist, and the electricity buzzing around the man's fingertips blinked out. It was grimly satisfying to watch fear bloom in the soldiers' eyes.

"Who the fuck *are* you?" said the man whose wristbone was in danger of being crushed under Noam's superpotent grip, struggling and failing to pull away.

"We're Level IV. Lehrer's students. Where is he?"

The man gestured mutely over his shoulder. Noam glanced toward Dara, who was too dazed to notice.

Noam turned back toward the soldiers. "Well? Are you going to let us in?"

"ID first," one of them said, not the one whose wrist Noam nearly broke.

Noam reached back into Dara's pocket and dug around until he found a wallet. Dara's name must've done the trick because the soldiers let them through, someone's magnetic power pulling back the barbed wire far enough to let Noam and Dara step over the knee-high steel blockade.

"Two blocks north of here," one of the soldiers told them. "They're holding against the loyalists near the old theater. Watch your backs."

They walked away from the riot but in the opposite direction from where the soldiers had gestured—away from Lehrer, away from the screams and gunshots that felt like they followed Noam a half step behind. He didn't like the way the soldiers looked at them, even behind this barricade. Their gazes lingered too long, fingers on triggers.

Without rioters, the street felt too empty, trash scattered across the sidewalk from an overturned garbage bin and tumbling along in the breeze. Noam hung on to Dara's arm like that was going to make a difference. Broken glass crunched underfoot. Noam kicked an empty tear gas canister out of the way, and Dara jumped.

"Sorry," Noam muttered.

"We can't," Dara said. He came to a sudden stop, yanking Noam to a halt with him.

At first Noam thought he was going to start up on the quarantined zone shit again, but then he followed Dara's glassy stare. A platoon marched this way, blue-ribboned soldiers with machine guns trained on a line of loyalist prisoners. Noam opened his mouth to say, *It's fine—they don't care about us*, but then there was a break in the line, and he saw the bodies slumped against the ground. Blood splattered against brick wall.

A fresh group of five facing the firing squad.

"Okay," Noam said, pushing Dara ahead of him toward the other side of the street. "Okay. Keep walking. Just keep walking."

His head buzzed with white noise. He kept taking in shallow gulps of air that never seemed to reach his lungs, heat pouring into his veins.

Pop-pop-pop-pop-pop.

Noam tripped over a loose brick on the sidewalk, and Dara heaved him up by the elbow. Their eyes met, and as if by silent agreement, they broke into a run.

Someone shouted behind them, but Noam couldn't make out the words. *Run.* Everything condensed to that. He barely felt the bullets bouncing off his electromagnetic shield.

"Just go!" Noam shouted at Dara when he turned around to look, shoving his hands against Dara's back. "Go!"

They sprinted down the next alley, both tapping superstrength to make each stride count. Bullets were one thing, but Noam didn't want to find out if that platoon had witchings. He sensed more soldiers up ahead, a tank.

"No—no, not this way," he said, and they changed direction again, up a lengthy street. Without cars and cabs and carts full of fruit and flowers, the road reminded Noam of a long black scar carved into the city's flesh.

They careened onto the parallel street, Noam on Dara's heels, and yes, *yes*—that was traffic far ahead at the intersection. They could lose themselves in the city, catch a bus to the Southpoint suburbs. Then maybe, maybe they'd steal a car, drive until they hit the fence that barred out the quarantined zone. After that, Noam didn't know, but they'd figure it out. They'd walk all the way to York if they had to.

"Freeze!"

Noam and Dara stumbled to a stop, the air cracking like thin ice under the weight of that shout. Noam spun around, hands up, not sure if he was ready to fight or surrender.

Soldiers, blue-ribboned ones, guns up. But no antiwitching armor.

No Lehrer either.

"We're Level IV," Noam said, because it worked last time. Only last time, his voice didn't shake. Last time, his mouth didn't feel like it was stuffed with gauze.

"Yeah," the lieutenant said, his slow smile unsheathing like a knife. "I know."

And Noam understood. He understood without looking, certainty shooting him like a lethal arrow—but he looked anyway, turning his back on the raised guns to face a worse threat.

For a split second, Noam reached for his magic, that silver-blue spark answering easily now. But what could he possibly do against 123 years of power? Lehrer would quench him like a struck match.

It was too late to run. Too late for anything now.

To his left, Dara was still—so very still.

Lehrer's hand fell to Noam's shoulder. In the bright summer sunlight, he looked like a hero straight ou legend, tall and fair haired with a streak of someone else's blood on his cheek. Like the revolutionary of the twenty-first century, stepped from the pages of a history book.

"What did he tell you?" Lehrer asked. His colorless gaze lingered on Noam's just a beat too long—then he lifted his hand.

Noam couldn't move. His feet had grown roots into the concrete, into the center of the earth.

Lehrer's fingertips grazed Noam's temple. It wasn't the touch Noam expected. It was light, delicate, like a caress.

Lehrer sighed. "I see."

His touch dropped again, this time to curve round Noam's neck, the edge of his thumb pressed against a knobby vertebra. Noam didn't dare breathe.

I won't be the reason you die, Dara told him, and Noam should have listened.

He should have listened.

"No," Dara said. "Please—don't . . ."

This was it. This was it, after all this—after all this time, this was how Noam died after all: the June heat seeping through Noam's skin, Lehrer wound tight into his mind like so many golden threads, Brennan's blood on his hands.

He looked at Dara—the last person he wanted to see. Dara's face, twisted with anguish and slick with feversweat.

"Don't what?" Lehrer asked. His fingertips slipped into Noam's hair. Noam couldn't have moved even if he wanted to. Lehrer was too strong. He kept him in place with barely any effort at all. "Kill him? My dear boy, there's an easier way. Pay attention. This lesson should be well learned. Now . . . Noam."

Lehrer leaned closer.

He smelled like iron. His words were soft.

"Forget everything Dara just told you."

And Noam did.

The moments that followed would return in fractured pieces, later, like images shot in a darkroom, the flash of a bulb illuminating still frames and freezing them in time.

Dara, sick with fevermadness, his hands on Noam's face. Saying, "You have to listen to me."

Over and over.

Lehrer, pulling Dara away like it was easy.

Dara screaming, *Don't let them* and *Please* and Noam's name, like someone praying the Shema.

The sickness in Noam's stomach.

Knowing he did the right thing. Hating himself anyway.

Gold-glitter magic.

The moment they won the day, Carolinia's blue banner unfurling anew over the government complex.

The crowd chanting Lehrer's name.

Chapter Twenty-Four

It was three days after the coup—three days after the military junta seized control, two days after the Atlantian refugees were granted citizenship by executive order, one day after Brennan's body was put in the ground—before Noam saw Lehrer again.

They lit fireworks in west Durham, dazzling bursts of color lighting up the sky, visible even from the courtyard of the government complex. Noam sat on a bench with Dara's flask of bourbon between his knees, face lifted starward.

He ought to be happy. They won.

He wasn't happy. His blood sludged through his veins, breath stale in his lungs and stomach swollen with something rotten.

Guilt, of course. He knew that. It was natural. Of course it was. He killed a man. He killed Brennan.

That's all he saw every time he shut his eyes. Brennan's dead gaze and the flare of blood on the wall behind his desk, red and vibrant as one of those fireworks.

Sometimes he saw Dara instead. Those times were worse, somehow, because he deserved to feel guilty over Brennan. He deserved worse than guilt. But Dara? There, at least, he'd done the right thing. Dara would be okay. Dara would be safe. Dara might not realize it yet, but soon he'd be healthy and happy and back to his old self.

If he survived these next few months, that is.

The last thing Dara shouted—the last thing Noam understood, anyway, before Lehrer's men took him away—was *kill me*.

"I thought I might find you here."

Noam looked up.

Lehrer had discarded his military uniform in favor of a plain suit. Understated. Political.

"Is everything all right?" Lehrer said.

He must have noticed the bourbon but pretended not to.

"I'm fine," Noam said. "Just . . . thinking."

Lehrer gestured toward the bench. "Do you mind if I join you?"

Noam nodded. After a beat, he even thought to pick up the bottle cap and screw it back on the flask.

Even sitting, Lehrer's body took up far more room than Noam's. He rested an arm along the back of the bench and shifted to face Noam properly. He looked at Noam like Noam was the only person in the world.

"This past week has been difficult," Lehrer said. "I know that. And I hope you realize you can talk to me."

Noam sat on his hands to keep from reaching for his flask. "I'm fine," he said eventually. He couldn't quite meet Lehrer's gaze, even now. Even after everything Lehrer had done for him, for Atlantians. For Carolinia. He stared at his knees instead and said, "Sacha told me about your power. Mind control. I thought you should know that I know."

He stole a glance, quick enough to catch the flicker of emotion darting across Lehrer's face: shock, uncertainty, a sudden tension. Noam braced himself for Lehrer to—what? Kill him, like Sacha said he would?

Noam knew Lehrer better than that, or so he liked to think.

"It's not *mind* control, Noam."

"Persuasion, then." Noam shook his head, discarding the semantics. That fear still gripped the base of his skull, white knuckled and refusing to let go. "I thought about it. I decided . . . I won't tell anyone. I'm sure you could *persuade* me to keep silent, or whatever, but you won't have to. Just for the record."

"I'd appreciate that," Lehrer said wryly.

In the far distance, someone set off a firecracker: a sharp snap and someone's answering whoop of ecstasy.

Eventually, Noam made himself say it.

"Have you used your power on me?"

"No."

Noam grimaced. "I suppose you'd say that either way."

"Probably," Lehrer admitted. "So, you're just going to have to trust me."

A hard gift to grant. Lehrer must understand that. He and Noam were alike in that way. They'd both grown up in environments where trusting the wrong person would get you killed.

When Noam was a young child, his grandmother used to tell him terrifying stories meant to keep him close to home—or make him Catholic, as his mother had always implied. It was no secret Noam's grandmother disapproved of her son's conversion to Judaism. So she told him stories about La Llorona, about El Boraro. About El Mandinga: the Evil One, a silver-tongued devil wearing the guise of a handsome man.

If he speaks, close your ears. If he follows, you pray. But never look him in the eyes; a single glance, and your soul belongs to him.

Noam met Lehrer's clear-glass gaze.

"What about Sacha? Did you persuade him?"

Lehrer didn't blink. "Sometimes."

"Did you . . ." Noam faltered. He swallowed. "Did you . . . make him . . . do all of that? To the refugees? Just to undermine him?"

"Of course not," Lehrer said, more firmly this time. "Sacha was a xenophobe and a bigot, Noam. You know what happened to witchings in the catastrophe. To my *family*. Do you really think I'd perpetuate that on another minority group?"

Heat flushed Noam's cheeks, but he couldn't just give in. Not now. Not after everything. "I have to ask."

"I used my power on Sacha because he had to be stopped," Lehrer said. "At *any* cost. I care about nothing as much as I care about this country. I was there when this nation was born, Noam, and like hell will I watch it die at the hands of a baseline."

There was a roughness to the way Lehrer said the words. The lighting out here reflected strangely in his eyes, like something moving beneath the surface of a lake.

"You turned me in to Sacha."

"I did." Lehrer's expression did not change.

"Why?"

"I needed Sacha to think he still had a chance. While he was distracted with you, my men surrounded the government complex." Lehrer seemed less human now than he once did. Now he was cold and utilitarian, as precise as an elegant machine. Those moments Noam had glimpsed true emotion were more fractured and unnatural than the mask itself. "And I knew if I sent Dara to save your life, he would kill Sacha for me."

Which Dara did.

All of them—even Dara, who had been so suspicious of Lehrer's motives—were just easy pawns in Lehrer's game.

The ache lingered in Noam's chest. When he turned his gaze toward the electric lights strung overhead, Lehrer reached over and set his hand gently on Noam's leg.

"I'm proud of you," Lehrer said. "I asked a lot of you these past several weeks. But you kept your head, even when all seemed lost. I've said it before, but it bears repeating. In many ways you remind me of myself."

Nothing Noam felt made sense anymore, as if his thoughts and his body were completely divorced from each other. He'd think, *I'm happy*, even as his lungs convulsed around a new breath. He'd think, *Everything is perfect now*, while his skin burned and his hands formed fists.

"How's Dara?" he asked.

Lehrer paused. His hand stayed where it was, but it had gone still, a heavy weight against Noam's thigh.

"He'll be all right," Lehrer said at last. "A few months under suppressants . . ."

"Those are illegal."

"They are. But to save Dara's life . . . he's like a son to me." Lehrer turned his face up as well, toward the lights. "I have him on a constant IV drip of suppressants and steroids to calm the inflammation. My personal physician is very discreet."

"Will that . . . work?" It felt like too much to hope.

"Eventually," Lehrer said. "Most likely. I'd hoped it wouldn't come to this. There's a reason suppressants are illegal—depriving a witching of his magic is a terrible thing . . ." He trailed off, and Noam didn't ask. Everyone knew what they had done to Lehrer in those hospitals. The torture, the experiments. Probably worse things, too, that Lehrer had kept quiet.

"Can I see him?"

"No. Not yet."

"When?"

"Soon. I promise."

They sat there in silence after that, twin minds floating in space.

Eventually, it started to rain.

That night, Noam dreamed about Dara again.

It was his building, where he grew up. The same wood floor creaking underfoot, the shadows peering from between the bookshelves. It was August 2120, cicadas in the window, too hot. Once, this scene was all Noam saw when he shut his eyes. And so Noam knew, he knew down to his bones, before he even saw the body.

But it wasn't Noam's mother hanging from the ceiling light. It was Dara.

Ghostly hands fell upon his shoulders, golden magic flickering through the night like heat lightning. A soft and familiar voice murmured in his ear: *You will do whatever I say.*

The next morning, Noam skipped basic. He sat on the edge of his bed and stared across the room at Dara's empty one. The duvet was unwrinkled, but a book lay open near the foot; when Dara had put it down, he'd planned on coming back.

What if he didn't come back?

When Noam thought back over that conversation with Lehrer in the courtyard, he felt like he'd swallowed grease, oil sloshing around in the pit of his stomach. He couldn't figure out what about it felt wrong.

Noam had the distinct sense there was something he ought to remember, something he *didn't*. The effect of shock, maybe.

Or maybe it was the way Lehrer had said, *You're going to have to trust me*, and Noam realized, in that moment, Lehrer easily could have *made* him.

Perhaps Noam should leave. It wasn't too late. He could pack his things right now and steal a car and drive until he broke past the border into the QZ. Until he was lost in the wild and fatal wilderness.

But then he went to the Migrant Center and saw the same faces he always saw—children who might be citizens but were still starving. Noam couldn't abandon them.

And what about Dara? Can you abandon him?

In the fear-splattered tumult of Lehrer's coup, Noam felt so sure that going back to Lehrer was Dara's best chance at survival. If Dara didn't get treated, he'd keep making antibodies, and those antibodies would keep attacking his own tissue. The brain now, but then his kidneys, his liver, his heart. Dara's body would fail in pieces.

But if Noam let him stay here, Dara would die anyway.

Noam didn't see the signs with his mother. One day she was smiling, singing in the kitchen and kissing Noam's cheek. The next night she'd killed herself, and Noam still, still, *still* didn't understand why.

He wasn't making the same mistake again.

He didn't plan anything. There was nothing to plan—he didn't have contingencies, no connections in clandestine places who knew how to make a man disappear. All he had was impulse and the flash-fire certainty that yes, yes, this was the right thing to do.

It was the middle of the workday when Noam grabbed a bag from his trunk and stuffed in several sets of civilian clothes, socks, and the copy of *Laughter in the Dark* from Dara's bed. Ames was the only one in the common room as he went out, lying on the sofa with one arm slung over her face to block out the light, still sleeping off the previous night. She hadn't been sober since her father died.

He couldn't undo the wards to Lehrer's apartment, but he could pick the lock to the study—and then all he had to do was knock.

Muffled footfalls on a wooden floor. Then Dara's voice, low and wary, said, "Who is it?"

Noam leaned in against the shimmering gold mesh of Lehrer's magic. "It's me. Can you let me in?"

Dara's sharp inhale was audible even from the other side of the door. "What are you doing here?"

"What do you think? I'm on a rescue mission, Rapunzel. Now let down your hair." He smiled even though Dara couldn't see it. He pressed his hand against the cool wooden frame and imagined Dara standing just a foot away, perhaps touching the same wood.

The seconds ticked past, one after the other.

Eventually, Noam said, "Dara? Did you hear me?"

"Yes. I . . . I can't undo the ward. No magic. I'm—"

"Suppressed." Obviously. Fuck. "Um. Okay. Can you tell me how to do it?"

He could practically see Dara's expression, probably derisive. Dara explained the process to him anyway, step by halting step. Noam's magic felt like a blunt instrument scraping against Lehrer's fine thread work, but at last it unraveled like a spool of string.

The door opened, and there he was, Dara, standing on the other side in civvies with an IV in his arm and a surprised look on his face—as if Noam wasn't who he expected to find standing there after all.

"It's really you," he said.

"Who did you think it was? Chancellor Sacha, risen from the dead?"

Noam grinned, and after a moment Dara smiled back, a tentative thing that didn't quite fit on his lips. Of course—once upon a time, Dara would have had his hands in Noam's mind already, fingers combing through his thoughts. He'd have known exactly who was on the other side of the door, even if Noam didn't say a word.

At least Dara didn't look like he was dying anymore—and he was coherent, which was something. Still.

Noam's heart clenched. He ignored it.

"We'd better hurry," he said and gestured vaguely toward the ceiling. "Lehrer probably felt me take the wards down. He'll be here any second, and I really don't want to go back to prison just yet."

But Dara didn't go get his things, didn't even tear the needle out of his arm. Instead he lurched forward and threw his arms around Noam, face pressing against Noam's shoulder. "I knew you'd remember," he murmured into Noam's neck. His brow, pressed to Noam's skin, was still feverish.

"I couldn't leave you here," Noam said. He slipped a hand into Dara's hair, resisting the urge to twist his fingers in those curls and keep Dara there for good. "What you said, after . . . I thought you might . . ."

Dara's mouth stayed silent. Noam closed his eyes and took in a breath of Dara's scent, sharp with the salt of sweat. It was several seconds before he could bring himself to grasp Dara's shoulders and push him back. Dara's cheeks were a dark rose now, and that wasn't just inflammation.

"Do you have anything you need to get? I brought some clothes," Noam said and lifted the pack demonstratively.

"No. Nothing." Dara hesitated for just a second, then ripped the tape off his IV site. The needle slipped free easily, ruby droplets spilling across Lehrer's polished wood floor. "I should have taken it out earlier. But Lehrer said . . ." Dara trailed off, rubbing the heel of his hand against the pinprick wound. When he drew his hand away, there was blood on his palm. Dara stared at the reddened skin and bit his lower lip.

At last, Dara whispered, "I didn't know what he would do."

Noam nodded slowly. Dara was right. Lehrer wouldn't have let Dara leave that easily, not with the stakes so high.

Which was why it was insane that he was doing this now. Dara could die. Noam knew that.

But if he left Dara in here . . .

Dara said he'd rather be dead, and Noam had believed him.

He pinged the security cameras. Lehrer was on the second floor and headed this way. He'd be here in less than ten minutes. He didn't look pleased.

"We gotta go," Noam said.

But Dara stayed where he was, pale and twisting his fingers together in front of his stomach. "Listen, Noam," he started. For one dizzying second Noam was so sure Dara was about to say, *I changed my mind*— but then: "Lehrer . . . he told me not to leave the apartment."

It took a second for those words to parse. Then:

"Oh. Right."

Of course he did.

Noam rubbed his eyes and tried to think. Did Lehrer's persuasion eventually wear off? Or did that only apply if you had a Faraday shield, like Sacha?

"Dara . . . ," he started, not sure where he was going with it, but then Dara said:

"Okay. All right. So, when I was ten, Lehrer invited some men over for dinner. I didn't learn until later that Lehrer had discovered they were Texan spies."

Noam stared at him, openmouthed. "Dara," he said, "this isn't really a good time for personal anecdotes."

But Dara kept going, barreling on as if he hadn't heard Noam at all. "They knew about Lehrer's persuasion, of course. So when Lehrer told one of them to drink from a poisoned cup, the others immediately knocked the glass out of his hand. It shattered. Whisky went everywhere."

Dara was fevermad. Of course he was. And now he was raving on about his good-old-time adventures with Lehrer from before he decided to hate him.

"And that was it. Without whisky to drink, the spy couldn't obey Lehrer's order. The spell broke, and Lehrer had to kill them all the old-fashioned way."

Dara met Noam's gaze, unflinching. Noam expected to see madness blazing in his eyes, but Dara was perfectly, horribly sober.

Noam frowned.

"Wait," he said. "Are you saying . . ."

Only, he knew what Dara was saying.

Dara was telling him, the only way Dara *could* tell him, that if Noam wanted to get him out of here . . . he was going to have to do it by force.

Blood dripped down Dara's forearm, pooling on the floor.

Lehrer had made it to the atrium.

Noam started forward, and Dara took a step back.

"I'm really sorry about this," Noam said.

He lunged for Dara, who ducked. Noam's hands closed around empty air just in time for Dara to jab a fist into Noam's solar plexus.

Noam choked, pain bursting like a star beneath his ribs. Thank god for basic, though, and sparring with Lehrer—Noam knew how to ignore pain. It washed overhead, then away. Noam caught Dara's arm, twisting it up behind his back so Dara had no choice but to stumble forward.

"Get off me," Dara growled and stomped his heel against Noam's instep.

Noam hissed but refused to let go. He tightened his grip even as Dara tried to yank away—Lehrer was so close now, and they didn't have time, they didn't . . .

He tapped superstrength. Dara cried out as Noam's fingers dug in, bruisingly hard.

"I'm sorry," Noam said again, all but pleading with Dara to believe him, but he couldn't do anything less—he didn't want to hurt Dara, but he couldn't waste time fighting fair. Not when Dara had years of training on him.

Dara tried to twist out of his grip, but Noam was too strong now. With magic it was only too easy to grab Dara's other arm and drive him toward the threshold.

Dara screamed, kicked Noam's shins, threw his head back in an attempt to crush it against Noam's brow. Dara fought without concern for his own safety, like he didn't care if he forced Noam to break bones.

Because, of course. Because Lehrer wouldn't be so specific.

Lehrer had said, *Don't leave*, and right now Dara would rather die than disobey.

Noam manhandled Dara through the doorway, and that last thrust of strength sent Dara toppling onto Lehrer's lush carpet. He scrambled to get up, but Noam was quicker—he pinned Dara down against the floor, straddling his hips and pressing both hands against Dara's shoulders.

"Stop fighting," he said, breathless.

Dara's short nails scratched at his wrists, Dara's whole body squirming beneath his weight. "You're hurting me," Dara gasped, and Noam, gritting his teeth, said, "I know."

Fuck, how long would it take? Dara said it would wear off—if Noam just—

But Dara was still struggling, cheeks wet with tears and pupils too large. And Noam hated it, hated himself for the way Dara was looking at him. Like he was afraid.

Afraid of *Noam*.

He squeezed his eyes shut and hunched forward over Dara, who still writhed. He had to make a decision right now. It would be quick, over in a moment. The lamp he sensed on Lehrer's desk was heavy enough. Noam wouldn't even have to let go of Dara; he could use his power to bash the metal base against Dara's temple. He'd have to drag Dara's unconscious body out of the government complex, but that would be easier than managing a Dara determined to fight him every step of the way.

But he'd just reached out with his power when Dara went abruptly still between his thighs.

Noam opened his eyes. Dara stared back, chest rising and falling with quick, shallow breaths—but he let go of Noam's wrists, hands dropping limp to his sides.

"Are you . . ."

Noam didn't know how put it in a way that didn't sound awful. *Are you still going to resist?*

"I'm okay," Dara said, but it came out almost like a question. He exhaled sharply. "I think . . . I think I'm okay."

Noam drew back the superstrength but didn't let go—not yet. "Are you sure?"

Dara shuddered beneath him, lashes fluttering briefly against his cheeks. "I don't know. I think . . . let me up?"

It could be a trick. It could be Dara, in Lehrer's power, trying a new tactic to get himself back across that threshold and into the dubious safety of the foyer. But Lehrer himself was on the stairs, taking them two at once, and they were out of time.

Noam let go.

Dara pushed himself up onto his elbows. He looked haggard. Sick. But he didn't try to fight again. So Noam slid off his lap, climbing to his feet and offering Dara a hand to pull him up. Dara wavered on his feet, clinging to Noam's shirt, then stabilized.

"Lehrer will be here any second," Noam said.

Dara took in a short breath and nodded.

Dara really was free. He'd fought, and he was *free*.

A question surfaced from beneath murky waters: Lehrer claimed he'd never used his power on Noam, but Noam didn't believe that was true.

Lehrer had told him to kill Brennan, and Noam had done it.

Maybe that had been his own decision, but what if . . .

What if Noam fought harder, resisted more? Would the idea have snapped in his mind like a taut cord, the way it had for Dara? Without Lehrer's voice whispering shadows in his ear, would he have killed Brennan at all?

"We have an hour until the suppressant wears off," Dara said as they darted across the unlit study and through the door out into the hall. Still empty—Noam had checked. "Until then, I don't have telepathy. Lehrer and I might still be close enough, he might be able to . . . or we might not. I don't know. We're going to have to think fast—no plans, nothing predictable. Do you understand?"

Noam didn't, really, but this wasn't exactly the time to argue with a fevermadman. Lehrer was one floor below.

"Yep, got it. Left. Let's go. Right now."

They took the fastest route out of the building, down the stairs and through the atrium and onto the street. Not that they were safe now.

None of the guards stopped them—Lehrer tried calling it in, of course, but Noam had blocked the transmission. Lehrer was a lot of things, but as far as Noam could tell, he still wasn't a technopath. Once Lehrer got to the atrium, he'd tell the guards in person—nothing Noam could do about that—but by then he and Dara would've lost themselves in the city crowds.

They ran up Blackwell toward Main, dodging cyclists bearing carts piled high with fresh summer fruit and barking dogs on frayed ropes, commuters heading to work, angry men in cars, a pickup ball game near the memorial.

"I called a friend of mine on the way over," Noam said, breathless and squeezing Dara's hand—Dara hadn't let go since they left the government complex. His palm was clammy. Noam didn't care. "He kind of owes me one. Sam. He'll get you anywhere you need to go—"

"No," Dara said, stopping abruptly. Noam stumbled on an uneven bit of concrete, power catching a streetlamp to keep from falling. "I told you. No plans. You think Lehrer won't find out about that? He knows *everything*. Everything you've thought of, he's thought of. Something else. Something new."

Jesus. Dara . . . Dara might be crazy, but he was right. If this was the obvious solution to Noam, it would be obvious to Lehrer as well. Lehrer had been there when Noam was arrested after the protests. He knew about Sam and DeShawn and all the others, had gotten their records wiped. He'd know everyone black bloc.

"Shit. Um. Okay." Noam scrubbed a hand over his jaw. Then: "Okay. New idea. Let's—"

"Don't tell me. Don't even think it. Just do it."

Dara shoved at his arm; Noam nodded. "Yeah. Come on."

It was a well-worn route, a sprint Noam's feet had learned from eight months of tracking it again and again. His mind was the white noise of adrenaline and blood pumping through his skull, Dara's fingers digging into the back of his hand, and this. This was perfect. They could keep running, just like this, all through Durham, into the neighboring towns, all the way out over the wall and into the quarantined zone.

They could disappear.

Noam's shirt was sweat soaked by the time they stumbled through the door of the Migrant Center, Dara's hair plastered to his forehead and the summer humidity hanging over their shoulders like a wet blanket. Linda startled to see them, nearly dropping the potted plant she'd been carrying to a windowsill.

"Noam," she started. "Sugar . . . are you—"

"No time," Noam gasped, chest aching every time he sucked in air. Fuck. He could've sworn he was in better shape than this after all that basic training. "Listen. Linda. You helped Brennan get people out of Atlantia, right? Refugees. You sneaked people over the Carolinian border."

Linda's gaze slid from his face to Dara's.

"You can trust him," Noam said.

Linda put the plant down on the table. It was several seconds before she said, "Yeah. Yeah, I helped."

"Can you take people the other way?"

"What?"

"Can you get people *out* of Carolinia?"

Linda stepped closer, wiping both palms against her skirt. "Honey, are you in some kind of trouble?"

"Not him. Me." Dara managed a grim sort of smile and shrugged. "I need to disappear. Fast."

"Is he . . ." Linda started.

"*Please*," Noam said. He was ready to beg if he had to. No telling where Lehrer was now, not without checking all the cameras from here to the government complex. He could be right outside. "Linda, please, just trust me. Will you do it?"

"Right now?"

"Yeah. Right now."

For a moment, he was so sure she was going to say no. That she might look at him and see what he had done to Brennan. Might realize he had no right asking her—or them—for anything at all.

But then she exhaled and said, "I have a car out back."

"Perfect," Noam said. It felt like all the blood drained from him at once. He could have lain down on the floor right there and slept for ten years. "Okay. Let's go."

Linda's car was an ancient black sedan, not even driverless, covered in a thin layer of road dust with smashed bugs on the windshield.

It looked incredibly generic. It was perfect.

Noam tossed the pack into the back seat and then turned to face Dara, who stood there with the door held open and an expectant look on his face.

Just looking at him hurt more than Noam had thought it would. Right now, Dara seemed almost healthy. The brightness in his eyes wasn't mania but adrenaline. The color in his cheeks wasn't fever, but exertion. He could have been the same boy Noam had held in his arms in the barracks bedroom, the same boy he'd kissed and touched and wanted so badly it ate him alive.

He was getting better. Lehrer's treatment was working.

If Noam sent Dara into the quarantined zone, where magic ran rabid in the water and ground, how long would he last?

"Why are you looking at me like that?" Dara said slowly. "Noam, get in the car. We have to go."

Noam's mouth tasted like copper. "Dara . . ."

"*Noam.* Get in the goddamn car."

"I'm not going with you, Dara." Noam stepped around the front of the car, toward the other side where Dara stood, staring at him with his hand still on the open door. "I can't."

"What are you *talking* about?" Dara's voice had its own blade to it now, pitch rising on the final words: both a question and a demand. "You—"

"I have to stay here. I started this." He gestured vaguely, encompassing the Migrant Center, Durham, Carolinia—all of it. All the things he'd done, the people he'd hurt. The one he'd killed. All those sacrifices, all for the greater good. "I have to finish it. The Atlantians are finally—Lehrer gave them citizenship. Did you know that? We won, Dara. I have to be a part of that. I can't leave now."

Dara's face was a mask of uninterpretable emotion, wide eyed and thin mouthed, his shoulders rising and falling in rapid, shallow motion. For one heat-seared moment, Noam thought Dara might actually attack him—but he didn't.

"You . . ." Dara wet his lips. "You don't . . . do you? Noam . . ."

"Dara, you have to go. Lehrer will be here any second."

"God. You—Noam, I have to tell you something, please—"

Lehrer was here. Lehrer was *here*—that was him, the angles of his face and slim lines of his suit captured on the security cam a block away.

Fuck.

"I know," Noam said. He tried to grin, but it felt weak. He said, "I love you too." And he grasped Dara's face between both hands and kissed him on his shocked mouth. Dara didn't resist. Dara didn't say a word, even when Noam pushed him back and into the car and slammed the door shut behind him.

"I'll take care of him," Linda promised. She patted Noam on the shoulder and gave him a sad little smile. Then she got in the car, and they drove away.

Noam stood there and watched the sedan vanish into the city traffic, watched until it turned the corner at the far end of the street and disappeared.

Lehrer found him still standing like that a minute later, watching the far traffic light change from yellow to red. Noam's pulse beat in his throat like a second heart, but he didn't run.

Lehrer didn't speak at first. And then he rested his hand on Noam's back, high up between his shoulder blades. It wasn't the anger Noam had been anticipating. It wasn't like that at all.

"I'm sorry," Noam said and didn't look at him. He shut his eyes instead.

"He'll die out there."

It hurt when Noam swallowed, like splinters cutting his throat. "Maybe. It was what he wanted."

Lehrer sighed and didn't say anything to that.

The distant streetlight went back to green. The color, through the heat waves, looked blurry and surreal.

At last, Lehrer's hand fell away from Noam's back.

"Promise me you won't go after Dara," Noam said.

"You're asking me to kill my own child."

"I'm asking you to let him make that decision for himself."

Noam turned toward him, squinting against the sunlight. Lehrer's expression was blank, unreadable. He could have been a still frame from a propaganda film.

Then the façade cracked, and Lehrer nodded. The lines of his face were sharper than ever as he said, "I promise."

Noam wasn't sure if he believed him. But for now he had no other choice.

"I almost went with him," Noam confessed.

"I know. I'm glad you didn't." Lehrer tugged at his sleeves. Noam felt it in the metal when his touch grazed the silver cuff links. Lehrer said, almost wryly, "I also know you aren't staying for me."

Of course Noam wasn't staying for him. Lehrer was every single reason for Noam to leave—to start running as far and fast as he could.

In all likelihood, by staying, Noam had signed his own death warrant. He knew about Lehrer's persuasion; Lehrer knew that he knew. In the best possible scenario, Noam risked becoming Lehrer's puppet even more than he already was. In another version of events, Noam wouldn't live long enough to learn if Dara survived.

But how else could this end?

Noam wasn't hiding. Not anymore.

"It's not over just because you granted Atlantians citizenship," Noam said.

Lehrer shook his head. "Far from it. I'd like to suggest you apply for Brennan's position, as liaison. And in time . . . you graduate in two years. As chancellor, I'll need people in my administration I can trust."

A small smile creased Noam's lips.

Good.

He wanted to be close to Lehrer, now more than ever. He had to make sure everything went smoothly. He had to be sure Lehrer, in his victory, didn't forget who'd helped him achieve it.

Everything worth doing had its risks.

And sometimes you had to do the wrong thing to achieve something better.

Noam was willing to gamble with Lehrer's persuasion if it meant securing a future for Atlantians. What kind of person would he be if he didn't? He could take precautions.

Brennan's blood on the wall.

He'd make sure Lehrer never forgot how useful Noam could be.

Lehrer's hand found Noam's back again, nudging him until he turned away from that horizon—until they faced the city again, the smokestack rising over the government complex in the near distance.

Dara was gone, but Noam was still here.

The war was over.

It was time to build something new.

Book Club Questions

1. Was Noam justified in his actions against injustice, even when he broke the law?
2. What hints were there early on that Lehrer was not all he seemed?
3. How did Dara's traumatic experiences shape his interactions with other people?
4. In the book, the characters sometimes chose to do terrible things in the name of the greater good. Where would you have drawn the line? What actions would have been "too far" for you?
5. Why do you think Noam chose to stay in Carolinia, with Lehrer, at the end of the book?

Acknowledgments

I used to think writing was such a solitary pursuit. Ideas came to you when you were alone, emerging in bits and pieces on your commute, unfolding from a line of music or a half-remembered dream. Then you wrote those ideas down, sitting by yourself in a café or sprawled across your bed with only your very bored dog for company. Now I know that isn't true. *The Fever King* is the product of so many people working together to sculpt a rough blob of clay into a finished piece—and without these friends and colleagues, writing would be very lonely indeed.

First, thank you to my incredible agents, Holly Root and Taylor Haggerty, for believing in this story and for helping me find it the perfect home at Skyscape. Your guidance and insight have been such an anchor. Thank you to my APub team: to my fearless editor, Jason Kirk, and to everyone at Skyscape who has labored tirelessly to bring this book to shelves—Clarence Haynes, Rosanna Brockley, Kelsey Snyder, Haley Reinke, Brittany Russell, Christina Troup, and many others. Thank you to my sensitivity readers; your work is invaluable, and I appreciate it so much.

I'd be incredibly remiss if I didn't levy about a thousand thanks on Pitch Wars and my mentor, Emily Martin, who helped me write and rewrite and revise and polish this book over the course of just a few months. All our long-ass phone calls and writers' retreats (which are really just excuses to set our dogs up on dates and go back to Durham, let's be real) paid off—our unfortunate faves now have their own real live book.

Thank you to my parents, who always supported my love of writing. To Amy, who's been there since my fandom days and who probably read early drafts of this book eighty billion times. To Ben. Ben, when I first let you read the beginning of this book, it was a baby draft four chapters long, and you were practically a stranger. Sharing this story with you was like exposing my heart, and it was the best decision I ever made. I love you.

Thank you, grad school colleagues, for putting up with my moodiness and bouts of self-isolation and for still wanting to go to Indigo with me even after all that. To Daryl, my PhD adviser, as well as the rest of the faculty in our department, for being understanding and supportive of my side gig.

All of my writer friends—there are far too many of you to list here, and you know who you are. You made it fun. You made me feel at home. Thank you for your support. Thank you for crashing parties with me, for soup dumplings and headcanons and tequila, for gifs and novel aesthetics and our favorite bartender Quinnbrook Ford, and for every text that read *how are revisions?* or *this guy on my bus looks like Noam.* Never change. #JusticeForDara

Aska, sweet doggo: Sit. Good boy.

Finally, to those of you who survived, who are still surviving: I am you. I love you. And I see you.

About the Author

Victoria Lee grew up in Durham, North Carolina, where she spent twelve ascetic years as a vegetarian before discovering that spicy chicken wings are, in fact, a delicacy. She's been a state finalist competitive pianist, a hitchhiker, a pizza connoisseur, an EMT, an expat in China and Sweden, and a science doctoral student. She's also a bit of a snob about fancy whisky. Lee writes early in the morning and then spends the rest of the day trying to impress her border collie puppy and make her experiments work. She currently lives in Pennsylvania with her partner.